IN THE EVER-SHIFTING NATURE OF GOOD AND EVIL— EAST MEETS WEST . . .

For centuries in the Orient, love and death have been an art. But this is not the time of the ancients. The time is now.

And new warlords who betray the ideals they are supposed to serve are in New York and Washington.

This is a labyrinth of evil that spreads from the Far East to America, where the underworld mocks the laws that can not control it.

Now it is the task of the Server, an American who has learned deadly martial arts from a Korean warlord, to put his savage strength in the service of purity and honor . . . as he poises his hands to rip apart a malignant plague of violence and greed. . . .

The Sign Of The Server

The Sign Of The Server

CHARLES DeLUCA

AN ONYX BOOK

NEW AMERICAN LIBRARY

PUBLISHED BY
THE NEW AMERICAN LIBRARY
OF CANADA LIMITED

PUBLISHER'S NOTE

This book is a work of fiction. Names, characters, places, and incidents either are the product of the author's imagination or are used fictitiously, and any resemblance to actual persons, living or dead, events, or locales is entirely coincidental.

NAL BOOKS ARE AVAILABLE AT QUANTITY DISCOUNTS
WHEN USED TO PROMOTE PRODUCTS OR SERVICES.
FOR INFORMATION PLEASE WRITE TO PREMIUM MARKETING DIVISION.
NEW AMERICAN LIBRARY. 1633 BROADWAY.
NEW YORK. NEW YORK 10019.

Copyright © 1987 by Charles DeLuca

 Onyx is a trademark of The New American Library of Canada Limited.

SIGNET, SIGNET CLASSIC, MENTOR, ONYX, PLUME, MERIDIAN
AND NAL BOOKS are published in Canada by The New American
Library of Canada, Limited, 81 Mack Avenue, Scarborough,
Ontario, Canada M1L 1M8

First Signet Printing, April, 1987

2 3 4 5 6 7 8 9
PRINTED IN CANADA
COVER PRINTED IN U.S.A.

for Sylvia

many thanks to John, Bruce, and Virginia

The man who in the view of gain thinks of righteousness; who in the view of danger is prepared to give up his life; and who does not forget an old agreement however far back it extends—such a man may be reckoned a complete man.

—*Confucius*

Prologue: 1950

The *Sylvia D*, fifty-three feet of a rich man's dream, sliced the ocean into ten-foot waves as I pushed her to thirty-five knots. "Waves gettin' too high, boss," Captain Jack snorted as he reached for the controls. I didn't answer. To hell with the waves. The *Sylvia D* could handle them. Besides, our quarry had broken water off the port bow.

The *Sylvia D* had been my fantasy for as long as I could remember, and once I'd sworn a silent vow to build her, she was as good as in the water. The finest yachtworks in the world, Crimmons and Sons of New England, had taken over a year to lay her out, but the moment they slipped her into the basin, I knew that the long wait had been justified. Seeing her that first time, I stood mute, awestruck. She was a beautiful yacht, and as I viewed her from the shore, I decided that the New York coast would have been naked had she never existed.

"Tuna off the port bow!" a deeply tanned crew member shouted against the ocean spray.

I pushed the throttle forward, realizing we'd stumbled upon an immense school of tuna. I guided the *Sylvia D* around the perimeter of the school, slowing her to a cruising speed. "Bait the water and set up the heavy-gauge poles!"

Within minutes, fresh chunks of bait were being cast across the ocean to slow the school while Captain Jack set up the heaviest of the poles. We'd awaited this afternoon with anticipation. Today we'd go home with tuna.

The school began to respond to the water baiting as I took a seat in one of the fighting chairs. I glanced toward Long Island, but couldn't see the South Shore, as we were better than ten miles out. I began to wait.

The tuna were obstinate most of the afternoon. They teased my line, nibbling at the free-floating bait as if they realized I was seated anxiously at the other end, awaiting some careless move. Several times the line pulled away, but never with the hooking power of a huge fish. I leaned forward in my seat repeatedly, only to relax again. The game was in the waiting. Patient, apprehensive waiting. Like all else in life.

I studied the succession of waves as they disappeared under the yacht. The school was congregated close to the hull and I instinctively sensed biting time. Behind me, I heard voices crackling from the electronic ship-to-shore monster I'd installed when the yacht was being built. My mouth curled into a frown but I never took my eyes from the line. Suddenly the line became taut, pulling me to the edge of my deck chair. Another pull and I could feel the tight press of the safety buckle across my midsection. My hopes for a record-breaking tuna were high.

The line screamed away and for the longest, most agonizing moment my mind roared for that damned fish to hook in—hard! I knew this was it and started letting the line away easily. My heart sank as the line suddenly turned limp.

"Put the engines forward to take up the slack!" I ordered over my shoulder.

"Ship-to-shore, sir," Jack responded dryly.

"Sylvia?" I asked, wondering if my wife was calling.

"No, sir. Maggie at the office."

"For Christ's sake. I told her not to bother me when I'm on my boat!"

"She says it's urgent, boss."

Jack took the pole, securing it deep into the chair lock. Unbuckling myself, I made my way across the deck and picked up the receiver.

"Yeah, Maggie, what is it?" I didn't try to hide my annoyance.

"Three gentlemen to see you, Mr. Dee."

"Tell 'em I'm out."

"But they said they're—"

"I don't care who they are, Maggie. Tell 'em I'm out."

She hesitated on the other end. "They insist on speaking to you, sir. There are two generals and a gentleman named Calloway."

I froze. We all have people in our pasts we never want to see again, and Calloway was one of those people.

Calloway. His name revived memories I'd long ago repressed. Memories of a fourteen-year-old boy; memories many years gone; memories of another life, another place, another me.

I

To Survive:
Death Rears
Its Head

1937

1

I went to the Orient because of Eddie Gardenia. Being fourteen in 1937 was no easy deal even if we were the two gutsiest kids ever to hit Long Island City. Most times, we just roamed the streets between Steinway and the bridge, but sometimes we'd venture out along Astoria or Vernon Boulevard to rumble with a rival gang or to grab our share of what New York City had to offer. In those days, half the country was out of work and the other half was waiting to be fired. Our neighborhood was typical of others in the five boroughs, a place where only the local whore and numbers runner made any money worth talking about. Naturally, everybody else was looking out for a few extra bucks. If you could survive here, you could make it anywhere.

Eddie was hardly a tough guy, even though he'd go along with the game. I knew my cousin better than anybody, and every time we were on the prowl, I could hear his insides shaking. He had guts, sure, but tough? Well, that just wasn't Eddie. Don't get me wrong. He was no coward. He was just an overly cautious guy who took more than his share of beatings. I'd always made it my business to be there when he needed me because Eddie was the only person I could trust, the only person I dared have any faith in. With no questions. It was that way ever since I can remember. Eddie, an orphan at the age of two, came to live with us. My mother and father treated him as if he was their own. As far as I was concerned, he was my brother.

We spent most of our time scavenging the dockside at night, where all the world's treasures lay haphazardly crated and practically unguarded. Sure, there was that old guy who'd been with Pinkerton's since the Spanish-American War, but he hardly ever got in the way. He wasn't interested in chasing kids, probably because he'd done the same things himself. We had a silent agreement: we didn't bother him and he turned his back on us. In those days, everybody was looking to survive, so whatever we grabbed was peddled fast and easy. I'm not saying there wasn't any competition, though. Other gangs from surrounding neighborhoods found their way to the docks too. There was sometimes bloodshed when Jimmy Moroni and his gang were involved. He ran the streets, ruthlessly taking from whoever he pleased because his father was a syndicate strongman. Moroni figured his father's rank gave him the right to do as he pleased. Word got around that Moroni was going to tangle asses with me on sight. It happened the night Eddie pried the lid off a crateload of Swiss watches.

"Goddammit, I'm rich!" Eddie laughed loud enough for me and the other guys to hear. "I'm fuckin' rich!"

We all ran over to stare at Eddie's discovery. The box had been small, not big enough for any of us to think about opening, but just right for Eddie's curiosity. We let him take the watches as we moved toward the remaining bundles. Each of us began ripping open various-shaped crates scattered around. I hadn't walked more than fifty feet when I heard Eddie shout again. But this time it was in pain.

I wheeled around to see Eddie surrounded by a group of newly arrived boys. They had emerged from the shadows after seeing that Eddie was unprotected, and fell on him viciously. I managed to pull a couple of lightweights off his back before seeing the gleam of a deadly blade reflected in the dimness of the night. Jimmy Moroni, a demonic grin across his face, lunged forward to slice Eddie's chest. I pushed Eddie to safety as the blade ripped toward me.

"'I'll fuckin' kill you, Dee."

Face to face, we stared at each other. Even though it was dark, I could see the fire and hate in Jimmy Moroni's eyes. In that split second, I knew I had to protect myself.

"Back off, Moroni," I warned, "or I'll lay you out."

As Moroni came at me again, I sidestepped his deadly jab and tore the knife out of his hand. As he regained his ground, Moroni's eyes darted from side to side, searching for a weapon. One of Moroni's boys tossed him a baling hook, which he caught by the wooden handle. Instantly he swiped at my face, barely missing. In desperation, I kicked him in the groin. His face told me how much it must have hurt, but that didn't stop him. I had the knife in front of me. My hand was visibly shaking. All I could think of was the hook and how close it came to my face.

He began screaming like a madman and came at me full force. His foot became untangled in some loose pier planking, causing both of us to topple over a pile of empty crates.

I thought he had gotten me because there was blood everywhere. The knife was no longer in my hand, but protruding grotesquely from his torn stomach. Time stopped. Then, as if all the cops in New York could hear the bastard dying, everyone ran. Everyone except my cousin.

"He looks real dead, Dee." Eddie was shaking.

I bent over to touch Moroni. He was about my own age and looked like any other street kid, rough and raw in appearance, with several scars marring his face. There didn't seem to be any vital signs.

"Aw, shit . . ." I kicked at a small crate, which skidded across the dock, then vanished out of sight into the dark waters. I looked back down at the boy. I'd never seen so much blood in my whole life. Did the human body really hold all that much?

"You gotta hide out, Dee," Eddie warned. "No sense you bein' around when the cops get here. You gotta take it on the lam."

In that moment I realized Eddie was keeping his head while I was losing mine. Hell, they'd just burned some guy at Sing Sing a few days ago and the tabloids were full of bloodcurdling death-house stories. I turned away from Moroni and found myself staring up at an awesome freighter moored behind us. I quickly made my decision. If I was going to hide, it wasn't going to be in New York. Eddie caught my drift real quick and a pained expression masked his face. And a disbelieving one.

"You wouldn't really . . . ?"

I looked back down at the still and lifeless kid lying between us. Then I did something I'd never done before. I walked over to Eddie and hugged him.

"Hey, we split the world between us, right? Always partners, y' know?" I tried to reassure him. "I just can't go hanging around while this guy dies on me. And I ain't goin' to no stinkin' jail. Understand?"

Eddie looked at me, a forlorn expression covering his face. "What'll I do, Dee? What the hell will I do?"

"Make like I never existed and I'll write you from somewhere, okay?"

Eddie nodded, tears running down his cheeks. We embraced a final time before he disappeared into the shadows. I was alone. I turned and looked again at the tramp steamer: the *China Star*. Its size overwhelmed me. It was the biggest thing I'd ever been close to, except for the Empire State Building. I moved to her, and like the city I was raised in, she proved to be a monster with many ways of devouring a young boy.

The forward cargo hold was bulging with crates of farming equipment destined for China. I found myself a nice comfortable spot between bags of seed and a few boxes marked "Hoes." For two hot, sticky days we sat in the port of New York before the *China Star* got under way. As I hid belowdecks, I knew Eddie was hanging around the docks waiting for the tramp to sail, waiting to see me off. And making sure I was okay.

He didn't have to worry. Three days into the icy North Atlantic, three crewmen found me and brought me to the captain, a crusty, leather-faced veteran named Carl Murvener. He wasn't overjoyed at the prospect of having a young kid on his ship, but I wasn't the first stowaway to cross his path. I was assigned to the galley, where I scraped cooking grease from the floor all the way to England. Even shorter on glory was the voyage to China, but once the weather turned warmer, it became endurable. Even foul weather and hard work beat spending time in reform school.

For most of the China voyage, I listened to the crew's tales of Shanghai. They made it sound like the most exotic place in the world. Shanghai, in 1937, was an international settlement with trading concessions granted to the European powers by the Chinese government. The British, still flush with wealth and power culled from their expansive opium trade a century earlier, ruled "International" China with an iron fist. The French, with the largest concession of land, followed as a close second. Most of the other nations— the United States included—were represented in this trading emporium but could not sway the brand of power associated with Great Britain and France. Except for Japan.

The Japanese emperor was hell-bent on consolidating all of Asia under the Rising Sun, and to accomplish this, he built the mightiest army since antiquity. And then he launched it against China.

By 1937 the Japanese had secured rural areas in northern China and were looking to capture the more populated cities. The slightest, most innocent incident would be enough to provoke the Japanese into an invasion of the more prosperous areas. Shanghai was divided into two spheres of power. The northern section of the city was under Japanese rule, while the southern zones remained in the hands of the European powers. The Chinese Nationalist Army under General Chiang Kai-shek was the only real bulwark against an all-out Japanese assault, but they were ill-prepared, understaffed, and sadly outgunned.

This was the Shanghai—a samurai sword driven through her heart—that I eagerly anticipated. The *China Star* entered the Whangpoo tributary at first light and I was thrilled by my first glimpse of the busy dockside. Scores of dockworkers chanted in low tones as they hauled tons of cargo from the huge motorized cranes.

What had been a scant crew of crusty laborers huddled about a fire as we docked in the early-morning light had suddenly exploded into a throng of hundreds of bustling longshoremen. I was still watching from the guardrails when a stiff, uniformed officer of the Japanese Imperial Army Customs Service intercepted First Mate Bellows and requested permission to board the ship.

I didn't have to see the procedure to know what would happen next. At dockside an immense throng of workers waited for the customs official to inspect the contents of each hold. Huge cranes would then drop into the bowels of the ship and begin unloading countless crates into huge webbed nets. When each net was secure, the crane would then lower the cargo onto the dock, where the men would disassemble the load and sort it according to the transport house to which it was assigned. It was a slow, but accurate process, repeated daily at every port in the world.

I didn't give two damns about crates or coolies. I wanted to see Shanghai. Every moment I waited seemed like an hour, watching coolies who never seemed to move fast enough. Finally I couldn't wait any longer. As First Mate Bellows came back on deck, I ran to him.

"Mr. Bellows, sir?"

"What is it, Dee?" He had a tired look in his eyes.

I guessed the Japanese customs official had given him a rough time.

"Request permission to go ashore, sir. I'd like to see Shanghai."

"You done with your tasks, boy?"

"Yes, sir. The galley's clean enough to eat off and I've already brought the captain his breakfast."

He looked at me. "You ever been in Shanghai before, boy?"

"No, sir."

"Permission granted." He started off, then turned and studied me. "Watch yourself, Dee. If you're takin' any money, take it in singles. U.S. dollars are valuable around here. If you gotta buy somethin', then make like that dollar is your last one, you understand? You can bargain the locals down that way."

"I don't intend on bargaining with anyone, Mr. Bellows, sir."

The first mate chuckled. "Sure. But remember this, Dee: this ain't New York. And the minute you decide to take a rickshaw, you'll bargain. Don't never accept the first price. Bitch and moan until you get 'em angry. Then they'll meet you halfway. And for Christ's sake, don't let 'em start tellin' you about their starvin' families or—"

"I think I get the message, sir."

"Okay, okay. Off with you. And be back by dark."

"Yes, sir!"

I picked my way through the crates heaped haphazardly upon the deck of the *China Star*. As I disembarked I noticed that Bellows had posted two crew members with sidearms and Springfield rifles. That was odd. We'd never had to post guards before. I told them I had permission to go ashore, then walked down the gangplank. Almost immediately, the Chinese seemed to zero in on me. But I was nobody's mark. I quickened my pace until I was completely off the docks and walked along the narrow streets leading into Shanghai. After a few blocks I stopped to get my bearings as the smells of the city assaulted me. There must have been a hundred different, exotic scents mixing with the dankness of pierside and the filth and closeness of the alleylike streets. It was intoxicating breathing in the smells of a busy city after so long on the *China Star*.

Turning a corner, I noticed a crowd separate to allow a large ornate sedan litter through. The litter was in actuality a huge, gaudily decorated box hoisted on the shoulders of four muscular Orientals. I watched as the men placed the litter down in front of a nearby tavern and opened the compartment door to allow a woman passenger to step out. As she extended her leg to exit, my eye caught a glimpse of her inner thigh.

She was beautiful, tall and yellow-haired, and towered above her servants like a goddess. Sharp-featured, she wore clothing of a decidedly European cut, and never even regarded the crowd around her. Nonchalantly she tossed several coins to a group of beggar boys who'd assembled nearby.

She could have been one of the many aristocratic women who fled Moscow after the Bolshevik revolution. Scores had come by way of the port city of Vladivostok, the final stop on the Trans-Siberian Railway and thousands of miles away from the advancing Red Army. The crew of the *China Star* had told me stories of such Russian aristocrats who had turned to prostitution to survive Shanghai's demanding life-style.

The woman disappeared into the tavern, leaving her muscular footmen to guard the litter. I was tempted to follow her but decided that was no way to see the city, so I began walking along the narrow street which appeared at the intersection of Kongping Road. It was there that I saw the first effects of war.

A demarcation line running the length of Kongping Road was secured by Japanese troops. The armed men were fresh, and showed no signs of battle fatigue, so I figured them to be part of the occupation force. Later I learned it was not unusual to see Japanese peacetime troops at this end of the settlement. On the opposite side of Kongping and northwest by the wharves, a small contingent of Chinese troops with cannon faced their Japanese counterparts. It was a curious situation. In the northern part of the country, these opposing forces were killing each other. Here, they warily eyed each other.

The narrow street which had taken me to Kongping Road brought me too far inland for my liking. Japanese troops were everywhere. I doubled back behind the Chinese lines and walked until spying a street sign proclaiming "Broadway."

Suddenly I felt at home, and thought sadly of my family. Along this wide, urban roadway named in honor of the American effort in China, I saw the grand Japanese, American, and German embassies perched along the Whangpoo. Since their territorial sovereignty included private wharves, I was forced to take the public roadways rather than attempt to cross the Soochow Creek through the heavily guarded embassy dock sites.

I walked along the narrow pathways bordering the Soochow, wondering how I was going to get across to the international settlement, when I noticed a huge red-and-black sign proclaiming "Foo's Transport Service." There, several fast-talking ticket sellers collected a dollar bill from me, returning several Chinese coppers. I think I was cheated, but decided not to argue the point. I lost myself in the crowded ferry so as not to be marked for robbery by my apparent ignorance.

We departed more than twenty minutes behind schedule because the overly industrious agents packed the ferry. From the upper deck I could see that everyone dockside seemed to be involved in some racket or other. Even Foo's ticket sellers. Several minutes before casting off, the legal ticket agents slammed shut their windows, turning away hundreds of potential passengers. The abruptly refused crowds then frantically stampeded the loading agents at the gangway to bargain for passage. Clearly, Foo's dockside employees made their living by pocketing this extra cash. When we pulled out under the high-pitched whine of the ancient engines, the ferry was riding far lower in the water than safety allowed.

The ride was tedious, the ferry weaving in and out among other overcrowded vessels racing the Soochow. We finally tied up at the Hoomi Road wharf. Along this stretch of the creek was the largest concentration of Nationalist Chinese troops I'd ever seen. Field guns were poised at targets on the Japanese side of the Soochow, with poor Foo and his rickety transport service directly in the line of fire, a good bet to be among the first casualties in the event shots were exchanged.

I started out along Hoomi Road, a street with more shops and carts and streetside vendors than I remembered in any other city. I soon reached the wide expanse of Nanking Road, rife with hundreds of shops advertising their wares with signs in Chinese characters. Each storefront was brightly decorated, and though I couldn't understand the language, all I had to do was take a look in each window to see what was for sale.

It was usually food, and the window shopping caused me to realize how long it had been since my last meal. At the corner of Nanking and Mohowk roads, just north of the racetrack, stood an ancient Chinese tending several sidewalk ovens. From a distance, I watched as several customers walked over, then selected potatoes baked by the vendor. For a single copper, they chose a polished stick, longer and thicker than a toothpick, then impaled the potato of their choice, biting through the roasted skin as they proceeded on their way. I couldn't resist.

The vendor smiled at me as I selected a large, dark brown potato. He nodded happily while I impaled the steamy potato. When I handed him a copper, his face turned suddenly cross and he shoved the coin back to me. Too late. I'd already taken a bite of his goods. He spoke in Chinese and held up two fingers. I held up one. He eyed me, this old man who must have been nearly seventy, and then came forward in a violent attempt to seize the potato while shrieking at me in Chinese. Believing everyone along Nanking Road was watching me, I quickly produced a second coin, which I tossed at him. Once the second copper was safely buried in his pocket, he smiled again.

The potato was delicious, but salty, so I began to look around for something to drink. Along Bubbling Wells Road, I came across a battle-ready contingent of American marines and they directed me to a café called the Alabama. I went in and took a seat at the bar several stools away from a sleeping marine. Young couples occupied most of the tables. I spotted a bartender and signaled him. He was a young, slick Oriental with an expansive smile and happy eyes. Wiping a glass as he approached me, he continued to bark orders to the nearby busboys who scurried about under the weight of steaming trays of food.

"You buy drink?" His English was clipped.

"Yes."

He pulled forth a bottle of Old Smuggler.

"No whiskey," I said, holding up a hand. "Beer."

He shook his head. "No have beer. Japanese blow up supply train from Woosung. Have only whiskey."

"Soda water then."

He glanced at me strangely, but took a dollar in exchange for a small glass. I waited for change, but when it appeared that none was forthcoming, I figured I hadn't so much as bought the soda as traded for it. At this rate, Shanghai would be too rich for my blood.

I finished my drink, then wandered back out onto Bubbling Wells Road, walking with my hands pushed deeply into my pockets until I came upon a newsstand. I bought a copy of the *North China Daily News* and quickly scanned the war stories originating in Chapai and Hongkew. In some areas, the fighting was escalating into fierce engagements. There were announcements by every government concerning the safety of foreign nationals should the Japanese unleash a full-scale attack. I looked around at the bustling, crowded street and found it hard to believe a war was being fought. Only an occasional column of smoke in the northern sky served as a grim reminder. I kept reading the paper while making my way back toward the *China Star*. By midafternoon I'd reached the Bund, where all the major banking houses were located.

Afternoon was definitely the wrong time to be strolling about the financial center of Shanghai. The streets were overrun with waiters angling large, steaming trays of food through a nearly oblivious crowd. The custom, it seemed, was to send out for multicourse meals and have them delivered. I figured that this way the large businesses could continue making money uninterrupted. Following several near-collisions with these boys, I learned to move more quickly. Not quick enough, though. A couple of them, whose trays I nearly toppled, were ready to drag me through the street, but I managed to slip away.

When my legs tired, I took Foo's transport back across the Soochow and worked my way to the pierhead where the *China Star* was moored. But it wasn't there.

I thought I was at the wrong pier, that maybe I'd taken a wrong turn someplace. I twisted my head, frantically searching in every direction. No luck. The ship was gone. I walked toward a boss man who was shaping up a gang of longshoremen.

"What happened to the *China Star?*" I tried not to betray my growing panic. The boss man regarded me as a pesty insect. He glanced toward the empty pierhead, then turned his gaze slowly to me.

"You follow."

A gut instinct told me to run in the opposite direction, but I didn't. It was my first mistake.

We walked along the massive dockside until we arrived at an oversize shed with the sign "Harbormaster" lettered in four languages over the door. I waited outside as the boss man entered. Five minutes passed. Then ten. I should have known something was wrong when several Japanese soldiers in full battle dress showed up, but they didn't threaten me. They just stood near the shed, occasionally tossing a glance in my general direction. I was getting nervous.

Finally the door reopened and the boss man and harbormaster moved out onto the dock. The boss man bowed, then quickly retreated as the harbormaster walked over to me. I knew by his uniform that he was Japanese, but his English was almost perfect.

"You ask for *China Star?*" He smiled slightly as his eyes narrowed to study me.

"Ah . . . yes. Did she sail?"

"You are crew member?"

"Yes. I'm the galley boy."

He nodded, then cocked his head in the direction of the nearby soldiers. "Arrest this boy."

"Arrest me? I didn't do anything!"

His response was curt, harsh. "*China Star* ordered from port. It is contraband ship which sought to deliver guns to the Nationalist Chinese Army."

Anger was winning out over fright. "Guns? There must be a mistake. We carried farming equipment and cattle feed."

"Oh?" The harbormaster's face betrayed nothing. "Let us inspect your so-called farming equipment. Follow me."

It was not a request. He led me behind the shed,

where several crates had been smashed open. I recognized them and read the stenciled word "Hoes" across the splintered wood. But the crates contained rifles. The smaller boxes resting nearby held hundreds of rounds of ammunition.

"But I don't know anything about this."

"Oh," he observed, and continued dryly. "Unfortunately, we did not seize the entire shipment. Only one small truck as it left the dock. Perhaps you know where other trucks were bound?"

"How the hell would I know that? I told you: I'm only the galley boy."

"Yes, of course." The harbormaster waved the soldiers over to where we were standing. "Take him to Kongping."

Kongping? What was he talking about? Kongping was the name of a street.

The Japanese soldiers led me away, shoving me into a waiting car parked near the narrow street leading to the dockside. Another pair of soldiers, obviously officers since they carried only sidearms, took over and locked me inside the car. The driver hit the gas pedal and we bolted onto the street.

The drive through the streets was nerve-racking, the driver leaning on the horn most of the time. Kongping? Where on Kongping? Then we passed a checkpoint which proclaimed "Kongping Road Prison." After halting to identify himself, the driver was waved onto the access road by several fierce-looking guards. I felt myself breaking out into a cold sweat.

Imperial Prison Number Four, Kongping Road, was a multi-story gray stone building surrounded by machine-gun nests. Even though it lacked the traditional high walls, the main holding building was encircled by cast-iron fencing reinforced with barbed wire. The Japanese high command had gone to extremes to escape-proof this place, and in a few minutes, I understood why.

I was led through the steel-lined doors to the sergeant of the guard, where the officers formally declared conspiracy charges against me. Two other guards shackled my wrists and I was led through a maze of corridors until we arrived at the commandant's office. Following a brief delay, I was led in.

The commandmant was dressed crisply in a clean brown uniform displaying the insignia of his rank. He was shaved completely bald, but his deep-set eyes and bushy mustache offset the harshness of his bullet head. As I waited in front of him, he searched through several reports scattered on the desk before him. When he was ready, he lifted his head and exchanged a few brief words with the officers before turning his attention to me.

"I am Nagata," he announced, "colonel commandant of Kongping Road. Have you a name?"

"Dee," I replied.

"You are an American?"

"Yes."

"You have papers?"

Now I knew I was in trouble. "No."

"This is surprising." Nagata rose and studied me. "Your country is usually quite thorough. How is it you have no papers?"

I thought carefully, deciding not to volunteer information if I could avoid it. "I was a cabin boy on the *China Star*. The ship sailed without me."

If he realized I hadn't answered his question, he gave no indication. "How unfortunate." Nagata reached forward to arrange a flower in the vase on his desk. "The *China Star* was a contraband ship. The harbormaster has charged you with arms smuggling and you'll be remanded here until a tribunal can be seated. You will not find us as tolerant as the Shanghai mixed courts. I warn you in advance."

"But I didn't do anything."

My protests fell on deaf ears. Nagata only smiled.

"I'm innocent."

"Naturally." He looked to the officers alongside me. "Take him to the holding pens. And see that he is placed among the other innocents."

As I was led away, I thought again of home and wondered how different things might have turned out had I not been so eager to slip aboard the *China Star* after my encounter with Jimmy Moroni.

2

The conditions at Kongping Prison were criminal. There were sixteen cellblocks on four floors, each conveniently within the sights of twin machine-gun nests situated in guard booths on the topmost floor. Rather than assign me a cell, the Japanese shoved me into a huge holding pen housing several hundred prisoners. Formerly a dayroom serving the four cellblocks on this floor, it was now another circle of hell.

From the moment the gates slammed behind me, all my previously held conceptions of prison life shattered. Almost immediately, I felt hands upon me. Some pushed, others shoved, and a few groped at my body. I began moving away quickly but had only covered about three yards when I tripped. Several prisoners pushed me upright and regarded me with mean, threatening glances. I sensed in their eyes a crazed, almost animalistic hunger for blood. I looked down to see what I'd stumbled across and was horrified to discover the crumpled body of an elderly man. He was way past ninety years of age, and had died in a fetal position. The rigidity of his arms and fingers indicated he'd been dead for hours. I clutched my churning stomach and forced myself to move forward, finally finding a corner in which to sort out my situation. As I stared at the other prisoners, trying to avoid their eyes, I slowly realized that there would be no trial for me. Kongping's overcrowding indicated that. As far as the Japanese legal system was concerned, just being here meant that one had already been found guilty.

Kongping bred filth, and within days I felt as though vermin known only to prisoners were crawling all over me. I kept moving as much as possible, but the sheer number of prisoners was far too great to allow anyone walking space. If anything, we shuffled very slowly as a group. I stayed far away from the corners of the dayroom, and for good reason. The Japanese had placed three or four urinal pots in each, resulting in constant, unending lines to use them, the pots always overflowing with excrement. Several times I was urinated on by prisoners standing nearby, but it wasn't intentional. The closeness of life at Kongping dictated that civilized traditions be shattered. Only the strongest survived.

We all stank. Every prisoner in that hellhole was cursed by a stench no one outside the prison walls would ever believe existed. Sweat pores which had remained uncleansed too long competed with the lingering odor of the communal pots standing sentinel at the room's four corners. I tried to dull my senses to the horror around me. It was impossible.

Before each evening meal, the Japanese observed a macabre ritual. An officer, accompanied by several sentries, selected a few prisoners, seemingly at random, as an overwhelming silence and stillness draped the room. The officer was always smiling, often cajoling the men he'd selected, mostly Chinese youths of fighting age. The chosen prisoners were then escorted from the compound and executed in the outer yard. Everyone seemed to accept this process of elimination. No one resisted or protested even mildly, least of all the Western prisoners, who were rarely bothered.

Shortly thereafter, the guard reentered the holding pens carrying large vats of food. There wasn't any type of line, but chaos didn't prevail either. The Japanese guards with their machine guns made certain no one became violent.

I never ate the evening meal. Or any meal, for that matter. It wasn't because I didn't want to, or need to, but because I could never get near the vats. Too many of the prisoners blocked me, and after countless attempts on the first few days, I began growing weak. The more I lunged for the food, the harder they'd hit me. After a while, I didn't seem to care.

For the prisoners who did eat, it was a degrading experience, accepted only because its alternative was starvation. No one was allowed any utensils except for a wooden bowl supplied by the Japanese. The first vat contained a gray-brown mixture which had been rice at one time but now appeared more like soot-stained snow. The second and third containers were filled with bread and water. Rice went into the bowls, water was slopped across the top, and a piece of bread was thrown in to be used as a spoon. The bread was consumed last, always with a degree of savor, as though a dessert. If it hadn't been of such disgusting quality, food-taking at Kongping would have been an art.

Days without food caused my stomach to curl in pain, but after a while I adjusted. Hunger came and went like a contagious delirium, causing weakness, fever, and real fear that I would lose my sanity. I tried to hold on to reality by observing the crowd around me, some shuffling, some eating, some dying. I once saw a nearby inmate keel over dead before finishing his meal. I made a grab for his unfinished bowl of rice and bread, but several other prisoners beat me to it.

There existed in Kongping another reality that would have made my procurement of food futile. Had I succeeded, older, larger prisoners would've slapped me aside, taking my meal for themselves. I watched as it happened daily to several other boys incarcerated in the dayroom. One skeletal urchin was seated in a corner near the chamberpots, consuming a bowl of rice, when a bulky Chinese with one eye gouged out demanded his meal. The boy refused, so the man merely took it. The undaunted boy went for the older man's legs, sinking the remnants of his rotted teeth into one of them, biting like some parasitic tick refusing to let go. Several other prisoners tried to pull him off, then crushed his head against the concrete. The boy died. His attacker followed several days after. I stumbled across his body and could see the fetid, gangrenous bite that had gone unattended.

The emaciated bodies and haunted eyes of boys my age scared the hell out of me. There were so many of them. I couldn't help but feel that their decaying presence offered me an accurate prediction of my future. Slowly, without realizing when, I gave up. There seemed to be only darkness at the end of this tunnel.

Until, on the fourteenth day, I met Kim.

As the evening meal was being fought over, I noticed a slight, almost beautiful boy my own age. He didn't seem as dirty as the other prisoners, and his eyes weren't laced with hunger pains. His hair was very black, while his facial features resembled a fine Manchu sculpture. His hands, clasped around the wooden bowl filled with food, were almost frail.

My first thought was to grab his food, but I was trembling too much from hunger and fever to dare such an act. Yet I couldn't help but wonder why this young, fragile boy went unmolested while the older, stronger men starved. The boy glanced up, his eyes meeting mine, and he immediately pulled his meal toward him to protect it.

I watched him for a long time, then took a seat next to him just as he was finishing his meal. There was only a heel of bread left with the faintest trace of rice smeared across it. He looked at me, and for the briefest moment I thought he would offer it to me. He didn't.

"I cannot give you food," he said quietly. "None of us have enough to eat. We all must struggle for what little we can keep. If I give you bread today, you will take my bread tomorrow."

"How do you know that?" My voice was not as strong as I wanted it to be.

"Because Western people have always treated Chinese in such a manner. But there are ways to acquire food in Kongping."

"What ways?"

The Chinese boy smiled as though dangling a secret before my eyes. I grew impatient.

"The prisoners form a wall around that food, a wall I can't climb."

"Most men think of scaling a wall," he said, "but a wise man makes use of what he has and goes around."

Wonderful, I thought. He'd succeeded in being cryptic but not in being understood. I started to rise, when I felt his hand on my arm.

"I am called Kim. What is your name?"

I stopped. "Is it important in this place?"

"Only if we are to become friends."

I considered this for a moment. "My name is Dee."

"Ah, an American, yes?" His eyebrows raised a bit. "It is truly uncommon for an American to be placed in here. Surely your own embassy will intercede in your behalf."

Kim was pretty well informed in the ways of Shanghai, so he was hardly surprised when I told him the basics of my story. When I finished, he shook his head.

"As with all of us behind these walls, you are a victim of circumstance," Kim said quietly. "But you do not have to starve to death." I waited for him to continue. He smiled slightly. "There are some men here who would enjoy the tenderness of a young boy. Someone like yourself. In all this misery, there are still those who wish pleasurable experience. It is the custom to share food for such favors."

I reacted with shock. "You want me to go with a man?"

"It is a suggestion," Kim explained. "There are worse fates. There is starvation, there is rape . . . or you could end up like the elder over there."

Kim pointed in the direction of an elderly man who was slowly dying, too weak to move toward the food, in too much pain to moan. A rat scurried toward his chest, sniffed his chin. The elder didn't move, didn't whimper. As I watched, the slight heaving of his chest cavity came to a soft, merciful halt.

I looked to Kim. "That's no way to die."

"Then permit me to help you."

I shook my head. "No. I couldn't . . . go with a man. I couldn't."

Kim shrugged. "You are wrong, my friend. You can. It only takes a place like Kongping to prove it to us."

Kim rose, advising me to sleep with my back against the wall. Since I wouldn't prostitute myself, my chances of being a victim of gang rape increased drastically. Then he moved off. Well, maybe it was easy for Kim to sell himself to survive. I just couldn't.

My eyes rested on the dead elder again. Within a short period of time, a pair of Chinese river pirates moved toward his body. I knew them to be pirates because they were part of a clique the other prisoners avoided. They were lean and tanned but vicious around the eyes and mouth. Within seconds they stripped the clothing from the elder's corpse, marveling at the durable and finely spun cloth. Then they stopped and I followed their eyes to a cryptic tattoo on the dead man's arm. It was a dagger with a fierce serpent curled around the blade. I'd seen many tattoos in my day, but never one like that. Quickly the Chinese pirates glanced around to see if any other prisoners were observing their actions. Then one of the Chinese stooped over and turned the corpse onto its back and began untying a leather thong hanging around the elder's neck. Attached to this thong was a long tube. The Chinese stood and opened the tube to reveal several multicolored, apparently precious stones hidden inside. Pocketing the tube, the pirates abandoned the body hastily.

I was puzzled by what I'd just witnessed. Obviously the tattoo was a key to the elder's past, a past which allowed him to build a small fortune in gems. But why had he permitted himself to starve to death when he could easily have bribed the guards for food? For freedom? What concept compelled him to accept death rather than enrich his enemies? My curiosity was bitterly stung as I realized this elder had died embracing secrets most men couldn't comprehend.

It was then that I first noticed a huge Oriental pressing through the crowd. He was tall, devastatingly powerful, with a mane of thick black hair. His head was lowered in contemplation but his eyes widened at the sight of the dead elder's tattoo. He raised his head, then glanced at me, realizing that I was watching him.

The immense Oriental knew exactly what he was looking for. He studied the tattoo, then searched for the tube. Noticing it was gone, he looked to me again. The fear within me heightened as his eyes locked with mine. Then, quickly turning away, he picked up the body in his massive arms and carried it to the entrance of the dayroom as close to the gateway as possible. The Japanese would be forced to remove the corpse for proper burial. Then he vanished into the crowd, leaving me with thousands of questions.

Hours passed during which I napped to the harsh sounds of a thousand surrounding men. The shuffling of bare feet against the concrete was annoying, but it was the heartbeat of Kongping.

"Boy, tell me who ravaged the body of the elder," a voice from behind me commanded quietly.

I turned around to see the Oriental. He stood precisely erect in posture so I could appreciate the fullness of his six-foot frame. A chill passed through me as I looked up into his eyes, realizing that this man could kill as easily as other men breathe.

"They were river pirates, I think." I didn't think twice about answering him. "They took the elder's clothing . . . and a tube."

I waited for a reply. There was none. He was gone as quickly as he'd appeared. I turned my attention elsewhere. Then I became scared. The river pirates would certainly kill me if they knew I'd talked to the Oriental. And Kongping was all eyes and ears. They would find out.

A pair of Japanese guards armed with polished nightsticks entered the compound, searching the crowd for someone. Their cruel eyes spotted me, then made a pathway through the mass. No words were spoken as they grasped my shoulders and pulled me to the gateway. A moment later I stood before Commandant Nagata in the corridor. He didn't waste time with meaningless greetings.

"The Kempetai has inquired about your role in the

smuggling of guns to the Nationalists. You will tell me of these intrigues."

He turned and led me away from the compound, and as I enjoyed the first lengthy walk in an un-crowded zone since being arrested, I considered what he'd said. The Kempetai were the Japanese secret police.

I tried innocence. "There is nothing to tell, Colonel Nagata. I was only the cabin boy and I wasn't even on the ship when the guns were unloaded."

"Ah, but you have knowledge that the guns entered Shanghai aboard the *China Star?* And you will sign a statement to that effect, yes?"

I thought quickly. All the crates had been shipped out of New York. The Japanese knew this by the stenciling on the boxes. I needed to lie to buy myself some time. But what?

I tried flippancy. "Why should I?"

"It would save you from the methods of the Kempetai," he answered simply. "They are very interested in you, but are at bay only due to my interces-sion. I assured them I would personally question you on these matters and provide them with prompt, truth-ful answers."

I tried lying. "There is really nothing to tell. We picked up the crates in Bremen, Germany, and—"

The commandant halted his stride before a stairwell leading to the cellars of Kongping. He turned to face me. His expression was hardly pleased.

"The crates were marked as being shipped out of the port of New York. How is it they were picked up in Bremen?"

I shrugged. "I don't know. We stopped at Bremen and that's where those crates were loaded. If the boxes were marked New York, then I guess somebody is trying to hide who really shipped them."

Nagata regarded me with half-closed eyes while con-sidering this information. Was I lying? And if I wasn't, did that mean that the Germans were secretly supply-ing the Nationalists? He knew, as I had learned on the voyage, that Bremen was one of the toughest paper ports in the world, a harbor where an inordinate amount of regulation made the captain's manifest a veritable nightmare. Anything that moved in or out of Bremen did so with the knowledge of the German government. That would include the clandestine shipments of guns. If Nagata passed on my information, the Kempetai would be forced to evaluate whether or not the Germans were Nationalist supporters. It could take months, and would buy me time.

We reached the cellars, and Nagata had not responded to my implications concerning the arms. The cellars housed the torture chambers run by the Kempetai.

A scream shattered the eerie silence and I froze. Nagata, sensing my hesitancy, placed his arm about my shoulder, urging me on in an almost fatherly fashion. We proceeded toward the end of the hallway, then paused before the blood-splattered archway opening into one of the subdivided rooms.

Inside this particular cubicle, a Chinese soldier was seated on a stool, his head resting on his chest as a result of a merciless beating. Two Japanese Army intelligence goons were leaning against the archway, sharing a cigarette. My eyes went back to the soldier. His eyes were blackened and his face encrusted with dried blood. He mumbled in Chinese, and the soldiers cut short their break and began to beat him again. As I watched in horrified silence, Nagata shifted his gaze to me.

"A mild inquisition," he said evenly.

"I guess so." I tried not to betray the extent of my terror. "He's not dead yet."

"He will talk," the commandant sighed. "They all do. Eventually."

Nagata steered me farther down the hallway and into a section where the guards were cleaner, more casually dressed. A crisply attired young man came forward to greet Nagata. He was small but powerful, with an air of confidence. I knew without being told that he was the resident officer of the Kempetai.

"Has the boy talked yet?" He spoke in English, probably for my benefit.

"He has offered a few things of interest."

The Kempetai officer smiled benevolently at Nagata, then without warning wheeled around and jabbed a nightstick deep into my stomach. I buckled and fell to the floor, the pain causing me to want to vomit, my empty stomach making it impossible.

I tried to focus on Nagata, who wore a worried, distasteful expression on his face. His eyes told me we had departed civilization for a gray area with no rules, each man at the total mercy of his captor. In that moment, I realized Nagata was just as much a captor of the dread Kempetai as I was his. And I vowed that this would never happen to me again.

Commandant Nagata waved the sentries over and indicated that I should be assisted to my feet. "Return the boy to the holding pens," he commanded.

As they seized my arms, dragging me to my feet, I watched Nagata walk to the Kempetai officer and speak. I couldn't hear what they said, but I watched as the officer's face began to turn dark as a thunderstorm. And as they led me away, dragging me until I was able to walk, I realized that they were in no position to discard my story simply because it couldn't be verified. The officer's stormy face was like a mirror of the turmoil in the Far East. I knew there would be a war, and that armies would win it. Information would sharpen the edge of the victor's sword.

And I realized, as I was being thrown back into the herd of starving prisoners, that I would survive Kongping.

Still hazy from the violent encounter with the Kempetai, I made my way through the vicious throng in the steamy dayroom, pushing along the fringes until reaching a corner far away from the entranceway. It was then that I noticed the bodies of the young Chinese pirates. Both of them lay like smashed dummies, and judging from the ring of blue-black bruises around their throats, each neck had been brutally broken. Looking around furtively, I thought to search the bodies for the tube I'd seen them take from the corpse, but as I took a step forward, Kim appeared, took my arm, and led me in the opposite direction. He didn't speak until we were several yards away, and even then he whispered.

"Leave them."

"Why?"

"The big Korean killed them," Kim explained quietly. "It is a matter of honor a Western man would not understand. But whatever the reason, no one in Kongping will question it."

"Who is this Korean? And why do you make him seem so important?"

Kim didn't answer immediately. First he produced a fresh pack of American Lucky Strikes, then lit one and handed it to me. I pulled in deeply on the butt, my hands trembling from hunger. The tobacco stabilized my stomach for a moment or so, but it wasn't the proper replacement for stale bread and tepid water.

"His name is not important," Kim finally offered as he continued to gaze around nervously. "Is there a reason why he would keep his eye on you?"

"I don't know," I replied, turning around slowly. My eyes picked the Korean out of the crowd immediately, and Kim was right: he was watching me. He caught my glance, stared at me for a moment, then took his spine-chilling attention elsewhere.

"Do not fall in his way," Kim warned quietly. "He is the cause of many graves."

Kim left me a few cigarettes and matches before meeting one of his clients. I looked through the crowd for the Korean, but he was gone. I knew he'd avenged the elder and wondered if he had plans to kill me too.

My thoughts turned to food again as the Japanese wheeled the large vats into the corridor adjacent to the gateway, the prisoners becoming apprehensive as the guards came into view. I pushed my way forward, praying to seize only a handful of rice or, better, a crust of bread. I shoved by several larger prisoners and almost reached the bread vat before they pulled me away. I fought back but they tossed me aside like so much garbage. This time, I came up swinging and smashed one of the men across the jaw. For a moment he seemed amused, but too soon his eyes flamed in hatred. He buried a fist in my stomach as another prisoner rushed to join him. Instantly there were three or four of them swarming all over me. I knew I would be beaten to death.

Massive fingers of yet another prisoner gripped my collarbone, and suddenly I was pulled free. My head swung about quickly as the crowd at the food vats fell silent. I was looking deep into the dark eyes of the huge, powerful Korean.

"Let the boy eat!" His bass voice reverberated at the wall of men surrounding us. "The boy eats first or I shall see the rats feed upon any who dare block his path."

The other prisoners retreated as the Korean pulled me to my feet. A few moments later, I was walking away from the vats with a bowl of soggy rice and a large, overbrowned end of bread.

I consumed the food and watched the normal chaos return to the line as I searched the crowd for the large Korean. I found him meditating against one of the walls. Before him were three bowls of food, which he had yet to eat. I squatted a few feet away from him but didn't speak until I was certain he'd completed his ritual of solitude. I moved closer as he picked up his first bowl of rice.

"Why are you here?" he asked without looking at me.

I was about to answer, when I noticed the tube of gems resting against his wide, muscular chest. The highly polished cylinder was attached to the leather thong, which was looped around his neck. Visions of the dead pirates flashed through my mind. My voice faltered as I answered him.

"I wish to thank you."

"A service deserves a service, but it does not answer my question. Why are you in Kongping?"

"I was arrested by the Japanese."

The Korean swallowed an edge of bread covered with rice, then smiled.

"There are four thousand men in this place. All have been arrested by the Japanese. What crime does a young Westerner commit against the Imperial Empire so as to earn him such a dread distinction?"

I told him what had happened to me and waited as the Korean quietly considered my story.

He studied me. "Did these guns ever reach the Nationalists?"

"Yes," I replied. "At least, I think so. The Japanese only got a small part of the shipment, from what I saw."

"Has Nagata interrogated you?"

"Yes." I had the strange feeling he already knew the answers to many of the questions he was asking. "The commandant was fishing. I guess he was under pressure from the Kempetai. I told him the shipment came out of Bremen. Thought maybe it'd buy me some time."

"So, you seek to play the Kempetai off against the Germans?" The Korean's smile widened. "Do you really think it would work, that the Japanese are so gullible?"

I shrugged. "Nagata has to tell the Kempetai something. My story is as good as any. He's in a bad place for someone who's the commandant of an imperial prison."

Above us, the prison lights blinked several times as though there was a problem with the generating system. Outside, the Japanese guards came to an alert. The Korean and I looked around, but everyone appeared fairly calm. We continued talking.

"Nagata's position is commonplace to him," the Korean told me. "Someday he will retire to his meek position at the Tokyo International Bank and cease being the savage he is now. Oh, he will dream horribly of a procession of dead men, but in the end, he shall outlive his contemporaries. In another time and place, he is a good man. A considerate father. A passionate lover. An excellent businessman. But all this is alien to us. His job is holding us in. Conquering us. For these unspeakable acts, his reward is an eventual return to civilian life."

"And us?" I shifted nervously as the lights flickered once again. "Who holds our reward?"

"I cannot speak for you, young friend, but my own fates have already plunged my life into the harshness of war." The Korean's face turned sorrowful. "My homeland is conquered by the Japanese. The family I loved was betrayed and slaughtered by a rival. Only one other of my bloodline survives. And I have become a prisoner not only of the Japanese but also of the unyielding devils who torture my soul."

Suddenly the Korean realized he was confiding in me and pulled back to his rigid, militaristic self. The person who had slain two pirates became evident again. His eyes were shielded by an iciness I couldn't penetrate.

The lights flickered again, this time accompanied by shouting outside the compound. This was followed by machine-gun fire and, as prisoners reacted, an explosion. Seconds later, the lights in the prison were extinguished completely as the first cannon shot burst against the prison wall, spraying flame along the concrete.

The prisoners screamed in the darkness as the second artillery burst blew in a wall on the opposite side of the prison, leaving a huge hole laced with burning pieces of concrete and illuminated by the moonlight. The prisoners began running toward the hole, and I gave in to the impulse to follow the herd. Only the Korean stopped me with his viselike grip.

"Get down and roll toward the wall," he ordered, pushing me in that direction. He didn't have to explain why.

The machine-gunners in the booths high above the dayroom opened up on the crowd below. Kongping became, in that moment, a living hell as prisoners screamed and fell dead as they ran. Many others were trampled in the blind charge for the opening.

More artillery fire from outside the prison blew several more archways into the ancient walls of Kongping. The Korean began pulling himself out of range of the guns and into one of the corridors leading to the cellblocks. Then, together, we were running the length of the prison to a section where the cells had been mangled by the artillery. The Korean knew exactly where he was going; and I followed as fast as my legs could carry me. Finally we went through the hole in the wall and began running outside on the streets along a wall of Kongping, the prison the Japanese had considered impregnable. Once we were past the Japanese patrols rushing toward Kongping, the Korean slowed his pace.

"We must separate here, young friend," he said flatly, almost coldly.

I became frightened. I didn't want to leave this man who'd saved my life, then guided me through the chaos to freedom.

"Can't I go with you?"

"No. It would be too dangerous." The Korean turned to leave. My voice stopped him.

"But I don't even know your name. And you've saved my life." I hesitated. "My name is Dee."

The Korean surveyed me as though remembering someone else. There was sorrow in his eyes, but his voice was strong.

"I am called Ducksun." He leaned forward when he told me. It was almost a whisper, so the rest of the world wouldn't hear. "Both my name and my life are in your hands, young friend, for the Japanese would trade half an empire for a single drop of my blood."

Ducksun didn't give me time to acknowledge. He turned, then vanished into the darkened roadway leading toward free Shanghai.

And I wasn't far behind.

3

Free Shanghai bustled around me. Several days had passed since the mass escape from Kongping prison. Bold, black headlines burst the story upon the European concessions despite a relentless Japanese propaganda drive to denounce the daring Nationalist thrust at liberating the prisoners.

Like hundreds of others, I was free of shackles yet a slave to my own hunger. I searched for work, but Shanghai was a harsh mistress, offering much, giving little. Most of the Chinese population was starving, and I watched as they groveled in alleyways and at service doors begging for food scraps, attacking the gutters for a handful of anything edible. I pitied them. I had better prospects. I would never be reduced to such degradation. Or so I thought.

After pushing back my hair and brushing down my clothing as best I could, I shoved my way through the heavy doors of a busy Nanking Road restaurant. As slender Chinese waiters rushed by me wielding huge bobbing trays of food with amazing adeptness, I asked to see the manager. I waited twenty minutes before he would see me.

He was a tall, handsome Chinese who enunciated his English flawlessly. He glanced at his watch. "You have two minutes."

I responded quickly. "I'm looking for a job."

He smiled as one would at a bad joke. "So you think you're a runner."

"I could try, sir. I need a job and I'm not afraid of hard work."

He studied me carefully. "The trays are bulky and heavy. You must maintain an excellent sense of balance. Do you think you could do that?"

I tried to hide my eagerness. "I'll do anything I have to, as long as it's good honest work."

He brought his slender fingers up to his chin and peered down at me. I could see by his apprehensive yet benevolent expression that I had the job.

"What's your name, boy?"

"Dee."

"Well, Dee, I usually don't hire Western boys. They never seem to work out. But I'm going to give you a chance. One condition, though. You're to use your first day's pay to purchase better clothing. I can't have my runners looking as filthy as you do. Now, go wash up and report to Hun. You'll be with his crew."

I was so elated I even hummed a tune to myself as I scoured the dirt from my hands, arms, and face. When I reported to Hun, I found his crew lounging nearby smoking fat, ugly cigarettes. The crew leader himself was engaged in a loud argument with the manager. It was over me.

They cursed each other in Chinese as Hun pointed to me and shook his head, then rolled his eyes heavenward as if calling upon some god to bolster his argument. But the manager's will prevailed and Hun reluctantly directed me to the trays. His English was broken but understandable.

"You work my crew. Do all I say or no job for you. You understand?"

I nodded. "What do you want me to do?"

"My crew run lunch trays to taipans at British Export Bank. Important men, no time for fools. Understand? We bring them food, set up meal like home. They pay me, I pay you when day over. We send food four banks. They know Hun's crew best in Shanghai, expect big amount service. We work fastly. No have even small problem, or no job for you. These all my customers. They want crew do proper job. Now, enough talk. Pick up tray."

There were five of us in the crew. The expert runners were assigned large oval trays of meats and poultry, while those behind, equally adept, handled soups and sauces. My tray, the lightest of the group, consisted of breads, salads, and various dressings.

My confidence sky-high, I figured to maneuver the crowded streets carefully but smoothly. This worked well while in the restaurant, but the moment we stepped out onto Nanking Road, the other boys began to run. With a single expert hand they held their trays high while shouting in Chinese. In seconds, only their raised trays were visible to me. They pierced the shifting crowds so easily that I decided to run too. Their simplicity, however, was a fiction. I managed only five full steps before tumbling the entire tray into the gutter.

I froze, certain all China had witnessed my stupidity. Then, as though upon cue, the homeless and starving people in the crowd dived for the spilled food. I ran from the scene and didn't possess the courage to return to the restaurant. I didn't even have the sense to get some of the food for myself.

My public humiliation kept me from trying to get work for several days. As my hunger heightened, I attempted to penetrate the crowds milling about the alleyways adjacent to restaurants in the district. Most of the time I was driven away, so I wisely decided to work the larger social clubs instead. Because these elite areas were well-policed, the crowds were sparse. It would be a piece of cake. I was wrong. The amount of consumable food in those trashcans wouldn't cover a small lunch plate.

I continued prowling the streets, searching out food and opportunity, but neither crossed my starving path. I weaved through the hustling crowds watching colorful singsong girls bouncing by in ornate rickshaws pulled by muscular Chinese, and well-heeled local criminals being carried in sedan litters followed by an entourage of armed guards. Even the lowliest beggars at their regular stations were better off than I was, for beneath their tattered clothing, each seemed at least well fed.

As I passed a place called the Little Dragon Pub, I paused to watch as a legless woman was assisted onto a small platform outside the doorway. While studying her method, I realized how unappreciated the fine art of begging was. Certainly I'd seen the woman's bedraggled counterpart in New York City, but the American fashion of apologetically asking alms wasn't nearly as polished a business as the Chinese form.

Near the stumps of her limbless thighs, the woman boldly displayed a bowl for dropped coins, and around her neck, tied to a thin length of rope, was a motionless infant who didn't cry or sob. I thought the child was asleep until the woman tossed it over her shoulder in order to keep it from blocking the tattered newspaper she was reading. She rested patiently until a prospect happened along, when she'd stretch out an arm, imploring tearfully in English or Chinese.

The Chinese ignored her but the Europeans wandering into the nearby tavern usually tossed a coin. Nodding and scraping respectfully, the woman gave a gracious thanks, then returned to the dog-eared copy of the *North China News*. In several instances she pulled forth the infant, holding the tiny body forward, hoping to evoke even more pity. It seemed she could extort coins magically with only a doleful glance. I decided to ask her for help.

While making my way toward her, I became acutely aware of two men standing at the corner. They came alert upon seeing me but then relaxed, deciding I wasn't dangerous. I shook my head. This racket was lucrative enough to support a pair of bodyguards.

The beggarwoman lifted her head as I approached, nearly commencing her act, but after sizing me up, figured it wasn't worth the effort and returned to her newspaper. When I didn't go away, she became suspicious.

"If you are thinking of robbery, I caution you," she said tiredly, probably the victim of many such attempts in the past.

"I'm not."

"Ah, then you've come to share your wealth with an old woman?" She brightened for a moment.

"I have no money."

"Then why do you stop? To gawk? To taunt? To

51

raise my hopes? Perhaps to listen in silent mockery as I implore for the lowliest of coppers?"

"I only want to talk to you."

She studied me through narrowed eyes. "Then say as you will and be gone before my business is darkly affected."

I took a deep breath. "I'm hungry."

She reacted with boredom. "So are thousands. My heart bears you little sympathy because you are a barbarian. Barbarians always eat because they take liberally from others. Are you a stranger to Shanghai?"

"Yes."

"And so you come to an old beggarwoman who can barely feed her own miserable self?"

"You did not become an *old* beggarwoman by starving to death."

The woman smiled, then laughed darkly. "Why does such an observant boy hunger for food? Is there not an opportunity for you to seize?"

I shrugged. "I'm not sure what to do."

She studied me again, then suddenly drew back the hem of her heavy sack dress to reveal the stumps of her thighs. The ends were seared an unsightly brownish-pink from the white-hot irons that had closed the amputation wounds decades before. I tried to look away, but her words pulled me back.

"Return your glance to me, boy!" I turned slowly and looked at her. "Look. You sought me out, yet you cannot face what is the truth."

"I didn't expect . . ."

"To what?" She slapped her thighs viciously. "To see life in all its benevolent splendor? Listen, boy, and I will tell you a tale. My parents before me were beggars, my mother blinded by Manchu soldiers, my father without arms. When they fell sick, I was but four or five and only I remained to collect enough coin for the day's rice. So my parents ordered a cart made for me, and my legs were cut off. My childhood was squandered rolling about the muddy streets. I was pitied, but we had bread every day thereafter."

"They cut your legs off on purpose?" I couldn't believe what I was hearing. "Your own parents?"

"Did I not say so? My effectiveness increased ten-fold because Europeans scream inside at the sight of maimed children."

I stood in stunned silence. Then from behind us came the clatter of a two-wheeled cart being pulled by an elderly man. He paused before the beggarwoman, exchanged a few words, then bowed ceremoniously. The woman reached inside her rags and handed him a few coins, which he tucked into a pouch near his waist. Then she pulled the baby forward by tugging at the rope around her neck. I don't know why I hadn't noticed the stench before, but it was starkly evident now. The baby had been dead for several days and was rapidly decomposing. She handed the tiny corpse to the old man, who in turn dropped it into a disposal basket attached to his cart. Then, from beneath the canvas covering the rear of the wagon, he selected a live baby boy. After scrutinizing the wriggling infant for defects, the old man handed it to the beggarwoman. The babyvendor bowed again while chattering in Chinese before continuing on to his next customer.

Paying little attention to me, the woman tied the rope around the cooing naked baby boy. "I hope this one cries," she pronounced to herself. "It's better for business."

"The other baby was dead." It wasn't a question.

"What? You still here?" But she showed no real surprise at my disbelief. "Yes, the baby was dead. Why you think I buy new one?"

"But they're real babies . . ." I forced myself to speak despite the horror I was feeling. "How can they be bought and sold? Aren't there any laws?"

The woman sighed heavily. "Questions, questions." She shook her head. "Young boy, people buy and sell anything in Shanghai. Legal, not legal. Laws mean nothing." She looked up at me lecherously. "There are those who would sell you to some pillaging warlord in Szechwan. Some of those men hotly desire a boy's flesh and will pay most handsomely. I caution you, boy, align yourself with friends while here, or you will end up an unwilling concubine to some lusty murderer. Now, go before you affect my business."

I tried one last time. "Is there work in Shanghai?"

"There is always work in Shanghai. Especially for those whose bodies are sturdy." The beggarwoman paused thoughtfully. "You could make a profitable Bertie."

"What's a Bertie?"

"Go into next street. Look for the small shop whose windows are brightly lit. It is the only one there open at this hour. We have talked enough." She signaled to the bodyguards lingering near the corner. It was time for me to go.

I began searching out the building in the next street over, and she was right, it wasn't hard to find. It was all lit up, and laughter was emanating from it. When I appeared in the doorway, the voices subsided and a tall Eurasian man signaled me forward.

"Well," he asked calmly in perfect English, "what do you want?"

"I need work."

He appraised my thin form. "You sure look it. What can you do?"

"A beggarwoman up the street thinks I'd make a good Bertie, whatever that is."

Before he could answer, two emaciated Chinese boys rushed into the shop, shoving me out of their path. Each had a can tied to his neck by a leather thong. They carried long broom-handle pokers whittled to a sharp needle point. The Eurasian inspected the can, nodded approvingly, then handed each boy a copper. The coins gratefully accepted, the boys dumped the contents of their cans onto a sorting table. Several hundred half-smoked cigarettes and cigar stubs poured out and were immediately separated into groups by the scavengers working the table. With nimble expertise they severed the unburned tobacco from both paper and wrapping leaf. The tobacco, mild or strong, greenish or brown, was then mixed into a large bowl at the end of the table. Two women stationed there added fresh, heavier leaves so the result proved consistent with cigarette grade.

The Eurasian picked up a freshly rolled cigarette from a nearby box. He lit it, then passed it to me. I inhaled, noting it didn't taste too harsh for rerolled tobacco.

"Now do you understand what Berties do?"

"Yes," I replied. "They walk the streets looking for cigarette and cigar butts, which you make into new cigarettes."

"Quite right." He nodded. "We sell our finished product to rickshaw boys, coolies, and other low-wage laborers who buy one at a time. It's cheaper for them than buying a pack of American tailor-mades. I pay a copper for two full cans. Full as you can get them, understand? You won't get rich, but you'll eat regular."

"When can I start?" I tried to cover the sense of urgency in my voice.

Silently the Eurasian directed me to the supply lockers in a nearby storeroom. He outfitted me with a litter poke and two neck cans. Then he wished me luck and I left.

I walked slowly while studying the gutter. Five agonizing blocks later, I realized the streets of Shanghai were cluttered with everything but tobacco leavings. During this luckless period I rescued a single half-smoked cigarette from the city sewer system. The situation was ludicrous. I could absolutely swear I'd noticed hundreds of people tossing partially spent butts into the road during my daylight travels. Where were all those unwanted cigarettes now?

After hiking a mile through a dismal section of the city, I'd collected half a can of butts. The putrid, stale odor of spent tobacco was beginning to give me a headache and I began to wonder if there was a more profitable way to corner the butt-salvage market.

As I turned a corner, the lights of a small B-grade nightclub flashed at me and I realized I'd found a gold mine. All I had to do was boldly enter the club and empty the ashtrays until I'd filled both cans. Hell, I could do that in a matter of minutes.

There wasn't any doorman to contend with, so I sauntered through the entranceway and by the hatcheck girl. She seemed to glance at me with slight inquisition, but since everyone in Shanghai has a racket, she let me pass.

There was a makeshift stage where a band went through several numbers of Benny Goodman, Tommy Dorsey, and Bunny Berrigan. A half-dozen singsong girls drifted quietly from table to table. The place wasn't a boisterous sailors' pub, but it wasn't designed for couples either. I nodded to the bartender, who acknowledged me warily but then went on about his own business. I strolled to a table and began my work.

"Excuse me, sir," I offered politely. "'Empty your ashtray?"

Most people cast me an annoyed glance, but I didn't care. I was really racking up the butts, and several tables later, the cans were overflowing. I'd grabbed my night's take in little more than thirty minutes, and I'd be able to eat tomorrow.

I departed the club cheerfully and feeling successful as all hell.

I was still smiling when two lanky Chinese boys stopped me just outside the club. A stream of Shanghai dialect brought the quiet street to life. I didn't understand their words, but the cans around their necks indicated I'd just violated their territory. I raised my poker at the same moment they did, because, Shanghai or Long Island City, territory is territory.

They stabbed at me simultaneously, but I managed to dodge their initial parries and whack one of my adversaries across the arm. He screamed in ungodly tones as my poker point broke skin, spilling blood. Then the other boy came at me like a maniac. He was completely unafraid and nearly gouged my eye out. I counterattacked, thrusting at his bony legs. I missed but didn't have a chance to regain my balance and attack again.

Suddenly other voices surrounded me. From the shadows ran the friends of the Berties I'd wronged. In seconds they were all over me. My poker snapped under the weight of the heaviest boy, and I felt some bastard knee my groin. I screamed for help, but as soon as my mouth opened wide, a hand ripped through my gums. The battering continued and soon I lost all concept of time. My eyes closed under the blows and I knew I was losing it.

Then I thought I heard the shrill screaming of tires and deeper shouts in guttural Chinese. Suddenly the boys scattered, leaving me crumpled on the pavement. But I was alive.

My first sight of her came through slitted bloody eyes. She was beautiful.

She was taller and older than I, with silken black hair piled high upon her head. She wore a three-quarter-length fur which was bunched sensuously around her throat, then dropped majestically to her knees. Her face, so classically Oriental, was the most stunning I'd ever seen. She glanced down at me, a determined expression across her proud face.

Beside her was a short Western cabbie who'd left his battered Buick idling nearby.

"Help me get him into the cab," she ordered in crisp, clear English.

The cabdriver was hesitant. "You sure you want to do this, lady?"

"If we leave him here, those boys will return and kill him." I didn't like the sound of that. She continued, "Now, help me take those ridiculous cans from around his neck and get him into the cab."

Friendly hands grabbed me, then pressed my body through the door frame of the Buick. As I fell back into the soft rear seat, my eyes closed completely. I was safe. The cab bolted forward.

And I slipped into darkness.

4

I slowly regained consciousness, realizing that I was lying on something soft and clean. My head felt heavy, my body battered, and my face hurt from cuts and bruises. I forced my eyes open and saw my muddy seaman's boots lying on the floor. I looked down. My shirt was open. Several feet away, thrown haphazardly across a barrel chair, was a fur coat. It seemed curiously familiar. Why? Everything was so fuzzy. Where was I?

She walked into the room carrying a porcelain washbasin and a bottle of alcohol tucked under her arm. God, she was beautiful. I couldn't take my eyes off her. She wore a simple coal-colored dress with a deep neckline which did little to hide her breasts. I watched her, eyes open as much as I could get them, as she knelt beside me.

"Oh, you're awake." She tested the water in the basin, pulling her hand quickly from the heat but managing to extract a washcloth.

"Where am I?" My voice was a hoarse whisper.

"Don't worry. You're safe." Her breasts swelled slightly as she spoke. "How do you feel?"

"I hope twice as bad as I look." I paused. It hurt to talk. "Where am I?"

"At my home in the French concession."

I looked at the fur coat again and it all came back. "You stopped those boys from killing me."

"Yes, I did," she replied. "I was on my way home. Tell me, what was a Western boy doing prowling around the streets of that area at night?"

I needed time to think. Even as she swabbed my face clean with the hot washcloth, I couldn't help but wonder why a total stranger would take me in. From the looks of the place and of her, she didn't need me or my problems.

I turned my face to look at her. "What's your name?"

"Crimson Orchid." She reached for the alcohol. "What's yours?"

"Dee."

We fell silent, appraising each other. Very rarely does a person meet someone whose name fits perfectly. Crimson Orchid did remind me of a fragile, delicate flower.

"Where do you live?"

"Nowhere."

"Everyone lives somewhere."

I shrugged. "Not me."

"Where do you sleep at night?"

"Depends pretty much on where I am. Doorways, sometimes. If nobody's sleeping there already. Alleyways in the restaurant district can be pretty comfortable."

She smiled. "I see you can joke about your plight." She finished wiping my face and set down the cloth. "Are you an urchin?"

"That would be a step up." I winced as she stung my face with the alcohol.

"Sorry."

Tears welled up in my eyes from the alcohol or from my whole situation, I don't know which. "It's okay."

She looked at me with concern. "Are you all right?"

I nodded. "It's just that everything's . . . everything's gone wrong ever since I docked in Shanghai. My ship left without me, I was arrested by the Japanese, thrown into prison . . ." I found I couldn't continue.

She studied me. She rose and started from the room.

"I will fix you something to eat. Then you can tell me all about yourself."

When she was gone, I gingerly touched my face, running my fingers over the bandages she'd placed there. I leaned back into the couch, realizing how lucky I was but still not understanding why. I looked around the living room, my eyes falling on the expensive furnishings, fine paintings, and distinctive Oriental artwork. High up on the far wall, centered between two immense candles, was a woodcut of the traditional Chinese dragon. The brilliant coloring of this powerful beast reminded me of the way China was depicted by the American newspapers. Until arriving here, I always thought of it as a large land hidden in darkness, a people awkward by Western standards. But China proved to be a lumbering, lethally deceptive giant, organized beyond the dreams of the average Westerner.

As I sat lost in thought, Crimson Orchid returned with a small platter of chicken arranged around various vegetables.

She set the platter down on a table in front of me. "Here. Eat."

I looked up at her. "It sure looks good. Thanks." I started in on the chicken and realized it was the first real food I'd eaten since I walked off the deck of the *China Star.*

"Tell me about yourself." She reached for a cigarette. "I'm very curious."

"There's not much to tell. I'm just another kid off the streets." I stuffed more chicken in my mouth to keep from saying more. My jaw actually ached from disuse.

"If you truly knew the streets, as you claim, you would not have been in the situation I found you in. Why did your ship leave without you?"

I took a breath, then decided I owed her some kind of explanation. "I don't think they meant to. I mean . . . well, I was the cabin boy on the *China Star.* When we docked in Shanghai, I got a day's liberty. While I was looking around the city, the Japanese ordered the ship from port. So they went. Without me."

"Why?"

"They claimed we delivered a shipment of arms for the Nationalists."

"Did you?" She exhaled a puff of smoke and I watched as it lingered in the air.

"Yeah, I guess so. It was then everything fell to smash. The Japs marched me off to Kongping prison."

She stopped smoking. "You were in Kongping?"

I swallowed, then nodded. "Yeah. Almost starved to death, too. Would have if I hadn't done some favor for a big Korean. He helped me fight my way to the front of the food line. I didn't eat well that day, but I ate."

She was watching me carefully now. "Didn't the Nationalists shell the prison several days ago?"

"That's how I got out. Christ, it was something else. On one side, the Nationalists were blowing the prison walls all to hell, and on the inside, the Japanese were gunning everybody down. I was one of the lucky ones. I managed to get through a hole blown in the wall. Then I crossed the Soochow and started another career in starvation." I looked at her. "This was real good. Thanks."

She nodded acknowledgment, then rose from the barrel chair and walked to the bar. "Would you care for something to drink?"

"Anything cold."

She nodded and quietly fixed herself a drink and got a beer for me. She brought me the drink, and after sampling hers, set it down on the cocktail table between us. 'Where is home to you?"

"New York City."

"Ah, then you are an American." She pulled three ornate pins from the pile of glossy black hair set in a sort of double bun at the top of her head. Suddenly her hair fell free and, with the slightest shaking of her head, came tumbling down to her shoulders. I watched transfixed as she continued. "You can simply go to your embassy and ask for help."

"I don't want them to send me back."

"You would rather starve?"

"Yes."

She considered this. "Do you have parents in America?"

"My dad died when a dock crane fell and crushed him to death. My mom's been sick and hasn't been able to support me for a long time. It's not her fault.

It's the depression. Things weren't exactly terrific in America when I left."

"But have you no interest in what has become of your mother?"

"Sure I do. I posted a letter to her from London, telling her not to worry about me. And I figure with me gone, she's probably better off. Anyway, like I said, I don't want to go back."

"You aren't stupid, Dee. You must realize that your chances in Shanghai are probably worse than in New York."

"I don't know. Maybe." We sat in silence for a minute before I decided to change the subject. "What about you, Crimson Orchid? You seem to be doing pretty well by yourself."

Orchid took a deep breath before answering, then spoke quietly.

"It is an illusion, Dee. All that you see are the gifts of men who find pleasure in my skills."

I think my mouth dropped a bit. "You're a prostitute?"

"I am. Are you shocked?"

"I think so." I looked at her. "You sure don't look like a prostitute."

She laughed gently. "And tell me, boy, what do prostitutes look like these days?"

I didn't realize she was teasing me. "Well, in New York, they were all painted up and . . . well, cheap. Even the singsong girls here look like . . . sorta phony. But you don't look like one of those. You don't look roughed up or anything. You're so . . . pretty."

"Those women you saw, they look roughed up, as you call it, because it is a brutal profession that wears upon a woman like the flame does the candle. We remain valuable only as long as we remain beautiful. Therefore, it is very important to me that I be beautiful. When that ends, my men will visit me no longer. And when that day comes, this illusion of prosperity will fade into the harsh reality of survival."

She looked down into her drink and I watched her. "Crimson Orchid," I offered softly, "you'll always be beautiful."

She looked up and locked onto my young eyes. In that moment I realized I was looking at a different woman. Then, quietly, and with little emotion, she told me the fragments of her life.

Sometimes people can speak of their own personal horrors only to strangers, to people they honestly believe they will never see again. Crimson Orchid must have believed that of me. She spoke of barbarity, of a destitute village in north China where the rice crop always failed and the children died young. She described the bandits who roamed the countryside and raped her mother. She spoke of her father, a tall and proud man, broken by the bandits, driven mad at seeing his wife violated. He had seized a makeshift pitchfork, turning it upon the marauding bandits straddling his bloodied, shrieking wife. For his effort, they impaled him, then marched his body around the village, striking fear into others who thought to resist. The bandits then took their rice, burned their home, and left.

Three years later they returned. Crimson Orchid was then fourteen, the perfect food for the hungry murderers. The bandits were harsh and gloated over their new discovery. They fought over her and killed Crimson's mother, who made a futile attempt to protect her child. Crimson Orchid became the property of the bandit leader. After two weeks of humiliation, she was sold to a wealthy landowner, who quickly took a liking to her and schooled her in the ways of etiquette. After spending three years with the wealthy mandarin, Crimson Orchid decided it was time to go off on her own. She ran away, came to Shanghai, and changed her name. When she buried her name, she buried her past.

Dawn arrived with the completion of her tale.

I didn't know what to say. I thought my life had been rough, but . . . "You didn't have to tell me all that."

"Yes, I did." She stood to yawn and stretch. "Besides, the thought struck me that I could use a boy about the house. It would be easier if I were friends with the person I decided to take in."

I wasn't sure what she was saying. "Are you asking me to stay here with you?"

"Yes. To work." She looked at me, then added, "You must obey in all that I ask of you. I will pay you fairly and allow you to board here. But you must not forget that you are my employee as well as my friend."

I considered this proposition for the shortest moment in my life. "I'd like that. I'd like it a lot. Thank you."

She smiled, and it brightened the room. "I think it's time for you to clean yourself and rest."

She left to prepare an extra bedroom. I stood and looked around the luxurious room and slowly shook my head. Maybe my luck was finally changing.

Crimson Orchid entertained several men each day, and I sensed she was more at ease now that I was around. I would frequently observe her fawning over a customer while leading him to the private areas of her home. Other times I could actually hear noises from her room, and a strange, aching feeling would come over me. There were moments when I'd imagine her making love to each man, visualize the exact expression on her face.

I was becoming possessive, though at the time I don't think I realized it. Yet I'd won her friendship and it blossomed as the days grew into weeks, the weeks into months. Our relationship was so comfortable, so familiar, I couldn't believe it was anything more than a fantasy. Nights alone in my bed, I would think of her and, in my own way, long for her. But I never brought up the subject of sex. Neither did she.

I ran errands for her, kept the bar well stocked, and on occasion served as bartender. I made certain the viperous laundry boys didn't cheat us out of any money, and I ran for the police when drunks or other undesirables fell anywhere near her doorstep. Once I even frightened off a burglar as he tried to jimmy a side window. Crimson Orchid sure kept me running, but at night, when I fell exhausted into my bed, I was happy.

As the months passed, she began to ask advice on

some little things. One day she paraded from the bedroom wearing a newly purchased pair of fur-lined panties.

She posed teasingly. "What do you think?"

The reaction on my face said it all.

I became accustomed to seeing Crimson Orchid in various stages of undress. Maybe "accustomed" isn't the right word. There were times I couldn't take my eyes off her, and others when I couldn't bear to look.

Her apparent sophistication mistakenly led me to believe that she was capable of handling any situation, but I came to discover over the months that what she couldn't deal with was the loneliness of her profession. It was then that she was most vulnerable.

One night, after the last customer had departed, I had retired to my bedroom and dropped right off to sleep. I awoke to find her curled up next to me.

I could feel the heat of her body next to mine. Her breasts touched my back, her foot touched mine. Her knees grazed the back of my thigh and her hand rested upon my waist. I moved slightly.

"Are you awake?"

I could barely respond. "Yes."

"I didn't mean to disturb you."

"Ah . . . it's okay." What was going on? Was she going to make love to me? Should I ask? I turned to face her. "Why are you here?"

She sighed and looked into my eyes. "Because sometimes a woman needs to sleep next to a friend rather than lie with a lover."

I never forgot her words. We both slept well that night, sharing each other's warmth.

Crimson Orchid enjoyed Shanghai's exotic bazaars and frequented those situated in the French concession along the ancient walled town which was the oldest section of the city. Along those narrow, colorful streets she discovered those tiny knickknacks and accessories which contributed so much to her happiness.

"Dee . . . look!" She tugged at my arm, stopping abruptly before a stand owned by a proud Chinese elder. "See that vase?"

"Which one?" There were hundreds, all arranged by size, shape, and color.

"The aquamarine with the wide handles." Orchid leaned forward, then gently lifted the vase from the display. "It must be over two hundred years old. What do you think?"

I hesitated, not knowing what to say, but was saved by the old man, who began to speak to Orchid in Chinese. She listened attentively, her head tilted respectfully, then turned to me.

"He claims it is one of several pieces which came from a Manchu treasure house in Canton. He asks, in your money, twenty dollars."

"Sounds like a steal." What did I know? I figured it wasn't worth more than two bucks, but the Chinese were funny that way. They mixed aged, valuable stoneware with modern, less expensive goods. I couldn't tell the difference.

"Do you think I should buy it?"

I gazed at the toothless elder smiling solicitously. "If you don't, the old man might cry." Her response was a look of reproach. "Ah, go ahead. It'd probably look good with a few flowers in it."

Crimson Orchid charmed the dealer into taking ten dollars, and he wrapped it graciously in a smudged old copy of the *North China News*. We bowed to him, then retreated into the crowd along the walled city's edge.

Both Orchid and I were getting hungry, so we stopped and took a table in a small café in the next block. As we sat, she admiring the vase, a familiar voice took me by surprise.

"Don't you greet old friends anymore, Dee?" said the boy handing me the menu.

It was Kim. In a moment we were embracing as Orchid looked on curiously. We broke apart, but I kept my hands on him.

"Kim . . . let me look at you. How are you?"

"I am well. And so, apparently, are you. I thought you died in Kongping. Few escaped alive." He looked to Crimson Orchid, then back to me.

I caught his look. "Oh, I'm sorry. Kim, I'd like you

to meet my friend Crimson Orchid. Orchid, this is my friend Kim."

Orchid extended a hand. "I am pleased, Kim."

"The pleasure is mine, Crimson Orchid." Kim looked at her carefully. "I must commend Dee upon his exquisite taste in women. Tell me, are you an entertainer in the French concession? I think I have seen you before. A singer, perhaps?"

"Hardly an entertainer of that sort," she laughed.

I tried to make it easy. "You're both in the same profession."

Crimson Orchid looked to Kim. "You are a prostitute?"

"Only when I need the money," Kim explained. "When one begins in the profession, one finds it difficult to quit. And it has saved my life. Otherwise I would have starved to death in Kongping."

I was uncomfortable and decided to change the subject. "How did you get out?"

"Through a hole in the wall. I watched as hundreds of men were gunned down by the Japanese, but I managed to survive by moving in the middle of a crowd."

"I got out the same way, with a little help from the big Korean. Then we split up."

I thought I saw Kim react, then cover. "The big Korean made it out?"

I nodded. "Yeah."

"What was his name? I've forgotten."

"Ducksun." I happened to be looking at Crimson Orchid as I answered, and at the mention of the name, she stiffened visibly. I realized I'd never mentioned his name before.

Kim nodded. "It was never his destiny to die in that awful place." He stood silent for a moment, then brightened. "You have found work?"

"Yes. I'm Crimson Orchid's houseboy."

"Houseboy?" His eyes shone mischievously, then looked upon Crimson Orchid. "I would watch him, Orchid. He is much too pretty to be a houseboy."

She smiled. "I noticed. Maybe I'll keep him around when I'm an old crone."

"I can't picture you old," I told her.

"We all get there, Dee. Beautiful whores and handsome houseboys alike. It's terrible to grow old, but even worse to die young."

For the briefest moment, my eyes locked with Crimson Orchid's and I received the distinct impression she intended a hidden message, but it went over my head. She turned away and picked up the menu. "I think I'll try the duck. Do they make it with real butter here, Kim? It's so scarce these days."

"Yes, and very delicately. And you, Dee?"

I shrugged. "I'll have the same."

He nodded. "Now I must return to work. I will leave you my address. I have rooms above a curio shop near Nanking Road."

He scribbled his address across the back of a napkin and then went about his business. Orchid didn't say much during the meal, picking at the duck. I could see something was bothering her, but I let it pass. I'd learned not to press her. It wasn't my place. Despite our friendship, I was still only her houseboy. If she had something to say, she'd tell me in her own good time.

We browsed through several shops on the way home, Orchid purchasing two finely polished sculptures representing a brave Chinese warrior and a demure, almost bashful Manchu lady. Upon arriving home, she placed them ceremoniously on the cocktail table.

"Do they look right there?" she asked.

"Why don't you try under the lamp? They'll catch the light."

She considered that, then nodded. As she moved the sculptures, the doorbell rang. A customer. Orchid sighed and disappeared into the bedroom. "Give me a few minutes to change."

I answered the door to find a young man leaning against the wall outside. He was one of Orchid's regular clientele and I knew him to be a fairly meek gentlemen, a stockbroker named Giles. He visited Orchid at least twice a week and was usually quiet and respectful. But today he seemed off his pins, and in a moment I detected the odor of whiskey.

"Where's Orchid?"

I was about to answer when he swept by me and wobbled into the living room. He got to the bar, then overturned a bottle of Scotch when reaching for a glass. The crashing bottle brought Orchid running.

"What's going on in here?"

"Fixin' a bloody drink. What's it look like?"

She glanced at me, still standing by the door. Her eyes told me to stay where I was. She would handle this.

"Giles," Orchid said softly, "why don't you go home and sleep it off?"

Giles downed his whiskey, then stared at Orchid. She was completely nude under the sheer full-length nightgown she'd slipped into. Giles slowly studied her body, a smile coming over his lips.

"Let's go find some fun, Orchid." He leered and grabbed her arm.

"Not today, Giles. You can barely stand up."

He grabbed her forcefully. "Bloody hell I can't." He pulled her close and brought his mouth down on hers harshly.

Orchid pulled away, a small trickle of blood coming from the corner of her mouth. She touched her fingers to her lips, then looked at the blood on her fingers. "Get out of here, you son of a bitch."

Giles came at her again, this time catching one of her breasts in his powerful hands. She screamed as he bent her backward over the bar, ripping at her gown.

I stood frozen.

"Dee, help me!"

I bolted up behind Giles and managed to get both my hands on his neck. His eyes bulged, but he quickly broke my grip. He turned on me as Orchid slipped to the floor. "You motherless little bastard. I'll bloody well kill you."

He was all over me. I took a hard right to the jaw, which sent me reeling into the cocktail table, then across it onto the couch. I lay there momentarily stunned as Giles swept the table aside with a single hand and then hoisted me by my shirt with the other. I slammed him dead across the eye, then again in the nose, but he was too drunk to feel it. Blood running from his nose, his eye starting to swell, he lifted me above his head and started walking toward the windows. In that moment I knew what he had in mind.

He never got the chance. Orchid got back on her feet and grabbed a lamp from an end table, jerking the cord from the wall socket so violently that sparks crackled in the air. Her sculptures smashed to the floor. I got a brief, surrealistic glimpse of her face; murder was written in her beauty. She smashed the lamp into a thousand pieces across Giles's head only a moment before he would have thrown me through the windows.

Giles growled, then collapsed onto the hardwood floor, taking me with him. Orchid sagged to her knees. My hands were trembling uncontrollably as I peered cautiously at Giles. He was unconscious. Then my eyes fell on Orchid where she sat, a small smile spreading across her face.

"Some protection you are."

"I tried. He was an animal."

She shook her head, but couldn't keep from smiling. "We'd better get him out of here before he wakes up."

Later, after cleaning up the shambles of her living room, Orchid and I were able to laugh. A bluish swelling was puffing out my cheek, so she made an ice pack.

"You should learn to defend yourself." She set the ice pack on my cheek.

"That hurts!"

"Keep it there."

"And I *can* defend myself. He just . . . well, took me by surprise."

"That would not happen if you knew the Gentle Way."

I removed the ice pack. "What's that?"

"It is a form of defense performed without weaponry, a martial art. Some of the more accomplished students are able to kill a man with a single well-placed blow."

"That's art?" I thought about Moroni lying on the docks of Long Island City, a knife protruding from his stomach.

"It is not the killing that comprises the art. It is the mastery of complete self-discipline that defines the Gentle Way. It is an inner force so powerful that it can break an ox's back as simply as you might snap a twig."

"I can't buy that." I put the pack back on my face. "I mean, I saw that judo stuff when we were docked in Japan, if that's what you're talking about."

She shook her head. "No. The Gentle Way is different, and far more effective. It is a symphony of lethal movement. I have a very close, dear friend who could teach it to you."

"You do?" This was starting to sound interesting.

"Yes. But I warn you, it requires rigorous discipline. Learning such a defense form is not child's play. My friend could school you in such precepts."

"School?" I remembered the public schools in New York, and my total aversion to them. "I don't think I could handle school again, but thanks."

She smiled. "I do not speak of a school of reading or writing. There, you will learn action and reaction. It is very physical."

"No, thanks. I think I'll pass."

"That is too bad, Dee." She paused, a mysterious expression coming into her eyes, the same one I'd noticed in the café that day. "It is such a loss for you. I believe the philosophy of the Gentle Way is something you have been looking for in a most unconscious fashion. You are different from most boys your age. You will be far different from men of your time. I sense this within you and I believe the Gentle Way is something you should study. Besides, I believe you have already met the man I would have teach you."

"Oh, yeah? Who's that?"

"His name is Ducksun."

5

Ducksun lived in a heavily guarded compound that included a greathouse, several outbuildings that had been transformed into barracks, and a few acres of open land that formed the southern border of the French concession. Following a week of friendly negotiations, Crimson Orchid was able to contact Ducksun. She told him my name and I was granted an audience immediately.

Orchid accompanied me to the compound but departed at the gate. Women were not allowed on the grounds of Ducksun's academy without his express permission. The training was of a covert nature. Only those directly involved in Ducksun's operation were permitted inside.

The Korean greeted me in the exterior courtyard. "And so, young friend, we meet again." Ducksun extended his hand. He appeared taller and stockier than when I'd seen him last.

"I never expected to see you again, Ducksun. You look well."

"I have been fortunate. And, I might add, so have you in discovering Crimson Orchid's friendship. She speaks highly of you."

"She's been terrific to me. She saved my life in more ways than one."

"I am well aware of what has transpired." Ducksun nodded. He began walking and indicated I should follow. "If you truly wish to do justice to Orchid's kindness, you will excel under my tutelage."

Ducksun led me into the greathouse. While walking through the corridors, we passed several Oriental guards. They were the most intimidating men I'd ever seen. They stood at rocklike attention and could be found guarding entrances, exits, and hall junctions. As Ducksun walked silently by them, each man bowed, then returned to his statuesque stance. I was impressed by the ingrained fealty these men demonstrated.

"It is only proper you be accepted directly into my household, Dee. Time is crucial because China is crumbling under pressure from the Japanese. We must utilize every moment in positive ways."

"Are your men ever sent against the Japanese?" I wondered aloud, suspecting they were partially responsible for the shelling of Kongping prison. Ducksun paused momentarily. I'd hit a sensitive subject.

"There have been days when my men have faced the Japanese," he answered. "From this moment onward, we shall become the busiest of men. There are many tasks to be accomplished. You will meet your instructor as soon as you've been assigned quarters. You will not see me often, but my adjutant, General Dang, will check upon you. He shall assist you in any way possible."

I moved my meager possessions into a cottage shared with several of Ducksun's Korean bodyguards. I liked the house and its grounds because it was one of the few homes left in expanding Shanghai with ample acreage. Ducksun left me alone to pack the small wooden footlocker assigned me. As I did, I couldn't help staring through the windows at several groups of men drilling in the grassy compound. They were repeating a series of moves like nothing I'd ever seen before. It did resemble judo, but it was somehow different. And, I suspected, far more lethal.

The house of Ducksun never rested. I was immediately placed under the guidance of Master Lin Soo. He was a kindly gentleman possessed of the fragility of a flower and the strength of an oak. He was in his mid-fifties but capable of challenging men far younger than himself. When I first bowed to him, Lin Soo was training two of Ducksun's bodyguards in advanced maneuvers of the Gentle Way. They weren't doing well, as evidenced by the dark expression covering the master's face.

"Are your minds sealed like some fat mandarin treasure house?" he stormed as they miscalculated yet another move. "Can you expect to protect the warlord when you are so vulnerable yourself?"

Neither man dared answer. They just stared at the elder with fearful respect. He indicated they should attempt the intricate assault again. They advanced on Lin Soo threateningly but did not get far. He let out a brief, horrid cry, then toppled both bodyguards in a split second. My mouth opened. This was no one to fool around with. Lin Soo then dismissed the men with instructions to clear their minds, then return for another session. He continued on to other students training for Ducksun's service.

He was truly a master at the Gentle Way and would subsequently play an important role in my life. He took time to work with me individually, accelerating the pace of my instruction. The initial training period was designed to develop all the body muscles so that when summoned, they responded instinctively and correctly to any given situation. I found a certain peace in physical exhaustion, a feeling of inner strength which gave me exquisite control of every function.

As I attained a new stage of increased physical strength through daily workouts, there came periods of severe depression. I felt guilt at abandoning my sick mother and regretted the likely difficulties my stabbing of Moroni had caused her and my cousin Eddie. I longed for home and had doubts about the path I'd taken. I feared I would never be able to return. Insecurities bared themselves, then just as suddenly vanished. I was falling into the abyss of my own worst fears and was forced to confront my deepest anxieties. Learning the art of killing, I had to face the fact that I had killed before. I was distracted and inept, and performed as badly as the two Korean bodyguards Lin Soo had admonished earlier.

Noticing my internal struggle, Lin Soo increased the pace of my training, hoping to shatter the psychological barrier the physical language of the Gentle Way had presented. My training became an emotionally and physically grueling punishment. At one point during exercises I passed out, falling face-forward onto the mat. Lin Soo left me there and went to assist another student. I regained consciousness some minutes later. Lin Soo never mentioned my blackout, but simply began taking me through my moves again. Several failures later, I threw up my hands in frustration.

"I'll never get it right. Why even try?"

There was a collective gasp from the other students as Lin Soo walked from the training area to a corner of the room. He knelt down, resting his buttocks on his heels, and bowed his head. Someone whispered, and the hushed and astonished words carried on the breeze to where I was standing.

"The master sobs. . . ."

Everyone gazed at me as though an apology was expected. I went immediately to Lin Soo, dropped down opposite him, then bowed my head respectfully.

"Master," I asked uneasily, "does the master cry for his unworthy student?"

"No, no, my son. The master cries for his own soul because he is a learned failure. A worthy student has thrown all to the wind, thus forsaking the intensity of the Way. It is for my own dishonor that I weep."

"But I just couldn't do it. It was me. It's not your failure."

"Ah, but it is. I have not inspired you, my son. There can be no greater dishonor than that of a teacher who fails to teach, yet calls himself still a teacher."

I lowered my head. "The dishonor is my own."

"You are uninitiated and therefore know only ignorance."

A silence fell between us that easily matched the solitude of the remaining students. They were all watching us intently, and silently wondering at the outcome. Finally I spoke.

"Master, the Gentle Way is difficult. Do men really come to such harsh terms with themselves?"

Lin Soo nodded as though he'd answered this question a hundred times before.

"If you cannot comprehend the truth of your inner self, then the universe is oblique. The Way is torturous but demands no more from the man than the man demands from himself." Lin Soo paused momentarily. "There is but one successful method handed down through the ages: train hard and you fight easy."

As the words rolled from his tongue, Lin Soo's eyes ignited like twin flames. Right then and there it all came back to me the reason for the unusual exercises Lin Soo had put me through from my first day of arrival. I had no idea that the Gentle Way held the secrets of the human body's pressure points.

The Budhist monks were fascinated by the manner in which the animals of nature defended themselves. The precision of the crane, the speed of the cobra, and the power of the tiger were all incorporated into this one method.

Movements were designed to direct and deflect blows at these critical life-points. One could strike with ease at these parts of the body, leaving an opponent helpless. This weaponless form of fighting caused a mysterious death.

The more proficient in the Gentle Way were known to possess the death touch. Now I understood how Ducksun easily killed the pirates in prison.

I rose, then went over to the mat. Following several breathing exercises, I began pacing myself. By day's end, Lin Soo had worked through the difficult maneuvers repeatedly. I surpassed the breaking point through fierce determination. Never again would I throw up my hands in frustration, because I'd learned walking away can prove far costlier.

As peace enveloped me, I began to entertain the thought of going home. Maybe, I thought, after I'd completed my studies at Ducksun's compound. Maybe then I could seriously consider such a move.

I hadn't seen Ducksun often, since he was away many days of the month. He spent many hours inspecting Nationalist troops or meeting with Chiang Kai-shek. What I did learn about him was sketchy and the direct result of casual conversations with General Dang.

Dang was a short, bullet-headed Chinese who'd been a farmer before turning soldier and politician. He followed Chiang's Nationalist banner passionately and was assigned to assist Ducksun when the Korean resettled in Shanghai. A warm friendship and stern loyalty developed between the two men. Dang knew more about the influential Korean than any other man in China.

"Why is Ducksun called the Warlord?" I asked Dang as we took a short walk around the compound.

"Because in Korea he was the most powerful warlord in recent history," Dang replied. "His family line is traceable to the reign of Queen Sondok, who ruled Korea some six centuries before the birth of your holy man Jesus Christ. He has a most interesting genealogy, which, in its time, has produced scientists, astronomers, and soldiers. Now, because of the Japanese invasion of Korea, there are only Ducksun and his daughter, Chen Lee."

"I never knew Ducksun had a daughter." I looked up at General Dang.

"She is quite an accomplished young lady. Ducksun has administered her education wisely. During peacetime, Chen Lee would be the most-sought-after girl in Korea. Other powerful homes would certainly send their eligible sons seeking betrothal."

"It's hard for me to picture Ducksun spending time with his daughter—or even having a family, for that matter. He doesn't seem the type."

"The Warlord is no different from other men in that respect, Dee. Ducksun's family was quite renowned in Korea until the Japanese invaded. I never learned the full story of Ducksun's flight from his homeland, but I'm led to understand there was a plot involving the betrayal of his family to the Japanese. His beloved wife and only son died because of this. Now, ask me no more."

We had been strolling through an orchard at the farthest extremity of Ducksun's compound. As we came out of the trees and into the finely sculptured garden, we saw a young girl walking toward us. She was slight of build and hardly as tall as I. Her coal-black hair was short and trimmed to fall just below her ears. Behind her walked two armed guards. For a moment we watched unobserved as she leaned forward to touch a flower. I thought she might pick it, but she merely touched it as though it were a fragile butterfly. Then she glanced upward to see us. Her demeanor stiffened until she recognized Dang. Then she relaxed.

I leaned toward Dang. "Who's that?"

"Ducksun's daughter, Chen Lee." Dang's voice acquired an edge and I could feel him pulling on my arm. "Come, we will take another path back to the greathouse so as not to disturb her."

"Can I meet her?"

"It would not be my place to introduce you to the Warlord's daughter, Dee. It would be a serious breach of protocol. That honor is reserved for Ducksun himself."

We took another path away from the garden but I couldn't help looking back. Chen Lee was watching us walk away with a sad curiosity in her eyes. Was she as lonely as I?

Dang and I were silent during our return stroll. At the house there was a tall young American man waiting for Dang. He wore a dark blue suit and carried a raincoat over his arm.

Dang excused himself, then went to speak to the American, leaving me to stand several yards away. They shook hands, smiling, apparently knowing each other well. Throughout this greeting, the American's eyes never left me. Nor mine his. I felt a cold chill inside.

The American had the eyes of a killer.

Several weeks passed and I progressed favorably under Lin Soo's teaching. Ducksun spent additional hours with me because his schedule lightened for a while. It began simply with a journey by automobile into the marketplace. I watched as Ducksun greeted various Koreans who, after fleeing the Japanese, had scraped together enough capital to open small curbside businesses. Those people were Ducksun's and they held him in the highest esteem. His enemies, of which there were a few, loathed him intensely. Because of Ducksun's generosity and intercession with the smaller banks of Shanghai, these Korean refugees were able to set up the businesses they had once operated in Korea. They considered Ducksun a protector because at home they had known him as a patriot.

On these occasions, Ducksun might meet with a Korean elder for a few minutes privately. While these reunions took place, I was allowed to roam through the bazaar as a way of passing time.

As I was thumbing through several English-language newspapers, which carried news about the death of Jean Harlow, a tall man stepped next to me and began browsing. I peered up absently but went rigid upon recognizing the killer eyes of the American who'd greeted Dang at the compound weeks before. He looked down at me, then spoke in a low tone.

"You're called Dee, aren't you." It was not a question. "I want to talk to you."

My first instinct was to walk away, but I was curious. "Who are you?"

"My name is Louis Calloway. I'm a lieutenant with the Office of Naval Intelligence. There's nothing to be afraid of. Just come with me. I have a car waiting around the corner."

"Forget it. I don't give a damn who you are and I'm certainly not getting into any car with you."

His reply was harsh. "Look, kid, if I'd wanted to abduct you, I could've done it weeks ago at Ducksun's compound. Just a stroke of the ambassador's pen and you'd have been on your way back to face criminal charges in the States. Now . . . it's up to you. Do we do this the hard or the easy way?"

I hesitated, then nodded reluctantly. Once inside the car, I turned to him. "How do you know about me?"

"No big deal, Dee. Ducksun's school for guerrillas doesn't accept Western boys. So when I saw you, I got curious. When I get curious, I check things out. You want to know what I discovered?" I said nothing, so he continued. "You're wanted on criminal charges in the United States, something to do with a stabbing in

New York. You shipped out on a tramp steamer called *China Star,* then wound up in Kongping Prison. Since the breakout, you've lived with a Chinese whore. Now you're studying under the most dangerous guerrilla in China." He paused. "Tell me, Dee, how does a kid like you end up under Ducksun's wing?"

"Just lucky, I guess." It was a gut-level reaction, but I really didn't like this guy.

"Be serious, kid. We're all on the same side, right?"

"What do you want?"

Calloway smiled. "Nothing much. Just keep me posted on Ducksun."

"No. What about Dang? You seemed pretty chummy with him."

"Hardly. Dang tells me only what he's ordered to tell me. That's the way this game is played, kid. But now I've got the joker, and the joker is you. You're an American, and I would think you owe certain loyalties to your country."

"Being loyal to my country doesn't include spying on my friends."

He studied me. "The criminal charges can be taken care of, you know. Someday you'll have to leave China and face them if you don't do something about it now. It's no secret that China will eventually fall to the Japanese. That'll put you right back on square one. So how about it? Do a little harmless observing for your country and I'll make sure you can go home without a worry in the world."

I considered the bait. I really wanted to go home, but I wasn't about to betray the man who'd saved my life and taught me to survive in a turbulent world. I could never live with myself if I did that.

"Like I said, Calloway, forget it. I'm not for sale. And as for those charges, I'll take my chances."

I started to get out of the car, but Calloway clamped a hand on my arm. "Reconsider it." His face was deadly serious.

"No."

He allowed me to get out, then closed the door. I took one look at his face through the open window and realized there was something else he wanted to tell me.

"What?"

"I thought maybe you'd want you know," Calloway said with careful calculation, "that your mother died two months ago. Tuberculosis."

I stared at his frozen eyes, knowing he really didn't give a damn. I felt torn with guilt because I hadn't been there when she needed me. If this was Calloway's intention, score one for the bad guys.

"Thanks." I disappeared into the crowd.

For the first time in years, I was crying.

I was seated on a granite bench in the garden when Chen Lee came into view. We still hadn't been formally introduced, so I rose to leave, avoiding her eyes.

"Stay." Her voice followed me in command. She was her father's daughter.

"I'd better not," I said, turning around to face her. "Your father may not like me talking to you."

"There is no crime in talk between friends. Come, sit across from me."

She indicated another granite bench. As I sat, I kept my eyes on the guards, who weren't thrilled about the situation. I had the feeling that they were going to memorize every word we said and report everything to Ducksun.

"Are you sure this is okay?"

She smiled, amused. "Of course. Now, tell me, why does a Western boy place himself in the Gentle Way along with the hardened men sworn to my father?"

I shrugged. "Your father and I are friends."

She seemed surprised. "Is this true? My father numbers very few as friends. How is it that a Western boy of my own age is granted such a lofty privilege?"

"Well, I was in Kongping prison with your father and . . ." I stopped because of her surprised expression.

"Can you be the one of whom he spoke?"

"Excuse me? I don't think I know what you mean."

Chen Lee sized me up with her eyes. "My father told me of a boy whose will for survival didn't compromise his values, even under the conditions of Kongping.

He said that this young boy had such potential that, in time past, he might even have become a Server. I was shocked when he claimed the boy was a Westerner. And now I find it is you."

"A Server? What's that?"

She shook her head in dismay. "Don't you know anything? Follow my reasoning, Dee. Server, from my language to yours, would mean one who lives for others. Hence the word 'server.' "

"I still don't understand."

"Then listen closely. In ancient Korea there were many warlords who carved the land into fiefdoms, spreading much intrigue and death. The strongest and purest of men of the time were known as the Servers. They were a secret brotherhood and the only men able to travel the length and breadth of Korea unhampered by bandits. Even the most notorious warlords granted them free passage."

I listened carefully, but it was still unclear. "Why?"

"Because to oppose the Servers was to war upon one's own angry fates. The Servers were special men with a special code. Anyone could approach them for a service. Their price was minimal because they elected to serve men of all castes. Were it not for the Servers, sanctuary would be but a word. A ruler could quietly dispatch a feared enemy through them, or anyone could seek prayerful intercession at their shrine. They adhered to several inviolate rules, one of which was never to take part in wars between the lords. For the longest period they were known as the Honorable Government because their service was based upon a personal plateau. Their needs were simple and their wants always fulfilled. There has never been a more accomplished gathering of silent warriors in all Korea. Some believe the Japanese Ninja have roots in the Servers.

"Each Server was himself the ultimate weapon. When my father compared you to them, I was surprised. He has never done this before, and for him a man could hold no greater honor."

I sat quietly for a moment, still not sure what she was getting at. "I still don't understand why your father could compare me to the Servers. I mean, they sound impressive, but they don't have anything to do with me."

Chen Lee was about to answer, when we both turned at the sound of footsteps in the thicket to our rear. The bodyguards came to attention as Ducksun appeared. How long had he been standing there?

He brushed past the guards, walking directly to Chen Lee and me.

"I see you have met my daughter."

I rose immediately and bowed to him. "Yes. We ran into each other here in the garden."

"It is just as well. I am now spared the imposition of introducing you. Has she pestered you with questions concerning the West?"

"Father! I was only curious as to who this Western boy could be."

Ducksun looked down at his daughter. "And is your curiosity now satisfied, daughter?"

"Yes, Father." She lowered her eyes.

"Good. You may now return to the greathouse. I wish to speak with this young man alone."

Chen Lee disappeared into the shrubbery, closely accompanied by her grim bodyguards. I figured they were going to catch hell for le.   Chen Lee and me talk. I figured I would too.

Ducksun led me away from the gardens toward the orchard. We walked silently and soon had traversed the length of the orchard and were standing upon the bank of a small stream which cut through the southernmost border of his compound. I watched as he contemplated the crystalline water. After a time, he glanced at me.

"There is such a stream near my lands in Korea. My son and I walked the wilds to that stream many, many evenings. He was a fine boy and would've been a remarkable man. Certainly not a warlord, but a leader of his people."

"You don't have to tell me this."

"Silence." He stood motionless, then continued. "You

have qualities identical to my son's, an inner strength which drives most rivals to envy. My days, my methods, are coming to an end. The power of the world is transforming from old ways to new. Slowly we are moving toward those men whose minds can be sharper than any sword, more precise than any bullet. I explain this to you as I would have explained it to my son."

I was uncomfortable. "Ducksun, sir, with all due respect, your son and I, well . . . we come from different worlds."

"Ah, but you are the same nonetheless. You aspire to identical dreams, ask only the same justices from this battered planet, and have a deep love of all men. This is very dangerous, Dee, to love all men. Your peers will perceive this, then use it as a sword with which to excise your heart. Once your generosity is realized, you shall never be left alone. Not for all your days." He paused, then looked directly into my eyes. "They shall consider you a Server."

That word again. Now I was certain he had overheard Chen Lee's and my conversation. But what was he trying to tell me? Somewhere in that cryptic speech was a message that escaped me.

"Ducksun, sir, I'm just a kid from New York who got left here and is trying to make the best of it."

He nodded and smiled. "Your denial is the proof I sought. And I shall tell you one more thing: there is more awaiting you than your dreams can foretell."

He leaned forward and picked up a large smooth stone. As he did, the shiny tube hanging around his neck swung free from his shirt. Ducksun tossed the shining stone into the stream. We studied the rippling effect until it disappeared.

"You know, young Dee, life is like the ripples in the water. It starts small, grows and grows, and then fades away. And throughout life, we must always remember one thing: nothing remains the same. It gets either better or worse."

Darkness fell as we returned to the greathouse together.

Ducksun took the time to have many such talks with me over the next few days, and each time his emphasis was the same: the world as he knew it was hurling toward an end. He was the most powerful Korean warlord, the man who had played the best game against a breed that reasoned with feudal cruelty. He was a complete dictator over his hard-won kingdom, and yet he realized that he would have to adapt or perish.

During his exile in Shanghai, Ducksun had begun many profitable businesses, some local, others in far-reaching parts of the world. It seemed that he commanded endless funds and poured much of them into his school and private army of guerrillas.

Ducksun had witnessed Korea's capitulation to the Japanese and was certain that China would follow. Then, on a crisp autumn day in 1937, the skirmishes between the Nationalists and the Japanese forces based in China erupted into a full-scale war.

The Japanese had always maintained a formidable military presence under the guise of protecting their concession, but what began as a guerrilla war suddenly turned into widespread hostilities. The Japanese, feeling justified at protecting the emperor's subjects residing in China, mounted a successful landing north of the city.

Hongkew, the northern district of Shanghai, was slowly devastated by fighting between the reinforced Japanese and the stubborn Nationalists. From his compound in the French concession, Ducksun intensified the underground war against the imperial forces.

Dusk had settled, and Ducksun and I were talking again in his garden. The distant Japanese artillery barrage punctuated the evening quiet like far-off thunder. Hongkew was burning and it was like watching hell bursting on the horizon.

"A great city falls because China's allies have no honor, no loyalty." There was disgust in his voice.

"Britain and America are negotiating for a cease-fire on China's behalf," I offered. "They're doing everything possible to convince the Japanese to pull out. I read it in the newspaper."

"They will negotiate until China falls and the problem evaporates. Then they will pretend the problem never existed in the first place. No, negotiations mean nothing. China needs loyal allies who will fight the Japanese."

I felt compelled to defend my country. "It has nothing to do with loyalty. I can hardly picture any of the Western powers declaring war on Japan over China, though."

Ducksun stared at me for a very long moment, then rose and leaned toward me. For a brief moment I was sure he saw not me, but his son. And I was sure he was going to strike me.

"Unteachable child! What do you know of loyalty? Must I spill blood on this very day to teach you more than any fable could ever do?"

I pulled back, frightened by this powerful man's rage. He turned toward the shrubbery.

"Do Osoao!" he shouted, ordering his two bodyguards to come to him immediately.

When they arrived, he ordered them to unholster their pistols, old Webley revolvers purchased from the British. Ducksun grunted in Korean and the men placed the barrels of their guns to the center of each other's foreheads. They stood frozen like this for several long seconds while Ducksun pondered his next command. I stood horrified, unable to move, my eyes locked on the sight of these two ferocious men, eye-to-eye, staring each other down, neither causing the other to flinch. Sworn to death, they were the calmest men I'd ever seen.

"A simple word from me, boy, and these men will die by each other's hand. They do not question my motives because these are honorable men. I surround myself with men of such character."

Then, at a wave of his hand and a word spoken in sharp Korean, the men were dismissed. I never questioned him on the subject of loyalty again.

*   *   *

My year of training at Ducksun's academy came to a close and I felt like my life had now come full circle. When I was permitted to leave the compound alone, I went directly to see Crimson Orchid.

I guess I didn't realize how much I'd changed, how much I'd grown in that year, but her face told it all.

"I sent away a boy," she said as she closed the door behind me, "and he returns a man. I am so pleased."

"I'm feeling pretty good about myself," I agreed. "I don't know how I survived Lin Soo's teachings, but I feel different now, like I know my own strength."

"Well," she said, a sparkle of pride in my accomplishments in her eyes, "at least I am in less danger now of losing another costly lamp."

Over the next few days I visited Crimson Orchid frequently. I knew I now had some important decisions to make, and I needed someone to listen to me as I sorted out my feelings.

We talked about many things, but no matter where I started, I always came back to the same thing: home.

One night, as she reclined comfortably on the couch, her robe partially open, exposing her breasts in the dim light, she forced the issue. "Dee, you have told me of your past, or at least as much as you have wished to, and each time you speak, your voice is tinged with pain and loss. When will you realize that you must go home?"

I looked at her, then took a breath. "I can't."

"But you must. You cannot remain in Shanghai forever. The Japanese will eventually occupy all of China, and no purpose will be served by your falling victim to their war."

"I killed someone, Orchid." I told her of that part of my life which I'd kept secret, of that night on the docks. She listened, her expression never changing.

"I suspected you were living with such a memory. But perhaps you are no longer hunted."

I shook my head. "I met this guy, Calloway. He's from the Office of Naval Intelligence. He said they're still looking for me."

She considered this for a moment. "I would not place much trust in the word of Calloway. He is an agent and would use any information at his disposal to motivate you. I suspect he would also withhold information if it was to his advantage. Now, answer me honestly. Do you want to go home?"

"Yes. More than anything."

She nodded, then came and sat down next to me. "Then we shall find a way."

I could feel her sitting so close to me, and looked down into her face. "I've missed you."

She smiled slightly, in the manner she usually reserved for her customers. "And I you."

She leaned forward and sought out my inexperienced lips, then pressed her tongue delicately into my mouth. Her hands came up around my throat, caressing tenderly until my face was framed by her soft, precious fingers.

Crimson Orchid showed me the art of touching a woman, showed me how my fingertips could caress and excite her skin. She soothed me and aroused my senses, letting me experience the tastes, and fragrances of her smooth and graceful body. She responded to my touch, urging me on in passionate hushed tones.

We slipped to the floor and she slowly removed my clothing and I hers. She kept me at a distance, urging me to use my hands, my mouth, my tongue. Her body quaked as silent waves broke within her. I looked into her eyes as she pulled me closer.

"Now . . ."

Crimson Orchid drew me deep within, loving me passionately for what seemed like hours. We awoke curled in each other's arms late the following day. The elders were said to describe a woman's love as thirty-three times sweeter than sugar.

I finally understood.

During my final weeks in Shanghai, I spent less time with Crimson Orchid as I saw Chen Lee more often. I admired her strength and her ability to accept the harsh reality of a life surrounded by bodyguards, cut off from most normal human contact. The Japanese Kempetai considered her a prize; her protection was the full responsibility of dozens of men.

Most things she needed were brought in from the outside, but on occasion she did travel to the city.

"There are moments," she once told me, "when I wish my father was only a poverty striken farmer rather than the leader of men. His politics have imprisoned me like the light frozen at the heart of a diamond."

"It's only until the Japanese are beaten," I offered. I knew that earlier in the week the British had announced a diplomatic breakthrough with Tokyo, which could lead to a major Japanese withdrawal. All Shanghai prayed as the Japanese considered the British proposal.

She shook her head. "I have seen what the Japanese did to Korea, Dee. Did you know that the earth can burn? I never did until I saw the Japanese do it. No, they will not be defeated. They will engulf every acre of land that lies before them. They are like the Demon Tide. Many will die. Nations will fall. But the Japanese will not be beaten."

"How can you be so sure?"

"Are they not in China this very minute? Are they not taking this country, inch by inch, while the world watches with disinterest? No, Dee, they will reign supreme among all the Eastern peoples until, one day, the blood of an Englishman or an American is shed. Only then will this war end, because Japan cannot defeat the West. That is why she strikes at China, to gain land and material for the final reckoning with the Western powers. It is an investment which shall eventually cause many of your countrymen to die on foreign soil as they try to stop the Japanese legions."

"You make it sound so grim, so inevitable, like Japan is out to conquer the world."

"Search your heart, Dee, and tell me that you do not believe that is the future."

In her happier moments Chen Lee would bombard me with questions about America, about New York City. Was it really glamorous and cosmopolitan? Did the glass buildings truly reflect the sunlight? Did the Empire State building really scrape the heavens? She seemed so breathless then, inquiring about Manhattan, her mind picturing a fantasy far removed from the reality of China's heartbreak.

I knew different.

Chen Lee enjoyed her forrays into the city more than any other moments life offered. She was confined to the compound for so many weeks at a time that she bubbled enthusiastically whenever these trips were planned.

"Father, can Dee come with us?" The question came as she was preparing to leave under General Dang's guard. "I'm sure he would enjoy seeing the marketplace with me."

I had been standing next to Ducksun when she surprised us with her request. The Warlord glanced at me, but obviously his mind dwelled on other, more important matters. It was rumored that Chiang Kaishek might visit Shanghai, and Ducksun was concerned. He waved his hand. "Would you like to accompany my daughter?"

"I would be honored, sir."

He nodded. "Then go. I am certain no harm will befall her when she is to be guarded by both Dang and yourself."

A moment later I joined the three-car caravan which would escort Chen Lee into the city. I sat up front in the second car next to the driver, while General Dang and Chen Lee sat behind me.

The lead car lurched through the compound gates and we followed closely. The third car came up dangerously close to guard our rear. General Dang strained forward, then turned about to look behind us, checking the placement of each vehicle. After a few seconds he relaxed his body, but not his ever-vigilant eyes. The ride proceeded quietly and we were well onto the main street beyond the compound before anyone spoke.

"I think I shall visit the elder with the porcelain dolls," Chen Lee said. "He promised there would be a final shipment from Korea when the Japanese lift the trade embargo. Do you think the dolls have arrived, General Dang?"

Dang wasn't interested in porcelain dolls. His eyes had caught notice of movement outside the car. I saw him stiffen, so I turned to look through the windshield. The lead car was being run off the roadway by a black sedan. Quickly I twisted to look at Dang again. There was a sickening crunch of metal as the rear car was intercepted.

My voice seemed to come from some other body. "Chen Lee, get down!"

General Dang threw himself down, covering her with his body as the shattering bark of machine guns foretold the fate of our armed guards. We screeched to a halt as the lead car erupted into flames. Men went screaming into the street, only to be gunned down. Our driver leaned forward to pull a pistol from beneath the dashboard. He never got the chance to use it.

The door on the driver's side flew open and he was faced with Japanese faces and gun muzzles. As he opened his mouth to scream, the barrels exploded, spraying blood all over me. The driver's body flew across the front seat and across my own, taking two slugs meant for me. A third grazed my forehead and stunned me. Barely conscious, blood running down my cheek, I could sense what was going to happen, but I was helpless to prevent it.

The Japanese pulled a screaming Chen Lee from the rear seat as General Dang bolted forward to protect her. There were two more shots and Dang's blood flowed into the car seats.

Chen Lee's screaming continued. Doors slammed, wheels screeched, engines roared. The screams became distant, then faded into silence.

Chen Lee was gone.

6

They had pulled me out of the wreckage of the three-car caravan hours ago. They decided I was unharmed, but I wasn't so sure. My head hurt like hell and the side of my face was bloody. But I was alive. And because I was, the questions began.

We were seated in a conference room at Ducksun's compound. Around the table sat Lin Soo, Ducksun, several ranking members of Ducksun's crack guerrillas . . . and Calloway. I was told he had been brought in because of General Dang's death, and it was he who conducted the repetitive, unrelenting interrogation.

I was tired, aching, and feeling guilty. "I told you everything I know. Twenty times already. What more do you want out of me?"

Calloway paced. "I want you to tell me again: are you certain you didn't see any Japanese uniforms?"

"I said I didn't. Why is that so important? It was the Japanese who took her, in uniform or out."

"It's important because we have to know with absolute certainty whether these men were Japanese regular army or members of the Kempetai. Now, one more time, are you certain you didn't see any Japanese uniforms?"

"Positive. The attackers wore civilian clothing." I looked to Ducksun, but his eyes betrayed nothing.

Calloway nodded to himself and continued to pace. "If Chen Lee's abduction was accomplished by elements of the Japanese Army, then the Western powers may be in a state of war. After all, the assault did occur in the French concession. The Japanese forces are supposed to respect all boundaries—"

"Enough." The Warlord rose and everyone fell silent. "We are aware of the politics of the situation, Calloway. Koreans and Chinese have been dying because of the Japanese for ages. The question here is not one of war, but one of rescue."

Everyone, including Calloway, could sense Ducksun's barely contained, seething rage.

"Oh, I agree with you," Calloway acceded. "But this is a very delicate matter. God only knows how the French will react to this affront to their borders."

"I do not care about the French." Ducksun's voice was so cold, I swear the temperature in the room dropped ten degrees.

"But the French may be able to exert sufficient pressure upon the Japanese to result in the return of your daughter."

"Ha." Ducksun moved around the table to face Calloway. "The French shall do with words what Chiang Kai-shek's tanks haven't done? No. You live in a world of opium dreams, Calloway. I have kept my part of the bargain. I have not dispatched any armed troops into Japanese territory. But I demand more than American-manufactured platitudes to secure my daughter's safe return."

Calloway faced Ducksun but did not flinch. "All available agents are trying to find Chen Lee. Arguing here among ourselves won't make things move any faster."

Ducksun fell silent, his eyes on me. His penetrating stare told me he wondered why I wasn't dead, why I was the only survivor, when every armed guard had died trying to save Chen Lee. Could it be something I hadn't said? I was shaken by the determined Korean's disturbing gaze.

Fear pervaded the room. Ducksun trusted no one. I didn't blame him.

"Fire between friends does no one well," Lin Soo interjected into the silence. "Possibly we should retire for a few minutes to collect ourselves."

No one had the opportunity to answer. The door to

the conference room opened and one of Ducksun's guards entered, approached the Warlord, bowed, and handed him an envelope. Ducksun had the envelope torn open before the guard was gone. He looked up, his face impassive.

"The Japanese have issued an ultimatum: I am to surrender within three days or Chen Lee will be eliminated." He stood in a silence that no one dared break. "It is over, gentlemen. I shall be forced into their custody if we cannot get Chen Lee back before that time."

Calloway, sitting again, was playing with a pencil. "My government won't allow that. Your life is far more valuable than Chen Lee's. Besides, even if you do surrender, there's no guarantee the Japanese will free your daughter."

"And how, Mr. Calloway, do you propose to stop me, should I decide to surrender?"

Calloway didn't even look at Ducksun. "We are prepared to place you in protective detention."

"Against my wishes?"

"If necessary."

"Then you will die trying."

Calloway realized he'd pushed too far and rose in a conciliatory gesture. "Ducksun, we cannot risk unlimited war in China any more than we can gamble with the life of an irreplaceable ally. My government, with the permission of the French consul, is now sending several detachments of United States marines to secure this compound. We cannot have you endangering the lives of everyone in the Western sector by attacking the Japanese. It will only provide them with an invitation to invade. I assure you, we will obtain your daughter's release through the proper diplomatic channels."

"You are sending marines to surround my compound? I am under house arrest?"

"Yes." Calloway looked up at the storming Ducksun. "The ambassador wishes to extend the fullest 'protection' of our American-based forces."

The look Ducksun directed upon Calloway was murderous. "I ask for assistance in securing my daughter's freedom, and in return I receive captivity."

The bodyguard entered again, and all fell silent. He whispered a few words to Ducksun and left. Ducksun looked to Calloway. "An official of your embassy is waiting in the hall. He wishes to have a word with you."

Calloway left, leaving Ducksun to sag into the over-stuffed chair. His harsh gaze now fell upon me. I wanted to say something, but what could I say? I decided to keep my mouth shut. The American agent had angered Ducksun beyond all reason, and I didn't want to be on the receiving end of that wrath.

Fifteen minutes of stone-cold silence later, Calloway reentered carrying a satchel. His expression was pale, his eyes averted from Ducksun's glance.

"It's worse than we originally believed. Chen Lee is being held at Bridge House." I watched everyone's reaction as he continued. "It's an old marine barracks that the Japanese now occupy. Further, it's now Kempetai headquarters. It's staffed with agents and a ruthless interrogation squad. It's situated well within the Japanese sector and very heavily guarded. No armed forces will be able to get within a mile of her without alerting the Imperial Army."

Calloway unfolded a map enlargement he pulled from the satchel and indicated the location of Bridge House. He then spread out several photographs and a floor plan of the former barracks.

Ducksun looked over the documents. "How did you learn this?"

"We have people who observe Bridge House on a regular basis. I can't go into detail concerning our contacts, but they have confirmed Chen Lee's presence. She was brought in by the Kempetai."

Ducksun spoke as if to himself, confirming his worst fear. "So the Kempetai do have her."

"Yes. Looks like they arranged and executed the whole plan. By the way, our deputy ambassador unofficially inquired about Chen Lee. The Japanese deny that they are holding her."

Ducksun's face sank; my mouth went dry. Since the

Japanese embassy denied any knowledge of Chen Lee's whereabouts, it would be a breach of decorum to carry the matter any further without any conclusive evidence. By then Chen Lee could be dead. In effect, Calloway was telling Ducksun to write his daughter off.

Ducksun, Calloway, and Lin Soo studied the floor plans and approaches to Bridge House as I looked over their shoulders.

The type of planning required to free Chen Lee necessitated a small, powerfully armed force capable of moving through the Japanese lines undetected. Upon reaching Bridge House, they would have to enter Kempetai headquarters unnoticed, locate and free Chen Lee noiselessly, and then escape with their prize from the Japanese zone without being captured. In short, only a squad of ghosts and spirits could succeed with such a plan.

Ducksun and Calloway ignored me while arguing the merits of several schemes. I began flipping through the photographs. Bridge House was an old four-story Victorian building surrounded by two checkpoints. Each gateway was closely guarded. Something gnawed at my mind.

Ghosts and spirits, I thought again.

I scrutinized each picture, trying to isolate every detail. "How long ago were these pictures taken?"

Calloway didn't look up. "Why?"

"Just curious."

"The dates are stamped on the back." Calloway went back to his discussion with Ducksun, dismissing any comments I might have. Only Lin Soo appeared to be watching me, suspecting I'd caught on to something.

Had I? Even I wasn't sure. I only knew there was something wrong with the photos, a slight detail—a ghost—missed by everyone. I continued to stare at the pictures. My eyes studied the shots of the fencing that ran adjacent to the guard booths. Suddenly I spotted the discrepancy.

At first glance, it seemed to be just a vague shadow. Closer inspection showed it to be not a shadow at all, but the ghost we needed. And I was the only one aware of it.

Very quietly, while Ducksun and Calloway argued, I rose from my chair and walked around the table. I picked up the floor plans of Bridge House as casually as possible and studied them.

"Where is she being held?"

Calloway looked up, annoyed at the interruption. "Maximum-security."

"In the cellars?" I formed mental images of dungeons and rats.

"No. The cellars are torture chambers. Maximum-security is on the top floor. Why the questions?"

I looked to Calloway and noticed that Ducksun was now watching me. ""Because I can get Chen Lee out of Bridge House."

Ducksun stirred in his seat and Calloway was about to say something when Ducksun silenced him with a wave of his hand. "How?"

"I'd rather not say. I know a team of armed men won't succeed. I also know that you've accepted that fact. If you'll allow me about two hundred American dollars, a pistol, and all the knowledge available on Bridge House, I can penetrate that place."

The Warlord considered this for a moment, then rose and walked to the window. He watched as the marines set up a guard around his compound, realizing that his movements and those of his guerrillas were not totally inhibited. Ducksun returned to the table, glanced down at the floor, then looked to Calloway.

"Can you brief Dee on the hazards of such a mission?"

Calloway was about to dismiss me, but thought better of it. "Certainly. If Dee will just outline his plan, I will tell him everything he needs to know."

"My plan is my own."

Calloway looked to Ducksun, then back to me. "Okay, kid, have it your way."

Calloway schooled me on every possible approach to the former marine barracks. He then went on to describe the interior. The Japanese had renovated the structure, making it nearly impregnable. Or they thought they had. I knew otherwise. Or at least I hoped so.

I left Ducksun's compound late that night. In my belt was a pistol, and I carried the satchel of floor plans and photographs. Ducksun had given me enough money to put my plan into action.

Now all I had to do was become a ghost.

It took me twelve hours to locate Kim. He was no longer working at the café and he'd changed rooms about thirty days before. Eventually I found him in a tavern. He was only mildly surprised to see me and we embraced, but the smile evaporated from his face when he felt the gun tucked tightly into my belt.

Kim and I left the bar and walked to his newly rented rooms. I explained the details of Chen Lee's capture.

"And she is being held at Bridge House . . ." Kim nodded to himself. "That is fortunate. I know the place. I was there several times before the Japanese transformed it into Kempetai headquarters. It is a most secure building, where only politically sensitive prisoners are housed. The only problem will be gaining entrance to the place."

"And getting out," I added. "And that's where you come in, Kim."

A moment later I had the satchel open and was handing Kim the photographs. He took a few minutes to flip through the series before glancing at me with a puzzled expression. Then I pointed out the shadows I'd noticed, and Kim's face broke into a smile. The shadows in the fencing, when studied closely, proved to be young Oriental boys carrying long, heavy sacks that dragged the ground.

"Rat hookers," Kim exclaimed. "The Japanese allow them entry and exit because someone must clean up the dead rats."

"Can you get us in?"

Kim thought for a moment. "It will be expensive. I must first locate the boy who hooks rats at Bridge House. Then I will have to buy his job from him for the day. His price will be high."

"But you know the boy?"

"No, but I have a friend who might be able to find him. How much money do you have?"

"A couple hundred dollars."

"Perhaps it will suffice."

I handed over the cash and he rose to leave the room.

"What should I be doing in the meantime?"

"Nothing." Kim tucked the money into his pants. "You'd best remain here. My friends do not trust Western boys. They will refuse to deal with me in your presence."

Kim left the room and was gone for hours. I tried to sleep, but found myself haunted by dreams of Chen Lee and the bloody death of General Dang.

Early the following evening, Kim pushed in the door. The stench of something rotting followed him inside. He was carrying an old set of urchin's clothing, two long sacks, and a pair of hooked pokers.

"We must hurry," Kim urged. "I located the boys just as they were leaving for Bridge House. The Japanese maintain a rigid schedule, so they will be expecting them."

Kim and I changed into the garments, then departed quickly with a sack and poker in each hand.

Rat hooking was the lowest form of labor, and the most dangerous. Most prisons experienced extreme rodent problems. The damp, inadequately ventilated buildings hosted huge rat populations that no one wanted to confront. Civil employees felt the risk of contracting plague too great and were unwilling to do the job, so it fell to pairs of starving street urchins. Prison administrations, even the Japanese, usually set aside sufficient funds to keep the hookers working. It was hardly a wage, more a starvation stipend.

Kim and I carried long sticks designed specifically for the collection of rats. On one end a steel point long enough to impale the rodents was attached. Kim explained that dying rodents were far too dangerous to be captured with bare hands. The opposite end of each poker was fixed with a large hook which could be lodged into the rat's mouth. We also carried canvas sacks eight feet in length in which to haul away the dead rats. A good night's work might net nearly two hundred pounds of carcasses.

If our masquerade succeeded, we could easily be admitted to Bridge House. The only problem would be to get out—with Chen Lee.

The rat hooker from whom Kim had bought our gear had confirmed Chen Lee's imprisonment on the top floor. According to the boy, she was there with several ranking officers of the Nationalist Army. And, he told Kim, those rooms on the top floor did not have bars, but oak doors, which the guards would have to open to allow us to clear out the rat population. That much sounded easy enough.

After ninety minutes of dodging Japanese patrols and picking through the war-ruined section of Shanghai, we stood outside the former barracks.

Bridge House was illuminated by a score of powerful searchlights, and appeared more impregnable than Alcatraz. At the street level were two rows of barbed-wire fencing and several heavily guarded checkpoints. This castle of death was our Goliath.

We approached the first checkpoint, canvas bags slung over our shoulders, hookers poised forward. From a distance, the sentries noticed us and began chattering among themselves. Finally three of these men shut themselves inside the guardhouse, leaving the remaining man outside. He hurriedly tied an old rag around his nose and mouth, then fixed a bayonet firmly on his rifle snout.

Kim turned to me and whispered, "You sure you want to go through with this?"

"I have to."

The guard was clean-cut, well-shaven, and sharply dressed. He was also annoyed with the filthy contact he was compelled to make with us, so he kept us at a distance with his rifle. We were forced to open the canvas bags so he could check for weapons with a flashlight. Once satisfied we were unarmed, he waved us on to the next checkpoint.

We crossed another fifty feet to the second barbed-wire fence. Kim and I halted at the wooden gate controlled by a Japanese sergeant. He seemed to be in charge of the outside guard patrol at Bridge House.

The suspicious nature of this crisply dressed sergeant caused a brief delay in our progress. His hand rested on a holstered sidearm as he questioned Kim in flawed but effective Chinese. Both Kim and I wore cotton neckerchiefs that were raised to filter the air and, in my case, obscure my Caucasian features.

"Where are the other boys?" the sergeant demanded. "The ones usually working this place?"

"They were ill," Kim explained. "Very, very sick. One of the rats gnawed through the bags on the last trip. A large vicious rat bit them as they tried to kill him. They are now feverish."

The sergeant retreated several steps but eyed us warily. "We have an arrangement, me and the other boys."

Kim faked surprise that the sergeant was trying to extort payment from us, though we knew Japanese payrolls were notoriously late in arriving from Tokyo. The soldiers subsidized themselves in any way possible.

"I know of no such arrangement," Kim replied, "but the boy is very ill and his mind wanders from the fever. He could have neglected to tell me. What is this agreement?"

"Money," the sergeant snapped coldly. "If you wish to work, you must pay."

"Well, I'm certain my ill friend will take care of you doubly when he returns," Kim promised. "But if you do not let us do his job, then certainly he will lose face with those who pay him. They may inquire why we were turned away."

The sergeant glowered at Kim because what he said was true. The Japanese administrators could be sticklers on even the smallest matters. Suspicions rose easily.

"And if the boy should die?"

"Then I will abide by this agreement. After all, must I not labor to fill my own stomach?"

The sergeant hesitated, then passed us on. I took my first breath. Step one accomplished.

Finally we walked through the lengthy wire-bound pathway to the main doors. We were still about twenty feet distant when several guards at the entranceway told us to halt, as they affixed protective masks to their faces. A moment later, we were urged onward. Again we were questioned concerning the regular rat hooker; again Kim explained, this time much more graphically. Satisfied, they opened the huge doors, then motioned us toward the Kempetai officer seated behind a desk in the hallway. He was dressed in plain clothing but displayed a captain's insignia on his collar. Peering up for a second, this squat little man frowned, then waved us by. We were, finally, inside Bridge House.

"Now the work begins," Kim whispered to me. "We must clean our way to the top floor."

I'd never considered this, but he was right. We couldn't just bypass the entire lower level and head directly for Chen Lee without arousing suspicions. We would have to arrive at the different levels at approximately the same time as the regular hookers would have. Earlier or later would signal trouble.

In the administrative offices we began our search for rodents. I was able to study the headquarters of the Kempetai there. These dread facilities must be well financed, because most of the desks were new and the file boxes affixed with an elaborate locking system. The offices were cleaner than anyplace I'd yet seen under Japanese rule.

We entered an office whose trappings were somewhat better than the others. Spartan and overly efficient in appearance, this office still retained the odor of death and isolation.

"This place belongs to Suri, the chief officer of the Kempetai in China," Kim explained. "That's his picture on the wall. He is the burly man standing beside General Matsui. His face haunts my countrymen and they dare not forget his features. Suri is known to be a very daring man who can appear at any hour of the day or night."

We continued on to the kitchen. The galley was brightly lit and staffed by a skeleton crew. It was the most dangerous part of the prison for us. Although the Japanese soldiers glanced at me curiously, they soon became uninterested and moved out of our way without asking any questions, probably fearing contagion. In any event, we finished the kitchen within forty minutes, filling a single sack with rat carcasses.

Bridge House was a rodent's paradise because it was situated above the main storm drains. The kitchen had been well-infested because of the hundred-pound sacks of grain and foodstuffs stored there. Several of these tightly sewn sacks had been nibbled through and grain had been strewn across the floor. No one had bothered to sweep it away. The rats feasted luxuriously.

We filled our sacks to bulging before proceeding upstairs. Kim explained that we'd be forced to dump them outside the prison grounds before continuing. I had qualms. Would we be able to regain entrance to Bridge House? Kim said we didn't have a choice but to risk it. He pulled the drawstrings on his sack tightly and we dragged them by the Kempetai officer to an area beyond the outside checkpoints. The sentries became accustomed to our coming and going and never questioned us. Several times during the night we headed for the vacant lot and quickly dug shallow holes, then dumped in the rat remains. Then we would return to finish working. Yet even the grotesque ritual of burying the carcasses didn't prepare me for the degrading infestations of the upper levels.

The cells were small and not very well guarded, because we hadn't reached maximum-security yet. Haggard, starving Chinese officers beseeched us to carry verbal messages to the outside world. We committed as many as possible to memory, but the load was staggering. Some of these men had been consumed by madness, so we listened without offering replies. These doomed inmates were confined in newly constructed cells which faced each other, destroying any sense of privacy. There was only a single guard stationed in the center of the cellblock causeway. Once he noted our purpose, he never glanced our way again, not even to nod a curt farewell.

Four sacks of rodent carcasses later, with only an hour or so left before sunrise, we were ready to work the maximum-security section. Oddly, it proved no more secure than any of the other levels, demonstrating the inflated confidence of the Japanese in the invulnerability of their fortress. The stairway leading upward was not blocked by any gateways. A guard sat quietly at a desk commanding a full, nearly unobstructed view of the confinement pens. He nodded to us, then indicated a key resting on the desk's edge. As a precaution, he unholstered his service pistol, placing it before him.

Behind the first two oak doors were elderly men dressed in remnants of once-proud uniforms. They had been in custody for so long that they hardly bothered to look at us. They were broken and oblivious of their surroundings. With them lived the rats. Some nibbled at the men while others congregated in corners. Here, in the dank cubicles, I saw defiant rats as large as alleycats. I heard them brush against each other while their tiny feet scraped at the floor. Then they squealed. First singly, then in unison. Sometimes they composed an unholy chorus that reminded the guards and prisoners of Bridge House's sole, inhuman purpose. Torture.

Kim led the way and was careful to open each door partway so as to contain the rodent population, just as a true hooker would have done. A pack of squealing, scurrying rats would've brought the guard to full, abrupt attention.

Kim unbolted and opened the third door, and there, curled in the room's farthest corner, was Chen Lee. She did not look up immediately.

"Chen Lee," I whispered.

She looked up, her eyes still sharp and clear, and was about to say something when I signaled her with my fingers to my lips. I then motioned her to stay down as we looped several rats near her with our hooks. Kim checked on the guard, then nodded to me: we were clear—for the moment.

"Is my father nearby?" Her voice was low, quiet.

"No. Now, be quiet and do what I tell you."

Quickly Kim and I tied a piece of linen across her mouth and nostrils. Then we spread open a partially filled sack. She peered into the carcass bag, catching a scream in her throat. She looked at me with fearful eyes.

"Get into the bag and we'll get you out of this place." I tried to make it sound simple; I wanted to divert her attention from the rats. It didn't work. She froze. "Chen Lee, it's the only way."

She hesitated, then stepped into the sack. Kim and I stood her up vertically, then tied the drawstrings at her head. That way the rats wouldn't rub against her face. Now all we had to hope was that the Japanese wouldn't inspect us too closely. Their fear of contagion was our only defense.

Kim and I spent several apprehensive minutes cleaning out the final room. We tried to do everything correctly, even to stopping at the desk to drop off the keys. The guard never even looked up. So far, so good.

My heart was pounding as we walked down the stairs to the main level. The Kempetai captain was rising from his seat as we approached. He was stretching and peering at his wristwatch. His replacement was scheduled to arrive soon, probably at dawn.

"Aren't you finished yet?" We stopped cold at the sound of his voice.

Kim turned, a smile growing on his face. "We have another load to bury. We should be out of here by dawn."

The captain nodded. Actually, he didn't really give a damn. He motioned us on, and Kim and I paced through the door of Bridge House as quickly as possible. The crisply dressed sergeant was still on duty but utterly bored with us. He merely scowled, then opened the gate. Just one more checkpoint and we would be away from Kempetai headquarters. It should've been easy. It wasn't. Several new, younger guards had just come on duty. They stopped us.

"What do you carry in the sacks?" one of the fresh-faced, seemingly dedicated guards inquired.

We began sweating. This guy was going to open our sacks. I just knew it.

"You want to see? Let me show you my pets." Kim sounded like a madman. He untied the sack containing Chen Lee as the guard approached. I untied my own sack, and suddenly the sentry pulled a flashlight, seemingly from thin air. Kim froze. Neither of us had expected the sentry to get that close.

Without thinking, I plunged my hand into my sack and pulled out a huge, ugly rat. Part of its head had been torn away by our hooks and it was all too gruesome.

"A gift," I said in Chinese, tossing the rat into the guard's face. He stood stock-still for a moment, then lost his composure and began sputtering. But his attention was now shifted away from Kim. And Chen Lee.

He dropped the flashlight and raised his rifle. Wonderful, I thought. I overdid it and we're going to get blown all to hell.

Then the unexpected happened. Several Japanese soldiers loitering nearby broke into laughter, diverting the sentry's attention. He glanced at his friends, realizing he had to save face in an honorable fashion. He couldn't allow two boys to best him. He forced a smile, then raised the bayonet to my neck. He pressed its point up against my throat, holding it there for a moment and letting me believe he was deciding what to do with my life.

Another stark fear overcame me. What if he picked up my mask and saw my face? I had to get out of this one. I became contrite by bowing my head, eyes closed. They were the only movements I dared attempt. The bayonet quickly vanished. I opened my eyes, then bowed fully from the waist as though this common guard were the worthiest samurai Japan had yet produced. He watched me sternly as I retrieved the rat I'd thrown at him. After I shoved the carcass into my sack, Kim and I walked by the guard. Behind us, we heard Japanese chatter and laughter.

We were free.

Kim insisted on returning to his own business, so I was alone when I returned Chen Lee to the compound. The Warlord met us in the courtyard, with Calloway right behind him.

Ducksun embraced his daughter, then turned to me. "I truly believed Chen Lee was lost. How did you accomplish this?"

"I'd like to know that too," Calloway's cold voice cut through the warmth of the reunion. "How the hell did you get into that place, never mind getting out."

The last thing I wanted to do right then was deal with Calloway. "It's not important. Chen Lee is safe, and nothing else matters."

"Wrong, Dee. You'll have to be debriefed. Routine, of course."

But it wasn't routine. Of course.

As I was led away, my eyes met those of Ducksun. In a moment of ultimate respect, he slowly closed his eyes and inclined his head toward me. It was the finest thanks I could ever have hoped for.

The first round of interrogation took place in Ducksun's compound under the supervision of Nationalist officers. They placed before me endless pictures of fellow officers believed to have been captured by the Kempetai and asked that I identify as many as I could. I did, adding the memorized messages the imprisoned men had passed to me. As it turned out, none of the prisoners identified were politically sensitive to the Nationalist cause. They would have to accept their fate as the fortunes of war.

Then the Office of Naval Intelligence took over. Calloway grilled me with the same basic questions the Nationalists had asked. I managed to contribute information that helped them redesign their schematic of Bridge House. I was tired and wanted to beg off any more sessions, when information was passed to Calloway that caused him to lose all interest in me. The Japanese had expanded their territory to include every ferry dock along the northern bank of the Soochow. Shanghai was capitulating and the people were beginning to flee.

As the roads to Nanking filled with fleeing refugees, I withdrew into myself. I'd had enough of war and found a kind of personal quiet in the resumption of my training with Lin Soo. I intensified my sessions and spent as much time with the master as possible. In a way, I think I was preparing myself, in both mind and body, for what I knew was inevitable: my departure from Shanghai.

Crimson Orchid visited me on a bright Wednesday morning, finding me idly paging through one of Ducksun's many volumes in the sitting room. I glanced up, surprised, and she stopped as she passed through the mahogany doors. As she stood there, her beauty and elegance before me, I realized this would be the image of her that I would always remember.

An awkward silence followed, which could only mean farewell. We moved to each other and embraced, then remained holding each other close.

"I have come to say good-bye and to tell a good friend that I will miss him dearly."

"You're leaving Shanghai?"

"Yes. I'm going up to Nanking. It will be safe there."

"Will I ever see you again?"

Crimson Orchid smiled and I realized that I already knew her answer. "I think not. You are going home." My face revealed my unasked question. She smiled in answer. "My own sources in the United States embassy have assured me that there are no criminal charges pending against you. As a result of my inquiry, a lower-level State Department official located your cousin, Eddie Gardenia. You will be pleased to know that the boy you stabbed, Jimmy Moroni, spent more than a month in the hospital recovering from the wound—he didn't die. Eddie followed his progress but knew of no way to get in touch with you once you boarded the *China Star*. So you see, you can go home."

Two days later, a car from the American embassy approached the compound. Calloway told me to pack my bag. I was being moved into the embassy complex for my own protection pending my return to the United States. Ducksun and Chen Lee were away in Nanking, where the Warlord was meeting with Chiang Kai-shek. I departed the compound with only the slight figure of Lin Soo to offer a good-bye. As the automobile sped toward the embassy, I asked Calloway about Ducksun and his daughter. I had wanted to stay at the compound until they returned, but Calloway wouldn't hear of it. And when I pressed again in the car, he turned cold.

"Forget about them." It wasn't a suggestion. "That part of your life is over."

I hated his tone and vowed never to forget either it or its implications. He tried to change the subject.

"You know, we're going to be at war soon in Europe. Asia, too. When you get back to the States, you'll have to do time in the military. Maybe you should do a little thinking about naval intelligence."

"I'll think about it."

I did. I was seventeen now, but even at that age, I knew it wouldn't work. I'd been my own agent from the moment I decided to go into Bridge House after Chen Lee. I'd always work for myself.

It was the only way to stay alive.

The deputy ambassador had arranged for passage on a French ocean liner scheduled to depart in five days. With the notable exception of Calloway, I had no visitors. I constantly inquired about Ducksun and Chen Lee, but Calloway's half-assed replies were usually that he'd left a message with Lin Soo but he doubted if Ducksun would chance a visit. I doubted it too, but for different reasons. I didn't think the Warlord ever got my messages.

I was due to depart at noon on an overcast Friday. I was depressed at not seeing my friends before boarding ship, so much so that I'd avoided Calloway earlier in the day. About ninety minutes before I was to be at the pier, Calloway knocked lightly, then entered my room.

I looked up, annoyed. "Don't you ever knock?"

"I did, kid. You just didn't hear me." I hated it when he called me that. I don't think he was more than eight years older than I at the outside.

"Yeah, yeah, yeah."

"You packed?"

I indicated a duffel bag resting on the floor.

Calloway ordered the marine guard accompanying him to take my gear down to the car and started to leave, then turned, as if he'd had an afterthought. "Oh, by the way, there's someone who wants to say good-bye. She's waiting in the library."

I found Chen Lee in the alcove overlooking the street. For the first time ever, we were alone. But it wouldn't have mattered if there were guards in every corner of the room. We rushed across the room and held each other tightly.

"We only just returned from Nanking," Chen Lee sighed. "Lin Soo told us they moved you here and were sending you home. Father is very angry with Calloway for not sending a cable."

"I'll be leaving at noon. I guess we haven't got much time."

She looked up into my eyes. "Dee, I did not think you would ever go home. You were always there when I needed you."

"You were there for me too, Chen Lee." I looked at her and forced a smile. "I'm glad you came. I wouldn't feel right about leaving without seeing you."

"Oh, Dee . . . will we ever, ever meet again?" She began to cry.

"I don't . . ." I stopped myself from telling her what I thought was the truth, but found myself looking into her large brown eyes. "Sure, Chen Lee. If it is meant to be."

We stood in silence, holding each other for a few minutes longer. Finally I broke the silence. "Did your father come with you?"

She nodded. "He is waiting in the car. He did not wish to enter the embassy for political reasons."

I took Chen Lee's hand and led her to the driveway alongside the embassy motor pool. The marines had brought around a staff car and were loading my duffel bag into the trunk. Then I spotted Ducksun's small caravan of automobiles. The Warlord was seated in the rear of a 1935 Packard. He indicated that I should sit next to him while Chen Lee got into the front.

"And so you depart from us." Ducksun smiled at me, a forced, almost sorrowful smile.

"They're sending me home, but I'd really rather go with you. There's' nothing for me in the States."

"No, boy, it is better that you leave China. This country will be in ashes in a matter of weeks. You should be home where you will be safe."

"But what about you and Chen Lee? What will you do?"

"We will go on fighting as we have always done." Ducksun was quiet, as if seeing into the future. "It is our fate and we accept it. Dee, you are so like the son I lost in Korea. If you have learned anything from me, from my culture, or from this devastated land, I hope it is the ability to accept your fate. Accept it, then master it. As the Servers would have done. We are always friends and shall always be at each other's service, even though half a world away."

I hit my fist against the seat. "Damn . . . I feel like I'm leaving you when you need me the most."

"Your time has not yet arrived, Dee. This is something I respect greatly, and I implore you to acknowledge my wisdom and do as your spiritual ancestors would have done. You have trained well. When the moment confronted you, you fought bravely. You liberated Chen Lee. Now, as custom dictates, I must do something for you."

"You don't owe me anything," I said. "If there is any debt, I owe you. You not only saved my life, but also gave it meaning."

Ducksun wouldn't hear me. He opened his coat and his hands went to his throat. I watched as he untied the leather thong holding the tube of gems. Then he leaned forward and tied the thong around my neck.

"They are yours."

I was stunned into silence, then found my voice. "I can't take them. They're worth a fortune."

"No, not a fortune, Dee. They are priceless. But I cannot hold them any longer. Codes of honor dictate that I may serve as custodian of these gems but that I may not use them. I was not born under the sign of the Server. You are guided by this sign, and these gems should rightfully pass into your hands."

"I am not a Server."

Ducksun stared into my eyes, his face impassive but the shine of some emotion in his eyes. "Time will tell."

I wanted to argue with him, but the marines were sounding a horn, telling me it was time to leave. I shook hands with Ducksun, but he surprised me by embracing me briefly. Chen Lee walked me down to the driveway, where the marines were waiting impatiently. She hugged me one last time, then walked back to her own car.

Even from that distance I could see that she was crying. So was I.

I was on my way home. The sergeant of the guard handed my passage to me. We shook hands and he wished me well. I glanced down at the ticket and saw that it was a first-class booking stamped DPL, which meant that the United States government had paid for it. First class. The route was to be Shanghai, Hong Kong, Sydney, Honolulu, San Francisco, the Canal, Havana, and at long last, New York City.

As I stood on the deck watching Shanghai fade into the horizon, I fingered the tube of gems that hung from my neck. I was going home. And this time I wouldn't be scraping the galley floor.

II

To Serve:
As a Way of Life

1950

7

I shook myself out of my memories and turned my attention back to the ship-to-shore receiver in my hand.

"He's no gentleman, Maggie. Throw Calloway out."

She never heard me. The next voice I heard was Calloway.

"Same old Dee. You never change, buddy."

"What do you want, Calloway?"

"We gotta talk, Dee. Immediately."

"Really? Funny, I don't think we've got anything to say to each other, 'buddy.' "

There was a brief pause; then his voice crackled over the receiver. "Hey, c'mon, Dee, let bygones be . . . you know."

"Let bygones be?" I kept my voice tightly under control. "A half-million you guys lost in Beirut two years ago, or did you forget? My money, Calloway, my business, and all I got for it was a goddamn apology."

"I did everything I could for you, Dee. You've got to understand—"

"Cut the crap, Calloway. You did everything but reimburse me. Now, get off the goddamn line and let me talk to Maggie."

A long silence followed, the receiver crackling with interference. Then it came, "Dee, this conversation is . . . a priority harpy. Do you read me?"

Harpy. The word denoted action of extreme importance, with decisions being made at the highest levels of power. Calloway had no right to use that tag without prior clearance. But what did they want with me?

"Okay, Calloway. We'll meet at my place, Maggie'll give you directions."

"What time?"

"In about two hours." I explained, "I'm about ten miles offshore."

"Nice to be rich," he said sarcastically.

"Ain't it, though?" I snapped back, then switched off the ship-to-shore.

Turning around, I saw Captain Jack struggling. Apparently he'd hooked a tuna and was having one hell of a job reeling it in. I walked over to him but didn't bother taking the pole. He was begging me with his eyes to take over.

Calloway. I thought of him, then looked across a sea being chopped by feeding tuna. He knew just when to show up, the bastard. Nicest school in weeks, and now the afternoon was shot to hell.

"For God's sake, help me!" Captain Jack implored, fighting the powerful, diving tuna.

I started laughing. "Sure." I pulled a knife free from my leg sheath, then cut the line while Jack gaped at me in horror. The tuna—probably the biggest daddy I'd ever catch—pulled out to sea dragging my severed line with him.

"Are you nuts?" Jack shouted.

"Probably," I answered. "Let's go home."

The primary reason I built my house on the bay was for the private dock leading down from the rear doors. Looking up the stone stepway from the water line, I saw Sylvia tanning herself on the patio, her slim body still in terrific shape, even after three kids. I guess that was because of the series of exercises Lin Soo taught us.

I'd found the peaceful elder in a refugee camp at the close of World War II. After I'd sponsored his entry into the United States, Lin Soo became our martial-arts instructor. Most of his days had been spent in solitude, but he'd managed to share the bulk of his knowledge with us before leaving.

Sylvia's beautiful body was his legacy. As tall as I, she wore her straw-blond hair no longer than shoulder-length. Her breasts were nicely rounded, in perfect proportion to her slenderness, and her legs were long and shapely.

"Hello, honey." I bent forward to kiss her.

She returned my kiss, not opening her eyes. "There are men waiting inside, Dee. I think one of them is Calloway."

"It is. Where are the kids?"

"Donna and Denise are at the town house with mother. She's taking them to the museum. Jeff's at a friend's."

"Good." I blew her another kiss and walked through the glass doors into the living room.

Calloway was there. He was now a large man whose clothing never seemed to fit correctly. Though he was barely thirty-five, the extra weight he carried made him look older. Flanking him were General Dillon and Colonel Bronson. I had met them before in Beirut, only their ranks had been different.

Calloway walked forward to meet me. "Good to see you, Dee." He offered his hand.

"I'll bet you are." I didn't take it.

Calloway was an agent of the newly formed Central Intelligence Agency. He'd served in G-2 with the OSS during the war and seemed to have made the transition to peacetime mayhem easily. Personally, I thought he was a maniac, but we were dealing with a world of fanatics. He seemed to fit right in.

I'd dealt with Calloway many times since I first met him in Shanghai. I always thought he was a complete company man, totally dedicated to the agency, but now I realized he'd always been for himself, and was dangerous as hell.

I smiled to take the edge off my comment, then offered drinks. General Dillon, who'd been first wave at bloody Tarawa, readily accepted. Colonel Bronson opted for club soda. He was definitely a climber, the silent and temperate colonel. Calloway I didn't have to ask—double Crown Royal over ice.

I led them to the recreation room, placed my drink

on a coaster, then unfurled the canvas mat protecting the pool table.

"Game?" I asked Calloway.

"No, thanks. The game aggravates me."

I smiled again. "It shouldn't. It's all angles."

Calloway didn't reply as I racked the balls into the tightest grouping I could manage. Even though I wasn't paying much attention to him, I could tell Calloway was gearing up, getting ready to offer his best pitch. I selected one of my custom-made cues and chalked the tip.

My break shot was clean and I pulled the fifteen ball back to the corner nearest me. Two balls broke from the rack and my second dead shot scattered the pack.

Calloway watched and waited. "Very nice."

"And very rusty." I glanced at him briefly before returning to the game. I took a long time figuring the angle on a rough side shot.

"We want you for a job," Calloway finally said. "A fairly delicate mission."

"I figured that one out all by myself, pal. No go."

I sank two more balls in silence. One was a gorgeous bank shot which never should have gone in, and the other was a hanger I couldn't resist. Calloway walked away from the table, turning the conversation over to General Dillon. He waited until I completed the third shot before interrupting.

"Dee, we've been getting our asses kicked in Korea since the Communists crossed the thirty-eighth parallel ten days ago."

"So I noticed."

"We're going to lose the peninsula unless 'alternative action' can be developed. General MacArthur is in complete command, naturally, but he lacks the hardened personnel that took the Pacific five years ago. He needs men with your talents."

"So what do you want from me?"

Calloway moved back to me. "The general is planning something calling for specialized personnel. We are not fully apprised of his strategy yet, but the general has reviewed your file and believes you'd be perfect for this mission."

"Mission? What mission?"

"Only MacArthur knows this," Calloway said. "We were ordered to contact you and, if possible, pass you along through certain phases, should you decide to accept. MacArthur would then explain all the details."

"You want to send me to Korea?"

"The possibility is very strong. However, in all fairness, I should warn you that we were informed that your chances for retrieval would be slim."

I laughed aloud, mimicking him. "Chances for retrieval would be slim." I shook my head. "In other words, it doesn't look like I'd be coming back. Kind of like my half-million in Beirut, huh?"

"Something like that."

"Real cute." I looked at my cue, handling it like a weapon. "G-2 may not have brains, but they've sure got balls. After losing my money, my entire Beirut operation, you come strolling into my house and ask me to go out and lose my life too. I worked my ass off to get that first export license to the Middle East. I had big plans to sell beef to the Lebanese. Where were you, Calloway, when the Lebanese government accused Dee Enterprises of being an information drop for Israeli intelligence?"

"I tried my best," Calloway answered, "but you know how touchy they are in the Middle East."

"Bullshit! If it was your money, your business, things would have turned out different."

"Look, Dee, I'm not going to spend all day beating a dead horse. Let's talk about a real problem. The information comes straight from the Oval Office."

Big deal, I thought to myself. All authority eventually finds a tunnel through the White House. "In other words, President Truman has been in close contact with MacArthur and agrees with whatever tactics the general is considering."

"That's fairly safe to assume." Calloway was holding back, and that made me edgy.

"Why do I get the impression you're trying to send me smack into the middle of a war?"

"Not exactly." Calloway's tone gave him away.

"Behind enemy lines? I'm not ready for suicide, pal.

Look at me, Calloway. I'm a round-eye. I'd be spotted in a minute."

Calloway measured his next words. "Dee, there is a surgical procedure in which your features could be . . . altered. That way, you could evade—"

"Drop dead."

"There's no other way. We make you an Oriental and—"

"No, you don't." I picked up the cue and, without looking, smacked the eight ball into a side pocket. "I'm not going. That's final. Now, get out of my house. All of you."

Calloway nodded to the military men to depart, allowing us some privacy. I was just lining up a nice cross-corner shot when he placed both hands on the table.

"Reconsider it, Dee." It was not a request.

"Fuck off. And get your hands off the table."

He stayed where he was. "MacArthur's a fair man. You know that. He's in the public eye and has to watch his manners. I don't."

"What a surprise. I never would have known that if you hadn't told me." My sarcasm was wasted; he had an ace up his sleeve.

"Remember Ducksun?"

Calloway had hit a nerve. I hadn't seen Ducksun since Shanghai. I knew he'd gone up to Nanking after my departure, so I figured he was lost to the Japanese when that city fell. The Warlord had been like a father to me, but for years I had considered him dead. I tried to keep my face impassive. I didn't want to let Calloway know he'd told me something I didn't already know. "What about Ducksun?"

"He's selling his services to both sides."

"Big deal. That's Ducksun's style. He's a businessman, you know that."

"True. But we'd write him off like that"—he snapped his fingers—"for the right reasons."

"Calloway, you couldn't get within ten miles of Ducksun."

"We wouldn't have to. The North Koreans would do it for us. All we'd have to do is let them know he's dealing with the West. Just a few innocent facts to the Communists, and Ducksun becomes a corpse. And if you won't help us, I can guarantee you that's exactly what will happen."

I kept my voice even, calm, though I don't know how. "Get out of my house."

In a moment he was gone, but his absence didn't cleanse the room any. It didn't change anything. Except now I knew Ducksun was alive. And in danger.

I poured myself a double Rémy, then dropped into the director's chair next to the pool table.

Ducksun.

If my old friend was in danger, then I knew I had to help him. Just as he'd saved my life when I was in Shanghai. It was because of Ducksun that I had had the capital to found Dee Enterprises. The tube of gems he'd given me had been more than enough to stake me to an empire. I owed him everything.

But going to Ducksun's aid meant leaving Sylvia and the kids. It meant putting my life and future on the line.

Sylvia. My beautiful Sylvia. . . .

8

The Tyson Building was located on Fifth Avenue. Whenever I entered the tenth-floor offices that comprised corporate headquarters for Dee Enterprises, my entire life flashed before me. Each event from the moment I returned from Shanghai was highlighted in my memory. The corporate climb hadn't been easy.

The morning I had docked in New York ten years before, Eddie Gardenia had been waiting for me. We had both matured physically during the intervening years, but there was no mistaking him. He told me nearly everything of importance that had occurred during my absence. Most of our conversation concerned Jimmy Moroni, the kid I'd stabbed on the docks. Moroni had recovered but was still holding a grudge. His father ran a crew for some mob guy along Mulberry Street, so it had been fairly easy for him to trace me, but when he found he couldn't actually get at me, Moroni had spent the next few years stewing in his own hatred. Returning to the United States meant I'd have to be careful. After what I'd been through, I had no intention of getting killed now.

Eddie had been working at the wholesale meat distributorship along Fourteenth Street. Within a few days a job opened up and Eddie was able to talk his boss into hiring me as a driver. Our duties included delivering forequarters, hindquarters, and other wholesale cuts throughout the five boroughs. I immediately saw the profit potential in the meat business, so I proposed a deal with my cousin. Using the gems given me by Ducksun, we bought our own truck and went into business for ourselves. We designed careful plans, then proceeded to lay the firm cornerstone of my business empire.

During this hectic period, I met Sylvia Pullman. She had been working in the accounting office of the Fourteenth Street distributor. She was a friendly blond who dressed well and was dedicated to her work. Within a few months of our initial meeting, Sylvia resigned her position to work for Eddie and me. Ironically, she was the person responsible for our expansion. At her suggestion, we purchased a new tractor-trailer and began hauling meat directly from the Midwest markets. Our profit margin soared as we competed aggressively with other local wholesalers. Our first rig was painted red, white, and blue and emblazoned with bold black lettering proclaiming "Dee Enterprises."

During the summer of 1941, Eddie and I were able to secure a government contract. The United States Army permitted us to haul away their reclaimable meat scraps such as tallow and fats, leading us into the rendering business. Soon we were profitably invested in the perfume and fragrance industry. Our refineries were a spinoff that enabled us to purchase our own sporting-goods-manufacturing operation. The number of first-class goods extracted from meat by-products was staggering, and we tried to invest in as many of these related businesses as possible. By the end of World War II, our business was well on its way to spreading across both oceans. And I was married to Sylvia.

The morning after the meeting with Calloway, I arrived at the Fifth Avenue address by limousine, then took the elevator to the tenth floor. The doors opened with a hydraulic hiss and I stepped forth, then studied the directory of my business.

Large gold-painted letters announced, "Dee Enterprises, New York." The twin subsidiaries I'd founded were listed beneath: "Far East Enterprises, Hong Kong," and "Far West Enterprises, London." I was hardly another Jardine, Matheson with a century of prestigious profiteering behind me, but Dee Enterprises was now one of the world's largest, most respected companies. And yesterday I'd been asked to give it all up.

I didn't want to leave Sylvia, but if Ducksun was in danger, then I had to go to his assistance. I just wondered if there wasn't some way I could do it without leaving either my family or my business.

First, though, I had to find out if Ducksun was alive, and if he was, what his position was. I passed through the main office to the secured area known as the "executive run." Along this corridor were the offices of the company's top men, the two most important being Eddie and myself. The rest of them could go play golf for all I cared. Turning into my three-room suite, I saw Maggie rise with her notebook clutched tightly between her fingers.

If anyone could be Sylvia's exact opposite, Maggie was. Her hair was dark and trimmed short, her figure thick. She was attractive, but hardly beautiful. But she was efficient and letter perfect.

"Hello, Maggie." I walked into my office as she followed me, flipping her notebook open as she moved.

"Good morning, Mr. Dee." She glanced down to her notes. "I placed the call to Edwards in our Hong Kong office late last night as you requested. He promised you'd have a reply sometime today."

"Fine."

She continued. "A Mr. Barringer called. He claims to be an attorney for James Moroni, so I transferred him to Mr. Gardenia. They're still talking, if you're interested. Also, our Sioux City processing plant called. Scabies has been discovered on several of our walking stock. Naturally they were destroyed, but the pen was slated for futures contract delivery. The usual speculation is flying around the Commodities Exchange. Several brokers called, but I told them you were unavailable for comment. And a Mr. Garfield from the advertising agency phoned twice. He said he'll call back."

I considered all the problems Maggie had fielded for me as I pulled loose my tie. There weren't any appointments scheduled for early in the day. At least, none that I knew of.

"Okay, Maggie. Issue the usual disclaimer on the scabies thing: the company is investigating, so on, so on. It's too nice a day to deal with Moroni, so tell Barringer I'm tied up. Be sweet, though, okay? And hold all my calls except Hong Kong and Garfield."

Maggie departed and fifteen minutes later I was finished with Garfield. His ideas were good, but not what I was looking for.

I sat lost in my thoughts, when a slight knock brought me back to reality. The door opened slightly and Maggie stuck her head in. "Mr. Gardenia buzzed, Mr. Dee. He would like a few minutes with you. He says to expect him in the usual manner."

"Tell him I'll be waiting."

When Maggie left my office, I turned my chair around to face the mirrors behind the bar and liquor cabinet. These mirrors obscured a secret passage which I could get access to by touching a button next to the cabinet. At either end of this hidden passage, two-way mirrors were installed so I could discreetly observe the way businessmen who were only allowed an approach to Dee Enterprises through Eddie would try to cultivate Eddie's favors. Most times they attempted recruiting him through handsome propositions. In order to offset this type of business strategy, we constructed the passageway so I could listen to the pitches being thrown at my cousin. We had used it on only a few occasions, but it had more than paid for itself.

A few moments later, Eddie opened the hidden door behind the bar and stepped from the dim passageway. He was dressed conservatively in a three-piece suit and his prematurely graying hair was combed neatly to one side.

"Good morning, Eddie."

" 'Morning, Dee." He quietly pulled up a chair. "How are Sylvia and the kids?"

"Fine. I'm meeting her for lunch later. Care to join us."

"No. Thanks. I've got lunch with the union reps. Seems they're blaming us 'cause some employees at our Midwestern terminals aren't organized."

"Sounds like fun."

"Sounds like they're angling for a new contract, Dee."

"Yeah. Watch your step, Eddie. Those boys can be tricky."

"Tell me about it. I remember all the problems we had with Moroni's union when we first started out. I don't feel like going through that again." Eddie consulted his notes. "By the way, a Mr. Philip Barringer phoned earlier."

"Maggie told me about it. What does he want?"

"Barringer claims to be an attorney for the Moroni group and wants to work out a deal."

"What kind of deal?"

"The fat-rendering business. Again." Eddie grinned.

I shook my head. "Jimmy Moroni's had his eyes on that operation since we got the army contract in forty-one. Claims we stole it out from under him."

"Yeah, I remember. He swore he'd buy us out someday. Anyway, he's offering three million."

"No dice. It's not for sale."

"I figured as much." Eddie smiled. "I already called Barringer back and told him to get lost."

Our brief conference was over and Eddie rose to leave. As he did so, I received the distinct impression something was bothering him. I couldn't quite put my finger on it; it was just a feeling.

"You okay, Eddie?"

"Yeah, sure. Why?"

I shrugged. "No reason. Get on that union thing, will you?"

Eddie had no sooner left than the phone rang. Maggie told me the overseas operator had completed a call from Hong Kong. A Mr. Edwards. Was I ready to accept? You bet I was. Several minutes later, an English accent crackled at the other end of the line.

"Mr. Dee? I say, Mr. Dee? Are you there?"

"Go ahead, Edwards. You're faint, but I hear you. What have you got?"

"Well, I was able to locate the party about which you inquired. Your suppositions were correct, sir. He is quite functional in every sense of the word. His dealings are, indeed, duplicate. Estimated worth: level number seven, with a turning of level three per annum. He has a considerable number of friends willing to listen to his every word and is presently quite safe, courtesy of opposing powers. However, there is no indication as to the future duration of this courtesy. Will I be making contact, sir?"

"No, Edwards." Then I thought about it. "Would contact be easy?"

"Quite, sir," Edwards replied.

"Thanks, Edwards. Draw a bonus for yourself. Take the wife on a holiday." We both laughed and he signed off, Edwards appreciating our standing joke. Edwards had never married but was somehow managing to keep two mistresses in separate Hong Kong flats. One was a delicate Chinese claiming mandarin background and the other a buxom German girl with shoulder-length blond hair. First rule: know your employees.

I put down the phone, hand still resting on the receiver. So Ducksun was indeed alive. And he was selling to both sides. His estimated worth was level seven, about a hundred million dollars. Those phrases about a "considerable number of friends" indicated he was still keeping a private army. But more frightening was Edwards' contention that he could get through to the Warlord. If a businessman like Edwards could reach Ducksun, a professional killer like Calloway would find the same task a piece of cake.

The whole deal bothered me. I spent the next two hours tossing it around in my head. Ducksun was the type of friend who understood the meaning of forever. Half a planet away, still a devoted sense of loyalty existed. Truly, he was a tiger, the last of a breed gone modern. Or dead.

I had a twelve-thirty reservation at Asti's to meet Sylvia for a light lunch. She'd made the trip into Manhattan in order to firm up the advertising details on the "Sylvia" line. On my way to the elevator bank, I ran into Calloway as he made his way to my suite. He did a swift about-face, then followed me into the express. The doors closed.

"You never give up, do you?"

"I can't afford to, Dee. Neither can my superiors."
He took a moment, then continued, "I conveyed your
answer to them and they would like you to reconsider."

"No."

Calloway took a breath. "That half-million is really
sticking in your craw, isn't it?"

I turned on him. "No, buddy. It's not the half-
million. I can make that back before sunrise tomorrow. What beats the hell out of me are people like
you, the lawyers of the world gone off to play cowboys
and Indians in somebody else's backyard. It's getting
too simple to send a man to war when you're not
going yourself."

Calloway softened his tone unexpectedly. "I'm just
a messenger boy, Dee."

"And you always will be while you're peddling the
blood of others. Try looking at the beauty of the
world, Calloway, instead of moving those drab green
armies around the globe."

"Sometimes those armies preserve beauty."

"Like in Dresden and Hiroshima?"

The agent drew in a deep, exhaustive breath. "Dee,
in the name of your government, I have been officially
dispatched to inquire as to your availability for this
mission."

I knew the words. The political and philosophical
bullshit was out of the way now. These were formal
words, and it wasn't just MacArthur asking, either.

"No."

"We will return the half-million, plus damages. I
personally will leave myself open to one request of
your choice. A matter of honor."

Calloway? Honor? The words were mutually exclusive.

"Sorry, Calloway. Tell your superiors I'm not at
liberty to take this mission. I've got too many respon-
sibilities here."

The elevator door opened. We shook hands, forced
faint smiles, then walked our separate ways. But I
knew he would be back.

Within seconds I was being driven downtown. I'd
always been partial to Asti's because it afforded the
type of solitude a businessman needed following a

hectic morning. The prime movers in New York managed a meal or a cocktail there at least once a week. I was no exception. Emil led me to my corner table, where my wife was waiting.

Lunching with Sylvia at the poshest spots had always been a weakness with me, the nicest moments money could buy. As I moved toward her, I realized that over the past few years Sylvia had been more than a lover, a wife. She was my true partner in every sense of the word. She was that one person I could trust with all the intimacies of my life. She understood the basics of my business, had a general idea of our net worth, and was written into our corporate documents as having overriding control in the event of my death. Hell, why not? She'd built it all with me.

Sylvia was smartly dressed in business gray, which lent her a subdued appearance. Her hair was swept back from her forehead and arranged to seem far shorter than it really was, accentuating the gray hat she wore.

"How was your morning?" I kissed her and took my seat.

"Fine." She smiled and I realized again how beautiful she was. "The people at the agency seemed to like my ideas."

"One of the many things they're being paid for."

She was about to protest my teasing when Emil interrupted graciously with a bottle of prewar Lafite Rothschild. My eyebrows raised a bit; most prewar Bordeaux was not only difficult to locate but also expensive when discovered.

"From the gentleman seated in the alcove," Emil announced quietly.

I turned to the rear to see a smiling silver-haired man seated between two bulky bodyguards. I raised my hand in acknowledgment, and from across the room Sam Terry lifted his own in reply. Sam Terry. I smiled because three months had gone by since we'd spoken last. But, then again, he was one of the men Senator Kefauver had sworn to interrogate when his Crime Commission arrived in New York.

"Emil, send the gentleman the oldest Château Latour in your cellar, with my deepest regards."

Over lunch, Sylvia and I spoke at length concerning the future of the "Sylvia" line, but I noticed that she kept glancing past me, as if someone to my rear had captured her attention.

"Is something wrong?"

"No." She smiled and her eyes met mine again. "It's just that the man you sent the bottle of wine to seems vaguely familiar to me."

I laughed. "He should. His picture is in the *Daily News* often enough."

I'd never mentioned Sam Terry to Sylvia simply because he was a part of my life which she only suspected existed. To all external appearances, Sam was a pleasant and considerate gentleman. But the pair of intimidating bodyguards flanking him underscored his position and his power. Sam couldn't go anywhere without them in New York because of the rival factions competing for his territory. And his prime territory, as any other ranking capo could have told you, was worth competing for.

I first met Sam Terry in the months following Pearl Harbor. On one of the rare occasions he slipped from character by walking the streets unguarded, two vicious street kids attempted to hold him up. They knocked him to the ground, kicked his ribs a few times, and were lifting his wallet when I happened along. How I broke them away from him really isn't important. Let's just say I had learned the Gentle Way; they hadn't. I helped Sam to his feet, then dusted off his overcoat.

After asking my name, but never revealing his own, Sam reached into his pocket for his billfold. I declined any type of reward, even upon his insistence. He asked me my business and I explained some of the plans Eddie and I were making. He repeated my name aloud, almost as if to himself, shook my hand, then walked out of my life. Until after World War II.

His name and position meant nothing to me until I saw his picture published soon after Lepke was executed in 1944. The Brooklyn *Eagle*, which broke the

Murder Incorporated story, was having a field day printing photographs of New York's foremost mobsters. Only then did a few of the strange occurrences in my business life take on meaning. One was the labor problems Eddie and I had experienced while putting our first trailers on the road. Those problems had vanished mysteriously. Picket lines went up and came down within forty-eight hours. The pressure completely disappeared and the union representative became a smiling, happy samaritan of the just cause between the worker and the boss. And I saw the signature of Sam Terry on the whole deal. His silent manipulation, no matter how slight, made my business life easier. Especially with regard to the Moroni family.

"Is he a politician?" Sylvia sipped her wine thoughtfully.

"You might say so."

She narrowed her eyes as she always did when detecting a secret. She was about to probe further when I caught her glancing upward. There was movement behind me and I turned to see the two bodyguards. Sam Terry was walking toward my table while issuing hushed instructions to Emil. Terry then came directly to me, hand extended. I rose respectfully to meet him.

"Dee . . . Dee," Terry said warmly. "It's goo' see an old friend again."

"Same here, Sam." I nodded toward the bottle. "Thank you for the wine. It's appreciated."

"No, Dee, thank you. The Latour was exquisite. Best of the prewar vintages, according to Emil. And nobody's going to argue with Emil."

"Tell me about it." We laughed, then I turned to my wife. "Sam, I don't believe I've ever had the occasion to introduce you to my wife, Sylvia."

She extended her hand, which Sam took gently.

"A pleasure," Sylvia offered.

"No," Sam answered gracefully, "the pleasure is all mine."

Sylvia smiled as Sam's attention turned to me. "Dee, we're running a fund-raiser for several villages in southern Italy. Seems like the Marshall Plan funding didn't exactly get down there, so the Church has adopted these starving towns. We would appreciate anything you could send down to Father Ceroni on Houston Street."

"Sure thing, Sam. I'll have a check messengered over today."

"Fine. I knew I could count on you, Dee."

"Anytime, Sam. You know that. Just ask."

Then he quietly said farewell and left, accompanied by his bodyguards. Sylvia and I finished our meal. As I motioned for the check, Sylvia looked up at me.

"Your friend Sam is charming. You should have him out to the house. He looks like he could use the sun."

"Someday." Charming? Good God. There were a dozen hoods at the bottom of Gravesend Bay willing to dispute that point. And if he really wanted the sun, Sam could stay at any of his many Florida homes. But I couldn't tell Sylvia all this, so I just nodded and repeated, "Yeah, sure, someday."

As we prepared to leave, we learned from Emil that Sam had picked up our tab in advance. I wasn't surprised, but Sam usually allowed me a moment to protest his generosity. Common courtesy, I guess, but he always paid anyway. Sam got his way in anything he wanted.

We left Asti's in search of our separate cars. Once I'd seen Sylvia off with a kiss, the valet brought my car around, then summoned my driver from the lounge.

"Dee, wait a minute. You may not be needing the car."

It didn't take me two seconds to recognize the voice. Calloway. Again.

9

"I'm too busy for this, Calloway. Take your mission elsewhere."

The agent moved closer to me as though to speak in seclusion. "It's different now, Dee. Situations change."

"It's only been ninety minutes since I saw you." I glanced at my watch. Where was that driver?

"My boss wants to see you, Dee. He wants you to reconsider."

"Don't bother me, Calloway. I turned you down and I'll do the same with him. Why don't you save us both some time and go away?"

Calloway's face assumed a near-satanic smile, like a man about to say "Checkmate" or a feudal baron set to claim wedding-night rights to a peasant's wife. Here it comes, I thought.

"I have absolutely no intention of carrying that message back to the President of the United States."

"Are you telling me that Harry Truman is your boss?"

Calloway nodded. "Yes and no. My affiliations are intelligence, but I've presently been detached to work the Situation Room in the White House. Our entire team is answerable only to the President. It's been like this since the North Koreans crossed the thirty-eighth parallel. We've got a real problem there, Dee. Nothing like the papers are reporting or the rest of the world believes. We're in the shadow of China and . . . Look, I know you're not crazy about me, but listen to the President. Hear him out. Then you can make your own decision."

Make my own decision. What a joke. "All right, Calloway. I'll talk to him."

Calloway ushered me into a new Cadillac, then closed the glass panel separating us from the driver. The chauffeur turned around, Calloway gave him the nod, and the ethnic neighborhoods of lower Manhattan passed behind us as we moved uptown.

The driver took Madison Avenue up to Fifty-seventh, took a left, then went the two blocks to Avenue of the Americas, swung right, and after another two blocks, turned right onto Central Park South.

The first thing I noticed was not the crowds walking or the amateur photographers, but the Secret Service men stationed around the Plaza Hotel. To the untrained eye they appeared to be average businessmen waiting for cabs, reading newspapers, talking. But I knew better.

When the car pulled up before the flag-draped entrance, Calloway got out first, spoke briefly with the doorman, who I then knew was also an agent, and in we went.

The government boys had taken control of an elevator for the exclusive use of the President's entourage. As we arrived, an agent was holding the brass doors for us. We stepped in. Without stops, the car rose to the designated floor and the door opened.

"This is where I get off, buddy." Calloway smiled and extended his hand. I never got a chance to take it. Two Secret Service men gestured me to a door.

The main drawing room was decorated in post-Revolutionary colonial style, probably a copy of some renowned mansion's sitting room. Alone, I looked around somewhat nervously when, without fanfare, Harry S Truman entered.

Less than a half-hour later, I was back on the streets, the President's words still alive in my ears. He'd made his points simply, directly.

Ducksun and his army represented the final bastion of freedom in South Korea, but he was under extreme pressure to commit to the North Koreans. He was presently holding his options open pending possible American intervention. A massive amphibious and airborne assault was being planned with the purpose of both surprising the North Koreans and providing a link-up with Ducksun. The President said MacArthur, if he were to succeed in retaking Korea and stopping the Communist march in the east, would require the perfect landing spot, the place the Koreans would never anticipate an army. And I was the man to find such a place.

But more important, the President felt I was the only person Ducksun would trust, the only person who could convince Ducksun that he would have American support should he throw in with the West. Truman was probably right.

I decided to walk back to the office, so many thoughts filling my head. In order to ensure my personal safety, I would have to submit to plastic surgery. A Dr. Green would take knife in hand and turn me into an Oriental, an operation that the President assured me was reversible. I hoped so.

By the end of the half-hour, I found I'd made up my mind. I asked for three days with my wife and family.

As I entered the Tyson Building, I thought of Ducksun. If what the President said was right—and I had no reason to doubt him—Ducksun's life was in my hands.

It was time to repay a debt.

10

Three weeks later, I was safely hidden in a secret base in Japan. My head was completely bandaged, with only the bleak, ever-present darkness to remind me of my future, the mission I was pledged to carry out. And in the nothingness, there were only images of Sylvia. My memory of her was the only solitude into which I could retreat. And with my memories of her came the searing, ripping pain of being away from that very special love. It was then that I found myself only a hairbreadth away from tearing off the bandages and returning to her.

Truman had given us three days in which to part. Sylvia never questioned my decision nor its probable impact upon her own life. She did as she had always done in the past: she very preciously gave me the moment.

During the first two days, I found myself making the preparations often associated with those who've found out they have a terminal illness: I spoke with my children, I updated my will, I turned my business over to Eddie Gardenia. But on that final night, we were alone in the house we'd built together.

We curled up before the fireplace, sipping the most delicate Bordeaux I could find. We wore matching black kimonos printed with blossoming red flowers which Sylvia had purchased only the day before. As she curled against me, I studied this woman. She was still the woman I'd fallen in love with, the woman I would always want. She was the mother of my children, the unifying force of our family. She was my lover, my wife, my friend. And I was leaving her.

Sylvia had been quiet for a long time. She then turned and looked up at me. "Why couldn't they find someone else?"

"There's no one else," I said quietly.

"But why, Dee? Why us? Did we work this hard to build a life for ourselves and our children only to surrender it all to some politician's whim?"

I touched her hair and gently kissed her forehead. "It's not that. And you know it has nothing to do with what some politician wants. I have a debt to repay, Sylvia, a debt I can't turn my back on. If I turned my back now, I'd never be able to live with myself. Do you understand?"

She fell silent, but moved closer to me until our bodies were pressed gently together. Then slowly her arms came around me as her lips moved to mine. She made love to me that night with more love, more passion than I could ever remember. We fell away from each other exhausted and complete. Then all too soon she was watching from the terrace as I vanished in Calloway's chauffeur-driven car.

The military can cut through even the reddest tape when priorities dictate. Within thirty hours I was at a small, compact, yet highly classified base somewhere in Japan. I was never told exactly where, but from the pristine environment beyond the electrified fence, I assumed we were far from any city. Another curious aspect was the number of specialized assault troops this base contained. Permanent as it appeared, this entire outfit—buildings and all—could be flown in C-147's to the nearest trouble spot.

Within a few hours of my arrival I was introduced to Dr. Green. He seemed a kindly man with thinning blond hair and mustache to match. We spoke of the operation for thirty minutes. In recent years the surgical procedure that would transform my Western appearance to that of an Oriental had become fairly common. A great many men had fought in the Pacific and more than a few had fallen in love with both the women and the culture they found there. I told the doctor I was well aware of the process, having heard the tales of countless seamen in Shanghai before the war.

"Sheer butchery at that time." Dr. Green drew in on a cigarette. "The better processes emerged from postwar Europe, primarily through independent laboratories in Switzerland."

"Is it reversible?"

"Yes. But only through a series of related procedures that require an extremely long and probably difficult recuperation period. The primary problem lies with the eyes, the grafting of replacement tissue to compensate for what must be removed at this stage. It's a very intricate process."

"How long?"

"A year, maybe longer."

I nodded, then inhaled slowly. Hell, it was better than not coming back at all. "Will my appearance be the same afterward?"

Dr. Green studied me, then cleared his throat. "Well, not exactly as you are now. You'd probably be better-looking."

We laughed the tension away temporarily, and following three days of preparation, I went under the surgeon's knife. The last thing I remember was the smiling eyes of the attending nurse.

As they removed the bandages, I spoke for the first time in weeks. "I want to see."

The nurse took my hand and led me to a mirror on the wall. Slowly I brought my eyes up to the reflection. No, it couldn't be. It wasn't.

I turned to look at the team of physicians, Calloway.

Calloway kept his voice light. "Well, hotshot, what do you think?"

"I think I want to be alone."

Calloway persisted. "Hey, c'mon, what do you think?"

I struggled to keep my voice under control. "Get out of here. All of you."

Calloway started to say something but thought better of it. They departed, leaving me alone with the mirror.

I stared at the stranger, the youthful Oriental with

my eyes, for a very, very long time, the stranger that was me. And I wondered if I would ever be able to go back to Sylvia.

I didn't see Calloway during the two days I adjusted to my new appearance. Dr. Green had constructed a classically Oriental face but he hadn't been able to take away the look in my eyes. Yes, I was Oriental, but I was still Dee.

When Calloway was finally allowed in, he seemed far more serious than I could ever recall. He brought a set of folded clothes that, when I slipped into them, complemented my Oriental looks.

"The general is here," Calloway said quietly. "He's been here for three days."

"When will I be meeting him?"

"There's a strategy session scheduled to begin in ten minutes." Calloway lit a cigarette. "We're included."

I nodded, then followed him out the door. The meeting was held in a Quonset hut guarded by several of the assault troops stationed at the base. Judging by the increased activity, this didn't seem to be a small meeting. In a tiny room adjacent to the conference area was a signal corpsman sporting headquarters insignia. He sat before a radio and was General MacArthur's ear on the world. This improptu base was a far cry from the Dai Ichi Building in Tokyo where the general ruled as military governor. The Tokyo headquarters were situated quite conveniently across a park from Hirohito's palace.

Calloway escorted me into a room wallpapered with maps and inhabited by khaki-clean offices. They peered at me, then asked each other hushed questions concerning my identity. Eventually General Douglas MacArthur entered and all attention was turned to him. He saluted everyone into position and then went to the wall to study the immense map of Korea.

The general, standing there, arms behind his back, appeared somewhat thicker around the middle than the World War II newsreels portrayed him. He also showed evidence of extreme exhaustion.

"Gentlemen," he began, "General Walton Walker

arrived at Taegu yesterday to personally command the Eighth Army. Let's hope he can do what Task Force Smith didn't."

Within a few minutes I knew about the ill fate of Task Force Smith. Calloway whispered some of their history as the meeting began. They were select elements of the Twenty-fourth Division, which was designated to stop the North Korean advance. Flown into Korea on July 1, they dug in near Osan along the main highway. Five days later, a juggernaut of Russian T-34 tanks decimated them in the first and most shattering American defeat of the war. The result was an overwhelming retreat of the UN forces toward the port of Pusan.

General MacArthur lit his pipe, then turned and stared at the men surrounding the table.

The meeting continued for nearly two hours as the various battlegrounds in Korea were discussed. Plans were devised, dismissed, revised. The expression on MacArthur's face was depressing. And why not? The Koreans seemed to have countless armies available to push the UN forces into the sea. Then the meeting was over.

MacArthur spoke briefly to several of his officers while the remainder left the room. When the last of them was gone, MacArthur took a seat at the head of the table and relit his pipe. It was then that he seemed to notice me for the first time. Calloway led me forward, performed the introductions, and waited.

"You may leave."

Calloway was about to say something, thought better of it, and left. MacArthur turned to me.

"A unique situation exists in Korea, Mr. Dee." He drew in on his pipe. "We're the best-mechanized, highest-trained army on the planet and we're getting our asses kicked by the North Koreans. As you may well have gathered, the official viewpoint in Washington is far different from the vantage point at the front. It's time we change that to our benefit."

For the briefest moment General MacArthur seemed a pathetic personage pitted not against opposing armies but against the tide of history. He was an officer accustomed to moving great armies across wide frontiers who'd now had his power halved by the complacency of peacetime, by a mentality which would have everyone believe that because there was no war there were no warmakers. And because a good many congressmen found poll-side profit in this doctrine, we'd been caught shorthanded in Korea: no armor, few heavy weapons, and troops whose last battleground was the high-school prom. This was MacArthur's army.

"What do you want of me, General?"

MacArthur crossed his legs, then ran his hand over his receding hairline. "Only what I'm asking of everyone these days, Mr. Dee. The impossible. Nothing more, nothing less. I want Korea and you're going to hand it to me."

"If armies can't do it, what makes you think I can?"

"The fact that armies do not maintain the standards the individual man does. My plan is to take this goddamn 'police action' dead to the Yalu River, where our frontier defense line should really be."

MacArthur paused and looked at me. "Find me the perfect landing area, Dee."

"Just like that?" I didn't believe Korea had a perfect anything.

"Yes. Just like that."

I fell momentarily silent. "What are the specifics, General? What, exactly, are you looking for?"

"A place to pack an army. I need enough clear beach to land the maximum number of troops with a minimum of casualties."

"If it's to be a rearguard assault, then we're talking about the west coast of Korea." I glanced over to the huge wall map. "An area entirely in enemy hands."

"I'm afraid so. The only other entry point to the peninsula is through Pusan. Inchon looks good, but we're not sure of the terrain. Your mission, Mr. Dee, is to confirm or deny Inchon as the appropriate landing place."

"What about Ducksun?"

"What about him?" MacArthur's voice was cold.

"Are we to link up with his men?"

"Provided he hasn't sold his soul to the North Koreans." MacArthur clearly felt distaste for this subject. "Maybe they should kill the bastard. I can't run a war depending on unstable, self-serving characters, whether they be politicians or warlords."

I began to understand Douglas MacArthur from a viewpoint no one in America could. If a Caesar he was, then indeed he was as tragic as his renowned predecessor. Only the North Koreans had crossed the Rubicon for him. Clearly he was not long for this war, even though he'd successfully moved awesome armies across Korea. MacArthur was hardly a fool, but he was blind to his own fate.

"Will I be in immediate contact with Ducksun?"

MacArthur shook his head, indicating he wasn't sure.

"Will I be reconnoitering the west coast of Korea by boat?"

"Yes."

I took a breath. "May I question the General about the physical aspects of this mission?"

MacArthur looked at me with glowing trust in his eyes and answered, "Calloway has arranged everything through G-2. I'm told you'll have a guide also. You do speak Korean, don't you?"

"I'm a little rusty, but I can get along. Who's my guide?"

"Someone who knows most of the shoreline but has no idea of the military requirements. Hopefully, your team will be successful."

"And the preparations for my retrieval?" I wasn't sure I wanted to hear the answer to this one. "I was led to believe this mission was as close to suicide as anyone could devise."

"True." MacArthur lit his pipe. "But all measures to pull you out have been taken. When you locate the beachhead I'm looking for, you'll contact a submarine that the Navy has agreed to submerge offshore. The code word is 'ballpark.' They'll come to you."

The general rose and I knew the meeting was over. He shook my hand and then watched as I walked to the door. Before closing it behind me, I glanced back to see MacArthur standing silently before the map of

Korea. I wouldn't have wanted his job for anything in the world.

Calloway was waiting impatiently outside. "Well?"

"When do I get started?"

"Immediately, old pal. We have a submarine waiting."

We arrived at my room, where I found a "treated" set of clothing piled on my bunk. By "treated," I mean the type a fisherman would wear. It came complete with stains, mendings, and an odor from the previous owner. I couldn't help but wonder what had happened to him.

Next I checked out the armory and was issued an eight-shot 9mm Walther PPK. I liked it because the caliber was on a par with the .45 automatic and operated like a revolver even though clip fed. Throughout all this, Calloway stood by silently.

I looked around at my room for the last time, then turned to Calloway. "Okay. Let's go."

11

The submarine transporting us to within shouting distance of Kunsan was a World War II model hastily welded together during the Pearl Harbor backlash of 1942. I wasn't comfortable being submerged from Japan to Korea, especially at night, when all decks were quiet and the submarine moaned in symphony against the exterior pressure of the sea. I couldn't understand how the crew became immune to those sounds of certain death.

Calloway bunked with me in the officers' quarters he'd appropriated through the captain. He explained that our meeting with our guide was to be far more complicated than previously planned. Prior to leaving Japan, he'd received a secret cable through MacArthur's office and had been ordered to make contact with a small group of terrain specialists. Those men were scheduled to exit Korea through the river mouth of Kunsan.

They'd been a small group commanded by Captain Percy Elser, who'd led them ashore during the initial fall of the peninsula. From what Calloway knew of their mission, this patrol of signalmen, cartographers, and infantry was to proceed upriver, charting the area in complete detail. They'd radioed for early evacuation because of an unforeseen enemy engagement. So, under orders, Calloway and I rowed toward Kunsan in a large inflatable raft, taking two additional craft. Within twenty minutes we spotted the fishing boat. It was the most unseaworthy wreck G-2 could locate; I was surprised it even bothered to float. The sampan was illuminated against the first rays of dawn, and beyond, huddled in the river mouth, was a battle-weary contingent of American soldiers. We came alongside the sampan but kept a safe distance away by using our paddles.

Suddenly I saw our guide. It was Chen Lee.

Now I knew why Calloway had never told me our guide's identity. He knew damn well that if he told me it was Chen Lee I'd never have agreed to the mission. Putting my own life on the line was one thing; endangering the life of Chen Lee was quite another. I looked at Calloway, who shrugged.

"I thought you'd like our little surprise."

I was about to respond, but decided it would keep. I'd deal with that manipulative bastard later. If there was a later.

Chen Lee leaned down to assist us onto the sampan, and I watched as her expression changed from one of expectation to one of disappointment. She looked to Calloway, but when he made no move to come aboard, her eyes darted back to me. Clearly she was very confused. I didn't expect to see her, but was she expecting to see me?

"Hello, Chen Lee," I offered simply. Immediately she recognized my voice.

She was about to answer but couldn't form the words. Her eyes did so explicitly, and suddenly she understood. I looked away from her to the quiet sound of Calloway pushing off from the sampan's hull. He was headed toward the river mouth to meet with the commandos. We were to await his return before sailing north along the coast. My attention returned to Chen Lee. She was no longer the little girl I remembered, but a mature, beautiful woman.

In previous years I'd often thought of her. Did she ever think of me? Did she even remember me? And now, realizing she'd be on this mission, I asked myself if the warm feelings of our past friendship would interfere. Could I sacrifice her as I would any other agent? Would I be forced to do so?

"Is it really you, Dee?" she finally asked. She stood

straight and proud, giving full command to her petite perfection. Her hair was not as long as I remembered as she had it trimmed to drop only as far as her neck. She was very slender, much like Sylvia, but not as full-figured. She had grown to be a stunning woman.

"It's me. Plastic surgery was the only way."

"I am sorry, Dee, to be the instrument by which they could do this to you, that my country's war should demand so much of you."

"No, Chen Lee, I'm the one who should be apologizing. I left you with one war and came back because of another." I studied her. "Why are you here?"

She smiled. "Because of you. I volunteered."

"But how? How did you find out?"

"The world is not so large a place, Dee." She moved to the edge of the deck and looked out. "I was going to school in Seoul when the North Koreans crossed the thirty-eighth parallel. I wasn't able to reach my father's citadel because Communist troops had completely overrun the area. I didn't even know if my father was alive. Until later. A young man named Smathers, who was attached in some minor way to the U.S. embassy, managed to get me inside the U.S. compound during the fighting. I had seen him on the campus several times but never knew he was an American agent. There I heard about the mission and your involvement in it. They needed a woman to be your wife, and I volunteered for the role." Chen Lee fell silent.

I was a stranger to her now, no longer the boy who had years before professed affection before leaving her in tears. Would I soon leave her in tears again?

"They didn't tell me you'd be my guide, Chen Lee. If they had, I don't know if I'd have come. I don't want to put you in such danger."

"In these times, all Koreans who support their country are in danger. I am no different."

I was about to respond, when we heard the rafts pulling up alongside the sampan. "We have much more to talk about," I whispered.

"Very much more," she agreed.

Calloway came into view. First his raft, then the two

others alongside. As the two continued to the submarine, Captain Elser and Calloway pulled alongside.

I could understand Elser's sentiment when he was aboard the fishing boat. He was muddied to the waist, and there were long bloody stains on his trousers where the leeches had gotten to him. Part of his camouflage shirt had been torn away.

"Brief them on the situation, Captain Elser," Calloway commanded.

Elser stared at me, impatience covering a face blackened by powder blasts and bloodied by cuts.

"Are you telling me, Calloway," Elser snapped, "that I left fourteen kids dead in that fuckin' river to give intelligence to some rice-paddy refugee? This is bullshit and G-2 is gonna know it."

"You think you got problems, Elser?" I said quietly.

Elser stared at my face. "Who are you?"

"Just another American trying to do a job for his country."

He nodded to himself, then indicated the maps he held in his hand. "Okay. The river is mean, fella. Stay the hell out. The North Koreans have cross-fired various areas with automatic weapons. They're not whole platoons, just one hell of a lot of machine-gun nests. We ran into five in as many miles. Kunsan is the battalion center for the river action, so stay away from there too." He studied me again. "Mister, I don't know what those bastards talked you into doing, and I don't want to know, but if you want my advice, don't go inland. At least not unless you got a friggin' army behind you."

"What about the coast?" I asked.

"North of Kunsan the enemy concentration seems to lighten up. I sent a couple of my boys north of the city to check it out. Most of the troops have been withdrawn to the Kum River line."

Calloway considered this fact. He turned to me. "I'm putting a team of frogmen ashore at Posung Mayon inlet in three days. Can you be there to meet them?"

"I'll try," I said, locating it on the map.

"Pass on to them whatever information you've compiled, okay?"

I just stared at Calloway. Something didn't sit right. "How do you plan to get us out?"

"If your mission is completed, you withdraw with the frogmen."

That wasn't good enough. "What about Chen Lee?"

"What about her?" Calloway was annoyed at my question. "She comes too. What do you think we are, barbarians?"

I didn't think he'd like my answer, so I didn't give him one.

Then he and Elser were gone.

Under any other circumstances, the Korean coastline would have been endlessly boring, but playing fishing couple with Chen Lee gave me a new perspective. All notions of my wealth and position vanished as I watched Chen Lee's slim, roughened fingers work the lines and nets in the early-morning hours.

"She has beauty?" Chen Lee peered up, inquiring. "The one you take for a wife. She is beautiful?"

"Very beautiful."

Chen Lee nodded and returned to the nets. She was satisfied with the answer, but I needed to explain further. "I never believed I would return, Chen Lee. You have to understand that."

Chen Lee's fingers ceased working the mending rods. "War has a way of bringing people back together." She stared at me for a few seconds, carefully selecting her words. "Dee, there are destinies which I fear you will never understand. When I last saw you, I sobbed at your leaving. I cursed the fates that interceded to keep us apart. But those same fates chose to guide us along separate roads only to bring us to the same place. And now the eagle returns, not because he is ready to love, but because he is a victim of circumstances. I am frightened, my darling Dee, that one road has taken you to the mountaintop while the other has led me to the sea. If we do not perish together, then I am certain we will return to those roads separately."

I had no response for her words, knowing that what she said was true and that I wanted it to be true. At least then, at that moment.

There was a sudden tug at the leader line and Chen Lee seized the opportunity to inspect the nets. Any tension between us dissipated when she pulled the minor nets back to reveal our first catch of the journey.

"Well, we shall not starve, husband."

I smiled. "No, we won't, wife."

Our living quarters were really a bamboo box in the center of the boat, but the boys from G-2 had rigged the hull with waterproofed false sides and flooring. Some brain trust had taken the components of a radio and arranged them so they could be placed into the floor like a pancake. Our antenna ran up the center of the mast, which had been drilled for just such a purpose. Within the false hulls were two sets of weaponry. Somebody at G-2 was really on the ball, I thought. Our automatic weapons were .45-caliber but modified externally to resemble Russian-issue, the same types the North Koreans were equipped with. The pistols looked like 7.65 Tokarevs but were redesigned to hold the apparatus for .45 automatics. All our grenades were Russian, as well as the plastic explosives, which bore markings from the old French armory at Haiphong.

I caught on quickly. If we were discovered during a routine search, we would never be able to explain away American issue weapons. At least with such a collection of Soviet hardware we might bluff them into believing our active sympathies were with the North. Somebody in G-2 was looking out for us.

I told Chen Lee what I was looking for—an unbroken stretch of beach a mile wide—and she directed us north away from the Kunsan basin and the river mouth.

We rounded the point late in the afternoon. With binoculars I studied the beach through the ventilation slots in our deckhouse. The beach seemed functional but the hills nearby were somewhat steep. I had Chen Lee direct the boat to shore so I could study the terrain from a better vantage point. I didn't need to go ashore to see that the hills had been slammed mercilessly by countless typhoons. Each had been dug out, forming a deadly overhang of sand. A landing there would be a disaster because the dunes were far too weak for scaling ladders, yet too high for the first wave of men to scramble over. The North Koreans, with a minimum of defenders, would effectively butcher a major invasion force. I never even considered naval or air support, because when it came right down to the actual fighting, it was the infantry, on both sides, man to man. Nothing else. And I also knew that whatever happened on the beach in the first fifteen to thirty minutes would decide the success or failure of the invasion.

Chen Lee guided the fishing boat north at an even speed, while I checked out other possible landing sites. I rated each in terms of assets and liabilities. Nothing. The only thing we were accomplishing was catching fish. I studied our map; the next lagoon was miles up the coast. We wouldn't be able to reach it until the following day.

As darkness crept over the western coast, I guided the vessel into a cove and anchored. Chen Lee cooked on the foredeck. I was completing my chores when she lit several oil lamps, and served bowls of fish and rice. Only then did I realize we'd be not only living but also sleeping as man and wife. The handwoven matting covering half the floor was just wide enough for two people, and it was the only sleeping area aboard.

We ate in silence. Neither of us said anything about the mat, but she must have noticed my preoccupation. Finished, she took away the bowls to clean and I stretched out on the floor. I was surprised. It was much more comfortable than I had thought it would be.

Chen Lee returned and wordlessly extinguished the lamps, removed her heavy sea coat, and curled up alongside me. There was silence, but I could feel all the years separating us evaporate. There was so much I wanted to say to her, but I had trouble finding the words. Finally I turned to her. She was asleep. I wished I could be that serene. I lay back and stared into the darkness.

13

The following afternoon, we sailed the boat through the narrows of the great lagoon. There were far too many coves which could be heavily armored on short notice by the enemy. We continued north to study the full stretch of beach, and it was along the rock-bound coast that I first noticed tidal discrepancies. Great areas of the lagoon showed signs of watermarking where the tide had unevenly eroded the beachland. Even more disturbing were the fresh water-level lines on the rock face jutting some twelve feet from the water. I wondered what could cause these significant heights to be attained at normal tide. I lowered the binoculars, deciding there could be no landing here. If some unforeseen force could flood the lagoon or just as likely suck water from it, landing craft would be left beached and the assault troops would meet a bloody end.

When our work in the lagoon was completed, I asked Chen Lee, "You attended the university at Seoul?"

"I was in my final year when the war began," she explained. "It was good fortune that your agent Smathers came for me when the capital fell. No one was safe. I am happy he remembered me."

"He was paid to remember you."

"Perhaps, but if so, he earned his wage. Besides, I knew who he was long before the invasion. He monitored many student demonstrations for your government. We had spoken and he warned me. For months prior to the invasion, North Korean agitators were enrolling at the university in hope of inciting huge demonstrations if not outright rioting. In the final days, it was hardly a safe place. The lowliest shopkeeper could sense the war coming. Smathers had to report all these incidents, Dee."

"Was he very outspoken?" Why was I so curious?

"He was a quiet man, but he chose to confide in me from time to time."

"Really."

Chen Lee looked puzzled, then smiled. "Why, Dee, your tone is so possessive." She laughed. "Well, if you must know, Smathers was the closest American friend I had at the university. I fear he is not a good agent and that his job will eventually consume him because of his unwillingness to compromise his strongly felt convictions of good and evil. I could see through to the softness of his eyes, and I knew that he wished me to be more than a friend. Much more. We spent a great deal of time together until my father learned of him."

"And I suppose Ducksun was overjoyed to learn of Smathers' interest in you." I couldn't seem to dull the edge in my voice.

Chen Lee smiled. "Father sent a car to bring me to the citadel. He was waiting for me in the garden. He told me of Smathers and inquired if I realized he was with American intelligence. I told him that I knew. Then Father cautioned me against forming close friendships with representatives of any government. I told him Smathers and I were just acquaintances, but he looked at me with narrow eyes. Ducksun looks at everyone in such a manner—it is merely his manner of expression. But at this moment he was firm with me. 'It ends,' he told me. I was to see this man no more because I had already been promised."

"Ducksun betrothed you?" Why was I sounding like a spurned suitor?

"In a way. He told me of a vow he made to my mother while holding her dying body in the face of the Japanese advance which forced us from Korea. She made him pledge that I would marry only a Server. That I should not consider any other man. Mother must have been delirious because the Servers died out five hundred years ago. But Father could not refuse the final wish of a woman so devoted to him."

"Isn't that just a little crazy?"

"Yes," Chen Lee agreed, "but I'd like to believe that men of such honor still exist. Before the war with Japan, there were a few men who still embraced the code of the Servers, but they were aged even then. One does not hear of any such men today. Or so it seems."

She looked at me with an expression I recognized—it was the look in Ducksun's face when he knew the answers to questions I had not yet asked.

The boat cleared the narrow neck of the lagoon and eventually we were back onto the open sea. I steered the craft west, then cruised with the wind up the minor peninsula which formed the lagoon's western edge. This slender formation of rock was part of a larger peninsula which reached into the Yellow Sea.

"Rocks ahead," Chen Lee warned as she pulled in our dragnets so they wouldn't snag on the submerged jagged edges.

By the end of the second day we were experiencing heavier seas and brisk, gusting winds. We were forced to search out a haven. I kept the boat offshore until sighting a cove that flickered with the lights of several fishing boats. Feeling safe, I put in to shore.

There were nearly thirty vessels packing the cove where we anchored. Decrepit in appearance, each boat was far more seaworthy than it looked, I knew. Ringed together, they formed a floating village. They were all shapes and sizes, the major difference being the hull paintings signifying varying points of origin. The hulls and sometimes the sails were painted with caricatures of various minor deities intended to invoke the successful intervention of the gods upon their fishing efforts. Each village recognized a different deity, creating competition between hamlets as well as supernatural beings. I then realized G-2's knowledge of Korean superstition was lacking. Both our hull and sail were blank. Hoping no one would notice, I anchored some distance away from the fleet. We ate, then retired for the night.

As the sky was turning pink with dawn, we were startled awake by shrieks and gunfire. I bolted from the mat, grasping the binoculars, then peered through the observation slots. On the beach adjacent to the fishing boats were two military jeeps and three small canvas-topped trucks with soldiers hustling about them by torchlight. The gunfire ceased and I observed the men removing a body from the shoreline. An old woman screamed hysterically, then threw her hands to the sky, invoking the fates.

"What occurs?" Chen Lee asked sleepily.

"I'm not sure. There are soldiers on the beach."

"Allow me to see." Chen Lee took the binoculars from my hand and studied the activity onshore for a few moments. She turned back to me.

"It is the conscription. You had best sail from this place before they take you to fight inland. The North Koreans must need reinforcements because until now, only inland villages have been affected. They shoot those who refuse."

I took the binoculars for another brief look. The fishing boats were moored so tightly together that the soldiers could walk from one deck to another with ease. After the first youth had been gunned down, no one dared resist and the guns remained silent. Fortunately, we were far enough away from the pack to escape into the Yellow Sea unnoticed. We caught an early-morning breeze and in a few minutes sailed away from the North Koreans. By late morning we had rounded the peninsula and were making our way toward a meeting with the frogmen at Posung Mayon inlet.

The Yellow Sea was serene and allowed me an opportunity to study several prospective beachheads. Two locations just west of the inlet seemed promising because the distance from surf to forest was a short walk, making a successful defense by the North Koreans possible only if they provided an army larger than MacArthur's assault force. The marines wouldn't remain on this beach very long. The only problem was the inland system of roads that an advancing invasion force would need to use. The troops would have to travel south before linking up with the major highways, and would almost certainly lose valuable time during which the North Koreans could direct a formidable counterattack. Yet, it was the most viable spot I'd located, and with air support striking inland, might just prove successful. Still, I couldn't recommend it because of the forced march south. Hell, I'd let MacArthur decide.

Our immediate concern was where to anchor at Posung Mayon inlet. The mouth was wide as a bay but narrowed to the inlet proper, which was fed by two minor waterways. From the bay I could see activity beyond the area Chen Lee called Kissing Rocks.

Kissing Rocks were three land formations which almost completely enclosed the inlet. They formed a deep, narrow entranceway which could successfully admit a large craft but not a ship. Realizing a submarine could never navigate farther than the bay, we maintained a safe distance. I prayed the frogmen would spot the lantern hoisted on the mainmast at dusk.

Chen Lee let our lines go, then observed the nets submerge without tangling or twisting. I had scanned the area, deciding no landing force could assault the mainland unless the inlet were seized beforehand. Such action required a commando night drop, and I doubted whether MacArthur would risk tipping off the enemy. I charted our position, noting we were closing fast on the thirty-eighth parallel. There would be no landing north of the demarcation line this early in the war because of outside intervention by Russia or China.

North of our bay anchorage were the islands of Taebu-Do and Yong Hong-Do, which border the channel in which the city of Inchon is located. Due east and several miles inland was the city of Osan, which G-2 designated as a major terminal in the Communist supply line. The map I was studying revealed the grimmest information. Unless I located a suitable landing area soon, we were going to run out of places to look. Further, we were strategically limited by the Han River, which flowed north of Inchon and into the capital city of Seoul. The river was heavily mined and too well fortified to attempt such an assault. If an amphibious attack were to become a reality, it would occur between our present position and Inchon. And I wasn't too crazy over the advance intelligence G-2 had supplied concerning that walled seaport. Chen Lee entered the deckhouse where I was working. Her expression was strained.

"Boat comes."

I jumped up and looked through the observation slot to see a patrol boat approaching. I hid the maps in the hull, then as an afterthought tossed my Walther PPK on top of them. I knew we were going to be boarded and, very probably, searched. Finding a pistol on a lowly fisherman wouldn't sit very well with the North Koreans.

"I'll talk to them," Chen Lee said. "Just work the nets, and whatever happens, don't turn around. I will tell them you cannot speak and your hearing is very bad, understand?"

I agreed. My Korean was rusty and would never stand up to intense interrogation by the North Koreans. I went to work on the nets but positioned myself so I could be effective, if necessary.

The patrol boat, flying North Korean colors, pulled alongside. I could just about hide the anger in my eyes because it was a surplus World War II American PT boat complete with four torpedo tubes, a row of depth charges, and two fifty-caliber machine guns, one fore and the other amidships. The North Korean officer waited until his men pulled near to us with grapnel irons. He boarded us alone but the machine guns were trained so they'd cut us in half at his command.

The North Korean officer was a dapper little man sporting a pencil-thin mustache and a crisply pressed uniform. He approached me but I ignored his words, causing Chen Lee to intercede. She would tell me later how the conversation went.

"He cannot speak," Chen Lee explained in Korean.

"Why is this?" The officer demanded.

"The Japanese," Chen Lee replied briefly, knowing the officer would understand. "He was a prisoner when they ruled Korea. He was tortured and now cannot speak."

"Shameful." His tone was uncaring. He looked directly into Chen Lee's eyes. "Where do you come from!"

"From wherever the fish swims." She kept her voice pleasant, calm. "We are going to the north."

The officer nodded, still glancing around curiously. I got the distinct impression that he felt something was wrong, and suddenly I realized it had to do with me. The lead lines of the net were tugging but I was too concerned with his presence to notice.

I rose too swiftly, and for the briefest moment I thought the machine-gunners would open up. I began pulling the lead lines to bring the net in close to the hull. The officer observed as I mutely indicated for Chen Lee to help. She bowed to the North Korean, then helped me swing the net onto the deck. We had picked up part of a school that had glided blindly into our netting. With the fish wriggling on the deck and the scavenger Gulls circling above, we were forced to work insanely, all under the increased scrutiny of the suspicious officer. Chen Lee said several words begging his pardon and continued indulgence. As we worked, she selected the seven finest of the catch and offered them to the North Korean.

"Fortune smiles upon us as it does the People's Republic of North Korea. We have more than we can ever use and you have brought us good fortune. Please, take these for yourself and your hardworking crew." She smiled a polite, shy smile.

The North Korean officer was stone-faced for an agonizing moment, but then broke into a wide, solicitous grin.

"Your man," he said, and indicated me, "is most fortunate with the sea. Can he be a brother or some other relative."

"He is my husband."

By this time I was seated once again and staring out across the water, watching our lines. The last thing I wanted was to catch any more fish.

"A husband who cannot speak but fishes well." The officer nodded again. "Any wife should consider herself most fortunate."

"He cares for his fishing," Chen Lee replied seriously. "Since the Japanese, well . . . it is his entire life."

The officer lifted a hand to Chen Lee's face, touched her cheek, then toyed with her silky hair.

"Is fishing all your husband cares about?"

I had a sudden urge to leap up and grab him by the throat, but I knew I would only succeed in having both Chen Lee and myself killed and the mission aborted. I gritted my teeth and pretended not to notice.

Chen Lee cast her eyes downward, causing the officer to retreat. He ordered his men to take the fish aboard the PT boat, then looked one last time at Chen Lee.

"Remain in the bay." It was not a suggestion. "We have mined the inlet with a type of device which could be detonated by your craft."

He climbed aboard the patrol boat, then idled away from us. When he was well into the bay, he increased his speed, then headed toward the cove nearest Kissing Rocks. I released a very long, heavy sigh. Chen Lee came to me and rested her head upon my shoulder. For the first time in our voyage, I put my arms around the woman that fate had chosen to accompany me into harm's way.

After dark, we dared not deviate from our usual pattern and the tradition followed by most fishing boats: we hoisted a lit lantern up the mainmast. The best I could hope for was that the submarine's infrared filter would pick us out so the frogmen could find us. I knew the North Korean coast watchers wouldn't see very much more than a flickering candle in the night if they trained their binoculars on us, which I expected they would do.

"What became of you and Ducksun after Shanghai?" I asked while keeping the night vigil. Chen Lee rested across from me, staring serenely at the Yellow Sea.

"When Shanghai fell, Father took me to safety at Nanking, but that didn't last very long, as the Japanese took that city in a few months. I remained in the interior for the duration of the war. After Shanghai and Nanking, I didn't hear another burst of gunfire until I returned to Korea. My father has been at war since 1930, and just when we thought there would be peace, more killing erupted. A rival warlord named Al Wong sent assassins against my father. For two years they hunted each other, until my father's men chased Al Wong across the border into North Korea. We haven't heard from him since, but I know he would sell his soul for my father's position, if he hasn't already."

"It hasn't been peaceful for you or for your country, has it?"

"Korea has been a toy thrown back and forth between Japan and China for a thousand years." She looked at me now. "But now we enter a new era—to be kicked back and forth between East and West."

I was about to reply when I felt the fishing boat pitch unnaturally. I waited a second, then felt the boat pitch again. Looking over the side, I saw the frogmen breaking water. Soon there was a line of them clinging to the combing. The leader lifted his mask, then removed his mouthpiece.

"Dee?" His voice was low, primitive, like that of a quarterback calling plays. Oh, brother, I thought.

"Yeah, here. Pull yourself aboard."

"Regards from Calloway," he said as he got his footing and extended his hand. "I'm Lieutenant Kane. Navy. You're Dee?"

I was getting tired of everyone's reaction. "Yes, I'm Dee. And I speak perfect English because I'm an American."

That seemed to appease him. "Christ. Coulda fooled me."

"That's the idea." I led him to the cabin. "Now, can we get on with it?"

We seated ourselves inside, going over my charts of Korea. Kane produced two matching charts and we exchanged information, his from G-2, mine from observation.

"Posung Mayon inlet is mined," I informed him.

"You sure?"

This guy was a moron. "No. I made it up."

"Dee . . ."

"Okay, okay, yeah, I'm sure. The North Koreans told us when they inspected the sampan today. I'm not up on mines, but they claim this boat would detonate them. Any clue in that?"

"Probably a mixed field, magnetic and low-pressure devices. Why the hell would they mine Posung Mayon?"

"Could be 'cause there's a coastal base there." Before he could react to this new piece of information, I continued, "By the way, tell Calloway they're using fully equipped American PT boats."

"You're joking. We can't even get our hands on any of them."

The words were barely out of his mouth when the sound of a PT, closing fast, broke in.

Chen Lee scurried into the deckhouse, her eyes giving a warning. "They return."

I pulled open the hull compartments, seizing each machine gun. I loaded one, then tossed it to Kane as I loaded the second.

He handled the weapon, then looked at me. "These aren't American."

"No shit. But they can kill just as good." I motioned him to the observation slot. "If we have to, go for the midship gunner, then kill the forward one if I don't nail him first."

I slipped out of the cabin and was able to hide the machine gun under our netting. What the hell had happened to cause this second inspection?

As the PT boat grappled us, I chanced a peek over our seaward hull. The team of frogmen had vanished beneath the waterline. Chen Lee approached the enemy boat very cautiously.

The captain was the same dapper North Korean we'd encountered earlier, but this time he was drunk. His crew wasn't in such great shape either, with the notable exception of the forward machine-gunner. Just my luck; he was stone-cold sober and watching our every move.

The midship gunner was resting his head groggily on the bolt box as the Korean officer stepped onto the fishing boat, bowed respectfully to Chen Lee, then indicated for her to come over to the PT boat. She refused. He insisted. And I tensed as the forward gunner sighted on me.

The officer grabbed Chen Lee's arm, pulling her toward the patrol boat, but she wrested her arm free, backing away, as his voice became louder and more abusive. My gut said go but I knew I'd be cut in half if I so much as moved a muscle. The officer grasped Chen Lee's forearm again, but again she resisted. The North Korean looked back at his subordinates with a leer, then, without warning, turned and ripped her coat straight down to her waist, baring her round, proud breasts. Chen Lee's face remained immobile.

They laughed loudly at her, leering, jesting, pointing. She stood alone, frozen in the cold glare of their prying eyes. But Ducksun's daughter did not move to cover herself, to shield her nudity.

The officer was still laughing his head off as he lifted his coarse hand to her breasts. He never made it.

I leapt from the deck with such fierce, vengeful speed that I was out of the forward gunner's eyeline before he realized what had happened. He had stared at Chen Lee's breasts for a second too long. And died for it.

My feet took out the North Korean officer's neck and nasal bridge while Kane blasted through the observation slot with his machine gun. The Korean officer was dead before he hit the water and the forward gunner died on his feet, never knowing Kane had blown his life into the salty air.

The power balance shifted violently as the frogmen boarded the patrol boat from the port side. The Communist crew resisted, but they were trapped between Kane and his men. Within a few minutes the action was completed, with no North Korean survivors. The patrol boat was back in American hands. Maybe Kane wasn't such a moron after all.

I said nothing to Chen Lee because there was nothing anyone could say. I helped her into the cabin as Kane emerged.

"She okay?" he asked quietly. "Anything I can do?"

"I'll take care of her. Thanks, anyway." I changed the subject as soon as Chen Lee was out of sight. "Well, you got yourself a PT boat."

"Damn sure did." Kane nodded. He turned to his men, indicating the torpedo tubes. "Those pipes loaded?"

The men checked the tubes and discovered they were fully armed with surplus American ordnance.

"Life's a bitch." Kane grinned.

"Tell me." The last of the Korean bodies had been splashed overboard, now only shark bait.

"Calloway said we should take you to the submarine, if you want."

I shook my head. "Tell him I haven't found what we're looking for yet. I'll be heading north in the morning." I didn't tell him any more. You never know when someone might get captured. "When I have an affirmative, I'll radio time and position."

Kane acknowledged, but his mind was on the PT boat his men were preparing.

"You say there's a North Korean base on the inlet?"

"Looks like," I confirmed. "Just outside where those rocks join to form the inlet."

"Do you think there are any more of these boats docked in there?"

"Could be. I don't know."

Kane seemed to be considering a plan. He looked up to me. "You'd better take this fishing boat out to sea. I'll give you a fifteen-minute head start."

He didn't have to tell me twice. I got the fishing boat under way, taking her north of the bay and out into the Yellow Sea. The earthiness of the Rolls-Royce engines was ear-shattering. It was the last sound we heard until the sky over Posung Mayon inlet exploded into red, orange, and yellow flame. Kane's men had floated the depth charges into the mine field, then turned their torpedoes on the coast-patrol base.

As the sky burned above us, I pushed on to Inchon.

13

Inchon bay was gray as hell's icebox in the early-morning hours. We guided the fishing boat by the lighthouse located in the center of the bay and then north to Flying Fish Channel. According to the map, this narrow channel was the sea route leading directly to the city's waterfront. Checking our charts, I could easily locate Yong Hong-Do island and its large counterpart, Taebu-Do.

Since the attack by the North Korean officer, Chen Lee had become quieter, more introspective. Though she didn't talk about it, trying to hide behind her duties on the sampan, I knew only time would dull the shock of that assault. And I knew that I'd never let anything like that happen to her again.

As we approached Inchon's sea walls, I noticed the island was connected to the city by an eastern causeway. The chart called it Wolmi-Do. On the hill overlooking the beach, I spied a fortress. I waved Chen Lee over, extending the binoculars.

"Know anything about that fortress?" I asked.

She took the glasses and studied the fortification for a moment.

"It is very old. Only ancestors of a slower world would spend a lifetime carving such rock into a fortress. There are many such in Korea and China."

"Could a garrison be housed there?" Already my mind was going to work.

"Yes. Not comfortably, but yes."

"How many?"

She continued to study the fortress. "Five hundred, maybe."

Five hundred men? It was a grim thought. A garrison that large could hold the channel until the last defender died of old age. That number could decimate any invasion force.

When Chen Lee returned the glasses, I studied the island again. Near the beach was a village with better than a dozen fishing boats anchored at makeshift docks. The natives seemed to be mending nets and performing other usual chores under the watchful eyes of the North Korean gun emplacements. From what I could see, the guns were 75mm artillery and there were ten of them spread from the edge of the village to the base of the fortress. I'd seen enough. I turned the boat about and headed south toward the lighthouse. As we broke from the channel, I noticed a slight surge in the speed of our vessel.

"Did you feel that? We're moving faster."

She nodded. "The Demon Tide."

"The Demon Tide?" She'd made mention of it once, many years ago, but I'd long since forgotten what it was.

"Yes. It is a tide that laughs at the sea gods."

Terrific. More Korean legends. As if I didn't have enough to contend with. "What does that mean in English?"

She smiled. "In antiquity there were gods to govern the sky, the air, the land, and the sea. Each god decreed the limits of all things natural. That the sky is blue, the air sometimes very dry, sometimes moist, the land either fertile or barren, the coming and going of the sea tides. The Demon Tide defies those limitations. It flows defiantly, as it pleases, its actions inexplicable. Why this particular area around the bay should be different from any other cove along the coast will always be a mystery."

"Wonderful," I said, thinking of an amphibious assault, "now we have Demon Tides."

As we followed the southeasterly current, I steered the fishing boat toward a floating village of similar craft anchored at the mouth of the strait separating Yong Hong-Do from Taebu-Do. I attempted joining this small fleet, but the tide kept pulling us away, and in less than thirty minutes the straits were a morass of ugly gray mud. The twin islands seemed to grow in size as additional land appeared where water had flowed only minutes before.

I trained my binoculars on the fishing boats and saw that they were stranded in the mud flats, each tilted at an odd angle. The Demon Tide pulled us into those flats and we tried to work our way toward a rocky cresent-shaped cove marking the northern landfall. Chen Lee lit several distress lanterns, hoping to signal the natives. A full hour passed before three villagers braved the mud to meet us. The trio waded through the hindering muck until able to grasp onto our hull securely. Chen Lee and I glanced down, then reacted with surprise when we saw that although two were villagers, one was a scruffy sea dog of medium height, wearing clothing that had seen better days. He greeted Chen Lee in Korean.

"Me name's Crimp. Harry Crimp. We seen your lanterns when you beached up. You're strangers?"

Chen Lee chose her words carefully. "We saw a storm forming on the horizon south and decided to seek shelter."

If Crimp realized she was lying, he let it pass. "Wise move, little lady." He turned to me, than back to Chen Lee. "He your husband?"

"Yes, he is."

The Englishman nodded to himself. "Don't talk much, do he?"

"No. He was tortured by the Japanese. He neither hears nor speaks."

Crimp studied me carefully, and I sensed that he suspected an irregularity in my appearance. But he said nothing, so I decided to play the game out.

"Yeah, the Japs tortured a lot of our boys when Singapore fell." Crimp nodded. "If the Royal Navy hadn't put me up here as a coast watcher only a few months before, I'd have been a prisoner myself."

"You've been here since the last war?" Chen Lee couldn't conceal her surprise.

"That I have, little lady." He laughed. "Kinda took

a shine to the village and its simple ways. When Singapore fell, the Royal Navy was in such a state it forgot all about me, and I wasn't about to go remindin' them."

Okay, so he was a renegade and probably wouldn't sympathize with either side in this war, doing only what was best for himself. He'd bear watching.

"The village," Chen Lee inquired, "is it far?"

"Not at all. Just beyond the beach clearing. These mud flats are quite walkable, and I'd be happy if you and your husband would come to my hut until the tide returns. We could talk better."

Chen Lee hesitated. I took the time to consider the possibilities. There were natives gathering on the beach, looking in our direction. Were they North Koreans? Was Crimp leading us into a trap? But I knew I had to take a look. We had to risk it.

I nodded my permission, then Crimp helped us down into the sucking, oozing mud. We walked almost a quarter-mile before reaching the beach, such as it was. As Chen Lee and Crimp chattered on in Korean, I considered the Englishman's motivation. I was sure he knew I wasn't Korean, though I didn't know how. I fingered the Walther PPK hidden in the folds of my clothing. If he showed the slightest hostility, I'd have to blow him away.

The Englishman's hut was more Western in appearance due to its larger size and definitive lines. He showed us into his living quarters and began brewing tea. All during this time, he continued speaking Korean with Chen Lee, but was observing me very carefully. Then, without warning, he switched to English.

"If I can spot you," he said almost casually, "the North Koreans will too."

I remained silent, waiting for his next move.

"First, there wasn't no storm brewing on the southern horizon. Second, you were never no prisoner, I'll be betting. You're in too good shape. And third, I never knew no fisherman with hands like that."

I looked down at my unworn fingers, then rested my hand on the gun.

"I could kill you right now, Crimp, and no one would ever know."

He shook his head. "An American. I should have guessed. Now, you could kill me for sure, but it's another twelve hours till the tide comes in. In that time, the villagers would catch you, try you, hang you, and leave your carcass for the vultures. Seems to me you should be thinkin' more about stayin' alive than killing me."

"Why should I trust you?"

He shrugged. "Why not? If I was really lookin' to kill someone, I'd go inland and fight the North Koreans. But Harry Crimp don't go looking for trouble, nosirree. I'm happy where I am, friend, tryin' to keep the peace on Yong Hong-Do despite the outside world. And I don't need none of you gents from OSS causin' me any problems."

"It's called CIA now." I don't know why, but I was beginning to feel I could trust him.

"Different name, same guns." He poured the brewed tea. "Let me tell you something, boy. There are three hundred North Koreans over on Taebu-Do and another four hundred up on Wolmi-Do. It took a lot of doing to get these villagers to resist, but they kept the garrison on Taebu-Do at bay. Made 'em realize this island ain't worth losin' their crummy lives over. So the Commies keep to 'emselves and we don't bother nobody. And I'd sure like to keep it that way. So"—he looked at me—"how about you have some tea, and in twelve hours, I put you and your lady friend back on your boat and we say good-bye, okay?"

"The North Koreans are gonna take this island someday, Crimp," I predicted. "And neither you nor anybody else will stop them. They've already captured all of Korea except for Pusan."

"But you will?" His skepticism emerged as weariness. "You and your . . . whatever it is you're working for? What are you gonna do? Land an army?"

Actually, that's exactly what I'd been thinking ever since we'd beached up on the mud. My first impression was of disaster; I could see thousands of troops caught in the mud being slaughtered by the North

Koreans. But then I had a strange hunch. If the proper intelligence could be secured, it might work. My thoughts must have shown in my eyes.

"You can't do that!" Crimp insisted. "It'd be bloody suicide!"

"Not necessarily," I replied.

He looked to Chen Lee, then back to me. "Why? Why land an army here?"

"You tell me. I never said a word about landing an army here. I just disagree that it would necessarily be suicide."

"You Americans. You all still think you're cowboys. Well, let me tell you a thing or two." He stood and paced. "First, who'd want this muddy piece of real estate? It's only as big as Liverpool but not as important. It's ugly as hell and would have to be defended year-round 'cause it's an ice-free port. The bloody place don't have any beaches to speak of, so any assault force would have to land in the heart of the city and fight it out house by house. And then there's the tides. The currents here run as much as eight knots and the bay is always blocked by disabled or sunken fishing boats. The tides themselves—from half a foot at ebb tide to a full thirty-two feet at high—I tell you, mister, it'd be suicide. You put an army in here, and it'll look like the biggest drowning since Moses parted the Red Sea."

I considered everything he said. Then I smiled. "You've convinced me, Crimp."

Harry Crimp's mouth fell open and he looked to Chen Lee, but she glanced away. He was about to speak again, when he heard screams from outside the hut. A number of villagers ran by the entrance and we joined them to see what was going on.

Upon reaching the nearby clearing, we saw a small, husky villager carrying a little girl in his arms. Behind him were two more men holding the limp bodies of children. They were dead, their bodies riddled with bullet holes. Up ahead, we heard the parents shriek as the men set the children on the ground.

Chen Lee listened in stunned silence, then interpreted for me. The children had wandered across the mud flats to Taebu-Do. Apparently they'd taunted the North Korean soldiers, who responded by shooting them down. I gazed from the dead children to Crimp, his face ashen, his eyes icy.

He turned and led us back to the hut, then closed the flap. "Tell me, cowboy, you really want to put an army in here?"

"Maybe . . . ."

"Maybe, hell. You listen to Harry Crimp and I'll tell you how to put ten armies in here."

So I listened.

We spent the next two days discussing the possibilities of a full-scale assault at Inchon. The more he told me, the more I saw what should be a textbook case for military disaster. Every tactical, geographical, and meteorological deficiency was in residence at Inchon. I knew MacArthur would wonder at my sanity, but there was one overwhelming thing going for it: the element of surprise.

Inchon was only eighteen miles from Seoul, the Communist terminal for military action in South Korea. The distance between landing and the eventual capture of the capital was less than a Boy Scout's regular hike.

"But be prepared to lose men," Crimp warned. "Hell, you'll be finding bodies thirty miles out in the Yellow Sea once the tide's out."

Everything revolved around the tides, which were unpredictable at best. I couldn't wait to see the expression on Calloway's face when I explained this proposal to him.

During the days I spent picking Crimp's brain of every detail concerning Inchon, Chen Lee remained aboard the fishing boat studying the movement and fishing patterns of the small fleet. She didn't report any naval vessels except for a single Chinese freighter that got stuck in Flying Fish Channel for a half a day.

We divided our days between guarding our own fishing boat and ingratiating ourselves with the villagers. I knew that one essential factor to any military success is the cooperation of the natives. The murder of the children would produce this cooperation.

On the third day, Crimp went off for a few days—fishing, he said—leaving Chen Lee and me his hut to stay in. Early one morning, just as the village was rising to a bright dawn, one of the beach watchers called the natives down to the shore. I left Chen Lee asleep in the hut and followed the small throng.

Out in the bay, resplendent against the rising sun, was a huge war sampan. The beauty of its impeccable rigging and sails contrasted darkly with the heavy armaments stationed along all decks.

"Who does it belong to?" I asked Han, the stocky village mayor as he came up beside me.

He shrugged, pretending he couldn't speak English, which I knew he could.

I decided on another tactic. "I've seen more magnificent sampans." I was thinking about the *Missouri*.

"Not in this bay," he said with pride and arrogance.

"Well, maybe, but it still looks like a poor man's sampan."

"Ha," the mayor remarked, "a poor man? You know nothing. That goddess of the sea is mastered by a warlord! A very powerful warlord. Can you not see its wake? Its immense engines?"

To tell the truth, I hadn't noticed. "And which warlord would that be? There are hundreds of warlords in Korea."

"I do not know his name," Han replied, "and I do not wish to know."

"But surely the mayor is influential enough to find out, if he wanted to." I hoped he'd take the bait.

Han's eyebrows rose and came together. I could almost hear him figuring what he would ask in trade. "I don't now. The warlord is said to be all the bad gods incarnate. He commands the fortress at Wolmi-Do. But I have relatives who might talk, some who are indebted to me. But it would be a considerable expense to the one who wants to know."

"And what would 'considerable' be?"

"A weapon," Han replied.

"A pistol?"

"Yes." The pudgy mayor smiled.

"I think that can be arranged." Hell, I'd give him

one of the handguns hidden in the hull of the fishing boat. "If you see your relatives today, you can have the weapon tonight."

While the tide was still in, we took the mayor's small boat north to Flying Fish Channel. He spent the entire voyage chattering of his self-importance. I smiled at his ravings.

I received my first really good look at Wolmi-Do, and it was far more impressive than I had first thought. Overlooking the beachhead of the village, it was a fortress carved into solid rock. From its parapets were several small artillery pieces trained on the channel. The upper levels were patrolled by men in traditional garb, while the lower extremities were infested with uniformed guards. I also noticed the water markings on the side of the fortress, just below the 75mm gun emplacements. The pier was secured by two more such field pieces. It was then that I realized that the island had to be shelled from the sea, then physically seized by raw manpower if Inchon were to be taken. But how to do that?

We found the mayor's kinsman mending nets and obviously unwilling to be disturbed. He was a gruff old man who turned completely pale when the mayor asked the name of the warlord commanding Wolmi-Do. At first he refused to answer any questions.

"Evil is buried in those walls," he said slowly. "I do not tempt evil."

He turned away, but Han was persistent. They bargained in Korean for a full twenty minutes before the mayor led me away.

"The warlord's name is Al Wong," he said as we returned across the bay.

The name was familiar. Hadn't Chen Lee mentioned it to me? Could it be the same man?

"Al wong," I repeated. "Is he heavily guarded?"

"There is a North Korean garrison at shore level, but his own men guard the parapets," Han explained. "There is no way to estimate how many men he employs, but judging from his elegant sampan, they are indeed a formidable force. The warlord keeps his own quarters on the topmost level."

"Is there any way of getting a closer look at the fortress?"

"Closer?" He seemed puzzled.

"Inside."

Han let a slow, sly smile creep over his face. "Certainly. You can stroll up to the walls and they will shoot you. Then Wolmi-Do will be the last thing your eyes will see."

It wasn't what I wanted to hear.

It was late afternoon before we made landfall at Yong Hong-Do. Upon arriving, I found Chen Lee had returned to the fishing boat. On the boat, I gave Han his gun and he departed.

Chen Lee, cooking on the foredeck, looked up at me. "You vanished this morning," she said. "Where did you go?"

"To Wolmi-Do." I sat down alongside her. "Why are you here? Didn't you like Crimp's hut?"

"I feel safer here."

"Oh?"

"There is something unstable, hostile in the air. I've been experiencing very strange feelings all day." She stopped, then shook her head. "It is difficult to explain."

"Chen Lee," I began tentatively, "didn't you once tell me about a warlord named Al Wong?"

She dropped the bowl she'd been preparing.

"I guess you did," I answered for her. "The mayor claims he's the ruler of Wolmi-Do."

Her terror was obvious. "If this is true, we must leave this place."

"You know we can't. I've got a mission to complete."

"Then allow someone else the honor. We are no match for Al Wong." She began picking up the pieces of the bowl. "Even my father, with all his power, must remain aware of him. He is a vulture, a trafficker in narcotics, a manipulator of all that pertains to the sale of vices. He is the sworn enemy of my father and . . ."

"And what? Why are Ducksun and Al Wong enemies?"

"Because powerful men always seem to rule from opposite sides of the fence." She stood and stared at me, her face cold. "Al Wong became a puppet of the

Japanese in hope of acquiring all my father's wealth, position, and power. Their feud stretches back across the years and much blood." She paused and looked at me, her features softening. "We have always believed Al Wong informed the Japanese of my father's escape from Korea before we went to Shanghai. He learned our route, told the Japanese, and they attacked us, killing my mother and brother."

"You *believed?* Are you sure?"

She shook her head. "We never really learned the truth, but if my father believes it to be so, it is. His suspicion of Al Wong's treachery is so overwhelming that he has vowed to . . . If Ducksun's eyes were ever to meet Al Wong's, one of them would be soon dead." She looked to me. "Dee, I beg of you, we must leave this cursed place."

"We can't, Chen Lee. We have to stay in spite of Al Wong. Or maybe because of him."

Chen Lee didn't argue the point further, but I could feel her increasing tension during the next few days.

I decided to contact Calloway. I removed the wireless from the floorboards of the fishing boat late one night and tapped out the word "ballpark" in Morse code. After repeating the transmission five additional times, I received the answer: tomorrow midnight, five lanterns.

I had no sooner replaced the radio guts into the flooring, secure in the knowledge that Calloway would be arriving the next night at midnight and would be looking for five lanterns strung along our mainmast, when I heard a boat pull up alongside. I looked up to see Harry Crimp in a motorized fishing sampan about the size of our own.

"Got a little job to do, mate," Crimp informed me. "I thought you might be interested in coming along."

"Job?"

"The children," Crimp explained. "Can't let that go unavenged."

I stared at him. "And I thought you were a peaceful man."

"Only when there's peace. If I let those Commies

get away with killing children, they'll do it again. How about it?''

I hesitated. "I don't know, Harry."

"You wouldn't be afraid of looking at those who would kill you, would you?" I detected a taunt.

"No, but it could jeopardize everything else."

"The hell it will. This is strictly a local matter and has nothing to do with your goddamned war. Now, make up your mind."

Crimp left me no choice. Avenging the murdered children was not worth wrecking the whole mission, but if he was captured, the North Koreans would surely torture my identity and plans out of him. I had to go, even if only to make sure Crimp didn't fall into enemy hands. Even if I had to kill him myself.

"I'm coming." I grappled toward his boat, then hopped aboard. Chen Lee watched silently, disapprovingly, as we pushed off. Crimp triggered the engines and we chugged forward in silence. He took his boat around the western landfall of Yong Hong-Do until sighting Taebu-Do in the distance. The Englishman headed directly for the wharves.

"The North Koreans built their barracks overlooking the piers," he explained with disdain at their stupidity, "right smack in range, dumb bastards."

"In range of what?" Then I saw the reinforced foredeck. Crimp had added a World War II machine-gun pulpit to his fishing boat.

"Pull the canvas back on the dinghy." He pointed to a small single-person boat tied down on the foredeck.

I lifted the canvas away to discover a fifty-caliber machine gun. Picking up the killing machine, I could smell the odor of fresh lubricant and knew this baby was well taken care of.

"Bought it off a gun runner in Seoul," Crimp explained with pride. "About six months ago. Knew there was gonna be a war eventually."

The machine gun was a United States military model overstamped with the word "Haiphong," meaning it had come from the French armory in Indochina. I set the weapon into the bolt lock of the pulpit, then took several boxes and belts of ammunition from under the canvas. When it was set to kill, Harry Crimp turned the navigation over to me.

"Bring her in as close as you can, and I'll blow the hell out of their barracks," he directed.

"What do they have to throw back at us?"

"Oh, nothin' worth mentionin'. Just a seventy-five-millimeter artillery piece, a couple of war-surplus mortars, and I hear they got a T-34 tank. But I doubt it."

"Terrific." Harry was out of his mind. And I was with him. As he took to the fifty-caliber machine gun, I found it very difficult to believe he'd sat out the last war.

I guided the boat as close to the pier as possible. We were at high tide, so Crimp's aim on the barracks was lethal. The low slapping of the waves against the hull seemed to punctuate the silence. I watched as Crimp leaned his weight into the murderous weapon, then hit the dual trigger heads, spewing forth white-red flame.

Immediately the fishing boat pitched, and from the docks the sounds of screams filled the air. As the shattering roar of the machine gun chewed the barracks to pieces, agonized shrieks followed as an echo.

I took the boat out of range, then watched as Crimp's arm indicated I should go in for another attack. I guided the vessel in toward the pier a second time while listening to the machine gun split the night in half. Up on the dock, several soldiers careened into the water, while others took cover and began returning fire.

As I turned around to the safety of deeper waters, the engines chugged, sputtered, and began whining. I hit the throttle and the boat lurched forward.

"Another pass, damn it," Crimp shouted.

"Forget it."

"I say bring her by again!" He was screaming over the sound of Korean gunfire.

"Hell, no," I shouted back.

He didn't argue. He didn't answer. Machine-gun fire from the pier had cut him in half.

Within minutes we were well away from the North Korean garrison. I went over to Crimp as we chugged toward Yong Hong-Do and pulled his bloodied body into my arms.

"We got 'em, didn't we?" he forced out.

"Yes, you did."

Harry Crimp died in my arms. He'd never asked my name.

Calloway arrived as anticipated, and I led him into the hut as Chen Lee kept watch with a submachine gun on the afterdeck.

"Inchon is the place," I said simply. I explained why, both pro and con, and watched as Calloway's face turned livid.

"Sounds like a catastrophe just waiting to happen," he observed. "Are you sure about this?"

"Yes. We've got the element of surprise on our side."

Calloway shook his head. "With a tidal discrepancy of thirty-two feet, I'd be surprised if the assault force even made it to the beach."

"There are no beaches, Calloway. The men would have to land against a seawall some sixteen feet high."

"The marines should find that appealing. Is this the best you can do?"

I nodded. "It's not the best, it's the only place. If we follow the tides according to what Crimp told me, we should have a successful landing with a minimum of losses. And once it's secure, a million men could come through here."

"What about the mud? What'll it support?"

"Not much," I conceded. "I wouldn't throw armored divisions in until definite routes have been established."

"What about this fortress, Wolmi-Do?"

"Well," I started, "that's a strange one. There are five hundred Korean ground troops on the island. Ten artillery pieces. Each a seventy-five-millimeter. But the fortress itself is in the hands of a Korean warlord named Al Wong."

"Friendly or neutral?"

"Definitely with the North." I decided against mentioning Ducksun's rivalry with Wong; I still didn't trust Calloway. "Wolmi-Do must fall if Inchon is to be taken. By the way, there's a causeway leading from

Wolmi-Do eastward into the city. I'd secure that before the North Koreans can blow it."

Calloway studied the charts a final time before folding them up. He placed them into his waterproof satchel, then rose to leave.

"Calloway, when do Chen Lee and I pull out?"

Calloway said nothing.

I pressed. "When, Calloway?"

He sighed with boredom. "Dee, I've got to verify this information. If it checks out and MacArthur likes the idea . . . well, he's going to want you to stay on as a coast watcher."

"Is this your idea of a joke? Because if it is, I'm not laughing."

"Look, Dee," Calloway argued, "you've come this far. If we verify Inchon and proceed with the plan, your presence could save a great many lives. All we ask is that you keep an eye peeled for new gun emplacements, fresh troops, or any unusual movements."

"You sound like you know MacArthur's going to go for it."

Calloway seemed to be holding something back. "Could be." He studied me. "Will you do it?"

"Yeah. Sure."

Calloway went back to his rubber raft and disappeared into the darkness. Seven nights later, at a prearranged time, I radioed the submarine for instructions. The message I received decoded as "Verification complete tentative. Continue as agreed."

Great. So now I was a coast watcher.

14

The last few days of July were hot and sticky along Inchon bay, but August was pure murder. Twice during the next thirty days Calloway resupplied me and I began arming several of the faster fishing boats with automatic weapons. Most of the younger men, especially those raising families, remembered the slaughter of the children and Harry Crimp's sacrifice and were only too ready to protect themselves.

By the first of September I had outfitted nearly half a dozen small sampans with American ordnance. My intentions were to block the garrison at Taebu-Do from attacking the village during the actual invasion. And I knew if we were to survive, we'd have to take care of it ourselves.

Calloway's actions during the few times I'd seen him indicated that the invasion was imminent, so Chen Lee and I continued our assignment as coast watchers. We worked in shifts, she watching the bay from our fishing boat by day, while I cruised around the islands in Crimp's motorized craft by night. All through August we noted no change in the garrison strength at Wolmi-Do. Then, in early September after days of mysterious quiet in Inchon, our worst fears were realized.

"More guns," Mayor Han told us as he pulled alongside in his small sampan. "New ones like the others we saw in Wolmi-Do."

"Where?" I wanted to know.

"Along the eastern shore of Taebu-Do."

"The eastern shore?" That hardly made any sense.

The eastern shore was separated from the mainland by extremely treacherous waters. No military craft would brave it, and I certainly couldn't think of a single reason why the North Koreans would place 75mm guns facing territory they already occupied. "How many guns did you see?"

"Ten, I think. Maybe more."

"Were there any ships nearby?" I pressed.

Han shook his head. "None that I saw."

I reviewed this fresh intelligence after the mayor departed. The garrison must have taken a freighter to pier during the night, unloaded the field pieces on the western shore, then pulled them overland. Chen Lee and I studied the maps but could discover no inland roads or docking places the North Koreans might wish to guard.

"Will we go to see these guns?" Chen Lee asked.

"Yes." We had no alternative. "We'll take Crimp's boat, and leave the sampan here. It'll be quicker."

She nodded, then guided our fishing boat toward the makeshift dock serving the village. After tying down our craft, we took Crimp's boat into the bay, heading west, then south. I sailed the long way around Taebu-Do island so that I might anchor off the newly armored eastern shore by dawn, thus being able to spot and record the gun placements while the rising sun was at my back. I'd have good enough light, but at the same time, the morning sunburst would obscure me from the vigilant eyes of the North Korean regulars for at least an hour. I didn't want them lobbing any practice shells at us.

The night was uneventful, the Korean patrol boats remaining exclusively in the bay area. At sunrise I was able to spot and chart the new guns, all 75mm field pieces. Aside from the ten counted by Han, I located an additional five. There were also three machine-gun nests on the beach. Strange. What the hell could the North Koreans be planning by placing all this heavy equipment on a strait that was hardly safe for daily traffic? Maybe G-2 could make sense of it. Certainly this shoreline was now the best-armored spot after Wolmi-Do.

While scanning the beaches and adjacent woodland a final time, I noticed a thin black wisp of smoke in the distance. I charted the position of the smoke, took my bearing again, then calculated it was rising from Yong Hong-Do. Without a second thought, I plunged forward into the rocky strait. It was slow, rough going but took less time than circumnavigating the island the way we'd come.

"Chen Lee!" I shouted.

She was instantly on deck. "Is there something wrong?"

I pointed toward the rising smoke.

Her face went white. "Yong Hong-Do?"

"Looks like." I kept my eyes on the water. "Check our weapons, Lee. I think we're sailing into a fight."

We made it to Yong Hong-Do in half a day. But it was half a day too late. What had once been a village, a pier, a small forest, was now only charred blackness. In silence Chen Lee and I navigated Crimp's boat as close as we could, fighting the receding tide and the mud. Soon the mud came up around the hull and we were forced to walk in knee-deep slime. Chen Lee and I, armed with submachine guns and extra clips, moved to the pier, neither of us able to speak.

I spotted our fishing boat half-sunken at its mooring, with most of its deck burned away, the mast and sails shattered. We headed toward the sampan, but the mud became unbearable. It pulled me deeper until I was almost up to my waist, Chen Lee in just above her knees. Upon reaching the boat, I discovered some of the embers were still warm, but I boarded the tottering wreck anyway. Easing myself onto a portion that was still stable, I began searching for the equipment G-2 had supplied us. If our radio had been discovered, the North Koreans would know there were agents on Yong Hong-Do. They might just be waiting for us in the village.

Our living quarters had burned and caved in, so I was forced to move heavy beams to clear the cubicle. But the radio was there. None of the compartments had been disturbed except for fire damage. Quickly I twisted a knob and several tubes lit up. Others didn't.

The radio would need work, but our lifeline to the outside world was salvageable. I went outside, where Chen Lee was standing in the mud, her machine gun at the ready.

"They didn't search the boat," I told her. "Our cover hasn't been blown. Yet."

"What about the village?" she asked. "We should go in to see if anyone needs help."

"It'll be dangerous. Maybe you should stay here."

"I will not." Her quiet voice was determined. "These are my people. I must go with you."

We struggled back through the mud, then began searching the village for survivors. There weren't any. And suddenly we realized we were trapped. The tide had returned, thus filling the bay once again. There were no boats left that we could use to return to Crimp's vessel, which was anchored offshore. Fate demanded we remain among the dead until the Demon Tide flowed back out to sea. We continued walking along the rubble of the dockside, when I detected a movement in one of the wrecks. Looking down toward a partially charred fishing junk, I heard a weak cry for help. Chen Lee and I managed to pull away the flooring of the half-sunken vessel. It began taking on more water just as we pulled the native from the wreckage. He was a little man, young, quite emaciated, but otherwise unharmed.

"Are you okay?" I asked him.

He nodded slowly.

I looked around. "Can you tell me what happened here? Was it the North Koreans?"

He shook his head. "No. It was the warlord. From Wolmi-Do. He came." Chen Lee's face froze as he continued. "He ordered the village burned. It was horrible . . ."

"Was there a battle?" I asked.

"No. Just fires. Endless fires." The shaken villager put his head in his hands, his body trembling. "I heard him my very self order everyone be executed and that the village be put to the torch."

"But why?" Chen Lee interrupted. "Why did he do it?"

"Why? Does the devil have reasons? No. The devil burns, and smiles at the destruction."

He fell silent and I couldn't bear asking any further questions. Chen Lee and I left him alone, then began walking toward the village ruins.

"This is senseless," I said as we walked.

"Not to Al Wong," she replied. "You can be certain he has a reason. It may not be one we could easily understand, but it is very real nonetheless."

"Is it possible that one of the villagers sold us out?"

She shook her head. "No. These are hardy people, Dee, but they do not involve themselves in politics. They would not go to the warlord willingly. But if put to torture, they would talk."

"In other words, maybe yes, maybe no."

She closed her eyes in assent. "We can be certain of one thing, Dee. If Al Wong thought we were here, he would be waiting for us. But I really don't believe the villagers betrayed us. No, Dee, there is another reason for this destruction."

We walked through the remains of the village and returned to the docks, boarding our half-sunken sampan. I'd made a decision. I would radio Calloway and tell him to pull us out.

For the next thirty-six hours Chen Lee and I worked on repairing the radio. We brought it over to Crimp's boat, then salvaged parts from a unit stored there. Finally we were able to transmit a fair signal. For five days following, I dangerously tapped out a message requesting Calloway to meet us at the prearranged spot near the mouth of the bay. When we didn't receive any acknowledgment, I assumed the Navy was maintaining radio silence. We sailed out to the rendezvous point and waited patiently until dawn. Calloway never showed up.

He'd thrown us to the wolves.

"We've been burned, Chen Lee," I told her. "Calloway pulled out on us. We're on our own and there's no submarine offshore to help us out in a jam."

"Maybe they believe we are dead. They must know the village is destroyed." I watched this woman, unafraid, very much in control. "We must ensure the landing, Dee. Calloway would not leave unless the landing was imminent. We are expendable, but this assault is essential if we are to provide for the liberation of Korea."

"What can we do? We've only got a few weapons and grenades left."

"Look, Dee." Chen Lee handed me the binoculars. "Look at Wolmi-Do." Several minutes passed before I was able to detect what Chen Lee had already noticed. High atop the fortress was a tall radio antenna. At such a height, this tower was capable of contacting Kimpo airfield. Or even Seoul.

"Al Wong must have erected this tower while we were anchored in the bay," I remarked. "It wasn't there when we left. From the look of it, he's probably got a radio situated at Wolmi-Do's highest point, and it's likely there's a generator close by."

"With this powerful generator," Chen Lee observed. "Al Wong could radio Seoul the moment he saw American ships in the bay. He could have reinforcements here in hours."

I thought it through, remembering the last time I'd passed information to Calloway. My strategic suggestions had been threefold: first, an all-out naval bombardment of Wolmi-Do to level the fortress; second, a contingent of American marines would land to secure the fortress and mop up any resisting North Korean forces; and three, the actual amphibious assault on Inchon. The only weak link in the plan followed the landing of the marines at Wolmi-Do. The tide would flow back out to sea for twelve hours, forcing the bombarding ships to leave Flying Fish Channel for the safety of the Yellow Sea. The marines would be alone during this period, and Al Wong could summon a hundred thousand North Korean troups to his aid in that time, with that radio.

Spotting the problem had been simple enough. I hoped the solution would prove as easy: to destroy the radio and its generator.

*   *   *

We rested the remainder of that night, and the following day set off in the motorized boat toward Wolmi-Do. We anchored in a position south of the fortress to blend in with the small fleet of fishing boats that filled the area. I didn't want to place us anywhere near Al Wong's huge war sampan. As dusk arrived and the fishing boats put in to shore, Chen Lee and I prepared the lifeboat for the journey to the southern shore. We waited well into the night before dropping the dinghy into the water and risking the treacherous currents. After beaching in a cove only a half-mile from the ominous fortress, we paused momentarily to gaze at the forbidding outline of Wolmi-Do from the shore. It resembled a three-hundred-foot tombstone with our names etched across it.

Chen Lee and I began the rocky climb up the southern face. The antenna was affixed to the northern wall, which meant we had to circle the fortress as we climbed, but because Wolmi-Do had been carved from solid rock, we were able to reach the north wall with plenty of footholds.

Wolmi-Do consisted of three levels. On the lowest level were the North Korean artillery digs. We passed those easily, as only a handful of sleepy regulars was posted to stave off the pilfering of the supplies by the natives. The second level became somewhat steeper and I had to assist Chen Lee when the rock face turned smoother. Following this was a long, interim level in which there were no guards. The North Korean soldiers kept to themselves while, above us, the vicious minions of Al Wong patrolled the parapets. We had almost made it to the top when I encountered three of the warlord's men. I froze, clinging tenuously to the outer wall as they stood blocking the walkway.

A trio of men stood speaking to each other, I turned my head to see Chen Lee holding tightly to the rock below. Her face was strained and as her eyes met mine, she shook her head. Her grip was loosening. She'd be able to hold on for only a second more, maybe only a moment. I turned my attention back to the guards, who'd fallen silent. Finally they proceeded to walk away. I pulled myself up, allowing Chen Lee an additional hold where my foot had been. I saw her scrambling, so I leaned across the wall, extending my arm. She reached up, missed my grip, tried again and finally was able to grasp onto my hand. In a moment she was over the wall and standing in the pathway with me.

"The antenna is on the north roof." I pointed toward the partially obscured tower, one small level up.

Chen Lee and I readied our machine guns, then moved stealthily toward the base of the antenna. In the distance we could hear the low whine of the generator. I was about to take my first step at the base of the stairway leading to the communications center when Chen Lee pulled at my sleeve. Again I froze.

I didn't hear anything, but I retreated into the shadows of the wall at her urging. A Korean armed with an automatic weapon was taking his sweet time walking down the stairs from the radio room. When he reached the bottom step, he paused. I lifted my machine gun, aiming it at his back from the shadows.

He just stood for a moment, but didn't look in any particular direction as my finger sweated on the trigger. The guard allowed his own weapon to slack forward, and I knew I had him if necessary. Suddenly the man belched loudly, then rubbed his stomach. Then he continued on his rounds.

Chen Lee and I sagged against the wall for a moment, then eased back toward the stairway. She nodded us forward and I peered around for a glance up the ancient stairs. There were no guards in sight. We ascended quickly, taking each step in its turn. The humming of the generator was louder and we had to strain to discern any enemy voices.

Upon reaching the top, we heard the static crackling of the radio. It rose from a room at the end of the short hallway. I pulled Chen Lee over to me for quiet instructions.

"You stay near the stairway to cover my back," I whispered. "The generator is in a separate room from the radio. I'll have to take them out individually."

She nodded, lifting her weapon to hip level. I slung mine over one shoulder, then walked quietly down the hallway. I stood for a moment outside the radio-room entrance. The operator was chattering into a microphone and, based on the words I could understand, he was speaking to Seoul. I chose to wait a moment until the transmission was complete.

I turned my head to Chen Lee, her expression a warning as she pointed toward the stairwell. Someone was moving toward us. I couldn't wait any longer, so I pulled the pin on the first grenade, then rolled it into the room so it fell under the transmitter. The first explosion roared down the hallway as the radio was blown into a thousand pieces.

I began running toward the generator room just as Chen Lee came face-to-face with three guards. I couldn't help her because she was in my line of fire. Putting her out of my mind, I pulled the pin with my teeth, tossing the second grenade under the whining generator. The second explosion rocked the tower, blowing sparks through the hallway.

As I hit the stone floor stomach-first, I saw Chen Lee firing from the hip. She'd gone into overkill, cutting down the guards in a split second, continuing to fire.

"Chen Lee," I screamed over the explosions, "Chen Lee!"

Suddenly her clip emptied and she snapped out of it. I scrambled to my feet just as several guards started up the stairway. Bolting in front of Chen Lee, I sprayed the steps with a short burst, then leaned flat against the wall opposite her. We had the stairway covered between us. Fully reloaded, Chen Lee stuck the snout of her submachine gun into the stairwell, firing wildly. Within seconds, a scream followed.

We were trapped. We could kill a hundred men but we'd never get down those stairs alive. I fired into the stairs, then jumped across next to Chen Lee.

With a gesture, I told her to run back toward the radio room. When she was near the corner where the antenna intersected with the north wall, I fired into the stairway a final time, then ran down to join her.

"Is this where we die together?" she asked. The shouting became louder.

"No, Chen Lee." I quickly boosted her up onto the platform where the antenna tower was poised into the blackness of the night. Then I followed her up, and suddenly we were on the roof of Wolmi-Do's highest point.

The guards were running down the corridor below us. I fired into the small trapway through which we'd crawled, killing the first curious pair. The rest of them backed off, trying to figure out what to do.

As they retreated, I pointed to the long taut ground wire leading down the side of the fortress. I told Chen Lee to start working her way down the wire while I held off Al Wong's fierce bodyguards. I knew I wouldn't escape even if Chen Lee did make it to the base of the fortress. The guards would cut the wire from above me and send me to my death. The only thing I could do was be certain Chen Lee got away.

I fired into the trapway repeatedly as Chen Lee shimmied her way to freedom. The guards below were shouting for reinforcements and soon more voices could be heard. Fifty men were jammed into the corridor and I was picking them off several at a time because their commanders ruthlessly ordered them into my line of fire. They were hoping to hit me out of sheer luck, and that's the best they could hope for. Until I ran out of ammunition.

Chen Lee had just about made it when I did. I threw the submachine gun to the side, pulled the Walther from my belt. I looked into the night but couldn't see Chen Lee's form along the wire. She'd made it. I raised the 9mm handgun and waited for the first head to appear through the trapway. I blew it into a thousand fragments when I saw it. Another North Korean head appeared and he died the same way. I was squeezing off each shot slowly, making them count and promising the last bullet in the clip for myself. I wasn't about to let those guys get me alive.

The Walther bucked three more times before jamming. In less than seconds, the guards were all over me. I tried to kick, punch, but it was futile. They had me pinned down on the roof, and I knew my time was up.

I was dragged through the trapway and into the carnage below. Bodies were strewn from the roof down the deadly corridor past the radio room and well into the stairway. We marched through the barracks area of the fortress with me in the center of a tight cordon, at least half a dozen guns pointed at my head. We then abruptly stopped before a set of ornate doors. The commanders entered first, walked across the length of the wide, finely furnished room, then led me to the balcony.

And out on the balcony, resplendent in his fine Korean garb, a red sash around his waist, stood Al Wong.

I remained silent as he studied me with murderous intensity.

"Who are you?" he demanded.

I said nothing, and he suddenly nodded to one of his commanders, who walked in front of me and, as two other guards held my arms, rammed the end of his rifle into my stomach. As I doubled over, hanging limply between the two guards, he swung again, this time smashing me across the face with the butt. As I struggled to remain conscious, I heard the commander explain to Al Wong the destruction I had caused in the radio and generator rooms. And he told of Chen Lee.

Suddenly the two men holding me let go and I fell to the floor. Al Wong stepped closer to me, then peered down into my eyes. I looked up, my eyes beginning to focus again, and I instinctively touched my bloodied cheekbone. Al Wong straightened up, then nodded to himself.

"So . . . you must be the man called Dee."

Again I said nothing, only struggled to get my bearings.

"I should have known," Wong continued. "But we thought you were dead when we destroyed Yong Hong-Do."

I got to my feet unassisted. "Apparently you were wrong."

Wong smiled. "Apparently. And might I assume that the young woman with you was Chen Lee, daughter of Ducksun?" I remained silent. He continued, "A pity she escaped. She would have been a prize of great value." He turned to his guards. "Comb the islands. Find her."

"You won't," I told him, holding a hand over my bloodied face.

"We shall see." Al Wong studied me again. "So, Mr. Dee of Far East Enterprises, Hong Kong, tell this humble man why you have chosen to live among the natives of my country, alter your face to appear one of us, and then tell me why you have come in the night to destroy my radio and my generator. . . . What, you will not talk to me? A pity. A pity because even though you are greatly respected in this part of the world, Dee, you have enemies."

I reacted to this, but tried to cover. He caught my reaction, though, and smiled. "Dee, I am by nature an inquisitive man who realizes life is often not what it appears to be. You have wrecked a fortress that I am sworn to protect. Why?"

I didn't get to answer. At that moment one of the commanders shouted, then pointed over the balcony to the bay. All eyes turned to see the vanguard of the invasion fleet under full steam toward Flying Fish Channel. Al Wong turned slowly back to me, comprehension on his face.

"So, your purpose now is very clear. They will invade soon, no?"

I didn't need to answer. One of the destroyers opened fire on the war sampan as it was trying to navigate away from its mooring. The first shell crippled the sampan by exploding just above the main screws. The following shells destroyed it.

Al Wong turned back to me. "You have made a very bad bargain, Mr. Dee." He reached across to touch my face. When he ran his fingers over my new bruise, I winced. "To change your race takes far more courage than most men could comprehend. For this, I respect you. It is the hallmark of a certain courage which modern times seem desperate to crush. You have more bravery than your enemies, Dee. Yet it is a simple matter for them to ordain your death. They are in safety, while you are. . . . It is a shame, Dee, a true waste."

I closed my eyes against the growing throbbing and pain in my face and gut, then opened them again to face Al Wong. "You keep speaking of my enemies, Wong. What enemies?"

There was an explosion in the channel and everyone turned to see the ships train their guns on Wolmi-Do. The naval bombardment blew away a portion of the beach.

"Your enemies . . . my friends. They have betrayed us both, Dee."

"You didn't answer my question. What enemies?"

Al Wong shook his head. "We are businessmen, Dee. Businessmen deal. The prize is suddenly larger: your life, my personal wealth."

"I don't deal with people like you." I was stalling for time as another salvo exploded at the base of the fortress. The ground trembled.

"Dee, do not make a terrible mistake," Al Wong warned. "Those ships in the channel can destroy this fortress, but they cannot save your life. I can."

I considered this for a moment, then looked at him. "You keep talking about my enemies. Do they have names?"

Al Wong nodded. "My associate is your enemy. His name is Calloway."

I was shocked into silence.

"Are you surprised?" Al Wong smiled knowingly. "Let me tell you more. Two nights before I ordered the village destroyed, Calloway met with me aboard my sampan. He contracted with me to kill you. He informed me that you were traveling with Ducksun's daughter and described your fishing boat. He did not tell me why you were here, but he did say you were very important in the business world and it was imperative that you not return to your world alive."

"But why? Did he say why?"

Al Wong shrugged. "Do we now make a bargain, Dee? There is much more to this story, but I will not tell it cheaply. I have failed to defend Inchon, and my North Korean friends will be sure I betrayed their trust. As the world will someday realize, they are incapable of bargaining. I will be forced to flee Korea. A man on the run needs all the money he can get."

I hesitated, then slowly, so as not to alarm my captors, unbuckled my belt and pressed a small snap. A six-carat blue-white diamond fell into my hand. The stone was a certified gem worth three hundred thousand dollars.

I fingered the diamond, then looked to Al Wong. "So tell me the story."

Another explosion shook the fortress, destroying the antenna tower and raining rocks and boulders down upon us.

"Calloway was acting for a man who does not want you to return to the States alive," Al Wong began. "His name is Moroni."

"Moroni? What does Calloway have to do with Moroni?"

Al Wong pretended unawareness. "Moroni wants you dead, for whatever reasons; Calloway agreed to arrange it."

As more shells continued to shake the fortress, becoming more frequent, I tried to make sense of what I was hearing. "How the hell do you know all this? Calloway didn't tell you, that's for sure."

"Mr. Calloway is no stranger to me, Dee. The politics of opium makes strange bedfellows. Your enemies, Calloway *and* Moroni, are well known to me. I have dealt with them before."

"It doesn't make sense." It didn't. Where did they tie in together?

"Mr. Calloway is Moroni's most important troubleshooter in Korea. It is his personal protection that allows Mr. Moroni's narcotics trade to florish. We've had the most interesting triad, Moroni, Calloway, and I. Many years ago, I am told, you were a young boy in Shanghai fleeing from your country for attempting to kill a boy your own age. It was said to be self-defense, but that is unimportant. The boy you had stabbed grew to be one of my partners, Moroni. My other partner is none other than your benevolent

Calloway. Isn't it ironic that you were instrumental in bringing Moroni and Calloway together?''

"How?" I questioned.

"While you were living with that Chinese whore, you refused to inform on Ducksun. Calloway was furious. He went to Don Moroni with information of your whereabouts, knowing he'd be rewarded. The don told him a young boy's death wasn't necessary, as his son lived. From that day on, Calloway was in the employ of the Moroni family. Now, the diamond." He held out his hand.

I handed it to him. I didn't know if he'd kill me anyway, but I had to chance it. I wanted to live—to get Calloway and Moroni.

Another salvo ripped into Wolmi-Do. The village vanished.

"A pleasure dealing with you, Dee." Al Wong bowed. "You are an honorable man."

"That and ten cents . . ." I turned back to Al Wong as a shell made a direct hit.

The last thing I remember seeing was the balcony fall away with Al Wong clinging to the railing. Then, from above me, I heard a crashing roar unlike anything I'd ever heard before.

The whole goddamned hill came down on me.

15

I remember feelings, sensations: lying in the darkness with an enormous weight on my legs, my chest, the taste of blood in my mouth. The air was too thick with dust to breathe; it seemed my arms were pinned under tons of rock. Suddenly there was a rush of fresh air, a shaft of light in the darkness. I knew I would live. And I slipped back into unconsciousness.

I know now that I was unconscious for months, lying in a comatose state in a heavily guarded room in Ducksun's citadel. It wasn't until much later that I was to learn that the invasion of Wolmi-Do was a success and that Inchon had fallen. And that a heavily armed party of Ducksun's most trusted men had pulled my broken body out of the rubble as the city capitulated.

Several days later, after friendly South Korean troops had finished their mop-up operation, Chen Lee came for me and, through Ducksun's intercession, transported me to safety within Ducksun's fortress.

The Warlord may have been the absolute power in the area, but Chen Lee quickly took command of everything involving my recuperation. She stayed with me during the long months of my coma, never giving up, always believing I would live, even when others had long given up on me. She knew I would come back. And slowly I did.

I remember the first time I opened my eyes. Everything was very much out of focus. Everything, that is, except the pain. I wanted to talk, to cry out, but suddenly I felt cool fingers on my lips, and then, before me, I saw the lovely face of Chen Lee. From that point on, she remained with me constantly, talking to me when I couldn't yet answer, reading my eyes and tending to my every unspoken need, helping me to help myself.

Carefully she explained my condition to me. My legs were both badly smashed, arms and ribs broken, my body a mass of bruises and contusions. But I said nothing; I couldn't. Several weeks passed before I was cognizant enough of my surroundings and condition to ask questions.

Chen Lee would never answer me. "Do not worry, Dee," she always assured me. "Everything is fine. Our mission was a success and General MacArthur is deep into North Korea now. But that is all we will discuss."

I wasn't strong enough to argue with her belief that worrisome news would only counteract my recovery.

Ducksun, however, took a slightly different view, but the Warlord and I were able to speak for only short intervals, and the information he provided me was fragmented. The armies devastating Korea were playing hell with communications, and accurate intelligence was difficult to come by. At least that's what Ducksun led me to believe.

The first time I saw him, he came quietly into my room and, thinking I was asleep, came over to my bed and put a hand gently on my forehead. I opened my eyes and looked at him.

"I do not believe it is you, Dee, that you returned to us." He paused, looking at me. "When Chen Lee told me you were at Wolmi-Do and possibly a captive of Al Wong I sent my men for you. I feared until today that they had arrived too late." He took my hand in his strong grip and studied my battered face. "Tell me, Dee, why did you take this mission? Why did you give up everything to fight in my land?"

I struggled to find my voice. "Because . . . you were in danger." I took a breath, then continued. "You were marked for death."

Ducksun narrowed his eyes. "I was marked? How was this? Tell me and I will kill the man marking me."

"I was told you were . . . faking neutrality. To put the North Koreans off-guard. If I didn't accept the mission . . . the Communists would be told about you. And you would be killed."

"Who told you this?"

I was so tired, but I had to tell him. "Calloway."

Ducksun took this in calmly, nodding to himself. "You came because of me." It was not a question. "You changed your race and left your world behind to assist an old friend."

"Not to assist, Ducksun. To save your life. If I could."

Ducksun almost smiled. "You are more like a son than any man dare ask for. I am angered to the brink of madness because your body is smashed and your life is in ruins. You came to my aid from friendship, yet were betrayed at the highest levels. And as though this were not sufficient, you willingly decided to give your life so Chen Lee might escape from Wolmi-Do. There are no words to describe the honor that guides your life, my son. The bond between us transcends war and is stronger than politics. You have my home as sanctuary and you have anything else you might desire. Rest and grow well, Dee. I will deal with your enemies?"

"Calloway?"

He nodded. "I will order his death." He stood, ready to leave.

"No!" I forced myself up and took hold of Ducksun's arm. "No, you can't. Not . . . yet."

Ducksun stopped, then gently forced me back down. "Tell me, my son, why I cannot."

And I did. I explained about Moroni, Calloway, and their connection with Al Wong. I told Ducksun of Moroni's grudge against me, of Calloway's duplicity, and of my encounter with his own rival warlord.

Ducksun nodded, then looked at me. "Where is Al Wong now?"

I shrugged. "I think he was killed at Wolmi-Do. The last time I saw him was on the balcony."

"Is he dead?" Ducksun demanded.

"Probably. I saw him clinging to the railing as it crashed down the hillside."

Ducksun was not satisfied. "This does not answer my question. Does my enemy live?"

"I don't know."

Ducksun considered this. "I must know of his death or survival." He was silent for a moment, then turned a cold gaze toward me. "Al Wong is not known for his mercy, Dee. Tell me, why did he not kill you?"

"I bought my way out."

"How is that?"

"Al Wong knew his game was finished but had no way to get to his funds, which I gather were banked in Europe. I traded a valuable diamond for my life."

Ducksun didn't answer immediately, and the expression on his face indicated he expected more from me. "Why did you not kill him?"

"Even though we were bargaining," I explained, "I was at his mercy. He could have killed me and taken the diamond. Instead, he kept his word. So I kept mine." I hesitated, then continued. "Ducksun, my personal code demands that I honor my enemies as well as my friends. It is the only way to effect true justice in one's decisions. And to be able to live with the consequences of choice. That is what separated us from Al Wong. He respects no one."

Ducksun sighed heavily, and for the first time I noticed the years creeping up on him. I, too, was tired, and closed my eyes.

"In your position, Dee, I would have done the same thing," the Warlord conceded. "Perhaps this old bull has yet something to learn from his adopted son." He rested his hand on my shoulder and I looked at him. "You must rest now and become well. I will look into these matters. There will be answers, but we must remain patient. And I will inquire into the welfare of your family."

He rose to leave, and I drifted off into a deep sleep.

Five nights after our conversation, fever took me. The doctors had warned Chen Lee to expect it, for my body was so weakened that I had no ability to fight off an infection.

With the fever came an aching delirium and severe chills. The doctors were concerned about the high body temperature, but they were more concerned about the instability that accompanied the chills. Chen Lee remained with me on a particularly cold night while an icy rainstorm pelted the stronghold walls. I remember waking to see Chen Lee wrapped in a blanket, seated in a chair near me.

I could feel my throat close with seemingly cold air as my voice stuttered through frozen lips: "I'm cold . . . so cold . . ."

My appearance must have frightened Chen Lee, for she immediately moved into action, throwing a blanket over me shouting for the doctors, ordering the servants to stoke the fire.

As everyone rushed to accomplish her bidding, she slipped under the heavy blanket next to me, pulling the woolen covering tightly around us, then pressing her body against mine. She spoke to me, her voice reassuring, gentle.

As more blankets were piled atop us and the fire increased, I drifted in and out of consciousness. Chen Lee never left my side, and after hours I could not count, my fever broke. And I knew I would recover.

Chen Lee was an utterly remarkable woman of seemingly endless energy. I don't believe she visited the inside of her own quarters more than a dozen times during the long months of my recovery. She was near me when I awoke in the morning, she was still with me as I drifted off to sleep each night. Time lost all meaning, my own reality becoming that room and the comforting warmth of Chen Lee.

"Why do you spend so many hours with me?" I asked one morning.

She smiled. "Dee, did you not risk your own life to free me from prison, and yet again at Wolmi-Do? Besides, it is very bad to be ill, and even worse to be ill alone."

It was almost a year after the fall of Wolmi-Do before Ducksun and I had another opportunity to speak. I was healing well, and within a couple of weeks I would begin exercising my legs in the hopes of walking again.

I was sitting up in bed when the Warlord entered my room.

"I have news," he announced as he settled into a chair.

"Al Wong?"

He nodded. "He is alive. My sources learned he sold the diamond in Hong Kong. Once he reaches his European banks, there is no telling what devilment he may devise. But one thing is certain: he will return to Asia."

"I'm sorry, Ducksun," I offered, "but there was no other way."

He sat silently for another moment, then continued. "I have news of your family."

I could tell by the tone of his voice that it wasn't good. Taking a breath, I steeled myself. "Tell me."

"You are dead," he said simply.

"What?" I was struck quiet for a moment. "How? Why?"

"Do not excite yourself, my son, and I will explain," Ducksun began. "I have opened contact with agent Smathers. He informed me that Calloway returned to the United States with the story of your heroic death at Inchon. He told the President that the landing could not have occurred without you and that you completed your mission successfully but that you were killed during the bombardment of Wolmi-Do. He said you were trying to destroy gun positions which threatened the ships in the channel. He even went so far as to claim you blew up two gun emplacements before being cut down by the North Koreans. The President summoned your wife to the White House, where a posthumous medal was awarded on your behalf. I understand Calloway was with her."

"But Smathers must have known I was alive. Why didn't he tell Sylvia?"

"And place her life in jeopardy? No, it would not have been wise, Dee. First, Smathers did not know of your survival until after the award, and when he did, he realized that if your wife or children were to know that you live, it could place them in grave danger. Your enemies, Dee, are closer to your family than you."

I thought a moment. "I have to return."

"When you are well and can protect them, you will."

The nights were long and dreary. I thought of my wife, a widow, and cursed my inability to recover more quickly. But I realized what Ducksun said was right. I couldn't go back. At least, not yet. I couldn't even let Sylvia know I was alive until I was able to be with her to protect her. Only then could I return to my former life.

But as the weeks became months, I realized something else was happening. My dependency on Chen Lee was beginning to turn to desire. I tried to deny it and knew I would remain faithful to my wife, but the feelings were there. And growing. I anticipated her visits with excitement, looked forward to her smiling face, her light fragrance, her gentle touch.

I was exercising, walking up and down the corridors, when Ducksun approached me. "We must talk," he said simply, and led me back into my room. As I sat on the bed, he looked at me directly.

"This is most difficult for me to tell you, Dee, but you must be told."

I tensed, sensing what he was going to say, but I forced myself to nod. "Yes?"

"Your wife has remarried."

I don't think my sense of loss would have been greater had he told me she was dead. "Whom did she marry?" I was finally able to ask.

"A man named Timothy Bridges," Ducksun responded. "I believe he was your lawyer."

I nodded. Timothy Bridges. A good man. I looked to the Warlord. "Ducksun, I'd like to be alone for a while." He nodded and left.

So it was over. Calloway had killed and buried me. My wife had mourned, recovered, and remarried. My children now had a new father. And as long as I was dead, they were safe.

One morning when I returned from my daily walk, Chen Lee came to my room.

"Dee, I would like to show you something."

We walked down passages of ancient stone which I hadn't known existed. Chen Lee led me to the rear of the citadel, where a gate bordered on the garden, one of the largest I'd ever seen. It was finely landscaped, with every type of blossoming tree imaginable.

"My ancestors called this place the Garden of Truthfulness. Legend claims that any man and woman who enter here cannot fail to search their hearts. It was to this place that Ducksun brought my mother upon their betrothal. It is said that here the truth in one's heart becomes dominant over any negative thoughts or desires."

I studied this beautiful woman and looked into her eyes. "What are you trying to tell me, Chen Lee?"

"When are you returning home, Dee?" she asked, then looked away.

"Why are you asking that? And why now?"

"Because now I have need to know." She paused, then turned to me. "Dee, do I displease you?"

I shouldn't have been shocked by her question, but I found I was. "No," was all I could manage.

She nodded, almost sadly. "The months have been long, Dee, but the distance between us is even longer. I wonder how far your heart must voyage before reaching its destination."

"I don't know, Chen Lee. I just don't know."

"Then know this. If you vanish from my life again, you will leave an emptiness that will never be filled."

"I never wanted to hurt you, Chen Lee."

"Then why do you evade my question?" She paused, then faced me directly. "When are you returning to the United States?"

"If this garden causes one to speak the truth, then I will speak it, Chen Lee," I said, easing her around to face me. "I now realize that my return there would cause much pain to me and those I love. I've seen more then enough hurt, and I'm tired. I am not returning, Chen Lee. I choose to stay."

I was surprised to hear myself say those words, but the moment I had, I knew them to be true. As I looked into Chen Lee's face, a cherry blossom fell. And then another, and yet another. I glanced up into the blue Korean sky as the breeze whispered through the trees, freeing them of loosened blossoms. They fluttered earthward, covering Chen Lee and me. Laughing, I began removing blossoms from her hair as she lightly brushed them from my shoulders. "It's snowing blossoms," I said quietly.

And I began thinking of a new life.

Chen Lee had taken to serving me an evening meal in the great hall, which had been furnished by her ancestors in the seventeenth century. Ducksun had ordered the hall restored upon returning to Korea, following the Japanese surrender. Somehow he managed to locate much of what the Japanese had plundered, and the hall was restored with accuracy.

We had just opened a bottle of wine and were reclining before the fire when a haunting feeling overcame me. The similarities with my last night at home—at home with Sylvia—became all too real. It was another time, another life. The wine had been a French white, the fireplace as warm as our hearts. As those memories flooded back, then ebbed, I looked down at Chen Lee, then slowly leaned forward and kissed her lips. Then I pulled back and looked into her eyes.

Chen Lee knew the phantom behind my eyes was Sylvia. For the briefest moment my past with Sylvia and the possibility of a future with Chen Lee tried desperately to meld within me. I leaned toward Chen Lee again, knowing I wanted her deeply, yet other feelings were standing in the way. But Chen Lee understood and I could see her move to meet, then touch my lips, offering me a soft sense of reality which would remain forever within me.

Her mouth found mine a second time as she relaxed in my arms, eyes closed, and sighed slightly. The fire crackled loudly as another log caught and was consumed by flame. I could feel both her hands moving slowly up and down my back as I cradled her slender form in my arms. My mind was racing. I was trying to anticipate what she wanted from me, how she wanted me. I knew I would make love with her, but not on this floor. Not below the hearth. I released Chen Lee unexpectedly and her eyes peered up at me curiously. Then I scooped her small figure into my arms and kissed her again.

She reached for the bottle of wine as we passed the large table. Her other arm snaked around my neck, pulling my lips closer to hers. Her tongue parted my lips expertly, then worked into my mouth, teasing and tantalizing with every delicate probe. As she kissed me deeply, I walked from the great hall, carrying her up the wide granite steps to the upper level. I passed my quarters and entered the large bedroom at the far end of the hallway. Once, during the eighteenth century, a woman had ruled the citadel. This had been her bedroom, and the succeeding warlords had pridefully avoided it.

Chen Lee smiled, realizing where I was heading, because this was her favorite room. She reached down to unlatch the door as I nudged it inward with my foot. The bed was an immense sea of downy mattressing canopied from four eight-foot posts of polished teak. I placed Chen Lee down on the plush coverings, watching her sink into the softness.

"I wondered when you would come to me," Chen Lee sighed.

"Is that why you were healing me so well?" I teased her.

"But of course." She laughed.

Our lips met once again. My deepest needs became a flaming desire for Chen Lee. I brought my fingers to her face, where they delicately touched her cheeks, then brushed her silky hair onto the pillows. She came up to kiss me again as I unsnapped the button holding her collar together. Once undone, the thin lapels parted, revealing a string of buttons leading to her waist sash. She teased me heartlessly as I went for each button in turn. As another came unfastened, Chen Lee brushed my hand away but caressed me erotically. Her every move was calculated to urge me on, yet she artfully prolonged my advances until certain all the urgency was gone. Then she helped me snap several buttons away so I could barely see her soft, tanned flesh in the opening. I reached for her breasts but she diverted my attention by kissing me quickly and continuously across my face and neck. I felt her mouth come up behind my ear while her free hand curled downward exploring my thighs. Swiftly heightening her feline taunting, she reached into my robe, held me gently, then retreated as waves of craving flowed through me.

I saw the desire in her eyes and knew she wasn't finished with her scintillating game. She pulled me closer, then began running her manicured nails down my back. Her free hand opened my buckle; then, seconds later, I was half-naked. She pulled the robe down around my arms, thus locking them to my sides. Then her fingers danced up and down the length of my spine, detonating tiny explosions wherever she paused. I started talking quietly in her ear, but she ignored me. Only her mouth and tongue seemed to answer by tasting and biting.

I worked my robe away while nibbling at her neck. My hands free now, I returned to the inviting opening at her lapels to unfasten the final button while undoing her sash. Chen Lee's robe parted completely, revealing her stunning body. I fell in love with the contour of her breasts. They were round and supple and attracted my hands magnetically. The slightest touch brought her nipples to life, triggering a wave of pleasure throughout her that I easily sensed. She raised her body boldly up to mine, wrapping her legs around my thighs demandingly. The teasing had ended, simply because we'd gone beyond our limits of resistibility.

We were good together and anticipated each other with uncanny intuitiveness. We moved like so many rhythmic waves against the shore and were as slow and certain as the tide. Each movement was a savoring within itself. Every caress was a portrait of our love. Chen Lee transformed before my very eyes as sensuality overwhelmed her. I discovered the woman I had never known. I detected her possessiveness in the way she held me and gave no indication of ever letting go.

The image of the sweet angel who had nursed me so devotedly for many weeks dissipated as she taught me this other side of her. A thousand emotions came together between Chen Lee and me. Our passion formed a turbulent rapid we'd committed ourselves to braving.

I told Chen Lee I loved her.

She smiled but didn't answer as I watched the past—my past—evaporate into the mists and warmth of her body. A mist and warmth that would stay with me forever.

III

To Secure: Death on Its Way

1962

16

Ten wonderful years seemed to fly away like silk in the breeze. Ducksun grew older, lost a considerable amount of weight, but appeared far more dignified with his silver hair. His influence in Korean affairs heightened as he became financially stronger. The days of warlords had ended as he had known them, and though he maintained a small cadre of bodyguards, he had long ago disbanded his small army.

Despite his age and history, Ducksun's thoughts and viewpoint were progressive. He questioned me endlessly about Western finance, developing a sharp appreciation for the nuances of the world economy. After functioning for decades in the treacherous political and financial waters of the East, Ducksun found the mechanics of Western business an amusing diversion. His business sense was so simplistic it was radical.

"Things which burn cease to exist," he observed. "The trick is to turn the ashes into gold."

He contacted his solicitor in Hong Kong, then bought up all the oil and coal stocks available on that particular market. He was wealthy enough to sit on those purchases and reap unbelievable profits.

Chen Lee and I retained our independence of each other, keeping our own separate quarters but sleeping together in the large bedroom in which I'd first made love to her. Love between us blossomed into a hardy, endurable life-style. A total acceptance of what we were capable of giving to each other made every moment we shared a treasured gift. The outside world was shuttered from us, and we wanted it that way.

Infrequently Ducksun brought news about home, about my children. He kept an open line to Smathers, who understood my situation and was happy to pass along whatever information he could learn.

I knew Donna, Jeff, and Denise were growing up without me. Sylvia was reportedly very happy with Tim Bridges, and Eddie Gardenia seemed to be prospering. Everything at home seemed to be well. Then one day Ducksun returned from a Hong Kong business excursion with unsettling news. He arrived at the great hall as Chen Lee and I were sitting down to dinner.

"Far West Enterprises in London has been sold," he told me.

"What?" I was stunned at the news. "That can't be true."

"It is," Ducksun assured me. "I have verified the report with the best sources."

"Who bought it? Who'd have that kind of money?"

"All I could learn," Ducksun explained, "was that a consortium of French and English bankers formed a holding company last year for the express purpose of buying Far West."

"French and English bankers? How much did they pay?"

"Twenty million dollars."

I stopped eating and considered what this meant. Far West was worth fifteen million when I'd left in 1950 and nobody was going to convince me it had achieved only five million in capital growth in that time. Something was wrong and I had the sickening feeling that Moroni was behind it all.

Ducksun left and Chen Lee turned to study me. "This concerns you greatly."

I nodded. "I built Far West Enterprises with my sweat and guts. And now it's gone."

"Will you return?"

I shook my head, then covered her hand with mine. "No, Chen Lee. There is nothing I could do. It is done."

Fifteen months later, Ducksun told me that Far West had been sold for a second time, this time the purchase price doubled the original. Again the identity of the purchasers was a closely guarded secret, but it hardly mattered anymore. The company was no longer mine and there wasn't a thing I could do about it. I'd been gone more than a decade, living in the solitude of Ducksun's citadel with Chen Lee. But I should have known that my solitude was coming to an end.

In the spring, someone came inquiring after me.

I was studying under the toughest master I'd yet to meet when Ducksun walked across the field to where we'd set up an outdoor gym. Even from a distance I could see the concern on his face. With a respectful wave he dismissed the master.

"Something's wrong," I said as I wiped the sweat off my face. "What is it?"

"You have a visitor," Ducksun announced. "From the United States."

"Is it one of my family?"

"No, but it is an old friend who bears news of them. Come."

I followed Ducksun into the citadel and through its polished walkways to the great hall. Inside, Ducksun led me to a young man with reddish hair. He was seated at the long oak table but rose upon our entrance.

Ducksun looked to me. "I don't believe you have ever met Smathers, have you?"

My eyes moved to the red-haired man. "You're Smathers? The one who helped smuggle Chen Lee out of Seoul when the city fell?"

"Yes," he said, offering his hand. "And you're Dee. I've heard a lot about you."

I took his hand and Ducksun silently departed. Apparently whatever Smathers had journeyed this far to tell me merited my ears only. I looked to the equipment he'd brought with him. The table held a tape recorder and a stack of reels.

"Is this about my family?" I asked while moving toward one of the hand-carved chairs.

"Yes." Smathers breathed heavily as I waited. "Eddie Gardenia is dead."

Something inside me died. Eddie? Dead? There had to be more to it. Smathers wouldn't have traveled ten thousand miles to deliver an obituary.

"How did he die?"

"Murdered," Smathers replied. "At least we think it was murder. We haven't found the body yet."

"Then why do you think he was murdered?"

"Because we have both intent and motive on tape."

As I watched, Smathers took several spare batteries from his briefcase, then placed them next to the recorder/player.

I watched as he set up. "Are these CIA tapes?"

He shook his head. "No, FBI. Let me explain myself. When the Korean War ended, I'd had my fill of intelligence work. I could see the Agency was going to have to take a far more ruthless stand if it was to survive against other intelligence groups. I really couldn't stomach that kind of play. Too much unnecessary bloodshed. So I took a position with the FBI."

"Go on," I told him.

"It's mostly investigative work, and I like it. And sometimes I even get to do something worthwhile."

"Like right now?"

He forced a slight smile. "Yeah." He was ready to begin. "And in case you're wondering, these tapes are originals. I left the copies back in the States. And no one knows I'm here, so let's try to keep it that way."

I nodded. "Understood."

"Okay." He continued, "After I started working at the FBI, I did a stint with the identification division and was then transferred to the rackets squad. We're a pretty small group with a huge job. If we had to track down and build a case against every top gangster in the U.S., well, most of them would be dead of old age before we could get them into court.

"In 1958 I was assigned to the Senate Investigating Committee on Organized Crime. We covered all the big ones, and even turned up a small-timer named Valachi, who squealed like a stuck pig. But, bottom line, we still couldn't nail the big ones. Evidence got real hard to come by. So we resorted to 'alternate methods.' " He gestured to the tapes.

"Smathers, if you're trying to tell me Eddie got mixed up with the mob and got himself killed for it, there's nothing I can say. He was my cousin and I loved him, but he knew better. Or should have."

"Dee, it's more than just the tragedy of Eddie's death. Everything you'll hear today is a schematic of how criminals can take over a thriving, legitimate business." Smathers put a tape on. "This first tape is between a Mr. Philip Barringer and James Moroni."

I was about to say something, but Smathers pushed a button and the tape started.

BARRINGER: Good morning, Mr. Moroni.

MORONI: Have you contacted Eddie Gardenia yet?

BARRINGER: Of course. But he doesn't want anything to do with us.

MORONI: Have you been able to confirm the extent of his interest in Dee Enterprises?

BARRINGER: Presently Mr. Gardenia holds thirty percent of the voting stock.

MORONI: That's all? I thought him and Dee were equal partners.

BARRINGER: They were.

MORONI: So why does he own only thirty percent?

BARRINGER: He signed away twenty percent of his stock.

MORONI: Why in the hell did the bastard do that?

BARRINGER: I imagine he felt you would pressure him if he owned a full fifty percent of the company but wouldn't bother him if someone else held the controlling interest.

MORONI: I'll be a son of a bitch! Who did Gardenia sell the twenty points to, anyway?

BARRINGER: Sylvia Bridges.

MORONI: Dee's widow?

BARRINGER: The same.

MORONI: So how much does she own?

BARRINGER: She's got seventy percent of the voting stock in Dee Enterprises.

MORONI: That broad has seventy percent of a
    multimillion-dollar corporation?
BARRINGER: That's correct. (Silence.)
MORONI: I want that company, understand? Start
    telling me just how we're going to get it.
BARRINGER: If you attempt a stock transfer over the
    open market involving her seventy percent . . . well,
    the Securities and Exchange Commission will come
    down on you. It's far too large a transaction. They
    could tie you up with investigatory procedures for
    six months to a year.
MORONI: Even if it's completely legal?
BARRINGER: Yes. Legality has nothing to do with it.
    They'll look so far down into you that they're bound
    to ask some embarrassing questions.
MORONI: Suppose Sylvia Bridges consented to
    sell me thirty percent of her stock. How long would
    that take?
BARRINGER: It's a simple deal. A few months at
    most. But I doubt if she'll sell. Word has it she's
    still pretty respectful of her deceased husband.
    Doesn't want to tear down anything he built up with
    her.
MORONI: Didn't she marry Dee's personal lawyer—
    what's his name?
BARRINGER: Timothy Bridges.
MORONI: Can he be bought?
BARRINGER: I don't know. I'll check on it, though.
MORONI: Yeah, Philip, you do that.

The tape whirred to an end, slapping a loosened tail
against the recorder. I looked at Smathers, who was
carefully removing the reel from the machine. Eddie
Gardenia had played it real smart in signing over a
portion of his stock in order to give Sylvia a top-heavy
interest in Dee Enterprises. I had to give my cousin
credit, but then, I always knew he could do it. He'd
survived without me, hadn't he? Or had he?

"How did you get these tapes?" I asked Smathers.
He placed another tape on the machine. "I was head
of the FBI surveillance team that assembled this collection. I became interested when your name and company kept turning up on the transcripts. I had no idea

that there was a business rivalry between you and Moroni going back so many years. I understand you took a government contract away from him in forty-one."

"Stabbed him, too, a few years before that. Street fight."

Smathers nodded. "Maybe you should have killed him."

"No shit."

"I knew you were alive over here because Ducksun's people alerted me. You know all that. Anyway, this next tape was taken from Philip Barringer's office. It's between Barringer and Tim Bridges."

He pushed the button and I listened. Barringer told Tim that a company called Overseas Trading wanted to get a portion of Dee Enterprises, a portion amounting to thirty percent. And that was the amount that Eddie Gardenia held. Bridges turned Barringer down cold, telling him he knew of Barringer's association with Moroni. Barringer denied the association, and the tape came to an abrupt end when the secretary interrupted and told Barringer that a man wanted to see him. A named named Calloway.

The second tape spun off the reel as I felt my stomach tighten. Calloway. I shouldn't have been surprised. But there were still so many unanswered questions.

"If you're wondering about Calloway," Smathers offered, "there is a connection between him and Moroni."

"I knew that ten years ago."

"Did you?" Smathers seemed impressed. "We only discovered it because Moroni's office was bugged."

"Moroni tried to have me killed, and damn near succeeded. Calloway set it up."

"Then it's true." Smathers nodded to himself. "It comes up on a later tape."

"Do they believe I'm dead?"

"Yes."

"What about Bridges? Did he go to Eddie with the deal?"

"We're not really sure." Smathers took a deep breath

before continuing. "You see, we could bug Moroni because he's an organized-crime boss. We bugged Barringer because he's Moroni's lawyer. We couldn't get into Bridges' offices. But we did get into Eddie's. Apparently Bridges did tell Gardenia, because your cousin began refusing his calls."

"Eddie wouldn't do that without good cause."

"Well, regardless," Smathers answered, "Sylvia stepped in to mediate between the men. Dee, you might find this next tape a bit unsettling. Sylvia's on it."

"Just turn it on."

I thought I could handle it but the sound of her voice jolted me back more than ten years. It hurt.

EDDIE: Sylvia! What a pleasant surprise!

SYLVIA: Good to see you, Eddie.

EDDIE: Please, please, sit down. Had I known of your visit, I would have . . . well, we could've met somewhere else.

SYLVIA: Your office is just fine. *(Pause.)* I'd like to settle this argument between you and Tim, Eddie. There is no need for these cold feelings.

EDDIE: There's no argument, Sylvia. I just have no intention of selling thirty percent of my stock to the Overseas Trading Company. Tim should know better than to approach me with anything concerning Moroni.

SYLVIA: As the legal representative for Dee Enterprises, Tim was legally bound to inform you of the offer made by the Overseas Trading Company.

EDDIE: Moroni is the Overseas Trading Company, Sylvia. *(A long silence.)*

SYLVIA: Do you have evidence supporting this?

EDDIE: Dee dug up the proof at the time we were awarded our first army contract. Sylvia, the Overseas Trading Company is only a Wall Street name for the Pan International Bank. They're the eighth-largest financial institution in the world.

SYLVIA: Moroni has an interest in them?

EDDIE: Better than that, Sylvia. Dee and I dredged up the original charter and certificate of incorporation of Pan International.

SYLVIA: But that was twenty years ago.

EDDIE: At the turn of the century, Salvatore Moroni bought an interest in the Mulberry Street Finance Company. He pumped some funding into it, then changed the name to the Mercantile International Bank. Most of his living was made as an old Mustache Pete, but he kept the bank clear of any illegalities. Around 1908 there was a rash of bank failures in the Italian colony along Mulberry Street. Salvatore Moroni managed to keep the institution afloat until World War I. He changed the name by merging with several large finance companies. The new name was Pan International. The original stock still remains in the hands of the Moroni family. The Overseas Trading Company is a holding firm which they use for special, discreet purchases. *(Silence.)*

SYLVIA: Have you told Tim this?

EDDIE: No. Dee and I agreed to keep the information within the family. That decision was made long ago. (Silence.)

SYLVIA: You don't consider Tim family, do you?

EDDIE: I'm sorry, Sylvia. To me Tim is just another lawyer. I just can't get used to the idea of you being married to him.

SYLVIA: Eddie, when I was told Dee was killed in Korea, all I could think of was my three children and the company Dee worked so hard to build. I was devastated. I needed someone to lean on. Tim Bridges was that someone. I know you don't think Tim is good enough for me. But if you would only give him a chance, you would understand why I married him. He was also one of Dee's closest friends, Eddie.

EDDIE: That doesn't make any difference to me. Tim would never have approached Dee with a deal from Barringer. Dee would've fired him on the spot. One of the reasons we lost Far West Enterprises was that I underestimated Moroni.

SYLVIA: Eddie! Far West's takeover by European bankers was hardly your fault.

EDDIE: I should have seen it coming. We were being groomed, Sylvia. And Moroni was behind it. Two of the French banks which assisted in coordinating that deal hold stock in Pan International. Moroni has every intention of ruining Dee Enterprises. Always has. Moroni has his eye on my thirty percent. *(Silence.)*

SYLVIA: Eddie, I didn't know any of this when I walked in here. Really, I apologize. I had no idea the extent of the battle you've been fighting. I can see Tim doesn't either.

EDDIE: I would prefer he doesn't know.

SYLVIA: Fine. *(Pause.)* Eddie, I think Dee would have pulled his family close to him during a moment like this. If anyone is going to defend Dee Enterprises successfully, it will be you and me. If we could meet again in a week, I think I can solve this problem once and for all.

EDDIE: What do you have in mind, Sylvia?

SYLVIA: I think I know what Dee would have done. A long time ago, he realized that anyone wanting to infiltrate Dee Enterprises would have to go through you first.

EDDIE: He thought I was weak, didn't he?

SYLVIA: Not at all. In any event, we'll talk again.

Another tape spun itself into silence as I looked at Smathers. Inside, I was shaking because they were both still living with a very real memory of me. It was as if, deep down, neither of them believed I was dead.

"Sylvia was some shrewd lady," Smathers remarked as he changed tapes. "The maneuver she pulled should have stopped Moroni cold. But she didn't realize whom she was dealing with. Or how ruthless he could be."

Smathers activated the machine.

MORONI: What the hell do you mean, a setback? I'm not in the mood for bad news, Philip.

BARRINGER: I would advise you to forget the Dee Enterprises takeover.

MORONI: Forget it? You must be kidding! I've been after that firm since the fuckin' war! Besides, I'm committed.

BARRINGER: Committed to whom?

MORONI: Ever hear of Emory Kraner?

BARRINGER: Ah, Jesus Christ! Not the same Emory Kraner that collects corporations?

MORONI: The very same, and he don't like to

hear no for an answer. We both are very interested in acquiring Dee Enterprises, so he bought into the Overseas Trading Company.

BARRINGER: Partners?

MORONI: Yes. *(Pause.)* Now, what's the problem?

BARRINGER: Gardenia sold his voting stock and stepped down from officership at Dee Enterprises.

MORONI: Who the hell did he sell to?

BARRINGER: To a holding company set up by Sylvia Bridges. The price of his thirty points was not disclosed, but my sources indicate he has been paid in bonded gold certificates. The lady's on the ball, Mr. Moroni. So the deal is off? *(Silence.)*

MORONI: Hardly. Now we deal with Sylvia Bridges on a level she can understand.

The tape ended and Smathers quickly replaced it with another one taken at the office of Sam Terry Wholesale Meats. "We have him positively identified as one of the most respected elders in the Mafia. It's Moroni and Terry."

I didn't dare tell Smathers of my connection with Sam Terry, but I mentally cataloged the thought that his office had been bugged.

Smathers started the machine again.

MORONI: Sam . . . Sam . . . it is good to see you looking so well. I heard of your unfortunate incident of a week ago. Did you find out who was behind the attempt?

TERRY: Thank you for your consideration, James. Be seated. No, we haven't learned anything, but . . . ah . . . these little eruptions must be expected. *(Silence.)* Hell, I've lived a full life.

MORONI: If there is anything I can do . . . You have my allegiance.

TERRY: I will bear that in mind, James. Now, tell me. What brings you here? This visit can't be purely social, can it?

MORONI: No, this is business. *(Pause.)* May I?

TERRY: Continue. I would be happy to listen to your proposal.

MORONI: Thank you. You realize my family has been placing more and more of their holdings into legitimate business. It was my father's wish. We now have an opportunity to acquire a large corporation. I would like to offer you a portion of my holding company. It is called the Overseas Trading Company, and we will be using it to make this acquisition.

TERRY: How much will your generosity cost me?

MORONI: Your humor is well taken, Sam. Generosity is expensive these days. But I intend to make a good profit from this purchase, so I can well afford to give points away. I have sixty points. Emory Kraner has forty points. I propose you accept fifteen of my own points.

TERRY: The name Kraner is familiar. Ah, the multimillionaire!

MORONI: That's correct.

TERRY: Which company are you interested in acquiring?

MORONI: Dee Enterprises.

TERRY: One of my competitors in meat packing. You intend buying the parent company?

MORONI: Yes.

TERRY: Have they agreed to sell?

MORONI: I understand Mr. Gardenia, the former president, has stepped down from full officership in the company. It will be run by a managerial team selected by Sylvia Bridges.

TERRY: This doesn't sound to me as though they are preparing to sell.

MORONI: They will. We will be opening negotiations with them shortly.

TERRY: And you are certain they will sell?

MORONI: Yes. We have the best price. *(Silence.)*

TERRY: Well, how can I refuse your generosity? Come, we'll have a glass of wine on it.

MORONI: Thank you, Sam.

The tape came to abrupt end.

"Those guys really know how to tear a carcass apart, don't they?" Smathers remarked.

"Yes." I thought a moment. "This guy Terry, did someone try to kill him?"

Smathers nodded. "About a week before this tape was made, two gunmen tried to nail him in front of the

Sheraton. One of his bodyguards was wounded and Terry was grazed by a bullet. Nothing much. Those gunmen must have been the worst shots in the history of hit men. They were right on top of Terry and missed. It's all in the FBI reports I read."

I considered this information while Smathers sorted through the spools of tape. Moroni probably had tried to scare Terry. The type of killers Moroni could afford wouldn't miss unless they were told to.

"Dee," Smathers said quietly, "from here on, the tapes are . . . Well, Moroni kidnapped your daughter."

I felt my control slipping. "Which one?"

"Donna. From what we were able to learn, Calloway grabbed her outside rehearsal. She's an actress in some off-Broadway thing. He got her coming out of the theater."

I squeezed my eyes shut and tried to remember how Donna looked. I still saw her as a little girl. And now she was in the hands of an animal. "Where could they be hiding her?"

"I don't know. Only one person does."

"Who?"

"Calloway."

It all came together. "I should have known. Why haven't you grabbed him?"

"He's still got strong intelligence connections, Dee. Nothing I can do." Smathers spread his hands in a gesture of frustration. "I had Sylvia's phone bugged, and we recorded a call from the kidnapper. He told her not to call in the police or the FBI and that instructions would be forthcoming. She got to talk to Donna, who assured Sylvia she was all right."

I tried to take it all in. Moroni had put this kidnapping together expertly. "What did they demand?" I asked.

"They haven't gotten back to Sylvia yet, Dee. At least not that we know of."

"How long have they been holding Donna?" Smathers shook his head. "I don't know. There were a couple of phone calls between Eddie and Sylvia. Eddie knew something was wrong and began asking questions. He must have guessed what Moroni had done."

"Did Sylvia tell him?" I asked.

"No," Smathers said bluntly. "But he found out regardless."

"How?" I wondered.

Smathers didn't answer. He just pressed the button on the machine, and familiar voices filled the room. First Moroni and then Eddie.

MORONI: Okay, what's next on the agenda?

UNIDENTIFIED VOICE: Well, there's the play in Harlem . . . *(Loud noise in background. Shouts.)*

MORONI: What the fuck . . . ?

UNIDENTIFIED VOICE: He's got a gun! *(Sound of gunshot.)*

MORONI: Grab that motherfucker! *(Sounds of a brawl. Shouting.)* You guys got him? Okay, hold him. *(Sound of a slap, followed by another.)* Whatta you think, you're still up on Steinway Street, Gardenia? *(Another slap.)* Come in here shootin' at me! *(Another slap.)* Sit this stupid son of a bitch down! *(Sound of chair scraping.)*

EDDIE: Where's Donna?

MORONI: You guys get outta here. I can handle this. *(Sound of doors closing.)*

EDDIE: Where's Donna, Moroni?

MORONI: You think you got Dee to back you up? My dear Mr. Gardenia, I've been waiting for this day ever since Dee stabbed me.

EDDIE: Where's Donna?

MORONI: So, you know, eh? *(Pause.)* She's in good shape. Just worry about yourself.

EDDIE: No, Moroni, you start worryin', because you just bought yourself one hell of a lot of trouble.

MORONI: Look who's threatening who.

EDDIE: I'm not threatening you, Moroni. When you grabbed Donna—when you fucked around with Dee's family—you unleashed all the demons in hell!

MORONI: What the hell are you babbling about?

EDDIE: Your life is hanging on the end of a thread, Moroni. If you think for one minute Dee is going to let you get away with this—

MORONI: Dee's dead, Eddie. He's been dead for better than ten years.

EDDIE: Nothing's going to make you safe. Not all

the bodyguards in the world. You're a walkin' dead man, Moroni. Dee will see to that. He won't let you hurt his family. He'll come after you. Even if he has to walk out of hell.

MORONI: The man is dead and Dee Enterprises will soon belong to me, Eddie. There's nothing you can do about it.

EDDIE: *(Laughing.)* The whole fuckin' North Korean Army couldn't kill him, Moroni. What makes you think you're safe?

MORONI: Because I had him killed, you fuckin' madman!

EDDIE: He'll come after you, Moroni. And you'll know it's him.

MORONI: Hey, Max . . . hey, Joey. Get in here! *(Door opens.)*

BODYGUARD: Yes, Mr. Moroni?

MORONI: Get this fuckin' nut outta my office. *(Chairs scrape.)*

EDDIE: Start counting every breath, Moroni. You got only one thing in life you can be sure of from now on. Death is on its way, Moroni. Death is on its way.

MORONI: I said get him outta here.

BODYGUARD: Any special instructions, boss?

MORONI: I don't wanna ever see him again. Understand?

The final tape ran out and I sat staring at Smathers. He appeared a bit edgy. Did death really show in my eyes? I thought of Eddie Gardenia. The little tough guy had tried to be me. Attempted going after Moroni just like he knew I would have done. Yet he was certain I was alive and would avenge my family. How could he know? I focused on Smathers again.

"Did you play any of these tapes for Eddie?" I asked calmly.

"No. But I did talk to him," Smathers said.

"Did he know I was alive?" I asked.

"He knew you were alive before I told him, Dee."

I thought about it and the answer suddenly came to me. Eddie and I always kept separate emergency accounts of personal funds in foreign banks. We called it "running money." The only stipulation with any of those accounts was that they must show some activity in order for the various countries not to declare them "dead" and seize the funds. It was a fairly common practice. Probably still is. So for the last decade, even though I had no real need for the money, I was forced to transfer funds from one account to another in order to maintain activity. Eddie, knowing where my accounts were located, probably had them monitored. So he knew I was alive but must have assumed I had my own reasons for not coming home. And he kept his mouth shut about it. Just like he had so many years before when I'd stowed away on the *China Star*.

"Dee, I'm sorry," Smathers offered. "Maybe I made a mistake in telling Eddie about Donna's abduction. If I hadn't, he might still be alive."

I stood and felt I was in full control again. "If anybody made a mistake, Smathers, it was Moroni." My voice was cold as death. "He tried to kill me and failed. Eddie Gardenia was right. I'm on my way."

Ducksun was waiting for me in the tower. It was the highest parapet in the stronghold, the place we went for our most private conversations. He was staring off at the vista this view afforded when I approached.

"Korea is beautiful in the spring," he said quietly.

"Yes, it is," I answered.

"You are returning to America." It was not a question.

I nodded. "I have to. Moroni kidnapped my daughter. And he's killed my cousin."

Ducksun was quiet for a moment. "The force of destiny is too much to overcome," he began. "I think all men know this. There is a plane waiting for you at Seoul airport. I have made the proper arrangements. Some of my men will meet you there. There is ten thousand dollars for you. If you wish to take my men, feel free to do so."

"Thank you, Ducksun. But this is something I must do alone."

He nodded. "Then allow me to give you advice, my son. Go exact your revenge, but do not lose sight of yourself. Vengeance is a two-headed tiger which habitually consumes its own tail. Know what you are going to do, because you must carry it in your heart forever. Think as a man of action, but act as a man of thought."

He offered his hand and I held it tightly, knowing he would always be there for me, that he had given me the strength to succeed at what I had to do.

"Where is Chen Lee?" I asked.

The Warlord looked away from me and remained silent for what seemed like a long time. Then he turned to me. "I have already explained the situation to her."

"I'd like to see her."

"For what, my son? To tell her good-bye? Again?" He shook his head. "No. My daughter loves you with all her heart. In this way, she is like her mother. But she is superstitious. She feels that if she tells you good-bye, you will never return. Chen Lee sends her hopes that you will return, do whatever it is you must do and then return to her. You have her love, Dee. You do not need her farewell."

Two hours later I was on the first leg of my journey home. Over the water from Korea to Japan, I reached into my suit jacket and pulled out the pure white envelope that had been handed to me by one of Ducksun's bodyguards as I'd boarded the plane. I hesitated, then opened it and read:

Dear Son,

I have always believed you to be a Server and have respected you as such privilege demands. Alexander the Great was born under your sign. If you are to succeed in your quest, you must be aware of your enemies or you may find the same end. Do not forget the betrayals in your past. Enclosed you will find the address of my trusted agent in your country. Mention of my name will render you the assistance you might require. Until your return . . .

Ducksun

The airplane droned through the skies, searching for the new, modern airport at Tokyo. There I would change to a jet and, eventually, enter the United States through the West Coast. Smathers and I had taken different flights back, but he agreed to help me as much as possible once I was back in the States.

I leaned back in my seat, then touched my face gingerly. My new face.

I would be seeing them all again: Sylvia, Donna, Jeff, Denise, Sam Terry, Tim Bridges, Calloway, and, in the end, Moroni.

Yes, I would see them all.

But they wouldn't see me. Yet when I was finished, they would all know I had been there.

17

New York was the same city I'd left twelve years before, only different. Or maybe I was different. I got out of the cab and began to walk. I wanted to see my home, but I couldn't. I wanted desperately to see my wife and family, but that was impossible. At least for now.

I rented a room near the Village, bought myself some new Western clothes, and returned to change. As I slipped on a new white shirt, I glanced at myself in the dresser mirror and stopped. Over the years, I had gotten used to my appearance, accepted it. But to those who had known me before, I would be a stranger.

I moved slowly to the mirror and studied the face that stared back at me. Even though I was in my early forties, the surgery had resulted in not only a new face but also a younger one. My body was in terrific shape, thanks to the Gentle Way. Only my eyes gave me away. They told me who I was, what I'd been through. I turned away quickly and buttoned my shirt with my back to the mirror.

I called Smathers at the Hilton, and we agreed to meet later in the evening. Hanging up, I realized there was so much I needed to know before I could even consider taking on Moroni. And I knew there was one person I could trust to help me.

I hiked over to Fourteenth Street, and turning the corner, found "Terry Wholesale Meats and Poultry" still emblazoned across the grimy brick wall of one of Sam's warehouses. As I walked toward the entrance, I couldn't help but glance down the street. One of my trailer yards had always been located near Sam's, and my first one was right down the block. I smiled to myself as I saw two of my red-white-and-blue trailers still parked in the distant yard.

I walked onto Terry's loading dock under the suspicious eyes of his crew. Though they were taking a coffee break when I arrived, sprawling around the dollies and crates like any other workers, they all knew of Sam's position and were his first line of defense. I reached the office, went for the doorknob, when the yard boss came up behind me.

"You want somethin'?"

I turned. "Yeah, I want to see Sam Terry."

The yard boss eyed me suspiciously, then nodded. "Wait here. I'll see if he's in."

I watched the man enter the business office, and then through the glass door I saw Sam himself stand up, look through the window, then shake his head.

The yard boss returned. "Mr. Terry says he don't know you. What's your name and what do you want?"

"Tell him I'm an old friend. The name is Dee."

The yard boss disappeared again and I watched as the aging don again stood up, gave me a careful going-over, then disappeared from my view, a cold expression covering his face.

I sighed. This wasn't going to be easy. I waited as the boss again emerged from the office. This time he had a hand threateningly in his pocket.

"You," he said. "Start walking. Second office on the left."

We walked down the hallway, me first, past modest business offices and into Sam's spacious private domain. As the door closed behind me, I looked beyond the enormous desk to face Sam Terry, a cigar in his mouth, bodyguards on either side of him. They, too, had guns poorly concealed in their pockets.

"If this is some kind of a joke, pal, I'm gonna have the last laugh. You got two minutes, starting now."

I gestured him quiet, then moved cautiously to his desk under the ever-watchful eyes of his guards. There I took a pencil and memo pad. I wrote: "Your office has been bugged by the FBI for some time. We can't talk freely here." I handed the note to Terry, and after reading it, he looked up at me.

"How do you know this?"

"I know." I wrote again: "You had a meeting with Jimmy Moroni here recently in which he spoke of Dee Enterprises and offered you fifteen points of a holding company he'd formed with Emory Kraner."

Again I passed the note to Sam. He read it, gave a startled reaction, then tore it up, and throwing it into the ashtray, lit it with his cigar. "Take this joker into the warehouse."

Ten minutes later I was seated on a crate in the rear of the warehouse, guarded by the ever-present yard boss. Sam Terry appeared suddenly from around the corner, pulled up a box, and sat five or six feet away from me. He gestured the boss out of hearing distance but within firing range.

"Okay, pal, your information is on the money. How'd you get it?"

"It doesn't matter." I hesitated, then decided it was all-or-nothing time. "Sam, it's me—Dee. And I need your help."

"I said your information was dead on, buddy. But that doesn't prove who you are. Dee's dead. Now, one last time: who are you and what do you want?"

"Sam, please, look at me. I had plastic surgery, but it's still me. Look, I can prove it."

"Keep talking."

I took a breath. This was my last shot. "The first and only time you met my wife was at Asti's in late June 1950. That was also the last time I saw you. You sent over a bottle of prewar Lafite Rothschild. And I had Emil send you a bottle of the oldest Latour—"

He waved me quiet. "How much did you pay for the meal, pal?"

I smiled slightly. "I didn't, you did. And it was lunch, before you ask."

Terry allowed himself a fleeting smile, then hardened again. "Okay, you've got my attention. Tell me more. From day one."

So I told him. From day one.

It was almost a half-hour later when Sam leaned back and relit his cigar. "Okay, you convinced me. Tell me about the face."

"I had to have it done for the mission, Sam. Couldn't have survived any other way."

"I heard you was a war hero or somethin'," Sam acknowledged, "but I never got the whole story. Can you talk about it?"

"I can, but not now, okay, Sam?"

Sam nodded, understanding without words. "You asked for my help. How, and with what?"

"Moroni is trying to take over my business. He's killed Eddie Gardenia and now he's kidnapped my daughter Donna. I need your help to make it all right, Sam."

Sam shook his head. "Kidnapped your daughter? *Infamia.*" He took another puff on his cigar. "My men, I'll have them on the streets now. We'll find your daughter. Then I send my boys in after her."

"Moroni will fight back, Sam. And hard."

Sam spread his fingers in a gesture of denial. "Let him. Should I let him hurt your family? What kind of man would I be?" He looked at me with compassion. "I didn't know, Dee, that he was gonna grab your daughter. Emory Kraner neither. But Moroni's gotten too big, too dangerous. And he goes outside the rules. To take a man's daughter . . . Wrong! Wrong! And he thinks I don't know it was him who sent a couple bullets in my direction."

"Just to try to scare you, Sam."

Sam nodded. "To try, yes. And for what? I didn't know until you walked back into my life right this minute." He sat silently for a moment, then continued. "He wants my help in taking over your company. He knows I was the shadow behind you all those years, and he hated me for it. Only he didn't come after me. Business is business, even he understands. But now we come to this thing. He offers me a cut of this Overseas Trading Company, he figures I don't say nothin' about what he does." Sam stood, his full height and girth still impressive. "But what he doesn't know is that I take his money, then I use it to buy him a funeral wreath. Finished."

"Do you know anything about Eddie, Sam? Where they might have dumped his body?"

Sam shook his head. "His death is news, Dee. I can't help you there. Yet."

I had a feeling he was going to say more, but we were interrupted by the appearance of a bodyguard holding a microphone he'd discovered in Sam's office. I took it from the guard, studied it, then dropped it to the concrete floor, crushing it under my shoe.

"Wireless model, Sam. Keep looking. If you found one, you'll find more."

Sam ordered his bodyguard to tear his office apart, then turned his attention back to me. "Tell me, Dee. If the feds can get this kind of information, why didn't they stop Eddie's killing?"

"Couldn't get there in time. And they didn't want to let anyone know they were involved in bugging. It's only being done on verbal authority."

Sam smiled. "They're doing it illegal?" He shook his head. "Used to be easy telling the good guys from the bad ones."

I thought of my whole life. "Nothing's easy anymore, Sam."

He studied me for a long moment. "Have you seen Sylvia?"

I shook my head. "No. Nor the kids. The only one I know anything about is Donna, and I'm going crazy thinking about what Moroni might be doing to her."

"Moroni wants money and power, not blood. Not yet, anyway. Donna's too valuable alive, and he knows it."

I stood and paced silently, my eyes staring at the floor. Then I looked up at Sam.

"I really want to see my children, Sam." I touched my face absently. "Have you heard anything about them?"

"Well, Donna made the columns about two months ago. Something about her and some actor here on location."

I still saw the little girl in yellow sundresses and sandals.

"Your Donna's not a little girl, anymore," Sam said, reading my thoughts. "I saw her once at the Copa and she's very beautiful. And she's got a lotta talent, from what I hear."

"You've been watching them, haven't you?" I smiled at my friend.

"Kinda," he told me, grinning slightly. "Nothin' elaborate, but I keep my ears open."

"How about Jeff?" I asked.

"What about him?" Terry frowned suddenly, shaking his head. "He grew up without a father and he resents it, I guess. He's a nice kid but he's got this steel hardness which . . . Aw, I don't know, Dee. I hear he can be pretty cold when he wants to be."

"And Denise?"

Sam's face brightened into a smile. "She's a little gem, Dee. Even me, I'm proud of her. She's a good girl, still lives at home, works, even does volunteer work at a hospital."

"She's working? She can't be more than nineteen." I could suddenly feel the loss of their childhood. "Donna's been kidnapped, Jeff's a hard-ass, and Denise isn't even in college. How can I make it all right, Sam?"

Sam put a hand gently on my shoulder. "They're your family, my friend, but they've been on their own for more than a decade. I'm not sayin' they forgot you, but they didn't forget that you weren't there, either. You can't make that up to them. Sure, you can settle the score with Moroni. And you should, for them. But do it because you want to, not because you want to buy them back."

I nodded. "I understand, Sam. Will you help me?"

"You don't even gotta ask, Dee. What do you want me to do?"

"See if you can find out anything about Moroni's next move. Anything."

"Done. Not easy, but done. Call me in the next day or so." He extended his hand and I took it. His grip was still firm, the handshake of a friend.

"Welcome home, Dee," he offered quietly.

I nodded a thanks. I don't know if he knew how much those words meant to me.

Back on the streets, I wondered about my next move. Then I thought about Maggie.

I found her address in the phone book and took a cab over to the refurbished brownstone on Third Avenue. As I climbed the steps, I wondered if she was still working at Dee Enterprises. Hell, I wondered if my offices were still in the Tyson Building on Fifth.

I paused at her door, then knocked. A moment later the door opened as far as the chain would allow.

"Yes? What do you want?"

It was Maggie, looking just as she had so many years ago. A few more wrinkles maybe, but the same.

"Maggie, it's Dee. I have to talk to you."

She recoiled, either at the sound of my voice, or my appearance, or the memories the name brought back. "Mr. Dee's dead."

She started to close the door, but I put my hand against it to hold it open.

"Maggie," I said urgently, "it's me. I had plastic surgery, but it's me. I'm not dead. I—"

She gave a shove on the door and it slammed shut. From inside, she warned me, "I don't know who you are, mister, or what your game is, but if you don't get out of here, I'm calling the police."

Strike one.

I went downstairs and found a phone booth, looked up her number, and dialed.

"Hello?"

I had to talk fast before she hung up. "Maggie, it's really me—Dee. If you'll hear me out, I can prove it. And if I don't, I'll never bother you again."

There was a long silence on the other end as she considered my request.

"The meter's running, buddy."

I took a breath. "Okay, Maggie, think back to June 1950. You placed a call to Edwards at our Hong Kong office for me. It was a priority-one call, remember? I phoned you in the middle of the night so the overseas

231

operator would have the connection ready by the time the office opened. Later that morning, Edwards did call. Then a man named Philip Barringer phoned but you referred him to Eddie. That was the same day some of our livestock in Iowa came down with scabies. You issued the initial press statement and—"

She cut me off. "So you found some letters."

"That wasn't in letters, Maggie. That was a confidential conversation between us."

"Keep going."

"Okay, the last two letters I asked you to write concerned the trust fund for my children. But I wasn't in the office that day. I called you from home and asked you to attend to it over the phone. Further, I asked you to write yourself a bonus voucher for a thousand dollars and have Eddie countersign it."

I stopped and waited for her next move. It wasn't long in coming.

"Again, that's in files, mister."

I rushed on, explaining about our codes, our salary system, anything I could remember that only I would have known. I finally ran out of words. She remained unimpressed.

"You tell a good story, whoever you are. And I'll grant you that the voice is familiar. But you haven't said anything to make me believe you're Mr. Dee, back from the dead."

I sensed she was about to hang up, so I threw out my last card. "Maggie, are you still in love with Eddie?"

There followed a stunned silence. Then, her voice broke. "You really are Mr. Dee."

"Yes, I am, Maggie. And I have to see you."

Her response was quick. "Come right up. I'll be waiting for you."

She was waiting nervously for me at the door, forcing a smile as I reached the landing.

"Please, come in." She gestured me into the apartment, then closed the door behind me. Her reserve was killing. But what else did I expect? Sure, I knew who I was, but to her I was an Oriental man with Dee's memory.

She turned to face me. "I'm sorry. I'm finding this all very hard to believe. Is it really you?"

I nodded. "How are you, Maggie?"

She shrugged. "Okay, I guess."

"Are you still with the company?"

"Oh. Of course. Eddie set up a foundation after you . . . didn't come back. I'm the director of research and educational grants. There's even a scholarship named after Mr. Dee. I mean, after you."

I tried to put her at ease. "That's just like Eddie." She didn't know about his death—that much I knew already.

"And your wife, too. I mean, Mrs. Bridges. She really oversees it. She . . . Did you know she had remarried? . . . I'm sorry. I didn't think."

"I know all about that, Maggie."

We stood in silence for a moment. "Please, sit down. Can I get you some coffee?"

I shook my head, then decided to plunge right in. "When's the last time you saw Eddie?"

"About two weeks ago," she answered thoughtfully. "After he stepped down from the presidency, he vanished. He never even cleaned out his office. But I guess he'll do that when he comes back."

I looked at her. "He's not coming back, Maggie. Eddie's dead."

Her eyes widened. "What?" She pulled back as if reeling from a blow. "How?"

"It's a long story, Maggie, all involved with the takeover of Dee Enterprises. It was Moroni, Maggie. He killed Eddie and . . . kidnapped Donna. That's why I'm back."

"Don't tell me this . . . don't." She stood and paced without direction. "He can't be dead. He can't be. I don't believe you. I don't—"

I moved to her and took her in my arms as she began to cry, her body trembling as she sobbed. After a time, she quieted and sat down.

"Tell me how it happened. I have to know," she said quietly.

I told Maggie what I knew, which seemed to provide her with more questions than answers. "But if

Donna was kidnapped, Mr. Dee, why didn't Sylvia call the police?"

"She was warned not to. Moroni's going to use Donna's kidnapping to pressure Sylvia into selling the company to him."

Something seemed to click with Maggie. "So that's what the secret meeting is about."

"What meeting?"

Maggie was in control again. "Mrs. Bridges phoned me today and asked that I arrange to have Eddie's office ready for a top-priority meeting. She told me to oversee the preparations personally and be certain that the office was stripped of any type of documentation, from loose letters down to blank memo pads. None of that was unusual, but then, just before she got off the phone, she asked if I'd ever heard of a man named Moroni. I said I had and told her that you'd had some dealings with him in the past. She didn't ask anything else and I didn't tell her any more. But now that I think about it, I'll just bet that meeting is between Mr. and Mrs. Bridges and that man Moroni. But I never dreamed it would be about a kidnapping."

"When's the meeting, Maggie?"

"Nine tonight."

I glanced up at the clock. It was nearly seven-thirty.

"Can you get me into the building, Maggie?"

"Of course."

"And are the offices still positioned the same as when I left?" I asked.

She nodded. "Everything's just as you left it. Eddie wanted it that way."

I walked over to the window overlooking Third Avenue. Something was bothering me. I didn't know what. I could feel it deep down inside as I prepared myself for what I had to do. I couldn't go in there with the slightest kink in my emotions, yet there was this little thing ticking in the recesses of my mind. Something to do with Donna, her kidnapping. But what?

"Maggie, I want you to take me to that meeting."

"But they'll never believe it's you. You—"

"Just get me in the building," I told her. "They'll never know I'm there."

"Yes, Mr. Dee. You know I'll do whatever you want."

I smiled, more with relief than happiness. "Okay, Maggie, you can start by getting your coat."

She stood and looked at me as if for the first time, and I knew she was seeing the man behind the face. She was looking twelve years into the past, when trusting each other had been a fact of each of our daily lives. I knew Eddie's death was still on her mind, but I also knew she realized that if I didn't win against Moroni, Eddie would have died for nothing.

She looked to me with a deadly serious smile. "Okay, boss," she offered, just as she had more than a decade before.

18

Maggie and I walked silently to Fifth Avenue and the Tyson Building. Lost in my thoughts, I didn't hear her question.

"Mr. Dee?"

"Oh, sorry, Maggie. What was that?"

"When was Donna kidnapped?"

I thought a moment. "About two weeks ago."

She nodded and we continued to walk in silence. Then it was my turn to ask a question.

"What does my daughter look like?"

Maggie smiled. "Donna grew up to be as beautiful as Sylvia. She's an actress, you know. She went to drama school at NYU and was just in a play off-Broadway. I'm told she shows great promise."

Donna. An actress. I couldn't help but think of her as the little girl with golden curls who trailed after Sylvia, imitating her every move. I used to call her my "little pumpkin," and she used to say I was the "bestest" daddy in the whole world. But the little girl was gone now, and a young adult had taken her place.

"Tell me about Jeff."

We had stopped at a traffic light, and Maggie waited until we'd crossed the street to reply.

"Oh, he's so handsome, Mr. Dee. And he does very well in school." She hesitated, then continued. "He might even substitute for a professor next semester."

I sensed there was a lot left unsaid. "But what, Maggie?"

She responded too quickly. "No 'but,' Mr. Dee. He's a . . . very self-sufficient young man."

I looked at her, then smiled. "You don't have to cover for him, Maggie. Rumor has it he's something of a wise guy."

She smiled, then looked at me. "Well, Mr. Dee, he can be cold sometimes. But he did grow up without a father." She stopped, then hurried on. "Not that I'm blaming you. I'd never do that. But he doesn't seem to want to have anything to do with Dee Enterprises. Eddie offered him a job, but he turned it down. I think he just plans to go on for his master's degree in the fall."

I nodded. No, it wasn't my fault. I'd just left home when they all needed me, that's all. "Tell me more, Maggie."

"Well, Jeff's been studying judo for the past few years. He's testing for his black belt soon."

"Really?" Memory triggered scenes in my mind's eye. I saw Jeff, the little boy, lean and strong, practicing moves of the Gentle Way with me. I had taught him balance, how an opponent can be put down easily, and how never to underestimate anyone. Ducksun had taught me that, and I'd passed it on to my son. "Where will he be testing?"

"At a special tournament at Columbia."

I nodded. "Maggie, tell me honestly, what's he like?"

"Oh, he's all right, Mr. Dee. Like I said, he can be cold sometimes, and I guess he's a little cocky, but I can't help but feel that it's because he's insecure. I'm not sure he's as compassionate as he should be, but he's hardest on himself. You have to know that. He's honest about it. I know he's a good boy, deep down inside."

We were about two blocks from the building as darkness descended upon the city. The night people were slowly emerging from the shadows to prowl the streets until dawn.

"And what about Denise?"

At the mention of Denise, Maggie smiled proudly. "Well, her 'Aunt Maggie' might be biased, but you've got one very special girl there. Did you know she's working at Dee Enterprises?"

I was surprised. "No. I'd heard she was working, but . . . How'd that happen?"

I don't know why I was surprised. As far back as I could remember, Denise was always the one who wanted to know what I did at work and how hard it was, and who always wanted to come downtown with me to play in the office. She always said she wanted to grow up to be just like me, and I guess working at Dee Enterprises was a start.

"She became interested in the business when she was fifteen," Maggie explained. "So she started coming by to visit Eddie and her 'Aunt Maggie' after school. Her visits became more frequent and lasted longer, and she finally said she wanted to start working. At first Sylvia said no, that Denise was too young. But you couldn't keep Denise down. She found out about our new computer operation, learned all she could about the hardware and software, then talked herself into a job. She's got three women working under her now."

"At nineteen?"

"Like I said, she's a very special girl." Maggie stopped, then studied me. "Would you like to see her?"

"Of course, but—"

"Then it's done. Stop by tomorrow. I'll introduce you as Mr. Chan from our Hong Kong office, and have her give you the guided tour."

"Thanks, Maggie."

Our conversation turned to an update on the business aspects of Dee Enterprises. Sporting goods proved an astronomical moneymaker during the fifties. We even had several world champion major league teams pushing our baseball line. Sylvia's cosmetic subsidiary had branched and expanded into the fashion business. Several top-name European designers provided master patterns for Sylvia's clothing line and a new young Italian designer was doing an exclusive line of swimsuits for the summer.

"What about the meat packing division?" I asked.

"Well, people still eat."

"In other words, not so hot."

"It's breaking even and then some, Mr. Dee. But, unfortunately, it's a little short on glamour."

"But long on memory. Or used to be. What happened?"

Maggie sighed. "Products became more expensive, union contracts kept escalating, I don't know . . ."

We arrived at the building and, upon entering, I stopped at the building directory. Dee Enterprises now occupied four floors. Not bad.

Maggie led me to the elevator bank and we rode to the tenth floor. When the doors opened, I saw the polished brass plaque and my life before Korea came back to me all at once.

The office was a corporate crypt by night. Only the far-off sound of the cleaning crew disturbed the eerie quiet. The offices leading to the executive suite had changed in the last few years. Modern equipment had been installed everywhere. Against one wall was a row of strange-looking typewriters. All were connected to a wide cable which disappeared into the wall. I was too curious to just pass it by.

"What are these things?"

Maggie stopped, then smiled. "They're terminals leading to our 'big brain,' Mr. Dee."

"And what the hell is a 'big brain'?"

"I think I'll let Denise explain it all to you tomorrow. This is her department."

Terrific. I've been away twelve years and now my own daughter is going to have to explain to me how my own business works. Twelve years is a long time.

I shrugged, then turned slowly and took it all in.

Maggie nodded. "Our total revenues hit the eight-hundred-fifty-million-dollar mark in 1960, but our projections for the next decade are even higher. We see ourselves as a multi-billion dollar company in ten years. Did you know we're into oil now?"

"Oil? How the hell did we get into that?"

"It was one of Eddie's last business decisions." Maggie stopped, then took in a breath. Talking about Eddie was hard for her. "Before Eddie . . . left . . .

he transferred a select team of parent company management people to Far East Enterprises. They're working under Edwards now. A deal was closed with several Asian investors for the production and export of fossil fuel from Indo-China. We even beat the oil companies to it. Don't ask me how Eddie managed to do it because it was all very hush-hush. It seems he learned someone was buying enormous blocks of Far East Enterprises stock on the Hong Kong exchange. Edwards investigated, but uncovered only a holding company with heavy financial backing which appeared sympathetic to the corporate aims of Far East. Apparently Eddie believed someone was trying to inflate the value of Far East so it could fall like Far West did. What eventually developed from this investigation was a fresh deal to form a separate division devoted to fuel oil and other forms of fuel."

"Eddie never found out who these mysterious investors were?"

Maggie shook her head. "No. At the time, we proceeded through a series of lawyers in Hong Kong to form this company, so everything is well shrouded in mountains of paperwork. I only know about it because Eddie had me handle the paperwork personally. It was done quietly because the company formed was not a speculating firm. It was a solid, operating leasehold for extensive areas of Thailand, French Indo-China, Laos and Cambodia. And some others."

It was the way she said "some others" that made me wary. "What others, Maggie?"

"Well, Mr. Dee, they were described only by latitude and longitude. So I checked them out on a map."

"And?" I could sense she was trying to hold something back.

"Mr. Dee, I thought Eddie had been either duped or that he'd gone off the deep end. The leases were a patchwork quilt of ocean between French Indo-China and Australia. They were mostly along shoreline, but some were outside the twelve-mile limit."

"Ocean? Eddie bought ocean?" Oh, terrific, I thought. I wondered if he'd optioned the Brooklyn Bridge too.

"Yes," Maggie answered, "and I don't understand it. It was such a big secret, you'd think there was buried treasure beneath the waves." She shrugged. "Well, it didn't make any sense to me, but who am I to question?"

Maggie led me from the computer banks toward my office. Her desk, the same one she'd had years before, was still where it had been. In fact, all the furnishings were. It appears that Maggie's only concession to the sixties was a new IBM typewriter sitting on her side-desk.

Maggie led me to my office door, but I froze. I closed my eyes, steeled myself, then waved Maggie aside. This was something I was going to have to do alone.

I walked in, then closed the door behind me. I stood in the darkness for a moment, then reached out and flipped on the switch. And in the light I could see that Eddie had kept everything exactly as it was the day I'd left.

Feeling years slide away, I walked to my desk, pulled back the heavily padded chair, and sat down. The calendar on the desk was open to June 1950. Nearby, a yellowed copy of the *Times* bore headlines concerning the outbreak of hostilities in Korea and the attendant sessions at United Nations headquarters in Lake Success, New York. I looked around. The walls had been papered in 1949 and hadn't been changed since.

On my desk were several file folders stained by aged dust. The telephone on the desk seemed to be an antique, while the nearby Manhattan directory was obviously much smaller than the current issue.

A soft knock pulled me from my reverie, and Maggie quietly entered. "They're here, Mr. Dee. What would you like me to do?"

"Moroni?"

She shook her head. "No, just Mr. and Mrs. Bridges. They went directly into Eddie's office. They never even saw me."

"Good." I nodded. "No, just stay here. I'm certain they won't come into my office. I can handle this alone."

Maggie seated herself on the couch as I walked

toward the huge liquor cabinet. I went behind the small bar, touched the button underneath, and watched as the cabinet moved the three feet to reveal the secret passageway.

I felt my way down the darkened corridor to the light at the opposite end, which was streaming through the two-way mirror set ornamentally into a matching liquor cabinet in Eddie's office.

I stepped up to the mirror, and for the first time in twelve years I saw Sylvia.

Her hair was still the shade of blond I liked so much and she was every bit as beautiful as I'd remembered. Maybe even more so. She was dressed in a brown-and-white business suit with an open collar. From what I could see, she was still youthful, but there was a pain, a fatigue in her eyes.

I looked beyond her to Tim, still well-built, even if a hint of a paunch was now appearing. I wanted to hear their voices, so I flipped the switch activating the hidden microphone.

"I'm worried, Tim," Sylvia said. "Suppose they've already killed Donna."

"You can't think that way, Sylvia." He sighed. "God, I wish Eddie was here. He'd know how to handle Moroni. It's not like him to walk out like he did."

"Maybe his disappearance is somehow tied to Donna's kidnapping," Sylvia offered.

"I seriously doubt that Moroni would attempt abducting both of them," Tim replied. "The risk is far too great."

"Tim, we are an eight-hundred-million-dollar company. Moroni would try anything to gain control," Sylvia remarked coldly. "Dee always said Moroni was ruthless. Now we know how correct he really was."

Tim's face darkened before he answered. "Well, Dee isn't here, Sylvia," he said, annoyed. "I wish you and Eddie would realize the man is dead. He's been dead for more than a decade, yet you act as though he's going to walk through that door and solve all our problems. Believe me, Sylvia, I think Dee was one of the nicest guys who ever lived, but he's dead. You and Eddie Gardenia—wherever he might be—are going to have to accept that unpleasant reality. Especially if you're going to get Donna back unharmed."

Sylvia didn't answer. She did what I hadn't expected her to do. She rose and walked over to the bar. Through the mirror, she was only inches away from me and I could see those blue eyes clearly. I studied her face while fighting back the urge to reach through the glass and touch her. Her face was still striking and the onset of middle age had brought a serene quality to her beauty. When she was finished mixing her drink, Sylvia looked into the mirror. She was gazing directly into my eyes but would never know it.

There was a knock at the office door, which caused her to turn. Tim went to answer it, but the guard from the lobby pushed the door open. He told Tim there were men waiting to see Sylvia. Five minutes later, Moroni entered the office flanked by bodyguards.

Tim greeted Moroni with a formal cordiality as Sylvia took a seat, acknowledging Moroni's presence with an impersonal nod.

"May I fix myself a drink?" Jimmy Moroni asked while waving his bodyguards away. The two bulky men waited in the corridor.

"Go ahead," Tim replied.

"I'm willing to help Dee Enterprises out of its present bind," Moroni said while mixing a drink. He was just as close to me as Sylvia had been. It was well within my power to shatter the glass and kill him with one blow.

"I'm certain you are more than willing to help," Sylvia said dryly. "What is it you want?"

"Want? Such a hard word, Mrs. Bridges." Moroni took a seat, then smiled at Sylvia. "You're a lot like Dee, you know that? Okay, this is the situation: your daughter is being held by kidnappers. You do business with me and I'll guarantee her safe return."

"How do we know she's not dead?" Tim asked. "It's been two weeks since she was taken."

"She's not dead," Moroni said, almost bored with the questioning. "The kidnappers have her alive and safe."

Sylvia stood and stared at Moroni. "The 'kidnappers'? You talk as if you don't know who they are. Well, let me tell you something, Mr. Moroni. I know you're the one holding my daughter, so let's stop all this game-playing. What do you want?"

Moroni eyed her coldly. "I want your signature on an agreement transferring fifty-five percent of the voting stock of Dee Enterprises to the Overseas Trading Company. You will be paid the current fair market price, so it's all legal. I get the signature, you get your daughter."

Sylvia was motionless. "Do you hate my late husband so much that you would stoop to hurting his daughter?"

Moroni shook his head in mock dismay. "Mrs. Bridges, this is not a personal matter. It's just business. You're having a board-of-directors meeting in about two weeks. I want this transfer effected by then. Then you get your daughter."

"This type of transfer could take almost six months to execute correctly," Sylvia hedged.

Moroni nodded. "True. But your signature gives me the voting rights at all board meetings during the transition period. You see, Mrs. Bridges, I know what I'm doing."

Tim pulled himself up to his full height. "I'm sorry, Mr. Moroni, but Sylvia will not sign over controlling interest in Dee Enterprises, despite this obviously illegal attack by mobsters such as yourself."

Moroni turned from Tim to Sylvia. "You don't have a choice, Mrs. Bridges." He reached into his pocket and pulled out a wallet and pocket watch, placing them on the desk before Sylvia. "The kidnappers are not joking when they say you won't get your daughter back alive unless you sign."

Sylvia looked down at the articles. "Oh, my God, it's Eddie's wallet. And the pocketwatch Dee gave him." She looked up to Tim, then to Moroni. "You've killed Eddie." She didn't pose it as a question; for her, it was a statement of rude fact.

"I mean business, Mrs. Bridges." Moroni got up and moved to the door. "You know where I can be reached."

Moroni left the office and Sylvia sagged into a chair. Tim moved to her, then put a hand reassuringly on her shoulder.

"We'll figure out something, Sylvia," he promised.

"I hope so, Tim." She nodded. "Take me home, will you?"

I watched as they left the office, feeling invisible, nonexistent. The Dee they knew was long ago dead and buried.

I made my way down the corridor to my old office. Maggie was still there waiting for me.

"How did it go?"

"Moroni is holding Donna, as we suspected. He wants Sylvia to sign over control of the company in exchange for Donna's safe return."

As the words came out of my mouth, an insistent ticking began in the back of my head. Some fact I'd overlooked was still trying to force its way through. Instinct told me it had to do with Donna.

Maggie stood. "Was Eddie mentioned?"

I nodded. "Moroni produced his wallet and pocket watch. And admitted Eddie was dead." I watched as Maggie kept control of her emotions. "C'mon, Maggie, I'll take you home."

Maggie decided to stay behind by herself. I knew she wanted to be alone with her memories of Eddie in his office for a while. I took a cab to Forty-ninth Street and started walking toward Broadway.

I had been away too long. Times Square had been transformed. Gone were the flashy street guys who formerly inhabited the theater district. The racketeers who'd made gambling the Square's second-most-prosperous business had been replaced by hipsters, hustlers, and more prostitutes than I'd ever seen.

I crossed Forty-second Street and headed south away from the bright lights. The streets became darker, more remote, reflecting my increasingly ugly mood. In the shadows I could see Donna's face, I could hear her silent screaming. Somewhere in the blackness, they were holding my daughter captive. Thousands of lights in hundreds of buildings flickered on and off as I realized Donna was waiting for me, waiting for me to find her. I closed my eyes against the impossible odds I faced.

"Donna, I swear to you," I said aloud. "I'll find you. Just hold on, pumpkin. Just hold on."

Only the Manhattan night heard me.

19

Early the next morning, I began piecing together information from my informal network of contacts. I phoned Smathers, whom I hadn't seen the night before as planned because of the Moroni meeting, and gave him an update.

"They made their demand last night," I told him. "Sylvia and Tim met with Moroni in Eddie Gardenia's office."

"Good," Smathers responded. "I'm glad it was there. We've still got a bug in Eddie's office, so everything said is on tape. I'll listen to it the minute I get into the office."

"Then what?"

"Well, as you know, we can't use it in any court as evidence, but I have friends in the U.S. Attorney's office who will seek an official judicial opinion on the matter. I already had them place the request through the Cleveland field office so no one would guess where the actual bugging operation is really located."

"That could take a long time."

I could hear Smathers sigh. "It could."

"I can't wait. There's no way I'm going to let Moroni get away with this just because some judge has to wait to make a decision."

"I understand, Dee, but there's no percentage in winning the battle in the streets only to lose it in the courts."

"We'll see." I waited a beat, but Smathers didn't

say any more. "If you've got to get me, go through Maggie Thorp."

"Okay. But call me tonight. Whatever you do."

"Sure." When I hung up, a strange feeling came over me. Was there something I should have asked him? That single recurring item I couldn't remember continued to nibble at me.

I called Sam Terry, but he was out. I replaced the receiver, then stared at it. Donna. How could I help her? What was I going to do?

I shook myself out of it. I had another daughter to meet, and Maggie was expecting me. I took a cab up Fifth Avenue, then got out a few blocks from the Tyson Building and walked. I needed the time to prepare myself mentally. Denise had been such a tenacious, inquisitive child. I remembered how she used to follow me around the house, how she used to be waiting for me in the living room each night when I came home. She was always so full of questions, so bright, so full of drive and energy.

When I arrived at the eleventh-floor office, a secretary greeted me. "Oh, you must be Mr. Chan. Miss Thorp is expecting you."

I took a seat and waited. Several minutes later, Maggie swept in, acknowledged me with a cordial, businesslike greeting, and led me to the elevator bank.

On the tenth floor, Maggie led me toward the computer terminals. Before each one sat an operator, all working furiously, feeding information into the big brain. Nearly half these terminals were equipped with small boxes that spewed forth long, continuous streams of paper.

Denise was standing at the center of a terminal, reading over an operator's shoulder. Her arms loaded with file folders, she was totally engrossed in her work. All I could see of her was her profile, but I recognized her right away. She was very much a young woman. She was about five-foot-seven and very slender, her soft brown hair with golden highlights pulled back into a ponytail. Her clothing was fashionable but practical. And she wore a pair of gold-rimmed glasses perched on the tip of her nose. She looked over to where Maggie and I were standing, straightened her glasses, smiled, and walked over to us.

"Aunt Maggie, hi."

"Good morning, Denise," Maggie answered, edging me forward. "Denise, I would like you to meet Mr. Chan from our Hong Kong office."

"I'm very pleased to meet you, Mr. Chan," Denise responded as she shifted the folders to free a hand, which she then extended.

"Mr. Chan, this is Denise Dee," Maggie continued. "She is the supervisor of our computer center."

I froze for a moment. "I am very pleased to meet you, Miss Dee." I held her hand for a moment too long as the little girl I remembered melded into the young woman before me. I dropped her hand and hoped she hadn't noticed the expression in my eyes.

Maggie turned to Denise. "Mr. Chan is in New York on a Dee Enterprise fellowship to study our entire operation. He's not an expert in computers, so I thought you could explain your section to him. I have a meeting now, but may join you two for lunch."

Maggie excused herself and left. I turned to my daughter, who had been studying me.

"Was your trip to New York pleasant?" Denise led me to the terminals.

"Yes, thank you."

"Have you had a chance to see much of New York yet?"

Did I see much of New York? I knew it like the back of my hand. But Mr. Chan wouldn't have that kind of knowledge. Ordinarily.

"Oh, New York is hardly strange to me, Miss Dee. I went to grade school here on an exchange program years ago."

She nodded. "That explains your English. It's great. And by the way, why don't you call me Denise? And I'll call you Chan. Is that okay?"

"Of course." I realized I would have to ask the question any stranger would pose. "I notice your last name is Dee. Would it be the same Dee the company is named for?"

"It sure is. My father was the founder of Dee Enterprises. But he's been dead for many years."

"I'm sorry. I didn't mean to—"

"Don't apologize," she said, cutting me off. "Everyone asks."

"Oh," I said, then turned to the terminals. "I am really interested in your computer system. Could you explain its intricacies to me?"

"I sure can."

And she did. For nearly two hours she explained every aspect of not only the computer but also Dee Enterprises. I could only stare at her as she outlined every individual operation, completely surprising me. Her knowledge of Dee Enterprises was so thorough that it wouldn't have surprised me if she were to become the first female president of the company. I was pleased and very, very proud.

Denise glanced at her watch, then took a whistle from her pocket. The shrill sound penetrated the consistent clicking of the computers, and within seconds each operator stopped and looked up.

"Finish up and take an early lunch," Denise told them. "Input stations one and two, transfer your work to station three and remain available for fresh accounting data. We'll begin again after lunch."

The machines clicked briefly as each operator finished her entry. Denise led me into her office.

"I don't get much of a chance to get out for lunch, Chan. Is it okay if I have something sent in?"

I nodded. "Whatever you like."

Denise picked up the telephone, taking the liberty of ordering for me. But my attention for the first time all morning was not on her. I was staring transfixed at a large painting on the wall behind her desk—an oil of the *Sylvia D* with me standing on the deck. I recognized the scene. It was painted from an old photograph Sylvia had taken. The sense of loss I felt was a very real and present pain in my heart.

"Is something wrong?" Denise asked as she replaced the phone.

I shook myself out of it. "No, not at all. I was just looking at your painting. It is very powerful."

She turned around, stared at the painting for what seemed a very long time, then turned back to me. "Yes, it is. It's my father on the deck of his most prized possession, the yacht *Sylvia D.*" She hesitated, then continued. "He died only two years after purchasing it."

"And what became of the yacht following your father's death?"

"Oh, it's still in the family," Denise said. "My mother hasn't the heart to sell it. She keeps hoping that my brother, Jeff, will take it out, but he doesn't seem very interested in that."

I nodded, trying to hide my pleasure. Sylvia had never sold the boat. "It's a shame that such a beautiful craft should fall into disuse."

Denise laughed. "Don't worry, I plan on taking her out myself next year. I have a lot to learn about seamanship, but there's no way I'm going to let that beauty rot in drydock." She sat down behind her desk, then looked up at me. "You know, when I go near that boat, I can almost feel my father. It's almost as if he's there—but that's ridiculous, isn't it?"

I didn't now what to say. "Perhaps it is the warmth of memories that you are feeling."

She smiled. "Maybe. But you know, when Dad went away, and even after we'd been told he was never coming home, I used to wait for him. I'd stand near the door in the living room and just wait, positive he'd be returning to us *that* night." She shrugged. "He never did. But I know one thing: there's a lot more to his death than we've been led to believe. And one day I'm going to get to the bottom of it all."

She said this with such determination, I realized that she would, in fact, do just that. "Why do you believe you haven't been told the whole truth?"

Denise sighed. "A lot of things. Different things. Stories we've heard from time to time. I don't know if they're all true, or even if any of them are, but one day I'm going to find out. And I know where I'm going to start. There's one story I've heard dozens of times— that my father was close friends with a barbarous Korean warlord. That's where I'd start."

I was about to force words from my stunned mouth when the sandwiches were delivered. So she'd heard about Ducksun. And she was going to get to the bottom of my story. And she would. And then she'd find out I was alive, that I was involved in intelligence, and then she'd stumble onto Calloway's connection. And from that moment on, she would be in grave danger.

"You have researched your father's life extensively?" I asked.

She nodded as she removed the elastic band from her ponytail, shaking loose her hair. "It's the only way I could get to know him. Sort of like the painting. You know, it took me two years to bring it to the stage in which you see it. Like all paintings, it still isn't complete. Once in a while, I'll notice where it could use added shading or toning or something, so I'll put it in. The painting is very much like the strands of my family's life: strong, sturdy, but changing wherever and whenever necessary. I keep it there because I love my father deeply. I respect what he stood for and hope to carry out his aims. There will always be a Dee on the payroll at Dee Enterprises. Before, it was my father. Now it's me."

If I ever wanted to hold someone in my arms and tell her how much I loved her, it was Denise. Without my even being here during her formative years, my daughter had far surpassed what I ever wanted her, or any of my children, to be. She operated in the present while cherishing the traditions of the past and eagerly planning for the future.

"Is it not odd that the youngest daughter would be the one to follow in her father's footsteps?" I asked as we ate.

"I guess. But my older sister, Donna, is an actress and is off doing what she does, and my brother, Jeff . . . well, he has a lot of trouble handling anything that reminds him of our father."

I must have reacted, because she continued, "I don't think I said that right. Jeff was really hurt by Dad's absence. And I don't think he's come to terms with his hurt yet. Speaking of Jeff"—she glanced at her watch—

"we're going to have to cut this afternoon short. I've already made plans to attend a tournament at two o'clock at the Columbia gymnasium. My brother's competing."

I raised an eyebrow. "In what does he compete?"

"The martial arts," Denise answered. "He's testing for his black belt."

I was suddenly very interested. "In which branch of the martial arts?"

"Judo," she said. "He even taught me some so I could defend myself. He's going to be on the Olympics team, so his training schedule between now and 1964 will be pretty tight. He's got to be ready for the Japanese. I hear they're the best in the world."

"The Japanese and Korean teams rank very highly," I observed. "I, too, am very involved with the martial arts and have studied under several Chinese and Korean masters renowned throughout Asia."

"Really?" Denise was fascinated. "I've just got to introduce you to Jeff. He'd never forgive me if I didn't. You see, he's really good at this, much better than his Olympic classification indicates. His only problem is that there aren't very many Americans as good as he is, so it's hard for him to find a teacher. He worked out daily with a Japanese master up until a year ago, by which time he'd exhausted the man of his methods."

"That often happens," I observed. "But the Oriental masters teach a simple yet rigorous remedy for such situations. They say, 'Practice against yourself and you defeat your most dangerous enemy.' "

"Oh, Jeff would just love you," she said. "Will you come with me?"

"I'd like that very much."

We reached the gymnasium at Columbia about twenty minutes late and stood at the edge of the bleachers watching the match, which was already in progress. Denise explained that there were four rival schools competing in this tournament. Halfway through the schedule, Jeff's school was due to stage an exhibition that would include his black-belt test.

"Has Jeff defeated everyone else in his school?" I asked.

"Yes," she answered, "but to get the black belt, he has to defend himself from attacks. But why am I telling you? You already know all that."

We observed the tournament, and what I saw shook me. Any of the masters I had studied under at Ducksun's citadel would have committed suicide before allowing their students to progress with the stylistic defects I witnessed. I took a good long look around the gymnasium and discovered the only two Orientals in the crowd were seated on the judging panel. They seemed fairly serious compared with the jocular American judges. Any of these martial artists attempting to use his skills in the Far East would be sliced to pieces. There was a noticeable lack of philosophy in the students I observed. The physical strength was evident, but the mental discipline just wasn't apparent. If Jeff was of the same caliber I'd observed, then he wouldn't survive the Far Eastern teams in the upcoming Olympics.

"Is your brother better than these charlatans?" I asked Denise pointedly.

She turned her head to me. "Why, yes," she said, surprised. "Don't you think these men are any good? Their movements are like a symphony to me, Chan."

"Then you have never heard real music," I told her. "Compared with the students in Japan, these men are like children at play. If your brother hopes to compete on the Olympic team, then I pray he is far superior to what I've seen."

"Well, I imagine you have a right to be critical." Denise nodded casually. "The martial arts are a way of life to your people, but to us they're just a sport."

Nearly thirty minutes passed before one of the judges rose and walked over to the microphone. He was a smallish man, and from his accent I decided he had recently emigrated from the Far East.

"It is now time for the trial of student Jeffrey Dee," the Oriental master announced. "This worthy student applies to the masters for consideration in the earning of his black belt in the martial art of judo. The masters have found the student worthy of trial, so if the headmaster of his school will present himself, we shall begin."

An American master stepped forward, bowed deferentially to the Oriental, then motioned for Jeff to approach the mats. A moment later, I saw my son. He was as tall as I, but with a younger, more powerful build. He stepped onto the matting respectfully, bowing first to the judges, then to the members of the four competing schools. He then turned to face his headmaster.

"*Sensai.*" Jeff bowed. "I submit myself for trial and pray to be found worthy."

The headmaster returned Jeff's bow, then stepped from the mat. The test began as the headmaster issued various commands, which Jeff obeyed. His hearing, intuition, and reflexes had to be accurate in order for him to complete the drill successfully. The first fifteen minutes were leisurely compared with the grueling pace of the final thirty. The headmaster was good. He knew his moves better than I had anticipated, and forced Jeff to carry out every torturous step of the black-belt drill. Forty-five minutes after the initial command had been issued, the headmaster abruptly ceased and bowed to my sweating son.

Most of the crowd in the bleachers began applauding, but Jeff did not allow himself the distraction of such accolades. Under cover of these loud hand-clappings, the headmaster nodded a silent attack to one of the students in Jeff's school. Jeff caught his opponent a full arm's length away and parried the probe expertly. A second and third attacker appeared. For a full ten minutes Jeff was assaulted from all sides; he effectively intercepted, then downed each consecutive opponent. They were no match for my son. When the exhibition was over, the audience applauded Jeff's victory.

I watched intently, noting the disgusted expression on Jeff's face. During the exhibition, he'd committed several tactical errors that my refined eye had captured, but nothing for which the masters would deny him the black belt. They were just bringing him the black robe and belt for the ceremonial award when

Jeff walked a few paces from the mat and approached the masters on the judging panel.

"Sensai," Jeff said loudly but respectfully. "May this student apply for a further test? An additional trial?"

The crowd buzzed with astonishment, then hushed to hear his words. A judge replied immediately. "Student, you have proven yourself worthy of the black belt through this exhibition of your proficiency. What more do you seek from us?"

"I respectfully request another test," Jeff explained. "I do not feel the attacks thus exhibited were ever really a threat to me."

"Allow me to comprehend this situation," the second Oriental judge replied. "Any of those blows directed at you by these accredited attackers would have maimed or killed the uninitiated. Are you claiming that your level of expertise surpasses that of the black belt?"

"It is not my intention to discredit the belt," Jeff responded with forced calm. "I do not want to be awarded this honor without earning it. I wish to win it beyond any shadow of doubt. Therefore, I challenge the three headmasters of the opposing schools, and if I defeat these three esteemed men, I will take the black belt for my own."

I was quietly shocked at this obvious desecration. The crowd, however, applauded and urged the situation on, much the same as every bloodthirsty audience since the days of the gladiators. In his own way, Jeff was correct in his subtle accusation concerning the level of expertise in the different schools. He knew that the inadequacy of his test made the belt he had been awarded worthless. The crowd didn't realize it, but Jeff was only being honest with himself. Despite this, I felt his attitude would be the factor most capable of defeating him in a true competition. I searched my mind for a way to help him.

"See what I mean?" Denise told me. She had been standing next to me as Jeff issued his unorthodox challenge. "He could've just taken the belt, and everyone would be content. But, no, he thinks he has to prove something to the world."

"Maybe he does," I said easily. "I think I understand Jeff better than he understands himself."

Denise didn't answer, only looked at me strangely.

By this time the headmasters were ready and approaching the mat. Once the obligatory salutations were completed, the assault began. Within ten minutes Jeff had downed all the headmasters a number of times, proving his point. As a fitting finale, the three men attacked him simultaneously, but their bodies were repulsed by Jeff's vicious, calculated defense. Two of the headmasters went down hard on the mat, and the other one was thrown clear onto the gymnasium floor. I watched Jeff carefully. The boy didn't realize how good he actually was! Only his attitude blocked him from the road to greatness.

The headmasters bowed, then moved away from the mat. The members of Jeff's school seemed impressed with his performance but weren't overjoyed with him personally. As they tried bringing the robe forward for presentation, Jeff beckoned to the crowd. "Is there anyone else who would care to try me?" he challenged harshly.

There was no further applause from the audience.

"Young sir," I heard my voice answering. Then I realized what I had done. I didn't want to go through with it, but I was committed.

"Who said that?" Jeff wheeled around to face Denise and me. He looked to his sister and then to me with a puzzled expression.

"May I accept your challenge, youngest *Sensai*?" I asked respectfully. "I seek the honor of approaching the mat."

Jeff stared at my face, fully deceived. He smiled and answered, "Normally I would accommodate you, but if you want to commit hara-kiri, I suggest you go elsewhere."

"In being granted this humble body, *Sensai*, I take full responsibility for its durability. If I could approach the mat and engage you, then possibly we could learn together."

Jeff ignored me, but the audience was relentless. Now there were voices from every section of the gymnasium urging Jeff to accept my challenge or stand embarrassed.

My son turned to me, his eyes and voice cold as ice. "I accept."

Bending down, I removed my shoes, then approached the mat, considering my tactics. I hadn't thought out what I would do, but there were two highly advanced techniques I was certain Jeff couldn't possibly be aware of. One was the result of a year's training under one of Ducksun's harshest Korean masters, and the other was the result of an equally grueling period with a tiny but powerful Korean. If possible, I would use the Korean method because it was lightning-quick and would require only the tip of a single finger. The master from whom I had learned it claimed that no more than eight men of the entire population of the planet could effectively execute this move. But beyond that, I realized that if I chose this particular move, Jeff would feel its effect but it would be too fast for the crowd to see. To them, only the result would be apparent.

As I stepped onto the mat, the crowd fell eerily silent. We studied each other intently, and I watched as Jeff's face registered the slightest indication of bewilderment. He tried to down it, then faced me in the traditional ready position. My own stance was so completely unorthodox, however, that he was unable to tell whether I was ready to attack or defend. And his confusion mounted.

He studied me, and I could see the doubt mount in his eyes.

I remained calm, my arms dangling easily at my sides. I stared at him as if I commanded his entire fate. I did.

And he knew it.

In that instant, Jeff became frightened. He defeated himself.

I whispered several words in Korean, and as he reacted with just a phantom of fear, I moved.

In the next instant I was peering down at Jeff, who

was lying on the mat staring up at me. His eyes asked a thousand questions; his memory was urging a thousand answers.

I glanced over to the judges in the stands. They immediately realized what type of man was in their midst and rose from their seats to approach me. I had to get out.

I glanced down at Jeff, still sprawled on the mat. As his hand came up to his chin, where a slight bruise was forming, he offered me a slight smile.

I smiled back, then turned and quickly fled from the gymnasium.

20

Two days following my impromptu judo match with
Jeff, I found myself at Maggie's apartment eating the
first home-cooked meal I'd had since returning to New
York. Denise had told Maggie of what had happened,
and both my daughter and Jeff wanted to see me
again, but I had to make myself unavailable. It was
too dangerous for them. And for Donna.

"Denise won't let the matter rest," Maggie warned
me. "You're just lucky she's drowning in work right
now, or she'd be after you just like . . . well, just like
she used to be."

"Something special going on to cause all that work?"

"Yes," Maggie answered with a hint of puzzlement
in her voice. "There seems to be a great deal of
activity on the Hong Kong exchange concerning Southeast Asia Fossil Fuel. Just since your return, the stock
has risen seven full points on the Hong Kong market.
It's as if there's been a sudden influx of fresh cash or
an increasing liquidity in assets. But I don't know for
sure, since the whole operation's still top-secret."

I wondered whose money was behind such dramatic
increases. "Have any of the leaseholds become active,
or have any strikes been reported?"

Maggie shook her head. "No, none. In fact, SAFF
has spent money for twenty-three additional leaseholds in Indo-china, and most of those sites will take
at least two years to even begin setting up drilling
operations. That kind of expenditure should have caused
the stock to dip, but instead it goes up. I'll tell you one

thing, whoever it is who's covered these purchases knows the inner workings of Dee Enterprises very well."

I wondered to myself who would invest that much capital in such a short period of time. "Maggie, it sounds like someone is pumping SAFF with cold cash—and one hell of a lot, too. Either that or the value is being inflated as a prelude to a corporate takeover. And we don't need to lose another subsidiary." I sipped at my coffee. "Are you still trying to learn the identities of the principals in SAFF?"

"Yes, I am, Mr. Dee. I telexed Edwards in Hong Kong but I was referred to Eddie Gardenia for specific answers." She paused, then looked to me. "We both know that's not possible."

I started to respond, when the doorbell sounded.

"Are you expecting anyone?"

"No," she answered quietly while walking to the door. She peered through the peephole, then turned to look at me. "It's Sylvia."

"She can't see me."

Maggie nodded, then gestured to the bedroom. "In there," she said as she cleared away my place setting. I exited, but left the bedroom door ajar.

The doorbell rang for the third time as Maggie opened the door. "Why, Mrs. Bridges, this is quite a surprise."

"Good evening, Maggie. May I come in?"

Maggie showed her in and Sylvia turned to her. "I know I should have called, but I have to admit I just came over on impulse. I hope I'm not interrupting anything."

Maggie smiled. "Of course not. Can I get you some coffee?"

Sylvia shook her head. "No, thank you."

Maggie waited expectantly for Sylvia to say what was on her mind. It didn't take long.

"Maggie, have you heard anything about Dee lately? Has his name come up at all recently?"

"Why, Mrs. Bridges, what do you mean? His name comes up all the time at the office, of course, but if you're trying to say—"

Sylvia stood abruptly. "I don't know what I'm trying

to say, Maggie. I'm not even sure about what I'm feeling. But,"—she turned to face Maggie—"I've had the strangest feeling over the past few days that Dee is . . . well, here."

Maggie tried to maintain her composure. "Whatever makes you think that?"

Sylvia forced a smile. "That he's still alive? Nothing, really. At least nothing tangible. It's just that I almost feel as if he's watching over me, even at this very moment."

I froze behind the bedroom door. How could she know? But she did. Our love had created a bond between us that neither time nor geography could break.

"Sylvia," Maggie offered, "when two people love each other as much as you and Mr. Dee did, it's only natural that you'd always feel a closeness toward him, even after death."

"It's more than just a memory I'm feeling now, Maggie." Sylvia turned and studied Maggie. "Jeff and Denise both told me a very strange tale. When Jeff was testing for his black belt, he challenged the audience toward the end of his test. It seems that a man, an Oriental man, accepted the challenge, and within a second had my son on the mat."

Maggie nodded, nervously twisting her hands. "Yes, I did hear about that, Mrs. Bridges, but—"

"But before he did that," Sylvia continued, "he whispered something to Jeff, something in Korean. He said, 'Never underestimate your opponent.' Dee taught those words to Jeff, words he said he'd learned from a Korean warlord."

Maggie was beside herself. "You're not suggesting that Mr. Dee is . . ."

Sylvia shook her head in frustration. "I'm not sure what I'm saying, or thinking, anymore. But I do know that those words had a profound effect on Jeff. He usually gets angry when he's defeated, but not this time. He said very little—Denise was the one who told me about it—and then, out of the blue, he said he was taking the *Sylvia D* out for a run. It's as if this confrontation triggered a series of emotions that are allowing him to finally come to terms with his own past. And his father's." She paused, then sat down. "I just don't know . . ."

Maggie moved to her, but had no words to share.

Sylvia looked off, then spoke as if she were alone in the room. "I can't help wondering," she said softly, "if I could handle the shock of finding out that Dee is alive . . ." She looked at Maggie, then sighed. "Tell me, Maggie, who is this Mr. Chan?"

"Mr. Chan is from our Hong Kong office. Did Denise mention him to you?"

Sylvia nodded. "Yes. And she told me he was the man who defeated Jeff. And she also told me that when he was observing the computer facilities, he asked a lot of questions about our family. Do you have any idea why he'd do that?"

Maggie stuttered a sound of hesitation, then looked at Sylvia. "No, I don't, Mrs. Bridges. And I had no idea he was the same man who defeated Jeff. If you'd like me to talk to him, I could—"

"That won't be necessary. I think I'll speak to him myself when I see him. You might pass that along to him, though. Tell him we will meet—when the time is right."

Sylvia departed, leaving a very nervous and shaky Maggie in her wake. I came out of the bedroom and Maggie looked over to me. "Did you hear everything, Mr. Dee?"

I nodded. "Yes, everything."

"So why don't you go to her, tell her who you are? She needs you right now, Mr. Dee. And I think you need her."

I smiled at Maggie, always concerned for others, yet living such a solitary life herself. "I can't, Maggie. Sylvia is remarried, has a new life. My children are grown and on their own. I can't complicate their lives now by dropping back in. There's another reason too, Maggie, and this one's a gem. If I'm alive, they'll all be dead. In order to save them, I have to deny who I am."

*   *   *

I walked down Third Avenue, and as I looked for a cab, my thoughts returned to Donna. I realized there was only a slim chance of my locating her unless Moroni made a mistake, a mistake that would lead me to her. As I waved down a taxi, I got that nagging feeling that there was still a tiny bit of information I wasn't remembering, something important. And then it was gone.

As I settled back for the ride to the Spring Street address I'd given the driver, it was impossible to banish my frantic fear over Donna's abduction and the knowledge that, if pushed, Moroni would go after Denise and possibly Jeff in his quest to swallow Dee Enterprises. I felt I had to take some action that would compel Moroni to play his hand prematurely, a move that would lead to some strategic blunder I could use to my advantage. But what? Moroni was a master of Machiavellian games and I'd been gone for a long, long time.

I left the cab at lower Spring Street and walked toward a sooty sign reading "Social Club." No other name was necessary; everyone knew what this place was. The club consisted of a suite of rooms specializing in after-hours alcohol while providing a modest gambling playground for high rollers who desired a walk on the shady side with women other than their wives. It was also a backroom caldron of multimillion-dollar deals between crime and political corruption.

During the daylight hours Sam Terry was an honest, forthright businessman, but his true kingdom and power emanated from these basement rooms that had gone unwashed for a generation. There was a decidedly old-world flavor to the place, and anyone who knew the world of organized crime in New York could almost sense the ghosts of Lupo the Wolf and Masseria and Marranzanno. This social club was one of the few remaining places the families considered sacrosanct because it had been founded at the turn of the century by Lupo and had since been used by every "prince" ascending to power.

As I entered the club, heads turned. Most of the faces were identifiable through the *Daily News*, and many of the gray-haired gentlemen in dark blue business suits probably remembered Luciano as a young man. All were friends of Sam Terry.

I imagined they all wondered at my Oriental appearance. Within a minute a burly guard approached me.

"Members only," he quietly informed me.

"I have an appointment with Sam Terry."

He studied me for a moment, then nodded. I watched as he walked to the rear of the club and disappeared. He returned almost five minutes later. "What's your name, sir?"

"Dee."

His expression relaxed and he almost smiled. "Okay. Follow me."

The thought crossed my mind that as soon as possible I was going to get this face fixed.

Passing through Sam Terry's domain was like strolling through the history of organized crime in the city. During his more active days, Sam would never have permitted such a gathering of powerful men, but since his retirement from the business and his general acceptance as a respected elder available to assist anyone, Sam had opened his life just a bit wider to allow the local businessmen and politicians to rub elbows.

The guard took me through two doors and then down a lengthy hallway until we seemed to have walked under the building to the other end of the block. We probably had.

We came to a large door etched with raised Florentine scrollwork. The guard knocked, then waited. I figured it was to allow Sam to let visitors who wanted no witnesses to their meetings with him quietly leave through a back door.

The guard finally let me in, then vanished. Sam was coming around from behind a large desk with his hand extended in friendship. Nearby stood the ever-present bodyguard.

"I was wondering when you would turn up," he said as he gestured to a stuffed chair for me, then indicated a box of cigars. "Smoke."

I shook my head and settled into the chair. "Sam, have you been able to learn anything about Donna?"

"I had my boys nosing around the past coupla days, Dee, but there's nothin' on the streets." He shook his head. "But I don't think Moroni's got his own boys guarding her. If he did, then somebody woulda put that information up for sale. Everybody's a rat when it comes to money. Anyway, if somebody had, I'd a bought it. But so far, nothin'."

I was about to answer when something went click in my memory, the little fact I'd been searching for. It surfaced for the briefest second, then buried itself again. Was it something Terry had said? If so, what?

"Are there any other rumblings from inside Moroni's organization?"

"Only one, which I find very, very interesting." Sam took a puff of his cigar, then continued. "I got it on good authority that Emory Kraner's pulled out of Moroni's Overseas Trading Company, money and all."

"Which means Moroni isn't financially capable of taking over Dee Enterprises."

"Not so fast," Sam cautioned. "Moroni's got to go through with it. He already promised me fifteen percent, remember?"

Sam was right. Moroni was not about to lose face with a man as important as Sam. He'd find the money—somehow.

"But he's still got to handle it himself, right?"

Sam shrugged. "Looks that way."

"Which would make him extremely vulnerable." I nodded to myself. "Which could lead to his making a mistake."

"A strong possibility." Sam fell silent, then looked directly at me. "Have you ever heard about a company called Southeast Asia Fossil Fuel?"

"Where'd you hear about that?"

"One of my boys picked it up from one of Moroni's people. Sounded to him like there was some kind of deal cooking between Moroni and that company."

Could it be? I asked myself. Could this be the one chance in a million that the silent partner in SAFF was actually Jimmy Moroni? Eddie might not have suspected Moroni's presence in the Orient, but I knew better. Had Eddie unwittingly sealed a pact with Moroni? If Moroni could order my murder amid the chaos of the Korean War, he was certainly capable of leading Eddie down the garden path. And suddenly, as all that came together, I realized that my entire corporate empire was about to be destroyed, with my daughter Donna just an expedient pawn.

"What's wrong, Dee?" Sam placed his cigar into a crystal ashtray and studied me.

"I think I've just seen a ghost, Sam."

"You look like it. So tell me about this Southeast whatever-it-is."

"It's an ultrasecret subsidiary of my company, founded by Eddie Gardenia before his death. Only a handful of people in this country even knew about it."

"That handful must have included some of Moroni's people, Dee."

I shook my head as if trying to clear it. "There's only one way I can figure it. Eddie must have blindly sealed a partnership with a front company controlled by Moroni. If he did . . . I can't think of any way to undo the damage."

Back on the street, I wondered if I, this one time, had underestimated my opponent. I found myself in front of a phone booth and decided to check in with Maggie.

"I was hoping you'd call, Mr. Dee," Maggie said after the usual exchange of greetings. "Your friend Smathers called not twenty minutes after you'd left. He said you were to call him immediately. He left this number."

In seconds I was dialing Smathers' number. It rang nearly twenty times before Smathers, out of breath and gruff, answered.

"Where the hell are you?" he demanded without any of the usual pleasantries.

"Pierce and West Broadway. What's going on?"

"Wait there," Smathers ordered. "I'm on my way."

I stood on the corner for only fifteen minutes before the FBI agent rolled to a stop at the curb in an innocuous Agency Chevy. I got in, he nodded to me, threw the car into drive, and took off.

Smathers drove through the darkness of New York City in silence. I figured when he was ready to talk, he would. I glanced at his profile as he kept his eyes on the road, and I could sense that he was deciding how to formulate what he had to say, almost as if he knew whatever it was would trigger some violent reaction from me.

He drove south along West Broadway to Canal Street, then wheeled the car into the hungry blackness of the Holland Tunnel. Within several minutes the stench of exhaust welled up around us and Smathers began to talk.

"The New Jersey state police found a body in a garbage dump not far from the tunnel exit. They cabled us for an ID and we sent some of our guys down there to secure." He hesitated. "From the description, I think it's Eddie Gardenia."

I took a deep breath. "Did the fingerprints check out?"

"No prints," Smathers answered. "This was a classy gangster hit, Dee. Two bullets through the head, hands and feet severed to obscure identification. There were no papers on the body. They told me the body's been there a few days, and decomp is setting in, but I figured if it was Eddie, you'd be able to tell."

He was right, but why was the FBI involved? "Murder isn't a federal crime, Smathers. What's your interest?"

"Murder isn't, but crossing a state line in the execution of a crime is. It's only a technicality, but a good one. If it's Eddie, we can finally, officially, get involved."

I considered his intention, fully realizing that Smathers would be compelled to reveal my identity to his superiors if the Bureau entered the picture. I could imagine the upheaval in the intelligence community were the story of my survival to surface. After all, they'd written me off a long time ago. If there's one eventuality which the Agency doesn't appreciate, it's an agent who can't stay dead. Or those, like Calloway, who go into business for themselves. Once the FBI began hunting for clues to Eddie's murder, they would stumble across Donna's kidnapping, a situation of which Smathers was officially unaware. They would keep hunting and double-checking and backtracking until ultimately arriving at the supersecret doors of the CIA complex in Langley, Virginia. Then the real investigation would begin. It would blossom into a festering political matter. Sure, the FBI could legally intercede, but such an action would get Donna killed.

"What do you plan to do?" I asked Smathers.

"First we have to identify the body."

"I know that. I just want to make sure that nothing happens that could put Donna in more danger than she's already in."

"We'll be careful, Dee. But you've got to know that I can't withhold information concerning your identity much longer. I'm not going to volunteer anything, but if asked directly, I'll have to tell the truth, understand?"

"You still didn't answer my question," I pressed. "What are you going to do?"

"I'm pretty sure it's Eddie, so I ordered all phone taps and bugs on Moroni's place discontinued. I don't want any taps in place prior to the time of demonstration of probable cause. Then I'll ask the court for authorization for legal surveillance. Then the bugs go back in and we start collecting legal tapes. And if you're wondering, it'll take a couple of weeks to get it all going."

I allowed this to sink in as we turned off a ramp, then headed south along the New Jersey Turnpike. In the distance, under newly constructed skyways, was the entrance to a dump. Flashing red lights and numerous vehicles were parked along the access road as several heavily armed state troopers checked identities. Smathers' FBI card gained us entrance, and within a few minutes we were talking to the agent in charge of the Newark office.

The following moments were a gruesome ritual. The law-enforcement officers spread apart, allowing us access. Lying in the tall weeds next to a mountain of garbage was a body covered by a rubberized sheet stenciled with the emblem of the New Jersey state police. Nearby, a medical examiner completed his on-site report. I nodded my readiness and a trooper pulled back the sheet.

There is no image on this earth like the face of death. It bears the screaming expression of someone staring wide-mouthed at the gates of hell as they swing wide open with abandon. A final moment of intense beingness is captured, then etched across muscles more accustomed to a smile or frown.

Eddie had died horribly. His life had ended swiftly enough to preserve that horror for my eyes to see. I saw that the back of his head was blown away; his face was sunken where there there had once been firmness.

"Is it him?" Smathers whispered.

I turned on my heel and walked away, heading back toward the parked Chevy. I watched as Smathers finished up his business; then he approached me. No words were spoken as we got into the car and headed back toward Manhattan.

"I assume you don't want to go on record," Smathers surmised.

"If I did, then I'd be subject to an inquest. I can't do that."

"But it was Eddie."

I hesitated, then finally nodded. "Yeah, it was Eddie."

As we turned onto the turnpike, I became silent. My mind flashed back to the days I had spent living with Ducksun in Shanghai, to one of the many stories of terror, vengeance, and revenge he used to tell. He had once told me a tale of a hired assassin who brought justice to a cruel prince in a strangely unorthodox manner. I remembered the story in vivid detail, then realized that Ducksun's parable of death was designed for just such an occasion as this.

Returning to Manhattan, Smathers dropped me near my room. When he was well out of sight, I walked into Chinatown and sought out the address of Ducksun's American contact. The old man I encountered looked up sharply at the sound of the Warlord's name.

"Ah, you are the one called the Server," he barely whispered. "We know of your arrival and have already pledged assistance to Ducksun. What is it you seek?"

The Server. The thought stirred within me.

I stared into the old man's eyes, reading the respect and obedience I saw there. It was the same look I'd seen in the eyes of Ducksun's two bodyguards as they placed revolvers to each other's foreheads so many years ago. The Server. I finally realized what the words meant.

I quietly informed the Korean elder of my needs.

The Server had finally come home.

Three nights later, I was perched high on the wall of Moroni's estate on the Hudson River. The unusual weapon I held in my hands, complete with appropriate attachments, was ready. Carefully I searched through the infrared sniperscope for my first target.

A lone Doberman came into view. I tracked him, waited, then squeezed off the first shot. The weapon's recoil was slight. The Doberman was dead. The weapon's accuracy was incredible.

A second dog appeared from the shadows. I reloaded, then tracked and pressed the trigger a second time. The second dog whipped backward, a hole ripping his throat open. I waited a long minute, then pulled in a deep breath.

The bloodletting was about to begin.

21

I returned from Moroni's estate both mentally and physically exhausted. What had transpired there from the moment I killed the first prowling dog until I faded into the night had so wrenched my humanity as to freeze my soul.

I'd dismantled the weapon, disposing of it in several sewer sites along the return journey, then found my way back to my room. I ripped off my clothing and forced myself under the healing spray of a hot shower. But even that couldn't wash away the smell of death.

Beyond tired, I crawled into bed, but my body, so woefully in need of sleep, fell victim to a vibrantly alive consciousness. As I stared at the overhead lightbulb, my entire life flashed before me. Like the proverbial drowning man, I replayed every detail from my first moment of human awareness to my present. I reviewed it much as if I too had died in the dark shadows of Moroni's guarded compound.

What was I doing in this place, at this time? The question had no answer. Fate had selected me to rescue my daughter. Destiny demanded it of me, and I obeyed.

I dozed, then woke several times during the next few hours like a man cradled in the arms of death as dreamy visions of my life emerged from the soft blackness. I could see everything up to and including the horror at Moroni's estate. I was death creeping silently across Moroni's well-trimmed lawns; I was the execu-

tioner's sword poised and ready to strike; I was revenge. But in it all, I was alone.

I had gone to terrorize Moroni into an error that
might reveal Donna's location. But as I stood in the
stark shadows near his plush home, I realized the
darkness of my intentions. Four guard dogs lay dead
in the grass behind me. Human henchmen lay ahead.
And as the sweat dripped from my forehead, I knew I
had reached the point of no return.

I had gone to kill Moroni. Yet he still lived.

From the depths of my dreams I heard a sound, a
pounding at my door. I shook myself awake, then
struggled to the door. "Who is it?"

"Smathers."

I unbolted the door and Smathers, briefcase in hand,
moved inside. He stared at me, then grinned slightly.

"You look like you've had quite a night, Dee. Been
busy?" I could tell by the tone of his voice that he
knew exactly what I'd been up to.

"What time is it?"

Smathers shook his head, then tossed the briefcase
on the bed. "Early afternoon. Did you dump the
crossbow?"

"How did you know what I'd used?"

Smathers moved to the briefcase, opened it, and set
up a small tape recorder/player. "You know, Moroni
doesn't know what hit him. Listen for yourself."

He pressed the button and the machine came alive
with the voices of Jimmy Moroni and Philip Barringer.

BARRINGER: Good afternoon, Mr. Moroni. This is a
   surprise. What can I do for you?
MORONI: Don't talk to me about surprises. I've
   had enough for one day, counselor. Somebody got
   into my house last night.
BARRINGER: Into your house? That's not possible.
MORONI: Really? Well, somebody did, and I got
   six dead bodies and four dead guard dogs to prove
   it.
BARRINGER: I had no idea . . . How did they . . . ?
MORONI: Kill them? With a fuckin' crossbow. One
   guy, acting alone, from what the cops said. And all
   the outside guards were found with twelve-inch steel

shafts stickin' outta their chests. Jesus Christ, one guy who's been with me for years bought it while lighting a cigarette. He never knew what hit him 'cause he died standing up. We found him nailed to the side of my house with a shaft that went through his neck buried in the wall. I still can't believe it. I mean, how close do you have to be to do that to someone? This crossbow killer must have been standin' right next to the guy.

BARRINGER: A crossbow? That's pretty hard to believe, Mr. Moroni. I mean, they're used against thousand-pound grizzlies, aren't they?"

MORONI: Philip, how in fuckin' hell do I know who goes around killing anything with a crossbow? Most of the guys I deal with use guns. I even asked the cops who would use something like that, and you know what the cops said to me? "Someone who hates you one hell of a lot, Mr. Moroni." As if I didn't figure that one out all by myself.

BARRINGER: Well, at least you weren't killed. Were any members of your family harmed?

MORONI: Harmed? Look at this. *(Pause while Moroni placed an object in front of Barringer.)*

BARRINGER: It looks like a lock of hair.

MORONI: You bet your ass it's hair. It's what's left of my daughter's ponytail. My daughter, you understand?

BARRINGER: But still, she wasn't harmed, was she?

MORONI: *(Very long pause.)* That's a stupid question, Philip. Of course she was harmed. She'll never feel safe again because this bastard managed to get into my house and slice off her ponytail, all without waking her up. In one night, this operator's made a shambles of my security system.

BARRINGER: *(Voice calming.)* Have you or the police been able to figure out how the guy got in?

MORONI: Oh, that one was simple to figure. He just went over the wall, killed four vicious, expensive guard dogs and six of my best men. Piece of cake, right? *(Pause.)* He crept through my home like some godawful ghost on a haunting. He sliced off my daughter's ponytail and then put it on my bedroom dresser so I'd be sure to find it. A calling card from people like that, I don't need.

BARRINGER: Mr. Moroni, it doesn't make sense that he would kill six guards and not touch you.

MORONI: Yeah, I know. I been thinkin' about that ever since I got up. What bothers me is that I know the best, most effective, highest-paid killers in the business. I know them and I know how they operate. You tell me who was killed and how the hit was done, and most times I can tell you who had the contract. But this crossbow killer I don't know. *(Pause.)* Before coming over here, I was on the phone for ninety minutes, making calls all over the country. Nobody knows this guy. No one's even heard of anybody using a crossbow on a job. The guy's an independent, Philip, I'm his target, and that scares the shit out of me.

BARRINGER: *(After long pause.)* Mr. Moroni, tell me about the killings. Did all the men die from arrows?

MORONI: Steel shafts, friend, with two little prongs at the end, prongs that rip and tear as they go through you. But to answer your question, the first four guards died that way. The other two were found in the house. The medical examiner said he'd never seen anything like it. Based on the bruises on their bodies, he claimed the man died of burst hearts.

BARRINGER: Burst hearts?

MORONI: Yeah, sorta like somebody shoved a stick of dynamite into the guy's ticker. The body in the kitchen was hit three times—chest, head, and neck. They're gonna say he died of a broken neck, but he shoulda been so lucky. The poor bastard had caked blood coming out of his ears, nose, mouth, and— catch this—his eyes.

BARRINGER: And no one heard this killer? I mean, not even the sound of a body dropping? C'mon, Mr. Moroni, it's contrary to the laws of nature that someone could kill ten living things without being heard.

MORONI: Well, whatever laws this guy lives by, they don't have nothing to do with nature. How else do you explain a phantom murderer who can pick off six guards, four Dobermans, and never bend a blade of grass? And what the fuck am I supposed to do? Seal myself inside a lead booth? *(Long pause.)* This scares the hell out of me, Philip. This maniac was standing only inches away from my daughter, Erica. I don't know what he planned on doing, but if he wanted to shake me, he did.

BARRINGER: But I keep coming back to the fact that he didn't kill you. You're not dead.

MORONI: Yeah. Philip, listen to me. I live in a world where any of my business associates could buy my life at any given time. Some gunsel could pop up from behind a parked car and I'm history. I've always been able to deal with that. It goes with the territory. But what I can't deal with is building a house far more secure than the damned FBI Building, hiring the best guards in the world, and then having some faceless killer play with me and my security system like none of it matters.

BARRINGER: Mr. Moroni, if this killer stopped short of killing you or of harming your family, then he must have meant this as some type of warning. Do you think someone like, perhaps, Sam Terry might be behind it?

MORONI: No. This smells more like . . .

BARRINGER: Like whom?

MORONI: *(Pause.)* Dee.

BARRINGER: *(Patronizingly.)* Mr. Moroni, he's been dead for years.

MORONI: Yeah? Well, somebody got into my house and left Dee's calling card.

BARRINGER: But he's dead!

MORONI: How do I know that? All I've got is Calloway's word that he's dead. They never found a body.

BARRINGER: I think you're grabbing at straws, Mr. Moroni. He couldn't have survived Wolmi-Do.

MORONI: I hear Al Wong did. *(Long pause.)* You know, if Dee walked into this office right now, I wouldn't bat an eye. *(Pause.)* Well, none of this changes the fact that someone left a trail of blood through my home last night, and I have a sickening hunch that it all ties in with Dee. I know it sounds like I'm claiming he could reach beyond the grave, but you had to know the man to understand what I'm saying. And I'm saying, on my mother's grave, it scares the shit out of me.

BARRINGER: What do you propose we do?

MORONI: I want you to close the deal with Sylvia Bridges immediately. The money is ready at Pan International Bank and the lawyers for the Overseas Trading Company have drawn up the appropriate papers. Just you make sure you close it, and fast. I'll be at the usual place.

BARRINGER: And about the girl?

MORONI: Call Calloway. He'll know what to do. Let me know when you've set it up.

The reel of tape spun to a halt and the trailing end slapped against the machine. I gazed at Smathers as a smile began to form on my lips. Deep in my mind something had clicked and I suddenly knew how to find my daughter. Hell, I'd really known all along. On another tape, one that Smathers had played in Korea, I had heard a conversation between Tim Bridges and Philip Barringer. At the end of their meeting Calloway had arrived at Barringer's office, telling the secretary to disturb the meeting so he could speak with the lawyer. Whatever it was that had forced Calloway to this indiscretion served to register the act in my memory. It linked Barringer directly to Calloway on a personal basis, and now, on this new tape, Moroni ordered Barringer to contact Calloway and expedite the deal. And so now I knew how to find Donna.

My violent play against Moroni had stirred his deepest fears, resulting in the mistake I'd hoped he'd make. A thousand different scenarios raced through my mind, but they all boiled down to the reality that I'd now have to squeeze Philip Barringer like he'd never been squeezed before. He was, indeed, the weakest link in Moroni's chain.

Smathers read my mind. "You heard something on the tape that I missed, didn't you?"

"Yet bet I did."

"What was it?"

"How to find Donna." I smiled with the first sense of satisfaction I'd experienced in days. "It's been bothering me ever since you brought me the original tapes in Korea. Up until this moment, I'd totally forgotten that Barringer had dealt with Calloway before and, most probably, would be able to contact him now. It would be the perfect way to insulate Moroni from the actual kidnapping while allowing him to retain total control of the situation. Barringer knows where they're holding Donna, and believe me, he'll tell me before the next sun sets."

Smathers drove me uptown to the suite of expensive offices Barringer occupied in the Colman Building. I told Smathers to wait in the car and I entered the spacious lobby. Once inside, I noticed a public phone and decided to call Maggie before seeing Barringer.

"Maggie," I said after getting a connection, "have you heard anything from Sylvia about a meeting?"

"No, Mr. Dee, I haven't," she answered. "Mrs. Bridges was in today but she didn't mention anything about one."

I nodded to myself. "Well, I have reason to believe that she'll be meeting with Moroni very soon. Keep your ears open."

"Will do, Mr. Dee. Oh, by the way, Southeast Asia Fossil Fuel rose dramatically on the Hong Kong exchange again. Ten points. I began wondering about it, so I took the liberty of placing a call to Edwards at Far East. He told me the increases were legitimate due to a secret but very valuable acquisition. He wouldn't go into detail, except to indicate that there is a large amount of fresh cash coming into the firm."

"Did he say who was spreading that kind of money around?"

"No, Mr. Dee. He would only admit that it was from within our own corporate structure. He refused to elaborate."

I considered it for a moment, but just now it wasn't a priority. "Thanks, Maggie. I'll check in again later."

I had just stepped away from the phone when the elevator arrived, and I rode it to the fourth floor. I walked down the long carpeted corridor to Barringer's office, stopping before the mahogany double doors with the plaque "Philip Barringer, Attorney at Law." Well, today Barringer was going back to school for a lesson in unwritten law. I pushed the door open and went inside.

The nearest desk in the wide, bright reception room was manned by a pretty blond. She looked up. "May I help you, sir?"

"Yes," I said quietly. "Mr. Chan to see Mr. Philip Barringer."

She glanced down at the appointment calender, selected a pencil, and ticked off each name before glancing back to me.

"I don't have you listed on my daily, sir. Do you have an appointment?"

I looked by her to another set of doors, knowing Barringer's office was behind them and, with any luck, Barringer himself. "I didn't think I'd need an appointment to see an old friend. Philip and I go back a lot of years. Went to college together, in fact. I'd really like to surprise him."

"In that case," she said as she went for the phone, "I'll buzz him and let him know you're here."

I had to stop her. "Don't do that. I don't want to disturb him if he's with a client. I can wait until he's finished."

She stopped, phone in hand. "Fine with me." She replaced the phone. "I'll get Mr. Barringer's attention when he's finished with this meeting."

The receptionist resumed her work while I seated myself. Several times during the next few minutes I felt rage build within me, but I contained it, knowing that I couldn't allow unbridled anger to wreck my single opportunity of freeing Donna. I couldn't just barge into Barringer's office and threaten him, with some unsuspecting witness watching. I had to be absolutely certain he and I were alone. And for that, I could wait.

Almost twenty minutes later, the receptionist rose and walked to the restroom, leaving her station unguarded. A few minutes later, the wide doors opened and two men emerged shaking hands. Then the younger man walked back into his office and I knew I would have Barringer exactly where I wanted him: alone.

The blond receptionist hadn't returned, so I moved to the doors unchallenged. I opened the door, walked inside, and closed the door behind me. Barringer, on the phone, looked up in annoyance.

"Just a minute, Joe," he said into the phone while looking directly at me. "Who are you and what the hell do you think you're doing here? Get out of my office."

In response, I moved to his desk and brought my left hand down on the telephone, shattering it into a thousand pieces with a single blow, severing his connection. As Barringer' eyes widened in surprise, I reached across the desk and pulled him forward by the throat.

"One time, Barringer," I hissed. "Where is Donna?"

"Who . . . are you?" he breathed, spitting blood.

"Where?" I demanded, tightening my hold.

He said nothing, so I brought my free hand around, located a pressure point, and touched it, sending ripping pain through his body in countless waves. He screamed, but no sound ever passed his lips because of my grip around certain key muscles of his throat. His eyes bulged and I let up, allowing the pain to subside. Barringer indicated he wanted to speak, so I loosened my grip once more.

"I . . . don't know . . . where she is . . . don't know . . ." he wheezed while gulping for air.

"Really? Well, listen well, Barringer. Last night I put a ponytail on Moroni's dresser. Tonight it'll be your head."

Barringer's face filled with terror as he realized I was the killer responsible for the carnage at Moroni's estate. But still he shook his head. "Don't . . . know . . ."

"Listen, you son of a bitch," I warned, "if you think what I did at Moroni's house was terrible, then you haven't thought it through. If you don't tell me where they're holding Donna Dee, I'm going to torture you right here, right in your own office, with help just beyond that door. Only you'll never be able to scream. Your heart will explode long before you get to make a sound."

Barringer choked blood and air and indicated again

that he wanted to speak. I loosened my grip but it took him several long moments before he was able to form the words. His voice was raspy, his body shaking, the smell of fear rising from his body. But Philip Barringer forced out the words revealing where my daughter was being held. In fact, he practically drew me a map.

When he finished, I looked down into his eyes as he silently pleaded for his life. I wouldn't kill him. He wasn't worth it. But I needed to buy some time, so with a single motion I put him out.

I walked out of his office, closing the door behind me and smiling just like any other satisfied client. As I passed the receptionist, she looked up at me with a friendly smile.

"I see you saw Mr. Barringer. Well, have a nice day."

I sure couldn't argue with that.

22

Smathers drove the government-issue Chevy for nearly three hours along Route 87 north as I watched the passing scenery with unseeing eyes. North of Saratoga Springs we turned onto a secondary road which would take us to Highway 4, if we were going that far. At the entrance to a private access road I spotted the sign I'd been looking for: Rockland Hunting Lodge. A few moments later we'd parked the car just off the road in a nearby clearing. The pine trees would obscure the car from the road.

"Now what?" Smathers asked. I sensed that he was nervous, as he had every right to be. Killing wasn't something Smathers did, and even assisting me put him just over the line of professional legality.

"We go in and get my daughter," I explained. "Barringer claims they're holding her here. Let's find out if he was capable of telling the truth."

We each took a high-powered rifle from the trunk, affixing silencers to the barrels, then adjusting the sniperscopes. We then started up the trail, myself in the lead. We were less than a mile away from the inn when night softly fell. A misty fog came down around us and the smell of the pine trees filled the air. The trail took us upward, then turned west.

We walked quietly, but not with total stealth because of Smathers' lack of training in the art of moving undetected. Suddenly I placed a hand on his arm. We both stopped.

There was a deceptive grayness around us, which

triggered something inside me. I motioned that we should split up, and we separated onto opposite sides of the road, Smathers disappearing into the forest while I remained on the shoulder. The sounds I had previously sensed became audible, and then I saw them: two guards, coming not from the road but from within the forest and heading directly toward where Smathers was hidden. There was no time and less opportunity to evade them, so I sat down on the roadway only seconds before they emerged from the dense shrubbery.

Both guards were city boys carrying automatic weapons. They spotted me simultaneously. I was seated now, one shoe off, rubbing my ankle. They approached cautiously, and in that instant I realized that my ruse might not work because I'd forgotten that the rifle I carried had a silencer attached to it. It was resting, partially obscured, in the nearby brush, and I silently prayed they wouldn't notice it.

"I am so pleased you gentlemen happened along," I said in as courtly an Oriental manner as I could manage under the circumstances. "I seem to have stepped into a hole of some sort. I suspect I may have sprained my ankle."

They studied me for a second, then dismissed me. It was their first mistake. "This here is private property, fella," the taller guard informed me. "No hunting up here while the resort's closed."

"I am sorry to hear that. But it appears that I will be unable to hunt in any case." I continued to rub my ankle and measure their eyes. "I sincerely doubt if I will be able to walk."

The guards edged a little closer.

"You got a car?" the second man asked.

"Yes." I pointed abstractedly down the roadway.

Both of them looked up, following the motion of my arm, and a moment later it was over. I came off the ground like a jet gone to afterburners. The tall guard's neck snapped awkwardly, and the shorter man died of a sharp blow above the eyes.

I was putting on my shoe when Smathers emerged from the forest. He studied the bodies, his face impassive. Inside, however, I suspected he was trembling. Without a word, he began to drag one of the bodies into the brush as I got up to help him with the other.

"This is new for me," he said, his voice quiet, controlled

"You were in Korea, Smathers," I answered. "You've seen death before."

"But this is different . . . somehow."

I shook my head. "It's no different. We had a good reason then; I've got a better one now. Let's go."

We walked the remaining half-mile in silence. The road led to the elegantly landscaped entrance of the Rockland Inn. I could see the large rustic hunting lodge surrounded by a series of bungalows and the cabins in the distance. The inn's colonial exterior was capped by a wide balcony that had been added after the original building was constructed. It extended across the entire length of the second story and directly below it stood a burgundy canopy over the polished oak doors.

From our position at the forestline, I could see four guards, a pair stationed on the balcony, with an unobstructed view of the parking lot and forestline, and two more patrolling the grounds. The only way to penetrate this fortress would be to take out all four guards. I turned to Smathers.

"Can you take those two on the balcony at the same time I take care of the two on the ground?"

Smathers was silent, never taking his eyes off the guards. "I can't kill in cold blood, Dee." He paused for a moment. "But I can wound them."

Understanding his reluctance, I nodded my agreement. We could still complete the mission if—I stopped my own thinking. A mission? Was I still thinking in terms of tactical moves and capabilities and eventualities? Did it all come back just when I needed it or was I placing my daughter's life in needless jeopardy? A cold chill went through me as I studied the guards on the balcony. As they talked, they would frequently signal to the men below, then return to their discussion. One of them was holding a small pamphlet. A scratch sheet? Anyway, they were paying little attention to the forestline obscuring Smathers and me. I explained my part of the plan briefly, then instructed Smathers to concentrate only on the balcony guards. He had to get them both out of action or we'd both be dead.

I circled the parking lot until coming abreast of the northern side of the inn where the fireplace was located. There weren't any windows on that side, so my sole concern was the guards patrolling at ground level. Also, I was not in the immediate sight-line of the balcony sentries. Ten agonizing minutes passed before I saw the two ground guards walking the perimeter of the building. They appeared so casual but both carried automatic weapons. Despite the sensitivity of their job, they had very little regard for their surroundings. Why should they? The resort was closed and the area was insanely solemn for miles. Once they'd rounded the path to the rear of the building, I ran across the roughened lawn, then pressed myself against the outcropping fireplace. I listened momentarily for footsteps. There weren't any so I made my way carefully to the front of the building without alerting the guards on the balcony. There was a finely cut, rectangular hedgerow framing either side of the oak door. I slipped behind one of these dense, stately shrubs, waiting, holding my breath.

Several long minutes elapsed before I heard the guards round the opposite end of the inn. They were speaking rather loudly and were incapable of detecting my presence. I blended into the hedgerow, eavesdropping and waiting for a pattern to emerge. These two trained, professional guardians would show me the easiest way to effect their quiet deaths.

It didn't take them very long.

Once they'd circled the building and were certain no one had evaded their notice, the guards allowed their weapons to slacken toward the ground. Their conversation turned humorous as they dug for cigarettes. Dusk was fast transforming to the blackness of night. As the guards lit their cigarettes, I took full and lethal advantage of the situation. They never knew what hit them because I came from behind the hedgerow without rustling a leaf. My surprise was death.

My arm exploded outward, the heel of my hand burying into the head of the nearest guard. He crumpled to the ground while I crossed over him to strike his partner, who was standing flat-footed, his mouth agape. He went down a moment later. Swiftly, effectively, I buried one foot into the neck of each man. A final, singular rush of air burst upward around my murderous heel, and the bodies settled into eternity.

On the balcony above, I heard a body drop. Seconds later a second body pitched forward, falling the twenty feet from the terrace. I eased myself outward to check if the guard had survived. A huge welt growing blackly around his throat indicted a broken neck. His shoulder had been ripped open by a bullet, so the fall must have killed him.

I looked across the parking lot toward the spot where Smathers was hidden. After allowing a full minute to pass, I realized the agent intended remaining obscured. I lifted my hand so he'd know everything was fine. Then I turned to the large oak door. There were windows on either side, so I peered through them into the lobby. There wasn't a single soul in sight, so I began wondering whether the guard inside could possibly be unaware of what had taken place outside. It didn't seem likely. Even quiet killing has a sound all its own. Either the inn was empty or the guards were well hidden.

I tried the door but it was locked securely from within. After checking the dead men for a key and discovering none, I wondered how they were able to enter and leave the building. Now I was certain someone was hiding inside awaiting me. The lock was an archaic device reinforced by a bolt. I approximated the position where the bolt actually met the door frame by pressing my hand against the lock plate. After easily determining the point of maximum resistance, I realized I could turn this protective bolt into a mini-battering ram that would shatter the door frame. I used *chi*, the secrets of my inner strength, causing the bolt resistance to become part of the energy flow from my body.

I placed my hand flat against the lock plate, exerting enough pressure so the bolt met the door frame tightly. I concentrated momentarily, then pushed forward with my entire body weight channeled through my hand. The bolt tore the frame apart and the door flew inward on its hinges. I pitched myself forward, hitting the carpeted lobby floor, then rolling to a sheltered position behind an oversize colonial couch.

For several minutes I could hear only my own breathing, but soon realized I wasn't safe behind this sofa. Bullets could tear through it easily. It was then I sensed someone else in the room. I raised my head cautiously to see Calloway standing on the landing of the stairway leading from the center of the lobby. In his hand was a .357 Magnum. When I was certain he wasn't going to blow my head off immediately, I showed myself totally. He indicated I should walk from behind the sofa. As I did so, Calloway walked down the stairs confidently, but never taking the barrel off a deadly line with my midsection.

He was smiling as he spoke. There were no hellos.

"When I heard about Moroni's estate, I knew you were alive," Calloway said easily. "That was some job you pulled, Dee. And the bit with the girl's hair was real cute."

"You didn't have to hear about Moroni's estate to know," I told him. "You knew I was alive all along."

"Well"—Calloway shrugged—"when your body didn't turn up, I figured it was a pretty good bet you'd gotten out, but I wasn't sure, and I sure as hell wasn't going to tell Moroni something went wrong. What'd you do back there, Dee? Get involved with that Korean broad and go native?"

I said nothing and he studied me.

"Have it your way." Calloway kept the gun trained on me. "Whatever your reasons, they sure served my purposes. Besides, just as an insurance policy, I had tracers out to every plastic surgeon in the world. If you'd shown up, I would have known about it."

"That's in the past, Calloway. Let's talk about now."

"So talk."

"Where's Donna?"

"Gone."

I didn't let my anger show. "Where to?"

"Manhattan," Calloway replied freely. "Moroni seals his deal tomorrow. Barringer called to warn us, so we transferred the girl."

It didn't make sense. Six men to guard an empty building?

"I don't believe you, Calloway."

He smiled. "So don't believe me. When Barringer called and described an Oriental man who'd attacked him in his office, I knew it was you. I wasn't about to tell Moroni that I'd failed and you were still alive. Hell, you're his problem, not mine. But I couldn't risk letting you slip by again. That's why I'm standing here right now. Sure, I had guards here, but nobody who'd be any problem to you. They were just an expendable diversion designed to give me an edge."

"You'll sell anyone, won't you." It was not a question.

"Inchon should have taught you that, Dee," Calloway remarked. "You were my passport to the luxury I've bathed in over the past twelve years. Moroni has a nice way of saying thanks."

"I'll bet he does."

We fell silent and I judged the distance between us. It was nearly thirty feet and I'd have a bullet to race. Calloway wouldn't miss, either. But then, neither would I.

The silence between us had persisted too long. "Whatever became of Al Wong?" I had to buy some more time.

"Al Wong survived," he said lightly, "and is now doing what he does best."

"Drugs?"

"Drugs, politics, women." Calloway stopped, cleared his throat, then continued. "You know, I'm surprised he didn't kill you at Wolmi-Do."

"He would have, but he found out about your double-cross."

For the briefest second Calloway's composure slipped. He glowered at me as my eyes transformed his body into a six-foot target. He sensed it, then took a step backward while raising the Magnum. Chance lost.

"Don't try it," he warned.

"You know, Calloway, I knew about you and Moroni years ago. When Al Wong realized you'd crossed him, he told me that Moroni had hired you to arrange my death. There's no way I could know that unless he told me. You contracted him for a simple murder, then made him appear a traitor to his North Korean masters. If I were you, I'd stay out of Asia, because warlords don't forget."

"Al Wong is the least of my problems," Calloway responded.

I ignored his comment and continued. "Your other mistake was going after Donna. That one will cost you your life."

"Really? I'm the one with the gun, Dee, remember?"

I kept my expression impassive. "That doesn't mean you'll live to use it."

A strangeness existed between us. Calloway could have ended it all by simply pulling the trigger, but he didn't. One simple squeeze of his index finger and he would have walked away virtually free. Moroni's plan would succeed without a hitch and my company would change hands under the dark hand of extortion and blackmail.

Suddenly the entire resort plunged into darkness. Every light had gone out simultaneously, and I knew I had Smathers to thank for it. Moments ticked by, but neither of us dared move. My skin felt the night chill yet remained dry. Then from across the room came the odor of Calloway's perspiration. He was trying so desperately not to move, to remain silent in the darkness, but his untrained body betrayed him. A sharp odor resulting from his Western diet told me of his fear. Then I heard the wheezing of each breath he drew. It was a repressed shallowness requiring extraordinary strength of muscles gone unused. Finally the vibratory power of his terrible fear touched me and I knew he was a dead man.

The room became a jungle, a landscaped battleground, a terrain of deadly, shuddering silence that was totally alien to Calloway. The politics of death had chosen a victim, and as usual, death was blind.

In the darkness I detected the slightest reflection from Calloway's untanned face. As I fixed his position accurately in my mind, I saw him, but not on any level that he would ever be able to understand. Because he was using all of his energy to restrain himself, thus protecting his precarious position, Calloway would not pull the trigger. I had to act first. He would react, nothing more.

I moved. He fired. But I was no longer there.

I was now behind him, but he never knew it. I spun around, then kicked the gun out of his hand. I felt him move, but there was no defense. I pivoted once more, this time delivering a kick to his lower back. He fell onto the couch and didn't move.

There was another flickering from the corners of the room as the red emergency lights flooded the lobby with an eerie, bloodlike hue that allowed us to view each other as if through the gates of hell. Calloway stood carefully, and I faced him, the distance between us less than fifteen feet. I now had the gun in my hand, and Calloway froze when he realized the balance of power had now shifted. He never knew how far.

I smiled slowly, then slid the gun into my belt.

"Is that the best you can do?" Calloway asked as he rubbed the spot on his back where I'd struck him. "Why don't you kill me and be done with it?"

My smile grew. "But I have killed you." My words were measured, even. "One needn't knock a man to his knees to claim his life." I paused as Calloway stared at me, the frightened question in his eyes. "In a few minutes, Calloway, your mouth will dry out and you'll start summoning saliva. But instead it will be warm blood from your perforated kidney. It'll work its way up through your senses with an ungodly pain until the only mercy left in your life is the moment of death. You won't go anywhere, Calloway. You can't. Death is on its way."

Then I walked by him as if he didn't exist. In a few minutes, he wouldn't.

I walked upstairs, figuring to check each room in case Calloway had been lying. He hadn't.

Outside the lodge, Smathers was waiting with the rifle tucked under his arm. He was casually smoking a cigarette.

"Is it over?" he asked.

Before I could answer, an agonized scream came from inside the lodge. For Calloway it was indeed over.

The first score was settled.

23

Smathers dropped me at my boardinghouse at dawn, where I showered and changed. I decided against breakfast and instead went to the phone to call Maggie. She answered, her voice still clouded with sleep, and I explained to her that I'd almost found Donna but failed. I omitted specific details.

"But I think the deal's going through today, Maggie," I told her.

"I think you're right, Mr. Dee," she responded. "Mrs. Bridges phoned last night and requested Eddie's office for a meeting sometime today."

"She didn't mention the time?"

"No, but she did say she wanted the office ready by the start of the business day. She also wanted me to have two additional security guards on duty by eight A.M."

I thought a moment. "Maggie, I've got to be in that passageway before the meeting starts. Can you get me in without anyone seeing me?"

She didn't hesitate. "Sure. We'll just have to get there before the guards arrive."

"I'll meet you in an hour." I hung up and called Smathers, arranging to meet him at a luncheonette near my room.

As I waited at my table, sipping a cup of tea, I watched the mix of day and night people as they began or ended their day. Teachers and toughs, hookers and helmsmen, the meek and the strong all mixed easily, and the longer I observed them, the more I realized that I didn't belong anywhere anymore. And that thought led me to thoughts of Sylvia.

Again she intruded upon my thoughts, taking command of my emotions. I realized I could have anything this world had to offer except for the woman I had chosen for my companion so many years ago. I then began to examine my reasons for returning from the dead. Certainly I was here to free my daughter. But I also wanted to see Sylvia. I wanted to assure myself that the memory I had carried for so many years had been, in fact, a reality. I wanted to see her, sense her, and know that she was all too real. And now I had seen her, and it hurt.

As I sat gripping my cup, a veil lifted and I saw, for the first time, a truth I had denied for many years. I had bartered my family's safety for the life of Ducksun.

I remembered Sylvia telling me that the government should find another person to carry out the business of world affairs. I recalled my answer: there was no one else. And at the time, it was the truth. No one knew Ducksun as I did; no other person would have been able to complete the mission successfully. By the same token, only I could return to the States at this late date to save my daughter. My principles remained unchanged; my road to those principles was littered with broken promises.

None of this would have happened if I had refused the mission or defied the fates and returned. I had forsaken, by choice, a wonderful, loving woman and three lovely children for the ideal of patriotism, an ideal long since eroded by time and treaties. I'd left home to fight against Communism, but when the rest of the world returned home to find a vague détente, I had remained at war.

And now I could never stay in the land that was my home. I had killed, and killed with a ruthlessness that no judge or jury would ever be able to comprehend. Moroni's goal had been to kill me, bury me. I wondered now if he hadn't succeeded.

I finished my tea, then went outside to wait on the corner. Smathers came along ten minutes later and we fought the morning traffic uptown. We pulled up a block away from the Tyson Building. I started to get out.

"Should I wait?" Smathers asked.

I realized I might need him before the day was out. "Yeah. But why don't you park it over there in front of the building. This could take a while."

He let a small smile cross his face. "I've come this far . . ."

I nodded and started for the building. I thought about Smathers and faced the fact that he had come to help me and had involved himself far too deeply to ever be clean enough for the FBI again. We both knew it; he'd twisted the rules and he'd have to pay the price. He was exhausted, both physically and mentally. I vowed never to forget him.

Maggie was waiting for me outside the building. She glanced at her watch. "Let's go. The meeting's at nine o'clock."

"Did Sylvia call?" I asked.

Maggie nodded. "Just after you did. C'mon." She tugged at my sleeve and we moved past the doorman and through security.

Minutes later we entered the hallway adjacent to my old office. Maggie explained that the security guards were to be stationed outside the elevator bank, and following Sylvia's arrival, no unauthorized personnel would be allowed to stop at this floor.

"If I have to leave the passageway quickly," I told Maggie, "I can't afford to be challenged by the guards."

"Don't worry, boss. I'll be here."

I smiled at her. "Thanks, Maggie."

As she went to her desk, I crossed my office and entered the passageway. Thirty minutes later I watched as Sylvia and Tim came into Eddie's old office. They both looked as if they'd been up all night. I flipped the switch so I could hear their conversation.

Tim was fixing himself a club soda at the bar. "It's not every day you trade a company for a kidnapped daughter," he was saying. "Are you certain you really want to go through with this? We can have the FBI here in a matter of minutes."

"I know that," Sylvia answered. "But right now the

only thing I'm interested in is Donna's safety. I will not risk her life for anyone or anything."

As Tim was about to respond, the door opened and in marched Moroni's bodyguards. Satisfied, they signaled Moroni in. He was followed by Philip Barringer. Except for some bruises around his neck and face, he didn't seem any the worse for wear. The bodyguards closed the door, remaining inside.

"Good morning, Mrs. Bridges," Moroni offered with a slight bow. "I'm sure you've met Philip Barringer. He'll be handling the legalities of the transfer."

Barringer extended his hand to Sylvia. "A pleasure, Mrs. Bridges. I've heard so much about you."

Sylvia stared from his hand to his face until, with a look of chagrin, Barringer dropped his hand.

Tim turned to Barringer. "You assured me you didn't represent Mr. Moroni."

Barringer smiled easily. "So I did. And it's true—technically. My retainer is through the Overseas Trading Company. I represent that firm, not Mr. Moroni."

"Then it is true," Sylvia said, her eyes intently boring holes into Moroni. "Mr. Moroni and the Overseas Trading Company and the Pan International Bank are all one and the same."

Moroni was about to answer when Barringer stopped him.

"That's partially accurate, Mrs. Bridges," Barringer told her.

Sylvia gazed up at Moroni with a long, condescending stare.

"Eddie Gardenia told me of your longtime association with the Pan International Bank, Mr. Moroni. I believe the Overseas Trading Company is the Wall Street name for that bank. So let's lay all our cards down. You intend to use the name of the Overseas Trading Company and the financial power of Pan International to acquire Dee Enterprises. Am I substantially correct?"

"You are very perceptive, Mrs. Bridges." Moroni nodded. "Philip has the notes drawn on the Pan International for one hundred million dollars. I believe this is the appropriate estimate in keeping with the most recent financial statement. Of course, we've included growth percentages for the period following the statement. Everything is in order, I can assure you."

Sylvia glanced over to Tim but he didn't wish to interject anything. The figures were, indeed, correct, and there wouldn't be very many papers to sign. Just the letters of intent and the additional promissory notes, which were payable upon demand. The actual time involved to legally process this transfer was several months, but the voting stock and privileges would pass to Moroni today. Within several minutes he would have Dee Enterprises grasped tightly in his fist. After that, he really didn't give a damn what the lawyers said.

"Where is Donna?" Sylvia demanded. "I assume you have brought her along."

"Unfortunately, Mrs. Bridges, circumstances compel us to leave the girl in a very secure place," Moroni explained. "You see, there was an attack upon my home in which someone attempted intimidating me by killing several of my bodyguards. The target, apparently, was my daughter. I suspect you may know something about this attack, so I took the precaution of leaving Donna at a place well out of your reach."

Sylvia regarded Moroni with a cross, vengeful expression.

"I have no idea what you are talking about, Mr. Moroni," she replied indignantly. "I wouldn't do anything that might endanger Donna's life."

"That may be true, but I'll have to insist you sign the transfer documents before I order Donna's release," Moroni stated.

"Moroni," Tim interrupted, "that wasn't the deal!"

"No, it wasn't," Moroni remarked agreeably. "The attack upon my home wasn't part of the deal either."

"But we don't know anything about an attack on your home!" Tim persisted.

Moroni only looked at his wristwatch, then turned his back on Tim Bridges. He spoke to Sylvia again.

"Mrs. Bridges, I can assure the safety of your daughter only until eleven this morning. I would suggest we finish the business at hand."

As though upon cue, Philip Barringer began removing papers from his briefcase.

"When will I see my daughter?" Sylvia asked quietly.

Moroni looked to Philip, who glanced up from the papers. "As you know, Mrs. Bridges, this is hardly a small transaction. The fact that there is a meeting of the board of directors of Dee Enterprises scheduled for Monday morning further complicates matters. Mr. Moroni wishes to attend that particular meeting, utilizing all the rights and powers inherent in his voting stock. Naturally, he will have total control through the Overseas Trading Company and the Pan International Bank. Undoubtedly this will spark controversy with the remaining directors. We intend holding your daughter until after Mr. Moroni assumes active control, which, according to our timetable, will be sometime Monday morning."

Moroni spoke up when Barringer completed his explanation. "You have my word she will be released immediately following the board meeting." The mobster bowed toward Sylvia as though faked humility would ignite her trust.

Sylvia studied him intently before answering.

"You ask a great deal, Mr. Moroni," she started. "I don't like the idea of signing these documents blindly."

"Your hesitancy is only natural, Mrs. Bridges, but I'm certain you see I must protect my own position," Moroni replied. "I assure you there is no other way."

Sylvia reached across Eddie's desk for a pen and the papers offered by Barringer.

"You shall have my signature, Mr. Moroni," she replied icily, "but my daughter will be delivered to my home on Long Island sharply at noon Monday. If she is but a minute late, I promise I will call the United States Attorney. Do you understand me?"

Moroni glanced at Sylvia, and for the briefest second a shaken expression crossed his face. Sylvia signed the papers but did not hand them to Moroni.

"I asked if you understood what I said?" she pressed him for an answer.

"You have my word, Mrs. Bridges," Moroni told

her. "Donna will be at your home before noon on Monday."

Sylvia extended the papers to him. While Moroni was affixing his own signature, which Tim Bridges and Philip Barringer were witnessing, there was a knock at the office door. A moment later Maggie entered the room, walking directly to Sylvia. She leaned over, whispered into Sylvia's ear, then awaited a reply. Sylvia looked away but I saw her nod ever so slightly.

From behind the mirror I watched as my company changed hands. My lifetime work was whisked from my family's control by the scratching of a fountain pen. But I couldn't help being curious at Maggie's unannounced entrance. What had she told Sylvia? I could easily see Sylvia straining to hide her own excitement. Deep inside, I wanted to fly through the mirror and rip Moroni's heart out with my bare hands. I knew the mobster better than anyone in the room and figured he would find another use for Donna. He would effect another scheme to milk my family of money or position. But I couldn't yet reveal myself, because I had no idea where she was being held.

A moment later the door opened, and standing in the door frame between two powerful Orientals was Ducksun. He surveyed the room with his eyes, then settled upon Moroni's puzzled face.

What the hell was happening? I was dumbfounded. Why the hell was Ducksun here? Was he somehow part of this obscene charade? Moroni was turning to depart but halted when his bodyguards came to attention.

"I wouldn't leave presently, Mr. Moroni," Ducksun said in quiet command. "We have yet to do business."

Moroni scrutinized the Oriental elder with a single uneasy glance. Ducksun was dressed in a black pin-striped suit and appeared anything but a warlord.

"I'm afraid we haven't met," Moroni stated evenly.

"I am Ducksun."

"Should I know you?" Moroni shrugged as though attempting to place the face and recall the name.

Ducksun stepped aside to allow his lawyer forward. At the same moment, both sets of bodyguards shifted to balance each other. An amused smile crossed Sylvia's face. She was enjoying Moroni's obvious discomfort. Then Ducksun's lawyer spoke in a bold tone.

"Pleased to inform Mr. Moroni that the honored and respected Ducksun is chairman of the board of the Southeast Asia Fossil Fuel Company, which was incorporated in Hong Kong through the auspices of Far East Enterprises," the lawyer announced.

Moroni's face brightened.

"Ah, then you are part of the corporation I have just purchased." Moroni was truly beaming by now. "Mrs. Bridges has only just turned Dee Enterprises over to me through an agreement with the Overseas Trading Company. I had heard Dee Enterprises was into oil."

"I am afraid you misunderstand, Mr. Moroni," Ducksun replied, shaking his head. "The Southeast Asia Fossil Fuel Company was incorporated through the laws in Hong Kong and is independent of Dee Enterprises. True, we have a reciprocal arrangement with Dee Enterprises on many levels, but we are independently financed and free of any encumbrance through United States law. No, Mr. Moroni, you would have to travel to Hong Kong should you desire to purchase our company, but that is quite impossible now, anyway."

"Get to the point," Moroni said roughly, impatiently.

"The point is simply this: Southeast Asia Fossil Fuel, under my direction, has purchased all the outstanding paper of the Pan International Bank. We have effected this through brokerages in Zurich, Hong Kong, New York, and London. Our accounting as of this morning, at the rate of fifty cents on the dollar, has given us nearly three hundred million dollars of Pan International's paper. May I point out that most of the notes we have purchased come due within the next thirty days, and I have requested my agents on the various world exchanges to secure payment or bring suit. At the ratios we have purchased, we now own fifty-seven percent of the voting stock in Pan International. Further, I have the signed proxies of an additional fifteen percent. The outstanding twenty-eight percent belongs to you, Mr. Moroni. Now, shall we do business?"

Moroni turned on Sylvia heatedly.

"What it this?" he demanded. "Some kind of double cross?"

"Don't ask me," Sylvia replied. "I never saw this man before in my life."

Moroni returned his attention to Ducksun.

"What kind of business?" he asked sharply. "My twenty-eight percent is not for sale. Never has been."

"The harsh reality of it is that your voting stock is worth only thirty-two million dollars," Ducksun explained. "You have a note with the Pan International for one hundred million dollars. Your note was included in the paper Southeast Asia Fossil Fuel purchased. I am pleased to inform you that you have been relieved of all indebtedness, as we shall now assume control of Dee Enterprises."

"You can't do that!" Moroni was truly panicked. "Philip, can he do that?"

Barringer took a sheaf of papers from Ducksun's lawyer. He read them over swiftly, then glanced at Moroni.

"It's all in order, Mr. Moroni," Barringer explained. "It's also been certified by a judge so we know it's legal. Apparently they purchased your note yesterday morning. It was the highest denomination of outstanding paper on the Pan International ledgers. The board certified the fact after learning some two hundred million dollars in notes had already been acquired by Mr. Ducksun. Obviously they had no choice. The bank was caught short, and only this abrupt intercession by Southeast Asia Fossil Fuel assured solvency."

"This is a goddamn trick!" Moroni shouted.

"There is no trickery involved," Ducksun asserted. "Only money."

"So, what do you propose to do?" Moroni seethed. "I've already paid Mrs. Bridges the one hundred million dollars for the voting stock in Dee Enterprises."

Ducksun smiled. "We foresaw such an event," he told him, "and have brought the proper papers, which rescind ownership as well as voting rights from you and place them exclusively in the hands of the Pan International Bank, which is now a subsidiary of the Southeast Asia Fossil Fuel Company."

Tim Bridges and Philip Barringer huddled over the papers for a few minutes. After trading their own brand of legalese, they looked to Moroni, but only Barringer spoke.

"They're covered all the pertinent points, Mr. Moroni." Barringer frowned.

"Damn it!" Moroni shouted. "They can't effect the transfer without my signature!"

"They were able to do so by proving your solvency doesn't exceed the purchase price of your stock in Pan International," Barringer continued. "Your annual cash flow could never cover the payments due for the first quarter. It's extremely complicated, Mr. Moroni, but they're on solid legal ground."

Moroni's face reddened as he looked to Sylvia and Ducksun.

The Warlord picked up the letters of intent signed by Sylvia only moments before. Along with them he collected the ownership documents for the Pan International Bank. He then turned to Sylvia.

"I have heard much about you, Mrs. Bridges," he said with deep respect. "I knew Dee many years ago. I knew him as an ambitious young man in Shanghai and later as the courageous young man who chose to leave his family and homeland to save the life of an old friend. It is because of him that I live today."

Sylvia leaned forward and forced her words out in a near-whisper. "Mr. Ducksun, there's something I have to know. Is Dee really dead?"

I held my breath, as did Tim Bridges. Ducksun smiled a tired yet kindly smile.

"Mrs. Bridges," Ducksun began, "do you not honestly believe that the answer to your question is within you, that only you have the ability to answer such a question?"

Sylvia thought a long moment, then nodded. "I believe you are right."

Again the Warlord smiled. "Now, if you will transfer the one hundred million dollars in promissory notes back to the Pan International, then I shall void any claim made through Mr. Moroni. Dee Enterprises will remain the property of your family."

"You would do that?" Sylvia asked.

Across the room, Moroni's face had turned blood-red as he saw his schemes disintegrate before his eyes.

"It is for this very reason that I have traveled ten thousand miles, Mrs. Bridges. It is an honor to assist the Dee family."

Sylvia thought for a moment, clearly torn by the situation facing her. "Mr. Ducksun, I hope you will understand, but I cannot sign the papers. Mr. Moroni is still holding my daughter, Donna. I can't allow her to be hurt."

"I am well aware of that fact." Ducksun nodded. He then turned and faced Moroni. "You will release the girl, I am sure."

Moroni's smile was cruel, and at a wave of his hand, both bodyguards stepped forward, guns in hand. "Your daughter was the purchase price, Mrs. Bridges. If the company is not transferred to me by the close of the business day, then I'll make it my business to see that your daughter's body is delivered to you by nightfall."

Moroni backed away from the desk, turning to leave the room. "You know where I can be contacted, Mrs. Bridges." He sneered and slid out the door as his bodyguards held everyone at bay.

Behind the two-way mirror, I realized my opportunity had come. Without a second thought, I made my way down the darkened passageway to my office. Maggie was waiting, holding the elevator. I got off in the lobby, and through the thick crowds I could see Moroni making his way toward the exit.

He spun around a few times to see if anyone was following him, but I was secure in the knowledge that he would never recognize me. Naked without his bodyguards, Moroni surveyed the crowd, and for one electrifying second he stared directly into my face. But he saw nothing. I smiled and continued to walk at a leisurely pace.

When Moroni passed through the wide doors leading to the street, I broke into a run.

I finally felt everything was falling into place. Moroni would now go directly to my daughter. I felt it; I knew it. He would react like a greedy king running to the vault to see if his own guards had, in his absence, plundered the treasure room.

And when he got there, he would find me waiting—just as I had sworn I would be.

24

As I reached the sidewalk adjoining the Tyson Building, Moroni's gleaming black Chrysler was roaring out into the Fifth Avenue traffic. I gazed around frantically, then spotted the government Chevy parked near the corner. I began running, knocking several people to the pavement. Smathers must have seen me in the rearview mirror, because he had the car idling as I pulled open the door.

"Follow that black Chrysler," I shouted.

Smathers jammed the car into gear and the chase began. Fifth Avenue was an explosion of horn blasts and screeching tires as, behind us, two cars collided with a metal-crunching sound. I kept my attention riveted to the Chrysler we were gaining on.

"Just tail him," I ordered, "but don't lose him. I have to know where he's going."

Smathers stared straight ahead. "Who is it?"

"Moroni. His deal was blown, so I think he's going to get Donna."

"He didn't bring her along as planned?"

"No." I thought for a moment. "But Ducksun showed up. You wouldn't know anything about that, would you?"

Smathers smiled in innocence. "Me?"

"How long has Ducksun been in New York?"

"Nearly a week," Smathers replied.

"You knew all along? And you never thought to mention it to me?"

"Ducksun asked me not to tell you," Smathers explained. "He claimed his presence was far too sensitive in nature, so I complied."

As I considered this, Smathers weaved through traffic while following the Chrysler deeper into the West Side. Then suddenly the Chrysler pulled away in an evasive move designed to shake any potential tails. For a moment I thought we'd lost him, but Smathers managed to remain on target by edging another car onto the curb. Quickly we skidded left and started downtown. We followed as Moroni turned onto West Thirty-fourth, heading toward the piers. Then we came to a screeching stop. Up ahead, a warehouse was on fire. An engine company had completely blockaded the street. And the Chrysler was gone.

"Where the hell is he?" I forced through clenched teeth.

We searched the street carefully with our eyes, but all we saw was an ever-growing crowd gathered to watch the building burn.

"Impossible," Smathers said in frustration as he pounded the steering wheel helplessly. "We couldn't have lost him. There's no place for him to go. He has to be stalled somewhere in this crowd."

We got out of the car and began walking. There was no way in hell Moroni could have escaped this block once he'd turned onto it. Yet he was nowhere to be seen. Then I spotted the aged, rusted sign: "River Metal Company."

The sign sported a small arrow pointing at a driveway cutting through the block to the next street over. This had to be the way Moroni had escaped.

"Bring the car!" I shouted at Smathers, while indicating the driveway. But I didn't wait. I ran along the accessway to find myself just opposite a storage yard alongside the old switching station.

Parked in one of the trailer bays was the Chrysler.

The fence surrounding the property was locked at the gateway, so I was forced to climb it. While twisting over the top, I heard people shouting for me to take cover. The fire at the end of the block had ripped through the pier, blazing dangerously near several fuel-storage tanks. The entire area was darkened with acrid smoke. In the distance I could hear additional fire engines racing to the scene as several more alarms were turned in. Ahead of me I watched the soaring embers form a hellish rain as they dropped like killer fireflies on the flat rooftop of the River Metal Company warehouse.

I was running toward the parked Chrysler when an explosion rocked the pier front. Surrounded by distant screams and the sight of a parked automobile turning itself over like some player in a surrealistic dream, the force wave struck me as it rippled toward the warehouse. Moments later I was flat on my back. The shock waves passed and I pulled myself up to see the hell I was trapped in. The fires above were spreading at a slow, lethal pace. Every square inch of tar and shingle was doomed to charred consumption. The bay doors were closed and bolted, so I went directly for the small entranceway at the top of several concrete steps. I blew the wooden door in with a violent kick, then hurled my body across the floor.

Gunshots whizzed before me, but I felt no pain. I bolted from the door instinctively, then felt someone's head snap at the edge of my knuckles. Then I was into another roll and unleashing a full attack on a second guard. He died instantly, his body reacting like a puppet whose strings had been cut.

The third guard was with Moroni at the opposite end of the dockway, surrounded by stacks of crates.

"Kill him," Moroni cried.

The guard raised his gun as I sped toward him. A split second later I was in the air with my feet fully extended. I smashed the bridge of his nose so deeply into his skull that blood began flowing from his ears and mouth. I came down, rolled forward, then righted myself. Moroni was going through a rear door as I came to my feet.

I bolted through the boiler room in pursuit. Unbridled anger became my path.

I followed the steps leading into the boiler room, knowing there would be no escape for Moroni there. Deep below, the twin boilers heaved. The empty room was wide but dimly lit. Cautiously I made my way along the walls. There was nowhere for Moroni to hide. The archaic coal bins were long since emptied of their contents and the few storage rooms were securely locked. Then I spotted the manhole cover.

Anticipation ripped through me as I realized Moroni had escaped through this hatchway and into the underground city of wires and cables. In a way, he'd gone through the looking glass to a time and place that had long since left our lives. He had returned to the city's womb to die.

Images of Steinway Street and the sewers flashed through my mind as I tore up the heavy metal hatchpiece and dropped my body into the hole. Memories and movements returned to me after three decades. The silent, pantherlike motions I'd learned and utilized as a boy came back to me, movements I'd learned to survive in the sewer. As I worked my way along the catwalks rendering access to the cable run, I realized we'd finally and inevitably come full circle. The service tubes led to the sewer system. I knew it because, as always, you could smell the sewers long before you reached them.

There was a series of traps leading from the cable tubes spaced every few yards, allowing workmen the maximum possible access. I dropped through one of the traps, knowing it led to a major storm drain, which in turn flowed into the Hudson.

I took the first few wet steps through the stench, hearing rats squeal as I upset their lonely, blackened wells. Then I stopped.

Ahead of me there was the spasmodic sound of another set of footsteps struggling through a tangled web of garbage. I listened, then discerned a splash followed by silence. As if by agreement, we both halted any movement. Then I took the initiative.

The putrid water was more than knee-deep by the time I reached Moroni. The crime boss was pulling himself out of a holding trap as a whirlpool of refuse that had traveled the long, arduous road from the glittering streets above swirled around him. Reflected light caught both our eyes simultaneously as we came within feet of each other.

He went for his gun but never got the chance to use it. My arm flashed toward him, smashing his wrist with a painful pincer grip while disarming him. His lungs bellowed in agony, and the first of his death sounds echoed along the viaduct toward the river.

"Who are you?" he demanded through his pain, but in his eyes I could see that what he wanted was a denial of the truth he couldn't bear to hear.

"You know who I am," I answered. I held him tightly as I stared down at him. "Remember Eddie Gardenia?" I asked quietly. "You enjoyed killing him, didn't you? It was almost like killing a little of me, wasn't it?"

"So it is you." Moroni nodded, trying to hide the pain of my grip on him. "I should have known. And it was you who raided my house."

"What did you expect? Eddie warned you I'd come back, but you didn't believe him. Remember what he said? 'Death is on its way.' You laughed at him while he squirmed in your office, knowing he was going to die. You said he was crazy, remember?" I loosened my grip slightly. I didn't want him to die yet. "You weren't satisfied with just killing me, were you, Moroni? No, the fact that you had arranged my death in Korea wasn't enough for you. You had to go after my family. You had to terrorize them. And for what? Some stupid vendetta you began over a fight we had on the docks of Long Island City decades ago? That's what it's all about, isn't it? Moroni, too many people have died because we couldn't live together. Countless lives have been shattered just so we could return to the sewers to settle a score that should have been forgotten."

I looked away from him in sadness and anger, and Moroni took the opportunity to try to go for me. He never made it. I grabbed his arm at the elbow and instinctively snapped it. He screamed, then passed out. As his body slackened and slid into the gray-black slime, I contemplated what I had become. I had almost killed Moroni once, and maybe I should have. Now I had a second chance. But I didn't know if I would take it.

I pulled him toward me and shoved his face into the

cold water to revive him. A few slaps and he began to return to consciousness. I waited as he coughed, then looked to me with venom in his eyes.

Then, through his pain, he began to laugh. "We're no different, Dee," he hissed. "Our tastes for revenge are the same. Only yours is going to cost you more. You couldn't let me go, you had to follow me. And because of that, your daughter will die." In that moment, everything became clear to me.

I reeled with shock. Donna! Donna was upstairs in the burning warehouse. Moroni's insane laughter echoed through the sewers. I pulled away from him as if his very touch would sicken me. I might have let him live then, but Moroni couldn't tell he'd been spared. He gathered up what strength he had left and came for me as I turned to find my daughter. I sensed him before he ever reached me, and I turned, my right hand exploding toward his neck. His last laugh blew forth a stream of blood. My clothes covered with his blood, I turned and left him to die, his unconscious body slipping into the trap where he'd become a feast for the rats.

The knee-deep water kept me from making any real progress. It was too thick to swim in, too deep to run through. I just had to take each step as it came. I finally reached the cable tube, then pulled myself up and into it. Moments later I was back through the manhole cover and into the boiler room. As the smoke swirled around me, I raced to the stairwell and up to the main floor of the warehouse.

The fire had spread across the roof, turning the entire building into an inferno. Through the smoke I could see Donna hanging limply from a support beam. Reaching her, I pushed on her chest, hoping to clear her lungs. With only sheer hope in my heart, I pulled her mouth open and breathed into her lungs forcefully. This would only give me a moment if she was still alive. My own breath became shallow from the ever-decreasing oxygen. Then I searched out the shackles. She had been chained to a metal loop bolt protruding from the support beam. There was only one swift, sure way to free her.

I retreated several steps, then concentrated on the small area of wood above the bolt. A split second later, I was in the air and my extended feet smashed the beam to splinters. Donna pitched forward. She was still shackled at the wrists, but she was free. I eased her upward, determining she was alive. But she wouldn't be if we remained where we were much longer.

She was in my arms now and I was running across the floor as the fire roared through the roof. Embers and shingling fell behind us, but we made it to the doorway. The sunlight blasted at us, and in the distance, fire companies battled the flames. The helmeted men moved toward us as the building caved in behind us. But we were safe. We were alive.

I set Donna down on the ground and she looked up at me. "Who are you?" she coughed, and continued to stare at me. "Who are you?"

I ran my fingers through her soot-stained hair.

"I always promised you I'd be there when you needed me, remember, pumpkin?"

She was vague, hazy with loss of oxygen. "Pumpkin . . . ?"

And just like years ago, she was safe and asleep in my arms.

IV

To Sever:
Death Buries
Its Dead

1962

25

Smathers took control the moment I stumbled out of the warehouse with Donna in my arms. Somehow he'd managed to summon several trusted agents. They hustled us to safety and managed to keep us from the harsh scrutiny of New York's finest.

Within twenty-four hours the newspapers were publishing accounts of the Dee Enterprises corporate raid and Ducksun's dramatic takeover of Pan International Bank. The Securities and Exchange Commission issued a press release announcing an investigation of the matter, but the full story never made the papers.

I could no longer remain in the country. Smathers had contained the situation but he couldn't completely hide it from New York's police department. There'd just been too many killings. I would have to return to Korea.

In the hotel room where Smathers had hidden me, I found I harbored no regrets. My family was safe and Dee Enterprises was intact. My mission was complete and I was at peace. I couldn't allow a family reunion, much as I wanted it. Sylvia, Donna, Denise, and Jeff had to get on with lives that didn't include me. Although I knew I'd never sever my emotional bond with them, I had to let them go. It was their world now and I was no longer a part of it.

Calloway continued to haunt me. From various intelligence agencies Smathers learned that Calloway had planted information concerning me, information that was only to emerge after his death. The reports indicated that I might still be alive, a dangerous renegade with allegiance to no one. Calloway's information could make me a target for life, and we both knew it.

On a crisp Wednesday morning, Smathers arrived at my room. We both knew we would never see each other again, yet neither of us could manage to say good-bye.

"There's a flight out of Idlewild in an hour," he told me. "You're booked on it."

I nodded. "How's my family?"

"Fine. Donna is okay, but they're asking her a lot of questions about that 'strange Oriental man.' I think Sylvia suspects it was you, but she's chosen not to say anything."

I smiled, seeing her before my eyes. "Yes, she would do that."

Smathers was silent for a moment. "Dee, if I can ever manage to bring any of your children to Korea, would you—?"

I cut him off. "No. Let them have their memories. I have mine."

Smathers nodded, then reached into his jacket pocket and pulled out an envelope. "Read this on the plane, Dee. It was discovered in Eddie's safe. We got a warrant to enter the office. I saw your name on the envelope and 'liberated' it."

"Thanks."

"The limousine's downstairs."

I nodded in reply and suddenly there were no more words between us. We regarded each other respectfully, but never said farewell. We shook hands and I left.

As I settled back in the limousine Smathers had provided, I saw a copy of the *Daily News* he'd left behind. "Crime Czar Slain in Sewer—Killer Unknown," the headline screamed. I smiled. Three decades of battling Jimmy Moroni had been reduced to a line of boldface type. I reached into my pocket and pulled out the envelope. I tore it open and immediately recognized Eddie's handwriting.

Dee,

By the time you read this, I'll be dead. Jimmy Moroni has kidnapped your daughter Donna. He is making a move to take over the company. I don't know your position, but I know you'll return when you find out about it. In case you're wondering, I've known you were alive since 1955, when I accidentally discovered activity in those Zurich accounts. I don't know why you haven't contacted me or your family, but I guess you have your reasons and I'll respect them. As you will probably learn, I have sold my interest in Dee Enterprises to Sylvia. I was paid in gold and transferred the bullion to your account in Zurich. I ask only one favor: please make sure that Maggie Thorp never wants for anything. I guess you know why. You've helped provide me with a good, full life, a lot more than anyone from Long Island City could ever hope for. You let me carve something out of this world, something I never could have done alone. Now, God willing I'll try to give you back your daughter. It's the least I can do.

Always,
Eddie

I folded the letter, then replaced it in the envelope. The limousine was cleared by airport security and directed to the TWA terminal. The driver pulled the car into a restricted zone, then got out and opened the door for me. He wished me a pleasant journey and I nodded a thanks.

Ten minutes later I was checked in and on my way to the gate. The airport, with its thousands of scurrying travelers, seemed so lonely to me. I melted into the crowd shoving through the gate.

As I walked toward the plane, a sixth sense told me to turn around. I saw Sylvia and my children moving toward the gate.

Sylvia walked quickly, Jeff at her side. Donna and Denise were only a step or so behind.

Not allowed beyond the gate, they gathered behind the glass. The man they knew only as Chan stood frozen, staring at them.

I couldn't turn back, but as I looked into the eyes of

each of my children and into the eyes of the woman I would always love, I had to acknowledge their presence.

Slowly I raised my hand in a gesture of farewell. Each of them in turn did the same. Donna was mouthing, "Thank you," while Denise waved good-bye to a newfound friend. As my eyes met Jeff's, I saw the sudden light of recognition flash in his eyes, and Sylvia, watching him, saw it too. She turned back to me and waved, then placed her open-palmed hand against the glass. For a moment, I held my hand frozen in the air in exactly the same position.

Then I turned to the plane that would take me out of their lives forever.

ABOUT THE AUTHOR

Charles DeLuca is a self-made Long Island businessman and an accomplished martial artist, yachtsman and horseman. He is married and has three children. This is his first novel.